WILDWOOD

Whit didn't feel lost, exactly: he had a compass with him and good geological survey maps, and in a pinch he knew he could find his way out of Wildwood simply by following running water to the flatlands, but he was at a loss, humbled, a blinded man groping to be informed; he did not fit his skin well today, and his bones, like dry bones he had transported from the scorched desert of his dreams, were alien here in this fiercely greening, richly fecund, breathing, murmuring, terrifyingly beautiful and treacherous place. The sensation he felt most penetratingly, as he struggled toward Tormentil, was one of rebirth. But by daylight it was not possible to recall the symbolic circumstances of his dying, symbols so infallibly ordered on the stage-set of sleep. So there was no meaning to be derived from the sensation that was as pure and chastening as hunger or sex; he had only the faint apprehension as he toiled through tangles toward the hidden sky and the mountain clouded by time and magic, that something crucial must occur before he would be allowed, or enabled, to come down again.

**Also by the same author,
and available from NEL:**

Minotaur
Nightfall
Son of the Endless Night

About the Author

John Farris is the author of SON OF THE
ENDLESS NIGHT, THE FURY and many other
novels of terror and suspense. Married with four
children, he divides his time between Puerto
Rico and Tennessee.

Wildwood

John Farris

NEW ENGLISH LIBRARY
Hodder and Stoughton

**To Su, for making
this possible**

Copyright © 1987 by John
Farris

First published in the United
States of America in 1987 by
Tor Books

First published in Great Britain
in 1987 by Hodder & Stoughton

First New English Library
Paperback edition 1988

British Library C.I.P.

Farris, John
  Wildwood.
  I. Title
813'.54[F]   PS3556.A777

ISBN 0-450-42644-0

Printed and bound in Great Britain
for Hodder and Stoughton
Paperbacks, a division of Hodder
and Stoughton Ltd., Mill Road,
Dunton Green, Sevenoaks, Kent
TN13 2YA (Editorial Office: 47
Bedford Square, London WC1B
3DP) by Richard Clay Ltd.,
Bungay, Suffolk

"Every exit is an entrance somewhere else."
—Tom Stoppard,
Rosencrantz and Guildenstern Are Dead

—— Prologue ——

November 1938

Crouched in concealment in the laurel slick, the quarry heard the hounds approaching, and feared them more than he feared the men with guns.

Around sunset there had been a momentary break in the low, chilling sky, a passing radiance without warmth. Now it was darker; rain had set in on the shoulder of the mountain. He was naked and shuddering uncontrollably. But there was some benefit in this new misery: perhaps the wetness would throw the dogs off his scent, which was enhanced both by his fear and the blood; he was slashed head to toe like a young savage undergoing a rite of passage.

He had no idea of how far he had run (so awkwardly) through the wilderness, at times only a few hundred yards ahead of his pursuers and their baying, leashed hounds. He had been, before his crossover, nineteen years old. He no longer knew how old he was, or where he was. He had become totally isolated by the hunting party, cut off from those who might have been able to

help him. Even by the most lenient standards of civilization he would not have been judged sane, although he
was harmless to himself and to others. What remained
of his rational mind focused on the image of ferocious
Plott hounds, bred for bear hunting in these remote mountains He once had seen another Walkout torn to shreds
by a pack of hounds, until what remained on the bloody
killing ground could not accurately be identified as man
or beast

Now there was little hope of escape; it could be his
time to die.

But the laurel slick was a vast hiding place on the
shrouded mountain. Long ago a landslide had carried off
a section of hemlock and hardwood forest, leaving a
bald spot that gradually became covered with a dense
thicket as high as a man's head—intertwined laurel and
rhododendron bushes that retained their glossy leaves
through the short winter. It was not possible to walk
upright through the slick. The hunters would find the
slick difficult to penetrate, even on their hands and
knees. But eventually the dogs would find him, well-
hidden but helpless. It was not his habitat. Instinct urged
him to seek the open air, in spite of his injuries, once he
had rested and could move again.

He heard the hunters calling to one another in the
twilight; there were many of them, and as many as two
dozen of the lean, scarred dogs. They had reached the
fringes of the laurel slick.

With his teeth chattering, the quarry looked up, toward
the fuming sky nearly hidden by overlapping leaves.
Tears ran down his cold face. Still crouching, he began
to move, slowly, away from the approaching hunters.
Keeping his balance was difficult. Another bad fall,
further injury, would finish him now He had to reach

open ground. Only the sky could save him. But he might have a long way to go through the heath. at an agonizing pace.

A different note in the baying of the Plott hounds: the hunters had unleashed them to track him through the maze of laurel.

The ground slanted beneath him: for a dozen yards he slipped and slid and floundered. The hounds still had his scent. in spite of the rain. They came leaping. crashing through the tangle of branches, separate yet building in momentum. their power radiating in waves ahead of them, the furor unbearable.

He came to a stop on bare rock. where no shrubs could take root. A long sloping ledge: beneath it, an abyss. Looking up, he saw the full moon through streams of clouds.

The light of the moon would betray him. But he couldn't wait. The dogs were only seconds behind him, ecstatic, aroused to kill.

He rose shakily from his knees. There was room to spare. He felt faint from horror. The dogs—or the guns.

Trembling, the quarry took three running steps, unfolded hawklike wings, and soared above the ledge.

Below him the first of the hounds, breaking from the slick and unable to stop, skidded on the wet stone and blundered into the airy gorge with a yelp of anguish.

The quarry beat his wings furiously in the sodden, windless sky. As he was only partly made for flying, he used up his blood too fast. clumsily striving for altitude and distance: the moon blazed in his frantic eyes as he flew away.

The dogs crowded on the ledge, milled on top of one another. snuffling and bellowing in frustration. The hunters at the edge of the laurel slick stared up at the pale

nude man with scimitar wings spread twice the length of
his body. He was almost half a mile away, and fading
now into clouds rising like a tide of ink just beneath the
moon.

One of the hunters swiftly raised his rifle and fired a
single shot.

The wingbeats ceased. For a moment their quarry
seemed suspended precariously in the air. Then the light
of the moon sank beneath the sea of cloud. They lost
sight of him.

The one who had fired the shot, the hunter with the
keenest eye among his companions. claimed he saw the
hawkman crumple and fall.

They argued about it for months; but Arn Rutledge
was too quick to reinforce his conviction, or obsession,
with his fists, and gradually the subject was laid to rest.

No one doubted that Arn had the ability to make the
difficult shot; he had honed his marksmanship since he
was old enough to carry a rifle, and later made good use
of his skill in places like Biazza Ridge, Chiunzi Pass,
and Ste. Mère-Église. But, although the hunters searched
long and hard in the gorge of the Balsam Mountain
range where the hawkman would have fallen, no remains turned up.

Of the ten hunters who had seen the hawkman fly,
four died during the next three years, in mysterious,
gruesome accidents in the woods. The others went to
war; only Arn returned in 1946. And continued to talk
about the hawkman, to argue the truth of what had
become a part of the folklore of his region, to look
stubbornly for what might be left of his trophy.

Eventually he found the lightboned skeleton of the
hawkman, or so he claimed. But that's only part of the
story.

—— Chapter One ——

April 1958

Long before they reached Asheville, Whitman Bowers wished he hadn't chosen to make the long trip down from New York by car. And by then he was afraid he had made a mistake in bringing his son along. It would have been better, perhaps, if he had postponed this trip and tried to entertain the boy in New York.

Terry had spring vacation the last two weeks in April, and his mother had plans. As usual. Custody arrangements worked out years ago provided for Terry to spend alternate holidays with his father, and six weeks each summer. At Christmas they had skied for five days at Col de la Faucille, and the reunion had gone okay. Terry was in his element on the ski slopes of the Jura Mountains, expert for his age. But he wasn't a kid anymore. He was shooting up and growing older, too quickly. Changing in ways that baffled his father. He would be fifteen in July—on the ninth, to be exact—and he had entered the world just about the time Whit Bowers was convinced he was going to leave it, as he parachuted into gale-force winds over the dark southern coast of Sicily.

The boy had been cool from the moment he cleared Customs at Idlewild, carrying his things in a small Air France nylon bag and his Alpine backpack. Whit was sure that Terry had added another couple of inches since Christmas. Taller than six feet now, and almost able to look his father in the eye without cheating by going up on his toes a little. Terry let it be known that he'd had plans of his own for this holiday period. Sailing with friends from St. Tropez to Corsica and back. Millie vetoed the idea: there would be no adults aboard, and the western Med could be treacherous at this time of the year. So Terry was letting his father know his displeasure. There were no welcoming hugs, not even a handshake. He was reluctant to smile. *I'm too old now*, his attitude said, *to be told where I have to go and what I have to do*. Whit felt both a pang of regret and annoyance that he was being made a scapegoat.

Charley Hodge, president of the division of Langford Industries that employed Whit, had four kids to Whit's one, and all of them were teenagers.

"Forget it," he told Whit, "the kid'll thaw out. They're all impossible to deal with at this age."

"So how do I handle him?"

"Be patient but don't take any smartmouth shit."

There was no overt rebelliousness on Terry's part, no petulance when he found out where they were going and was told the purpose of Whit's visit to the Great Smoky Mountains. His mother had raised Terry with a firm, sometimes iron hand, and from the age of six the boy had attended elite schools where most of the subjects were taught in French. He was well-traveled, moving with a cosmopolite's confidence and a certain aloofness through the hurly-burly of international airports, the lobbies of five-star hotels. In many ways he was more European than American. His manners were above reproach, but the distance he kept between himself and his father from the time they left Manhattan and motored into the mild emerging spring of southern Appalachia became a trial for Whit. They would have ten days together, and Whit had planned side trips: Washington to view the usual monuments, then the Luray Caverns of Virginia and on to Colonial Williamsburg. Terry accepted each diversion with a polite lack of enthusiasm.

"I think we'll stop in Asheville for the night," Whit said as they drove southwest on the Blue Ridge Parkway through some of the highest mountains in North Carolina. It was the afternoon of their fourth day on the road, the next to last leg of their trip.

Terry yawned and stretched in the front seat of the rented DeSoto sedan. He looked vulnerable coming out of a doze: a reddened crease along one cheek, mouth softened, greenish eyes opaque. A bit of mustard at one corner of his mouth, left over from a hot dog lunch, was fetchingly childlike to Whit's eye. But the child was gone forever; Whit had to deal with new complexities, a maturing, challenging male he feared he might never get to know very well.

Terry spoke for the first time in two hours.

"What's in Asheville?"

"Oh—Thomas Wolfe was born there, I think. Have you read anything by Wolfe?"

"You Can't Go Home Again."

"Did you like it?"

"It was okay. Too long. I like Hemingway better. And Irwin Shaw. I talked to Shaw at one of Mom's parties. He's a ski nut, like me."

"The Biltmore mansion and gardens are in Asheville. It was a summer house for one of the Vanderbilts. All those nineteenth-century millionaires were trying to outdo one another building imitation European chateaux. If you want to have a look—"

Terry shook his head. He said, "I've seen a lot of chateaus."

"I'll bet you have. How about a plain ordinary American movie tonight?"

"That sounds okay," Terry said, nodding, his coarse blond hair falling into his eyes. He wore it longer than kids in the U.S., and Whit tried not to nag him about the length. Brushing his hair back with one hand, Terry gave his father a sideways glance and a slight, optimistic smile.

At five-thirty they checked into a motel, the units of which were miniature replicas of Mt. Vernon. It was a little hazy in Asheville, the sun just hanging on above the grasp of the horizon, a full plum in ether. The temperature was a chilly fifty-five degrees. But there were two imposing Japanese magnolias in bloom on the motel grounds; the hill immediately behind the horseshoe arrangement of units was a glowing tapestry this third week in April, pinkish dogwood and flame azalea, earthbound clouds of white rhododendron. In their room they had a wood-burning fireplace, a TV with phantasmal images.

After chicken dinners in the motel's restaurant they drove to downtown Asheville and looked over the available movies.

Terry chose *The Beginning of the End*, a low-budget thriller about grasshoppers that ate a radioactive substance at an agricultural station, grew to heights of twelve feet, and proceeded to terrorize Chicago. Terry sat with his knees propped on the seat in front of him in the nearly empty, cavernous theater, munched popcorn, and snickered often. Whit chewed gum and tried not to think about smoking.

As they were driving back to the motel Terry said, "Grasshoppers that tall would fall apart if they tried to walk."

"They would?"

"Sure. Their joints would collapse, unless they were lined with something as hard as diamonds."

"That's interesting."

"Remember when the army was hitting them with flamethrowers and cannon and stuff? All they really had to do was throw a few rocks."

"Why?"

"Grasshoppers are arthropods. Their skeletons are on the outside of their bodies, and they're always shedding them and getting new ones while they grow. The new skeletons are soft, and if you hit a twelve-foot grasshopper with enough rocks, you'd make so many dents, he'd kink and fall over."

Whit laughed, popped a spearmint Chiclet into his mouth, and offered the last one in the box to Terry.

"So you didn't like the movie much."

"Yeah, I liked it. Sometimes dumb things are fun."

While Terry took his bath in their motel room Whit built a fire on the stone hearth. Then he dialed the only number he had for Arn Rutledge in Tyree, which he had obtained from the 505th Regimental historian. But the number was long out of service. Information had listings for several other Rutledges in the western Carolina area, possibly a relative or two of Arn's. Whit thought he might try them tomorrow if he didn't have any luck tracking the sergeant-major down, but it had been a long time.

Arn had attended only one 505 reunion, in '48, a reunion Whit had missed. If he was dead, then the historian would have known about it. Although it was difficult to imagine Arn in circumstances so straitened he would leave his birthplace, he might have been forced to move up north, to Detroit or Cleveland, and find employment on an assembly line.

Whit did one sit-up and one push-up for each year of his life, then showered when Terry was finished in the bathroom.

Afterward they lay in their beds with the lights off, lulled by flames in the little ovenlike vault of the fireplace, feeling, as wanderers had always felt while holed up on unfamiliar ground, shielded and protected by their fire, by unknown gods propitiated. Terry, whose biological clock was still trying to adjust from Paris time, usually fell asleep by nine-thirty. But tonight, although he yawned frequently, he also twisted and turned and seemed to be searching for a way to get a conversation going. He settled for a further critique of the movie they'd seen.

"If a twelve-foot grasshopper, which would have to weigh about four tons, fell off the Wrigley Building, it wouldn't just get up and walk away. It would be a grease spot. That's a function of mass and momentum."

Whit said genially, "They're not wasting your time where you go to school, are they?"

"I guess not," Terry said, secure at least in this area of acknowledged superiority. "Dad?"

"Uh-huh."

"Did you ever see a paratrooper jump and his chute didn't open?"

"Couple of times."

"What happened?"

"The first one bounced about two feet off the ground; probably every bone in his body was shattered. The other roman candle came down through some pine trees at Bragg and walked away with scratches and a dislocated shoulder after falling seven hundred feet. He was a chaplain, by the way."

"I don't think I could do what you did in the war. How scary was it?"

"Jumping was bliss, compared to getting there, all but one time at night, usually in miserable weather, with inexperienced or panicky transport pilots who had trouble locating the DZ. Going into Sicily from North Africa, some of our pilots got lost in the dark, and a lot of C-47's were shot down by friendly fire from the navy standing off the coast at Gela. Most of us were so sick from dysentery we'd picked up in Tunisia, our bowels were like running faucets. Counting 'chutes, we each carried at least a hundred and twenty-five pounds of gear. Anybody who wasn't hurt or killed on landing was just lucky. I had a trick knee for three years after Sicily."

"How many jumps did you make?"

"Maybe forty in practice. Four in combat. Sicily, Italy, France, and Holland."

"You never were scared?"

"I was always afraid of screwing up and getting my men killed."

"Did you ever screw up?"

"If I had, I surely doubt anybody would have noticed." Whit's Texas drawl and phrasing became more noticeable when he was being ironic. "Except for Salerno, our combat missions were either inadequately planned, badly timed, or improperly executed due to circumstances beyond anybody's control. But . . . hell, no, when I think about it, there's not much I would have, or could have done differently. The only way to get out of a snafu is to keep moving and improvise."

"Snafu?"

"Military term for screwup."

"Oh," Terry said. After another yawn he stopped turning in the bed. Whit looked at the luminous dial of his chronometer. Ten after ten. In the fireplace a burning log broke apart, the flames flickered lower. He looked over at Terry, and was surprised to see the boy's eyes were still open. Appraising him.

"Mom said she couldn't sleep in the same room with you after you came back. You'd wake up yelling and screaming and scare the hell out of her."

"Yeah, I know it was a problem for Millie. Wasn't doing me any good, either."

"You don't have nightmares anymore, do you?"

"They're few and far between." Whit felt a change of subject was in order. "How's your mother's new book coming?"

"She's into revisions. It's about Eleanor of Aquitaine. I've read all of Mom's books, but history's my worst subject. I get bored except for the sex scenes. Don't tell her I said so."

"They make a lot of money. Five best sellers in a row."

"Yeah," Terry said, uninterested in the subject of money, which he had never lacked. "What were some of the other problems?"

"Between your mother and me? Well, the war lasted a long time. I shipped out to North Africa before you were born and by the time I got home you were potty-trained and had a two thousand word vocabulary. And your mother had the fastest-selling novel in the country. I was a burned-out bird colonel with such a bad case of the shakes I couldn't hold a glass at all those literary cocktail parties in her honor I was obligated to attend. Millie didn't understand what was wrong with me and I didn't know who the hell *she* was anymore. She owned clothes I couldn't afford to buy her, and she was on a first-name basis with movie stars. I felt like I had to go it alone for a while. In the time it took me to get my bearings and adjust to being a civilian, Millie met André on the Washington social circuit. You know the rest.''

"Mother's got a new boyfriend. His name is Raphael. I think he was an assistant director on one of Pagnol's films. Raphael is a lot younger than she is. She says she's never going to get married again.''

"Probably a wise decision.''

"Are you?''

"Am I going to get married? Not much chance, Terry.''

"What about, you know, I met her last summer on Long Island. The painter. Wasn't her name Ellen?''

"Elaine. We see each other occasionally. She doesn't come into town that often. She's getting ready for a show at her gallery.''

Terry didn't reply.

After a couple of minutes Whit turned his head on the pillow and looked at his son. His eyes were closed. His breathing had slowed. He twitched a little, nervously, beneath the blankets, exhaled sharply, then slid deeper into sleep. His face was shaped like his father's. A little long, but with a good chinline. He also had the slightly protruding density of brow that sheltered the eyes; theirs were not faces open to quick inspection, snap appraisals of character. They had, in the same spot, similar harmless moles, on the jaw near the left earlobe. Almost everything about the boy was Whit, from the way he was hung to the slimness of hip and a tendency to saunter. But Terry had his mother's keener, skeptical, sometimes acerbic witch-hazel eyes, and her excellent teeth. Whit felt a tug of appreciation, a momentary impulse of comradeship. He yearned to smoke a Camel. But he had quit again because of the troublesome coughing and was determined to build up his wind, which in turn he hoped would quicken his step on the courts. He'd been playing like a tired old man lately.

He wished there'd been time tonight to try to explain to Terry how people are changed, permanently, by circumstances. We come together, we cling to each other for a while, we are, inevitably, separated. He was reminded of a cliché that Millie the novelist might have scorned. The river of life. Human beings caught up in a timeless flow, now drifting, now hurtling through rapids, colliding with one another, slipping away, sometimes nearly drowning, everyone destined for that unimaginable waterfall at the end. Every day, by chance, countless bondings both biological and psychological occurred. *I need you. I love you. Stay with me forever.* But the river became too swift, too tricky: there are many other bodies swirling nearby, counter forces combining with cataclysmic events in the roaring depths, ceaselessly at work to separate the paired ones.

So Terry was curious about him, about the relationship out of which he had been born. A dialogue was under way, perhaps; the slight but persistent tension between them seemed to have lessened in the moments before he fell asleep. Whit didn't try to fool himself into thinking they had reached a new level of understanding. Nothing so profound. Whit already had missed too much of his son's life. They had little in common. He worked hard to keep the relationship going, but more out of duty and a sense of guilt than from love. The deep love for his flesh and blood that he knew he ought to feel. But it had been a long time since Whit Bowers had felt something stronger than a superficial attraction to anyone. The end of his marriage to Millie had been a relief. Burned-out bird colonel. But he wore the Academy ring. After extensive R&R he might have gone on faking it, swung the prestigious Pentagon post or Occupation duty, accepted the promotion to brigadier merited by his war record. But there was a surreal feeling about staying in uniform once the shooting stopped. He had gone to war expecting that he would die in battle; convinced that he must die. It was the destiny forecast in the dreadful dreams of childhood. Better men than he had been killed, seemingly at random; he had come home after months of bloody fighting on three fronts with only nicks from shrapnel, a steel pin in one ankle and some decorations for heroism under fire. His proof that he had been among the quick and the victorious. The dreams that had nothing to do with the war he had fought began to recur almost immediately, and the message was plain: his destiny was unfulfilled, unforeseeable.

Terrifying.

Now he was forty-eight years old. The lucky ones, he sometimes thought while in a sink of morbidity, lay peacefully beneath uniform white crosses in foreign countries. The unlucky were still struggling to pull their lives together. He found himself in between, steady for now but on a tightrope that sometimes shrank to the diameter of a human hair. He had stopped his heavy drinking, going from job to job, living off his contacts from the Army's Old Boy network and his father's revered name. He was doing acceptable work in a not very demanding position with Langford Industries. Not enjoying himself, but not hating it either. Making enough money to indulge in strenuous hobbies. He skied and played a respectable game of tennis and went after billfish whenever possible. He had learned several methods of diverting his mind when the brooding, potentially debilitating thoughts intruded.

Elaine, his sometime lover whom Terry had inquired about, had been in analysis for several years and, at the most intimate stage of their relationship, she urged him to give it a go. He needed to get in touch with himself before it was too late, Elaine insisted. No, not for him, not ever; sorry. So he had backed away from Elaine; they were still on cordial terms but seldom made the effort to see each other. Someone else would come along, though the river was swifter now and he felt more alone than ever in its rapids.

And now it was turning into one of those nights when he was weary from the long drive but not within reach of sleep. If he did drift off, it would be into the territory of the childhood terrors. Whit got up and walked into the bathroom, took a sleeping pill from his shaving kit and swallowed it without water. Debated taking another. He decided that two of the pills would make him groggy and possibly irritable in the morning. He walked back to the bed in his skivvies, shivering, the fire all ash and red-eyed coals now, the squat electric heater not doing much to warm the room.

—— Chapter Two ——

Terry Bowers was wide awake at five A.M., and restless. It felt like ten o'clock to him. Half the morning gone. He was a habitual early riser wherever he happened to be.

In the twin bed three feet away his father snored placidly on his back. The motel unit smelled, not unpleasantly, of warm birch log ash in the fireplace. There was a streak of twilight where the blackout drapes didn't quite come together over the windows. The old heater glowed lifelessly in one corner like an electrocuted June bug. Birds were chirping in the bushes outside. He heard a truck in a monotonous middle gear on the road a hundred yards away.

Terry got up, used the toilet, gave his hair a lick with the brush, and dressed. Chinos, penny loafers, flannel shirt, rust-colored leather jacket with a brass zipper and elastic cuffs. He let himself quietly out of the room and stood on the small roofed porch, looking around.

There was a low-lying mist drifting in bursts across

the landscape as if from silent, unseen guns. Overhead, stars so faint they disappeared even as he tried to focus on them. From one of the rooms around the semi-circular drive he heard a baby's thin squawl of hunger. He'd always been observant; he was slowly, unconsciously cultivating the artist's mania for seemingly pointless conjecture. That rusted car with Illinois plates (Land of Lincoln), one stove-in door covered with plastic sheeting taped to the body; how had the owner managed to drive his wreck this far, and where was he going?

Judging from the number of cars and pickup trucks parked around the drive, about half of the motel's rooms were occupied. What if, under some kind of spell, everybody had to come out now, get into a car that didn't belong to them, and drive off in a totally unplanned direction? The red and white Corvette was destined to be someplace else tonight, maybe five or six hundred miles away. It might be in Texas. How far was Texas from Asheville, North Carolina? He could look it up later in the Rand McNally road atlas. His father had been raised in El Paso, on the Ft. Bliss military reservation.

He walked slowly down the drive made of smooth brown river stones, toward the Blue Ridge Parkway, past the motel's restaurant that wouldn't open until seven for breakfast. He remembered the eyes of the girl who had waited on them last night, the school ring she wore on a gold chain around her neck. She was lavaliered, she had explained. It meant she was going steady. She had said, in a quietly amazed voice, "Paris, *France*?" when he told her where he was from. He liked her western Carolina accent and her delicately boned face and the way she would look at him and then look away with a slight smile as if he'd given her something weighty and interesting to think about. What if she walked out of the mist right now, wearing her green-and-white checked waitress's uniform, thick-soled white shoes that had smudges on them, and he pointed his finger at her and suddenly they were together on the Champs-Élysees. What would she say when she saw the Arc de Triomphe in front of her? When she smiled at him again, tickled and bemused, he would take her by the hand and they—

Nothing came or went on the road. He forgot about the young waitress when he saw a black dog with four white paws, run over in the night and dead for hours. The dog lay stiffly on its side, snarling mouth caked with dried blood. If it had been his dog, he thought, looking at the white paws, he would have called it "Sneakers." No collar. The dog probably didn't belong to anyone and had no name. His mother had two dogs. Toy poodles, both a kind of dowager, blue-rinse color. Mitzi and Miou-Miou. Terry tolerated the poodles but wished he owned a Great Pyrenees, his favorite breed. But he knew he wasn't going to have a dog that big (they often weighed two hundred pounds), not while they lived in a seven-room apartment. Maybe if his mother bought that restored olive mill with six acres in the countryside near Nice—

His hands smarted from the cold, and he put them in the pockets of his jacket, walking south along the parkway. A rooster crowed in the distance. The mist was thicker in places along the road. Looking back, he could make out the elevated blue neon of the motel sign, but not the motel itself. He kicked at trash in his way. A Nesbitt's Orange Soda bottle, a squashed Marvel Mystery Oil can, a bread wrapper. Almost every step of the way there was litter.

Americans could be such pigs, he thought scornfully. Thinking in French, as a Frenchman.

Terry hadn't walked far, only about a quarter of a mile, when he came to one of the roadside rest areas that afforded, when the weather was clear, vistas of mountains and valleys. An unhitched house trailer was parked well off the road, listing to one side. He had seen a couple of others like it on the way down from New York: it was a dull silver color, and shaped like a loaf of bread. There were small windows covered with venetian blinds. One of the tires had gone flat and was half off the rim, which accounted for the tilt.

The narrow door in the side of the trailer was standing open. Terry thought he heard someone groaning inside. The groans were soft, intermittent. He had heard his father make similar sounds in his sleep. The trailer was about fifty feet away in the mist. There was nothing particularly interesting about it except for the door that was open on a cold morning. Yet he felt rooted, unable to go any closer, reluctant to turn and walk away.

The groaning had stopped.

Another sleeper, troubled by his dreams.

"Boshie!"

The cry from within the trailer caused Terry's heart to jump.

"Help me—help me!"

He wasn't immediately frightened, but he didn't know what to do. Maybe there was someone else in the trailer who would respond to the plea for help.

"Where are you? I need you! Please, Boshie!"

The pathetic cries indicated that he was alone, or thought he was. Instinctively Terry moved closer.

A large man in a monk's hooded robe appeared, lurching, limping badly, from the other side of the trailer. He slammed the door shut. He looked odd as a walrus in this setting. But he was carrying something in his other hand, a club, or—Terry backed away, a sudden freeze in the region of his bowels.

The crying and pleading continued inside, but on a rising note of insult and pain, as if the slammed door had been a heartbreaking rebuff.

"What do you want?" the man in the monk's robe asked Terry. "Where did you come from?"

With his head bent the man's face was unseeable within the bulky cowl. It wasn't a club he held, Terry observed, it was a croquet mallet. The man also seemed off-balance, like the trailer; his right foot protruded beyond the hem of the russet robe. The foot looked grotesquely swollen, shapeless. On it he wore only a filthy white athletic sock.

Terry felt as if he'd taken a wrong turn into a forbidden area of a medieval cathedral; a crease of superstition, like a small bone in his throat, made it difficult to speak.

"I—I don't want anything. I was out for a walk."

"Are you staying at the motel?" He had a deep voice, which was neither threatening nor angry. But there was an inflection of command; sometimes Terry's father sounded that way, when he was talking to certain taxi drivers or obnoxious maître d's. Their rudeness always vanished, right away.

Terry nodded, answering the question, but he liked this less and less; he was poised to run. The hooded man seemed to realize it.

"Why don't you go back there?" he suggested. "This is no place for you to be—not at this time of the morning."

"Is somebody sick?" Terry asked. "Do you want me to call a doctor?"

When the man replied his voice faltered, descending on a scale of emotion from sadness to futility.

"No. A doctor won't do him any good. My brother has come home to die."

"Oh—I'm sorry. What are you going to do about the flat tire?"

"The others drove into town to buy a new one when the Goodrich store opens." The man raised his head. The pious cowl fell back and Terry saw that he had strange, bulging eyes that looked in different directions—simultaneously to heaven and to hell. "We'll be on our way soon. There's nothing you can do. Go back to where you came from, boy. Leave us in peace."

"Okay," Terry said, a tremor running through him like a quick furry animal. There seemed to be no point in repeating that he was sorry.

As he was turning to leave he heard a clatter of metal blinds at one of the small windows of the trailer. He looked up. He saw aged hands with long yellow nails holding the slats apart. A human throat with the runnels and wrinkles of old age. A trembling mouth with only a few teeth remaining.

What else he saw broke Terry's nerve and sent him flying, the sounds of a jeering, birdlike scream trailing after him.

"Geeeeek! Geeeeekkkk!"

He was beneath the flickering blue neon sign of the motel before he stopped running, winded, and bent over with his hands on his knees. He looked back to be sure that nothing—nobody—was following him, stalking him relentlessly out of the mist.

As soon as he could he jogged across the motel

grounds, around the drained pool and the children's playground, ignoring a severe stitch in his side. He let himself into the room and quickly bolted the door behind him.

He was sitting on the edge of his bed, hands between his knees, when his father woke up with a kind of wary readiness in his face, lying at full length but inobtrusively up on one elbow before Terry could blink.

"Hey—Terry. Time's it getting to be?" Whit looked at his chronometer. "Ten to six? Might as well get up."

Terry didn't move. Whit became aware of the clenched hands, his son's drawn, worried face.

"You okay? Something wrong?"

Terry almost blurted it out, everything: the silvery trailer with one tire crushed down to the axle, the limping man in monk's habit, the— He took a long breath and shook his head. He delivered the simplest explanation possible.

"I was—I went for a walk."

"Still waking up too early, huh?"

"Yeah. Do you think we could get going?"

"Now? They won't open for breakfast here for another hour, aren't you—"

Terry suppressed a shudder. "No. I'm not hungry. We can eat later, can't we?"

"Sure, I guess so." Whit sat up, stretching. "Be ready to roll in fifteen minutes."

"Okay," Terry said, as his father got out of bed and went into the bathroom. He sat staring at the door he had double-locked, lips tight, half-expecting something really bad to happen momentarily.

They knew he was staying at the motel, he'd foolishly told them that. But they wouldn't know in which room to look for him, would they? Even if they did, they couldn't get inside. But if they broke the door down—

His father could handle them; his father would stop them.

Wouldn't he?

—— Chapter Three ——

B Y the time they reached the summit of Waterrock Knob in the Plott Balsam mountains, forty-eight tediously winding and upturning miles from the motel outside of Asheville, the sun had risen and the rental car was overheating again from the altitude. At this point the Blue Ridge Parkway was the highest motor road in the east, and they had been traveling a mile above sea level for most of the way; here they were at six thousand feet.

Whit Bowers pulled off onto the graveled crescent of an overlook, to give the radiator a chance to cool down so he could pop the cap and add water before they made the long descent through Soco Gap. It was cold on the knob, not much above forty degrees. The air thin but invigorating. Whit pulled on his thick wool sweater, with the oil still in the wool for shedding cold pelting Alpine rains. Rising mist hid the pinnacles of fir and red spruce, but the sky above the mountain ranges surrounding them in oceanic waves—the Balsams, the Newfounds, the Great Smokies, the Cowees—was barefaced, with a becoming blush, like a young girl rising from sleep.

On the rock wall around the overlook he unfolded a geological survey map of the area to look for reference points. The Qualla Reservation of the eastern Cherokee nation lay immediately below them, in its settlements a slovenly place of unwanted people, extending north to the boundaries of the national park on the North Carolina–Tennessee line. Clingmans Dome, at the heart of the Smokies, was unmistakable, an indigo giant shedding torrents of smoke in a westerly direction.

He had never laid eyes on this imposing land, but he had done some background reading, he knew its history well. All of the mountains in this near-primeval region, untouched by glaciers or the heated seas of distant epochs, were heavily forested to their summits despite the best efforts of lumbermen, whose venality, in the first four decades of the century, had been criminally inflamed by a million acres of virgin timber green as new money. Whit used his binoculars and located, to the northeast, a sparkling thread of river in the valley of the Cat Brier, and Tyree, the only town of any consequence in the moistly radiant, sapphire-and-gold valley.

"Where's Wildwood?" Terry asked. He'd been keeping his eyes on the road, but they had seen only a few cars on the parkway since leaving Asheville.

Whit drew a rectangle on the map, the low side of which intersected the Balsam Mountains less than a mile north of Waterrock Knob, and shared part of the eastern boundary of the Cherokee reservation.

"Wildwood covers all of this area." He handed the binoculars to Terry. "About eighteen square miles. A third of it is inside the park now, but the company still hasn't deeded the land over to the government. Langford

Industries has been fighting a holding action for the last
twenty years, but eventually we'll have to compromise.
There's enough scenic land outside the park boundary
for what we want to do."

With his pencil he shaded a small area inside the
rectangle.

"The lake would go here, near the headwaters of the
Cat Brier. Tormentil Mountain is fifty-three hundred
feet high, and there should be room for a dozen good ski
runs on the slopes."

Terry seemed to be forcibly concentrating, trying to
show interest.

"Ski runs? Does it snow much this far south?"

"No. But we're looking ten to fifteen years ahead.
By then we should have the machines for making artifi-
cial snow economically."

They heard a car coming up the grade to the overlook. Terry put the binoculars down quickly. The car, a
big tan Olds, came into view. There was a trailer hitched
to it—a silvery Airstream with the familiar breadloaf
shape.

"Oh, shit," Terry said under his breath, instinctively
getting a grip on the sleeve of his father's sweater.

"What's the matter?"

"Let's go."

"I have to fill the radiator." Whit stared at Terry,
whose lower lip was bloodless between his teeth. The
boy raised the binoculars for a fast look at the driver as
the car and trailer pulled off the road and came toward
them. The car had Pennsylvania plates. The Keystone
State.

A heavyset man got out, rimless glasses flashing in
the sun. His hair was white, planed down to a stiff

flattop. He brushed crumbs from his cardigan sweater and gray twill pants and smiled.

"Say, this road's a killer. Just about pulled the guts out of my Eighty-Eight. But you can depend on Oldsmobile. Surrrre you can. Never bought any other make of car since I was old enough to drive."

A woman was emerging slowly and unsteadily from the other side of the car, like a sickly chick from a litter of eggshell. She also wore glasses and was noticeably bow-legged, but otherwise they looked normal to Terry, an ordinary couple.

"Don't forget the camera, 'Stelle," the crewcut man advised her. "This is the big view we came up here for. Now where're you going?"

"I need to get an Alka-Seltzer from the trailer, Joe, and use the toidy. It's your fault. You never should have tempted me with those cinnamon doughnuts."

"Now, now." He had a slight accent that reminded Terry of Lawrence Welk, the Champagne Music Man on television. He turned and winked at Whit and Terry. "Joe Kunzelman's my name. Homestead, P.A. I walked out of the plant gates for the last time Friday a week ago, and the little lady and me, we're seeing the country. Been looking forward to this trip all my life. 'Stelle, she'll get her travel legs eventually. Just wait till we come to New Orleans. She'll like that. Surrrre she will. The French Quarter. Ha-cha!" He winked again.

Terry, unsmiling, asked, "Do you have anybody else with you in the trailer?"

"No, there's just 'Stelle and me. Care to have a look inside? After 'Stelle gets off the toidy, I mean. These Airstreams are just wonderful for long-distance travel I'm not exaggerating when I tell you we've got all the comforts of home. Built solid, too. Nine thousand rivets!"

Terry shook his head. "We're in kind of a hurry. Aren't we, Dad?"

As they were driving through Soco Gap Whit looked for a third time at his uncommunicative son. Even Little Richard and Fats Domino on the car radio hadn't lightened his mood. He was chewing at a hangnail, chewing it to the quick.

"Why did you ask him if there was somebody else in his trailer?"

"I don't know," Terry mumbled.

"You must have had a reason."

"Skip it."

"Terry—" Whit's jaw was bunched ominously over his wad of gum.

Terry almost shouted at him.

Okay, okay! This morning I saw a trailer just like the one at the overlook and in that trailer was an old guy who had curly horns a foot long growing out of his head, and ears like an animal. Is that what you want me to tell you?

Just thinking about it made him feel as crazy as he suspected he would sound; never mind the fact that he was absolutely certain of what he'd seen.

So he bit his tongue hard enough to make it bleed and sat back with his arms sternly folded for a minute. Then he said abruptly and a little wildly, "Is there an airport around here?"

"I suppose so. Why?"

"Because I want to go home! I don't like it here."

"Home to Paris? Your mother isn't—"

"I know she's not there! Claude and Berthe can look after me if everybody thinks I need looking after so bad." They were the couple who had maintained the eighteenth-century apartment on Île St. Louis for as long as Terry could remember.

"I thought we were starting to get along," Whit said in exasperation. "Why the change of heart?"

Terry sat rubbing his forehead with the heel of one hand, a self-mesmerizing gesture that had a gradual calming effect, allowed his common sense to rise to the top of his brain. The truth was (he would never doubt it) he'd seen a living gargoyle no less intimidating than many of the medieval ones in stone and soot grimacing down on the oblivious city in which he lived. Undoubtedly the horned man was a freak of some kind, unless Terry was prepared to believe in the existence of the devil; he was not, he decided, although he had run through the mist this morning half-convinced he was escaping from a traveling sideshow of hell. *My brother has come home to die,* the other man had said. All but hidden in his monkish robe, exhibiting the goggle eyes of a lizard, a big lump of club foot in a dirty sock. The croquet mallet in his hand not necessarily a threat. Adding everything up, the facts of his escapade looked different to Terry. Probably the Airstream trailer and the dying old man were traveling in a different direction by now; even in this sparsely settled region he should never run into them again. What a shame. Squirming on his seat, Terry was uncomfortable: the morning sun through the closed window hot on his right cheek, his father's unspoken questions silently grilling him on the other side.

"It isn't you," Terry said finally, giving Whit a quick conciliatory look.

"Glad to hear it." The bulge in Whit's jaw smoothed out, he chewed his gum slowly. "You know it isn't practical for you to go back right now. There are things

I need to accomplish here. Get a close look at the area,
see if any of the railroad spur line is salvageable. I'll put
you on your flight a week from today. Until then maybe
you'll do your best to cooperate. It's really beautiful
around here, if you take the trouble to appreciate what
you're seeing."

"Yeah, okay," Terry said glumly. "I told you I was
sorry."

"Not exactly." But Whit smiled, relenting.

Billboards were everywhere as they neared the intersection with U.S. 19, advertising junk attractions and
souvenir shops at the fringe of the park, tribal handicrafts in the Cherokee nation. Whit drove east, toward
Tyree.

"I think you'll like Arn Rutledge. If I can locate
him."

"Is he a moonshiner?"

Whit laughed. "Wouldn't suprise me to find out Arn
was in the whiskey business; he used to talk about
'shine, how it was made. His father and most of his
other male relatives earned a living from stills before the
war. But the government's making it more difficult for
them these days."

"You depended on him a lot in the war, didn't you?"

"He was the best squad leader I had; I was a company commander going into Sicily. His troopers were all
tough country boys or mountaineers; nobody got their
respect unless he earned it. We missed the DZ, jumped
too high and too fast, and I lost track of Arn's stick. The
battalion was scattered over a wide area in the dark;
none of us had any idea where the hell we were, except
we knew we were behind the lines. I regrouped part of
my company and we headed south toward the beach-
head, raising hell with small patrols, making as much

trouble as we could along the way. We cut telephone lines and blew up bridges. Some of our kids had shaved their heads back in Tunisia, and they were wearing war paint. The civilians we ran into were terrified; the Germans had told them that all American paratroopers were convicted murderers, parolees from death row. Counting walking wounded, we had less than four thousand troopers roaming around as far south as Santa Croce Camerina, about twenty miles from the DZ. But by dawn the Italians and Krauts were convinced it was more like sixty thousand. Intelligence wasn't very good on either side. We didn't know there was a Goering Division Panzer unit in Sicily until we ran into a column near Biazza Ridge. We didn't have antitank weapons, nothing that could even slow down a sixty-ton Tiger. We dug in anyway, down about eight inches into bare rock, and held until we got some help from a battery of .155's on the beach. There were so goddamn many tanks on the ridge, all they had to do was fire for effect. I rounded up all the able-bodied men I could find—clerks, cooks, riggers, you name it. We crawled forward a few feet at a time, knocking out pillboxes—until we ran smack into a big Tiger sitting in a ravine and drawing a bead on us. I thought we were goners. But the top of the tank popped open and there was Sergeant Arn Rutledge grinning at me. He'd surprised the tank crew outside having a smoke and a piss, polished them off with a grenade. Then he crawled inside to take a look at his new tank. 'Hey, Captain,' he said to me, 'if we can figure how to turn this fuckin' thing on, we'll have the area policed up directly.' "

"Did he get a decoration for taking the tank?"

"The first of many. A couple of nights later he was burned pretty badly pulling some British commandos

out of a glider that crash-landed. In France we had days
of going from hedgerow to hedgerow, house to house,
flushing out the Krauts. I don't know how many snipers
he killed. Mountaineer's savvy. He had the old squirrel-
hunter's knack for knowing where to look, where to
shoot, before they spotted him.''

"How long has it been since you've seen him?''

"The summer the war ended. I had to miss the '48
reunion. It was a testimonial to the sergeant-major,
so some of the guys made damned sure he was there.
They told me Arn stayed drunk for three days, not very
drunk, just enough to keep his distance and maybe his
dignity.''

"What's a sergeant-major?''

"Highest ranking noncom in the army. There's only
one per company. Arn could have had battlefield pro-
motions on up to major if he'd wanted them. But he
never cottoned to the idea of being an officer. Held most
of us in contempt.''

"But not you.''

"I never behaved in any way he found disgraceful.''

Terry smiled slightly. "Do you think he'll take us to
Wildwood?''

"If we can find him and he's not busy doing something else. I'd like to have him along. He must know
every foot of the way.''

Now they were driving through the Cat Brier Valley.
Cove country: woodlots in pale green leaf, pastures
smothered in wildflower. Phosphorous yellow and coolly
passionate lavender. Lolling cows enclosed by the zig-
zag of split rail fences, old gray wood weathered hard as
iron. They crossed the river, not a torrent but full to its
banks, and clean, entered the town between two churches
facing each other on hillsides. The Baptists in tall white

frame and with a belfry, tombstones haphazardly spaced over most of the rest of their hill. The CME church was brick and blue shingle, squarish, utilitarian, a red, white, and blue crusader's shield over their doorway. The grave-yard near the CME church was of old dismembered vehicles, rust-red hulks half buried in tenacious kudzu like collapsed tents.

Tyree, North Carolina. Population 1705 The Lion's Club met on the last Friday of each month at Fulcrum's Cafe. The BPOE had their own shacky place, next door to a John Deere dealership. Machines more formidable than the grasshoppers in *The Beginning of the End* were grouped on the gravel of the front lot as if mounting a long-term siege. There were signs of life: a tall man in slouchy Big Smiths was talking to another man, bald as Eisenhower, who wore a yellow John Deere cap back-ward on his head. Big Smith pulled away in his running-board pickup as Whit turned into the drive. The man in the John Deere cap sat in a wooden armchair beneath a sagging rust-stained tin roof and regarded the newcom-ers with a tilt of his head. He had one stale eye and a contented manner, as if he'd fathomed the strategy of the machines, and couldn't be bothered.

"Help you?"

"I'm looking for a man who grew up around here," Whit said. "Arn Rutledge. Do you know him?"

"Everybody knows Arn."

"Could you tell me where I might find him?"

The man turned his head so that Whit could see only the stale eye, which was like having a door shut in his face, one with a Closed sign dangling in it.

"We were in the war together," Whit explained. "Eighty-Second Airborne, 505th parachute infantry regiment. I was his commanding officer. Thought I'd like to say hello, long as I was down this way."

"And you would be—"

"Whit Bowers."

"New York plates on your car, but can't place the accent."

"Texas."

"Well, howdy," the man said, as if they were starting over, and favored Whit with his good eye. "The five oh five, eh? Heard tell that was the toughest outfit in the U.S. Army."

"We liked to think so."

"You just might of come a piece for nothing. Arn ain't the easiest sort to get hold of. What you could do is, drive on into town to the traffic light—they's but one in Tyree, and buddy I don't know what we need that'n for—then you go left and from the lumberyard it's three-quarter mile on up the cove. You'll see his store there on the left-hand side the road. Cash grocery and gas, and he's got him some cabins scattered back there 'mongst the tall trees. Rents to a few tourists ever summer but he's off the main road and the sign he put up out the other side of town don't pull 'em in none too regular. Arn, he's around the store sometimes. Hard to say when."

"How does he run a business, then?"

"Wife's there. And his nephew, Jewell, who is not too strong in the head but can make change."

"Okay, thanks."

"Arn did himself proud in the war, hear tell."

"He's a good man. Nobody I trusted more."

The man nodded, but cautiously. "Well, there's not too many would call harm agin' him. On the other hand, not so many claim him as a friend. Men have a way of changing, I suppose.''

''Why do you say that?''

''Been a while since the war. Must have changed some yourself.''

''That I have.''

''You come across ol' Arn, give him my kind regards. Name's Ripley. Believe it or not.'' The man doubled up slowly, convulsed, then let out a whoop of laughter.

Whit said with a smile, ''The boy and I are thirsty.'' He had noticed a soft-drink box around by the side door of the building. ''We'd like to get a couple of sodas from your box.''

''Yesterday's ice is mostly gone, but them drinks'll be cold enough, I reckon. They's dime apiece.''

Whit paid him. Terry slid the corroded top of the drink box back, felt around in the numbing six inches of water until he fished up a Grapette and an RC Cola from the murky bottom.

''Want to try to find some breakfast, or go on up to Arn's store?'' Whit asked.

''I guess I'm hungry now.''

Three blocks away, at the corner where the blinking yellow traffic light was suspended over a deserted intersection, they found Fulcrum's Cafe. A dozen cars and trucks were parked diagonally in front. A trio of Walker hounds in a dog box in the back of a stake-sided pickup truck raised a ruckus as they went by, up two high steps to a sidewalk and the roof jutting out over the cafe entrance and steamed-up windows.

Inside there was a crowd, men in fedoras and denim and heavyweight, triple-stitched brown duck overalls doing some serious eating beneath the heavy blue float of griddle smoke, waitresses busy and chatty at the same time. Two stools left at the counter, with an unfriendly looking black-jowled man seated between them. But he moved over with a nod to Whit so Whit and Terry could be together.

"Mornin' to you," one of the waitresses said, placing laminated menus in front of them. She had straggly red hair pinned up, and freckles everywhere, even on her gums. Teeth going every which way in her mouth but a good-humored smile for all that.

They ordered mountain flapjacks with sorghum molasses, which the waitress referred to as "short sweetenin'," big ovals of grilled ham, a double ice-cream scoop helping of grits covered with red-eye gravy, two eggs over easy. The food was better than any they'd eaten thus far on the road; it was, in fact, superb. Terry cleaned his plate and let the waitress talk him into having a second glass of rich buttermilk.

"Where y'all from?" she asked, when she had a few moments to catch her breath.

"New York."

"Paris," Terry said.

"That be Paris, Tennessee, or Paris, Kentucky? My second cousin Hallie Norton's married to a ole boy from Paris, Kentucky. Maybe you've heard of—"

"No, uh, I live in France."

"You don't say! Why, you are a *long* way from home, darlin'. Come all this way to visit the park? It just may be the prettiest season there is for wildflowers, but gets right cold at night; see that you dress warm if you're pitchin' camp."

The man who earlier had moved over one stool wiped up egg yolk from his plate with a piece of biscuit and turned his unkempt bearish head to stare at Terry. Because of the close set of his blue eyes his scrutiny could be taken either as menacing or moronic. He filled out his unpressed wool shirt in great heaps and bulges. The rye and acid odor Terry had put up with through the course of his meal seemed to take on added sharpness as the man focused his full attention on him. Apart from his size, which was considerable, there was something disturbing about him: edgy, secret, outlaw.

"Where do you live in Paris?" he asked.

Terry blinked at hearing faultless French, and was a few moments in replying. "On the Quai d'Orléans, near the St. Louis bridge."

The man nodded. "With a splendid view of Notre Dame, I should imagine."

"From my bedroom windows."

"I was three years studying at the Sorbonne. Have a good day."

He got up abruptly, laid down a quarter for the waitress, who had scooted away momentarily to refill a coffee mug, and departed without another word.

Whit, whose French was only fair, asked Terry to translate the brief conversation.

"He wanted to know where I lived in Paris. He said he studied at the Sorbonne."

"Studied what?"

"I don't know."

Whit watched curiously as the big man paid his bill, helped himself to toothpicks from the dispenser beside the cash register, and walked out. He said to the freckled waitress, who was back within earshot, "Do you know who that man was?" He pointed at the stool next to Terry.

She deftly picked up the quarter and dropped it into her apron pocket.

"I believe his name's Jacob. Somebody did tell me that."

"You don't know him? He's not from around here?"

"Surely weren't born here. He started comin' in, could be two, even three years ago. I'll see him ever' meal for a couple days, then I won't see him the longest time. Ain't never spoke ten words to me, 'cept to order. Not much for conversation." She wrinkled her nose; his odor had stayed behind like a homeless ghost. "Baths nuther."

"He speaks French," Terry said.

"Do tell. Now that's somethin' else I know about him. Speaks French and rides a ole Harley motorcycle and lives way off up in the woods. Just wants to be left alone, I reckon." She beamed at Terry. "What else can I get you?"

"I'm full," he groaned.

"Hon, what're you talkin' about? Call that *breakfast*? Won't be ten o'clock you'll be hungry again and snackin' pie."

Chapter Four

THEY got back into the DeSoto and turned left at the one-eyed signal; within a couple of blocks the town of Tyree was mostly behind them. They saw, pulled off on the apron of a station that sold an unknown brand of gas, a muddy black motorcycle. The French-speaking man was hunkered down beside it, one hand on the throttle as he revved the engine and listened to it misfire. They passed the lumberyard and the road climbed gradually past small mean houses with chicken yards and beanpole gardens freshly hoed, into a thickening of graceful cove hardwoods: yellow poplar, buckeye and sugar maple with new dill-green leaves woven like lace eighty feet above the ground. Beside the two-lane blacktop road where the sun was unobstructed, smaller trees and shrubs had reached a peak of radiance a blind man could have distinguished through his skin. The streaming air had a sweet-sour tang to it, subtly narcotic. Speeding through this byway of nature in its surge of renewal Whit Bowers felt perversely melancholy, humbled, and barren. He drove faster than he knew he should in an unexplainable pique, tires squealing on a deceptive curve, and Terry shot him a look.

When the road straightened out a large sign appeared, framed in split knotty pine that had been stained and varnished to stand up to the weather. The sign was neatly lettered. ICE*GROCERIES*BAIT 500 FEET, it said. And LAST GAS BEFORE THE PARK. And TOURIST CABINS/HEAT.

The store was set back from the road about thirty yards. with a big graveled parking area in front that showed a few sprigs of dandelion. Otherwise the area was neat and well-policed, as Whit would have expected of Arn's establishment. He dispensed Good Gulf gasoline from two pumps. The store had the customary sheet-metal roof to shade a concrete porch slab, but the roof was in good repair and only slightly stained by rusting nailheads. Both the frame building, painted a pale yellow. and the slab porch rested on concrete block pillars. There was a Double Cola logo painted on the screen door. A Kern's bread truck was parked near the steps and the route man had stacked some cartons of bread and rolls on the porch.

The young man in faded jeans and undershirt who had been watching this operation took his hands out of his back pockets and accepted an invoice from the route man. He concentrated on signing his name to the invoice. putting as much energy into it as if he were wrestling a bear.

He had to be Jewell, Arn's nephew, Whit thought. He certainly fit the brief description provided by the John Deere dealer in town. Jewell looked just savvy enough to get out from under a falling tree. His eyes were pale and vague. too insubstantial for the depths of their bony sockets. His mouth was a little agape from the weight of an uncouth lantern jaw. He was slat-thin but had a girlish tummy, not a manly beer-drinker's mound over his belt.

"There you be," Jewell said, handing down the clipboard. He smiled expectantly at the route man and fidgeted. The route man turned away whistling to his truck and shut the double doors in back. Jewell's expression changed from dull amiability to pained concern. He opened his mouth but didn't speak, then slumped as if heartbroken against a vine-covered post.

The route man paused, still whistling, gazing a little dreamily at the clipboard. Then he suddenly snapped the fingers of his free hand and looked up at the porch.

"I forget somethin', Jewell?"

Jewell nodded eagerly, hopefully.

"Yeah, sure 'nuff did." He opened the doors again, rummaged inside for another, smaller carton, tossed it to Jewell but making him reach. Jewell fumbled and dropped his prize, then went down on all fours after it.

"Almost forgot your cupcakes," the route man said. He locked the doors. "Now listen careful, Jewell. Won't be no more free cupcakes, less'n—"

That got Jewell's attention. He looked up in the act of tearing the lid off the white carton.

"Unless you tell Arn in no uncertain terms he's got to cut out lettin' his account run so long. Tell him that comes straight from the boss man. He don't pay up soon, I got to drop him from the route. Now what'd I just say?"

Jewell's hands trembled. He breathed deeply, staring into space.

"Tell Arn—"

"In no uncertain terms—"

"Uncertain terms, he's got to cut out lettin' his account run so long."

"That's the boss man talkin', not me. Sure you got the message?"

Jewell nodded.

"Okay. So long. Why don't you try to make them cakes last this time?"

The bread truck drove away. Jewell sat back against the wall of the store next to the screen door. He tore at a cellophane package with his teeth and extracted a devil's food cupcake with a squiggle of white icing on it. He had paid no attention to the arrival of the DeSoto and didn't look up from his treat until Terry and Whit reached the bottom of the steps.

"Hello, Jewell," Whit said.

Jewell pinched a couple of dark crumbs from his gray undershirt and carefully popped them into his mouth. "You need gas?"

"No, I don't need anything. I'm looking for Arn."

A hint of wariness wrinkled the fair brow. "Don't know that I seen him yet this week."

"Do you know where he is? Where I can find him?"

Jewell licked a grimy finger. "I like these Hostess cupcakes the best, they got the cream fillin' in the middle, you know? Ain't supposed to eat nothin' sweet because of my sugarbetes condition, but just get to cravin'?" His voice had a way of ending on a questioning high note, as if he doubted the wisdom of what he was saying, or had been told, too often, to keep his mouth shut.

"Jewell."

"Huh? Oh, you want Arn?" He pondered his uncle's absence. "When Arn goes, he just goes. Don't tell nobody first. You could ask Faren? Maybe Faren knows when he'll be back."

"Who's Faren?"

"That's Arn's wife. Now, she's not here nuther. She's down at the reservation? But Faren told me she'd be back before noon. I don't recollect what time it was she left."

"Mind if we wait around?"

"Heck, no. Why should *I* mind? Come up and set a spell." He looked around the porch. There was nothing to sit on except some upended yellow Coke boxes against the wall.

"Give you a hand with that bread," Whit suggested. He and Terry picked up a couple of boxes each. Jewell scrambled to open the screen door.

"That's nice of you," he said, as if he were amazed to have someone go to any trouble on his account. "That's *real* nice."

Inside the one-room store there was a scarred counter on one side half taken up by big glass storage jars each partially filled with cookies and soda crackers. There was a cash register at one end. The metal bread rack was in front of the counter and they put the boxes down there. A coil-top refrigerator hummed noisily in one corner next to a butcher's refrigerated case. Whit noticed a scarcity of canned goods on the shelves. The deep sill of the window that faced the gas pumps and the road had a long strip of sticky paper with a line of extinguished but otherwise intact flies adhering in a row, looking like quaint aircraft from a Lilliputian war.

Whit got around to introducing Terry and himself. Jewell waved a hand at some wooden chairs surrounding a black Franklin stove

"You could set over there, you got a mind to wait? But Arn—he took the dogs with him."

"Has he gone hunting?"

Jewell opened the door of a refrigerator and took out a bottle of milk that was half empty.

"Mainly he just goes a-lookin'," Jewell muttered. Then he glanced around at them, lowering the bottle before it touched his lips. "Offer you a drink of this?"

Whit and Terry declined. Jewell tilted his head back and swallowed most of the milk that was left in the bottle, dribbling some of it on his gray undershirt. He put the bottle back into the refrigerator.

"What's Arn looking for?" Whit asked idly.

Jewell looked for a place to stash the opened carton of cupcakes behind the counter, disappearing for a few moments. They heard him laugh, deep in his chest: *huh, huh, huh*. Then he popped up partway, head and shoulders above the countertop, his face woodenly serious, like a character in a puppet show that sooner or later all the other characters were going to take a whack at.

"Oh, we don't talk about it none. He lamed me right upside the head one time for sayin' it out loud, couldn't hear so good out of this ear for the longest time." He put a thin arm up on the counter, and pointed at the assaulted ear. Then he got to his feet, leaned out, and looked at the rack in front of the counter.

"Reckon I'll just put that bread up. Won't sell half of it nohow."

"I think I'll go outside," Terry said. Being around people like Jewell made him edgy after a time.

Whit, looking around, had seen a pay phone in the corner where the stove was.

"Go ahead. I need to call the office."

Terry walked outside on the porch, screen door slapping shut behind him. A young tabby with a stylized face like one of the lions in a Rousseau painting gazed at him from a corner of the porch, then swatted at an insect buzzing around its head. Terry wasn't a cat person and didn't try to get acquainted. Hands in the pockets of his suede jacket, he went down the steps and looked behind the store. Undershirts like Jewell wore were drying on a carousel clothesline; presumably he lived in a room behind the grocery—there was a back door and a single window with a cheap yellow shade pulled halfway down. Terry walked past a pile of bald tires stored in a scrap lumber bin, a rusted barrel reeking of partly burned, compacted trash. A little farther on he came to an outhouse. He had never seen one before, and had to open the door and glance inside to be sure of what it was. Like a *pissoir*, but fetid and spider-webby under the roof. Kudzu vine had been halfway cleared from a hillside and left in piles to rot and a few trees were logged off, leaving stumps around which new shoots of kudzu were winding. There were two beehives on the hill, and dozens of redbud trees in blush shades of a color between pink and purple, dazzling where the sun touched the boughs. The gravel road went back a hundred and fifty feet and looped around a big shagbark hickory that looked as if it had been clawed by lightning more than once. There was a string of modest tourist cabins beneath the hill. Opposite them, a one-story clapboard house with a stone chimney and a deep screened porch distinguished by filigreed woodwork. Jonquils and daffodils and a few tulips had been planted where they would have sun for the longest part of the day. Behind the house stood a cluster of peach and sassafras trees, fronting a long grassy slope to a stream with a tile springhouse on the bank. Half a dozen large brown birds with topknots were strutting in the shade beneath the trees; they had loud and irritating voices like geese, and seemed to be upset by his presence. Downwind there was a henhouse and dirt yard populated by fat pullets having chicken-brained disputes about nothing much. A dog kennel that appeared deserted. A garden plot enclosed by more chicken wire reinforced with palings to keep rabbits and other vegetarian nibblers out. Little clumps of wildflowers everywhere, like drippings from an artist's palette. Hepaticas thriving in the rotted hollow of a stump, violets splashed up against one side of a corrugated metal building with an air-conditioning unit that took up most of the window space on one side.

He heard tires on gravel and turned to see a '55 Pontiac station wagon. He stepped off the rutted road to let it go by. The dark green wagon, with simulated wood siding, stopped in front of the house. The woman who got out had a dark russet face and short black hair, Italian-cut, high, slanting cheekbones. Her widely spaced eyes were of a darkness somewhere between the tone of her skin and the raven sheen of her hair. Her expression was neutral as she looked him over, but sunlight on her lips suggested a willingness to smile. A strand of hair loosened by the breeze came down over one strong eyebrow. She flipped it back with a little toss of her head.

"Hi," she said. "I'm Faren. Are you looking for me?"

"No. We were—we came to see Mr. Rutledge."

"Arn's my husband," she said. "He isn't around today, I don't think. Who's we?"

"My dad and me. My name's Terry Bowers."

"Ohhhh." She was wearing a V-neck black sweater over a white Ivy League shirt, a tan culotte, and sturdy-looking harness-leather sandals. She appeared tall to Terry, but it may have been an illusion because of her slenderness, the length of her throat, the short haircut that covered all but the lobes of her ears and left the nape of her neck bare. "Your father's not Colonel Whit Bowers from the 82nd Airborne, is he?"

Terry nodded. Her smile came and went so quickly, he had only an impression of perfect teeth, a whiteness that startled and left him with a momentary sensation of having been tapped smartly at the base of the neck with a pointed rubber hammer. He seemed to have forgotten how to breathe. But the smile was gone; she put the backs of her wrists on her hips in a way that was feminine and aggravated, and looked around.

"Well, Arn's in for a shock," she said softly. "If and when." She looked back at Terry, the storm in her eyes cooling and whirling away, leaving her face a little squarish and rigid until she managed another, fainter smile. "Did you just get here?"

"Yeah, little while ago."

"Where's your father?"

"He's using the phone at the store."

She nodded. "I want to meet him. Maybe you could give me a hand with something first."

"Sure."

Faren Rutledge opened the back of the wagon, which was loaded with digging tools, a rolled-up tarpaulin, and several of the five-gallon cardboard drums that ice cream for stores came packed in. But these drums were old and contained damp clay.

"I'm a potter," she explained. "Don't want this stuff to dry out before I can use it." Apparently she had dug the clay herself. Her hands looked a little beat-up, the nails all broken off to the quick, the only thing about her

that wasn't exceptionally attractive. She still had traces
of the red clay ground into the minute whorls of her
fingertips, outlining the abused nails. Now that she was
standing next to him, Terry could tell she was about
five-six: half a head shorter than he. Her jewelry was
silver, handcrafted, it looked tribal. Terry remembered
what Jewell had said about her going down to the
reservation, and he wondered—

Faren pulled two clay-stained butcher's aprons out of
a sack and handed one to Terry. "This will protect your
clothes. Clay stains worse than pulcoon root."

"What color is that?"

She laughed. "The color of my skin," she said.

"Are you—"

"I'm Cherokee, yes. Full-blooded."

"Oh. You don't—"

"Don't talk like an Indian?" She was busy tying her
apron behind her back. "How are we supposed to sound?
I only say 'ugh' when I step in some chickenshit. Cherokees were a literate people a hundred and thirty years
ago, with their own syllabary. I have a master of fine
arts degree from East Tennessee State."

Terry's cheeks were hot; she knew he was embarrassed without having to look at him. She picked up one
of the drums of clay and leaned it against her chest,
sighing a little from the effort.

"That was kind of a put-down. Everybody tells me
either I run off at the mouth or I don't talk at all. I'm
sorry. Why don't you grab one of these things and
follow me?"

Faren led him past a covered cistern at the back of the
house and along a path to the door of the iron shed that
was her workshop.

"What's a syllabary?" Terry asked, when he began to regret her silence.

"It's a list of characters, like Chinese writing, that stand for the syllables of a language. An alphabet—sort of. Our written language was invented by Sikwa'yi, or Sequoyah, a mountain Cherokee who didn't read or understand English. But he took characters from an old spelling book, turned some of them upside down, any which way, added little curlicues and symbols he thought up. The result was eighty-six different signs, one for each syllable of Cherokee speech. He spent twelve years doing this because he wanted to preserve our heritage. There were Cherokees who thought he was possessed, and ought to be put to death."

"What happened to him?"

"Annihilated with the rest of the nation, I guess, in 1838."

"Annihilated?"

"Better not get me started," Faren said. She put down the drum she was carrying and opened the workshop door. "Once we were a nation; now we're a poverty pocket in no-man's land."

The workshop was illuminated through a makeshift plastic skylight covering a hole cut in the sloping iron roof. There was just enough space for some deep shelves knocked together from packing crates, an electric kiln, a sink, her potter's wheel and worktable. Examples of her art, painted and glazed bowls and storage jars, lined the shelves. She liked earth tones, speckled tans and off-whites, crudely drawn geometrical designs into which she'd worked barely recognizable totem shapes: bears, birds, deer.

They made three trips with the cartons of clay. She covered each with wet sacking, then pulled a handkerchief from a sleeve of her sweater to dab at perspiration on her forehead.

"Gets fierce in here in the summer," she said, "even with that little air-conditioner going. Thanks for the help, Terry. You know, you look a lot like your daddy, pictures of him I've seen. But it's been some time since Arn pulled his wartime album out."

"Where did you learn to make these?" Terry asked, looking at her pottery.

"Oh, I took a couple of courses at school; after that it was just trial and error. Need to get back to work, the big buying season's June till about Labor Day, when the tourists come swarming around the reservation."

They walked to the grocery store. Whit was off the phone, sitting on the top step of the porch looking at one of his maps.

"Where do you go to school, Terry?" Faren asked him.

"*L'École du Sacre Coeur*. That's in Paris. I live there with my mom."

"Paris? Lucky you. I wouldn't mind seeing Paris. Maybe I will someday." But as she spoke she was shaking her head slightly, as if the possibility seemed ludicrously remote.

She went striding ahead of Terry to the porch steps, and introduced herself to Whit.

"If Arn has a hero in this life, I guess it would be you, Colonel Bowers."

"I've been retired from the army a long time, Mrs. Rutledge. So if you'd just call me Whit."

"And nobody at all calls me Mrs. Rutledge."

"Fair enough. How is Arn?"

She smiled, at the same time drawing up her shoulders, clasping one hand briefly over the back of the other, as if the casual question was, too abruptly, in a sensitive area, like the prick of an unseen needle.

"I expect you'll find him changed a good bit. After all, it's how many years?"

For the third time that morning he had the impression that there was something difficult in Arn's character, a difficulty that people were reluctant to step right up and name. What was he doing, drinking too much? Helling around? Or was it darker than that, perhaps criminal?

"Fourteen years," Whit said.

"We've been married since '53." She fell then into a bracing posture, arms across her breasts, perhaps obliquely expressing an opinion of the marriage. "I know Arn'll be tickled you're here. Wish there was some way I could get word to him. But there's no track where he goes when the mood takes him. How long can you stay? Are you here on vacation?"

"No. The company I work for owns a big piece of land—"

"*Wildwood,*" she said, dark eyes widening, her pupils suddenly odd, as if their polished density had been heated and then fractured by an overload of light; there was something at once stern and mystic in her lovely face. "Arn's there. He just won't ever give up—but you shouldn't have come—" She blinked and looked confused, like someone trying to sort out signals from a distant flashing mirror, tension building in her slim body. She dropped her hands and leaned forward, and he sensed that she wanted to take hold of him, to communicate, words having failed her.

"What's wrong, Faren?"

A prewar Buick pulled up to the gas pumps and a woman hailed her. Faren shivered almost imperceptibly, lowered her eyes, glanced back up at Whit sharply, turned to the Buick with a wave of her hand, called, "Jewell! Gas."

He came out of the store at a lope, excusing himself as he squeezed past them and went to the car.

Faren said pleasantly, " 'Morning. Mr. Dryman. Good morning. Wilty. How's your new grandson?"

"Right fair chunk of a boy," the old woman replied. She had tiny black eyes. Her face was softly circular and mottled. like a plump snake curled up in a basket. "Where's that rascal Arn?"

"Oh. he's cooterin' around somewhere. Mr. Bowers, here, he'd be a friend of Arn's from the war. And this good-looking boy is his son Terry."

"Mighty pleased," Wilty Dryman said, looking the two strangers over with a toothless smile that was like a dimple in the body of the snake. When they had their two dollars worth of Good Gulf and Jewell had checked the oil level ("Believe I'll add a quart next time," said Mr. Dryman), the Buick grumbled sootily uphill.

Faren said. "Wilty's a long-tongued woman, so it's always a good idea to get straight with her who's who and what's what before she can think of a more interesting story to tell."

" 'Long-tongued,' " Terry repeated, grinning. "What's that?"

Faren put an arm around him and gave him a rough hug. "Means she's an ole gossip, and you better get used to the way we talk around here." Terry's grin was bigger and his cheeks were reddening again. "Now, tell me how long you'll be staying," she insisted, addressing Terry. her back to Whit.

"A few days, I think—" Terry glanced at his father for confirmation. "I have to be back at school the thirtieth—"

"Well, until then you're staying right here with us. Wouldn't have it any other way."

She released Terry and turned to Whit. She looked wryly embarrassed and avoided his eyes, almost as if he were a lover whom she had met in the dark, was unsure of what face to put on the affair now that their passion had been spent. She kicked fiercely at the head of a dandelion, scattering tufts. He sensed fear in her.

"What is it you don't like about Wildwood, Faren?"

"Everything. You name it." Head down, she located another dandelion to demolish with a swing of her foot. "Nobody goes there if they don't have to. Hunters have met with some pretty strange accidents. Even moonshiners, who truly like their privacy, they stay clear of Wildwood."

"Why?"

"Oh—well—I expect since you work for the Langford people, you know Wildwood's history. Since the disappearance, the tall tales have taken on the stature of Holy Writ. It's superstition—but, maybe not entirely superstition—"

"What disappearance?" Terry asked.

Faren looked at Whit. "Haven't you told him anything about Wildwood?"

"Not much."

"Has he heard about Mad Edgar's Revels and the enchanted cottage?"

"What's this going to be, a fairy tale?" Terry asked skeptically.

Whit laughed, and Faren looked briefly amused.

"Sort of," she said. "The story's about a mean old wizard who took a beautiful princess away from her rich family and made her live down here in the wilderness while he built his cottage—"

Terry groaned. "Come *on*."

"You tell it," Whit said to Faren. "I can't do half as well."

"Terry, I'm only pulling your leg a little bit. First of all, Wildwood starts up the road there about half a mile; then it's eighteen square miles of virgin forest and mountains and a couple of pretty little lakes, Arn says. I wouldn't know; I've never set foot in those woods. Anyway, it was all owned at one time, long before they thought of having a national park in the Smokies, by a man named Edgar Langford. He was one of the sons of—" She looked to Whit for help. "What was his name again?"

"John Alvin Langford," Whit said.

"The old man, if I've got this right, was a crony of Cornelius Vanderbilt and, later on, John D. Rockefeller and Jay Gould, and the same kind of highbinder. That's another word for a rich man who steals and gets away with it. He made a ton of money from other people's misfortunes, merging railroads, forming cartels to fix prices, forcing competitors to go broke by busting the stock exchanges during the financial panics that caused the Great Depression of 1873 to 1896."

Terry said patiently, "What disappeared?"

"Coming to that. When old man Langford died, he left his railroads and all the rest to the sons who were of the same stamp as himself, and not likely to lose back what he'd gobbled up during the Depression. His other son was Edgar, who was no businessman. All Edgar got was money. About a hundred million dollars. In those days, that much of an inheritance made him richer than some nations."

"Uh-huh," Terry said, fidgeting, trying to keep his interest alive; it sounded like a history lesson to him.

"Edgar Langford was born in Paris in 1863, where his father took the family so his oldest sons wouldn't have to fight in the Civil War. Edgar was the last of his children, his mother must have been close to forty then, and you know children born that late sometimes turn out to be the runts of the litter. Edgar never enjoyed good health as long as he lived. But he was a scholar; had Latin and Greek down cold before he lost all his baby teeth. Have you heard of Mesopotamia?"

"No."

"Mesopotamia was the Greek word for Iraq, which the Bible tells of in Kings and Isaiah and Revelation. If you've studied your Bible, then you must know about the Babylonian Captivity. Anyway, that's all Edgar cared about, ancient civilizations that go back, oh, five thousand years. He spent a lot of time and money digging up old cities—places like Ashur and Nineveh and Babylon itself—and unearthed all sorts of valuable relics. There were statues of gods and kings, the chariots they rode in, jewelry, gold daggers, and better bowls than I know how to make. Some of them carved out of big blocks of obsidian, which is brittle stuff to work with, or so I've heard. They had wonderful craftsmen, even that long ago. Well—it was Edgar's money, and he wasn't about to hand over the treasures he found or bought from other diggers who were swarming over the ruins to any government or even a museum. By the time he was thirty Edgar had spent a couple of summers in the Asheville area, recovering from lung trouble—all it does is blow dust in Iraq—and he began to buy the parcels of land that make up Wildwood. He'd already determined he was going to build himself what the rich people in those days called a "cottage," build it high up on Tormentil where, I imagine, the view is second to none. And build it big enough to hold all the beautiful things he'd brought back from his digs and stored in warehouses. He had a chateau designed like some he'd seen and admired in Europe, and set to work. That was in 1904. The cottage, which covered twenty-four acres of ground, wasn't finished until 1916. Just a couple of weeks before it vanished, along with Mad Edgar and all the guests he'd invited down for a housewarming."

"Why did you call him 'Mad Edgar'?"

"He started out in life a little eccentric; a genius more or less. But when he was still a young man, on one of his first trips to the Middle East, he got bit by some kind of poisonous insect, a centipede or scorpion. He was partially crippled from that bite, and almost died. It seemed to affect his mind as well as his body. From that day on they say he was never free from pain. You have to feel sorry for somebody in that state, but he really did act like a madman at times. He liked to play mean jokes on people. He thought he was a greater magician than Houdini, and claimed he learned the secret of making himself invisible from inscriptions on some clay tablets he'd found in Mesopotamia."

"So he made himself disappear?" Terry asked with a slightly wary frown, as if he anticipated Faren had a joke of her own in mind.

"No, no, that's not what happened. It was just a freak of nature that brought down the cottage and all the people in it. Like I said, this was the summer of 1916. Ole Mad Edgar invited about five hundred guests to a week-long party; his Revels, he called them. A lot of big shots, the upper crust from New York and Boston. They came by special trains, in sixty-five deluxe Pullman cars, the fanciest private varnish anywhere. His party was written up in all the newspapers and the magazines at the time; created a sensation. When I was in college I did a term paper on Langford and the Wildwood mystery, so I've read most of the old accounts. A masquerade ball was supposed to be the highlight of the Revels. But the night of the ball a storm the old-timers still talk about hit the mountains. And we do get some incredible electrical storms around here. A fire started that burned off part of Tormentil. Then it began to rain, and Lord, it poured down for two weeks straight, real freaky weather. You couldn't get in or out of Wildwood; nobody had the least idea of what happened to the cottage and all those people. The truth is, not a single soul who took the train to Mad Edgar's Revels was ever seen or heard from again. Imagine that! Some of his guests had survived the sinking of the *Titanic*. It's my belief you only have so much luck in this life, and when that's used up, well—''

''Did they all die in the fire?''

''Maybe. There's another explanation. Some of them could have been trapped when part of Tormentil gave way during the rains and tons of mud and rock piled on the cottage. Mad Edgar and his enchanted cottage and the rest of those poor people were buried, just like one of those Mesopotamian civilizations a long time ago.''

''Why didn't somebody dig down and try to find out if—''

Faren shrugged. ''You need to understand just how difficult it is to go tramping around deep in Wildwood without getting yourself bad lost. To this day nobody's been able to say for certain there ever *was* an avalanche on Tormentil. Nobody in this part of the country had airplanes to fly up there and take a look. The railroad spur line was the only way in, and the trestles flooded, beginning way up by the mountain; one span would go and wash downstream, taking out the next one, and so on. After a few weeks the War Department in Washington ordered the North Carolina State Guard cavalry to go in and look for survivors. But there was something in the air for years after that big storm, kind of a will-o'-the-wisp that burned the skin and seared the lungs and lit up the whole mountain at night, surrounding it with a fierce blue flame. Wilty Dryman remembers it well: she could tell you how the flame looked from her front porch. And there're old-timers who claim they still see traces of the will-o'-the-wisp on summer nights, when the air's charged a certain way.''

"All those people were killed?" Terry said. "But nobody ever did anything?"

"There's always been some interest in Wildwood and the cottage. Could be tens of millions of dollars worth of valuable jewelry buried up there on Tormentil. Now and then little groups of fortune-hunters show up with metal detectors and the like. But they never make it as far as the mountain. They have accidents, or get so sick they can't walk and have to be carried out. Arn says there's sinks and vapors in Wildwood you need to be careful about.''

She looked hard at Whit.

"Maybe not a good place for what you have in mind.''

"I don't think I told you what we have in mind for Wildwood,'' Whit said with a perplexed smile.

"But I can guess. Some sort of development. Summer homes and a golf course or two, and a big lake for rich people to scat around on in their powerboats.''

"If it's feasible, then the company wants to develop a few sites. Most of Wildwood wouldn't be touched. We know that indiscriminate development would spoil its scenic appeal."

"But people come from all over, and the land gets spoiled in spite of your good intentions. Already happening up there in the park, and when they put that new interstate through east of here, it'll get worse than ticks on a bald dog."

"Do you think Arn would be willing to guide me up to Tormentil?"

She put her hands deep into the pockets of her culotte, a gesture of resignation, of withdrawal: she had done a lot of talking with accompanying graceful hand movements, and he felt a vague sense of loss.

"You'll have to ask him. I doubt it. Even Arn never goes that far. And he's real touchy about Wildwood—more than any man, he feels it's his own private preserve. Anyway, he just might not be back here before you have to leave."

"Did he tell you when to expect him?"

"He never does. This time he took all the dogs. That could mean serious tracking; a week, two weeks—"

"What is he tracking?"

"We don't talk about the hunts," she said, and there was a searching look in her eyes momentarily, as if she were trying to think of something they did talk about that mattered. "Maybe he's after a Rooshian. That's wild boar. Arn does get a craving for boar meat now and again."

Whit had a strong sense of being lied to; the act of lying deadened her whole face. But there seemed to be no point in pressuring her for a revised explanation.

"While we're waiting for Arn, Terry and I might charter a plane and fly over Wildwood. I want to get a closer look at the terrain and take pictures."

"Lon Bramlett owns a flying service. He's in Waynesville, the county seat."

"Thanks, Faren."

"I'll get the big cabin aired out for you. If you want to leave your luggage at the house, I'll see to it everything's put away for you. And maybe you'll plan on having supper tonight with me—with us, figuring ole Arn gets back?"

"That sounds good. How do we find Bramlett?"

Her hands were out of her pockets, she held her head high again. "Back down the road here to Route Nineteen, then head east and follow the signs to Waynesville. That'll be Lon's hangar and his collection of junker planes sitting around the field half a mile outside of town."

Chapter Five

WHIT took his new Hasselblad camera with him, and two changes of lens: one telephoto, one for wide-angle photography. They found Lon Bramlett tilted back in a chair against the side of his Quonset hangar, trading jokes with a youthful mechanic who was working beneath the cowling of a war surplus Aeronca. Lon had an overdeveloped upper body and short bandy legs, a reddish nap of hairline that had receded almost to the center of his flat skull. He chewed Mail Pouch tobacco and wore aviator's sunglasses with one cracked lens, and an old khaki shirt, darned in many places, that had a faded Air Corps insignia hanging by a few threads on one sleeve. Lon got up from his chair as soon as Whit's ring told him he was shaking hands with a West Point graduate.

"Whitman Bowers? Not related to General Blackie of the 36th Texas, are you?"

"He was my father."

"Well, I'll be dog. I flew your pap around a couple of times, Salerno and Utah Beach."

"Grasshopper pilot?"

"Yes, sir, the whole war. You know that old man of yours wasn't afraid of nothin'. He was all the time tellin' me to get lower, *lower,* Lon. And I'd try to explain to him, hell, General, this ain't no Mustang I'm drivin', we're so low now the krauts could shoot us down with a half a pint of spit."

"Sounds like Blackie."

"No offense intended, you must've come off a tall branch of the family tree somewheres, 'cause you surely don't resemble the general as I recall him. He was a plucky son of a gun, but he needed a stepladder to see over a dime."

"I was a foster child. Blackie and Ruth adopted me just before I went off for my plebe year."

Lon nodded. "I see. Well, sir, what can I do you for this fine mornin'?"

"Faren Rutledge told me you might be willing to fly us over Wildwood long enough for me to take some pictures."

Lon rubbed a stubbly jaw. "Ain't much in the way of photo opportunities from up top. Just trees and more trees. Let's see now." He looked around his field. In addition to the Airknocker the mechanic was working on, he had a couple of Piper Cubs in stages of disassembly, a Twin Beech 18, an old bi-wing Tiger Moth, a pale blue and gray camouflaged Navy Six, and an L-9, more war surplus. "The Beech'll run you sixty-five an hour on account of those big Pratts are gashogs, 'course you can't beat the comfort. But the Stinson is my best rag-wing. A three-seater, and I can fly her the rest of the week on a sawbuck's worth of fuel. I know she ain't much for looks, but Termite—he's my mechanic there, ain't much for looks nuther but he's got his A&P ticket—he keeps that engine purrin' like a whore on a hundred-dollar date.''

Whit looked over the airplane: it was painted, tentatively, several shades of red, as if Lon had been unable to make up his mind which he liked best.

"How long would it take to fly up to Tormentil mountain and back?''

Lon said with a slightly sour twist of the mouth. "Oh, figure half hour. Twenty-five bucks be okay?''

"Okay.''

"Before you spend your money, only fair to tell you I don't like to joyride in that particular area. Tormentil: 'the Tormentor,' we 'un's call it.''

"Why?''

"I was personally involved in some incidents near the mountain. One time, came near to crashin' a old Cadet I later traded off. Engine just died. And summer before last, took up a couple photographers *Life* magazine sent down here. They wanted photos of the area where that crazy old coot built his chateau way back when. Reckon you've heard of him?''

"Company I work for owns Wildwood.''

"That explains your interest. Well, I know the Stinson was in perfect workin' order when I took her up. But I come to the mountain and they wanted me to fly over it, and I couldn't. Geezo Pete, all of a sudden it was like pushin' against a big wall. That ain't a word of a lie. Couldn't make no headway and I was down to stallin' speed before I could bat an eye. Veered off. Tried again. Same phenomenon. Then I started gettin' vibrations that worried me, so I hightailed it out of there. and when I got her on the ground I discovered there was a bend in the prop hadn't been there before, and it was causin' cracks in the metal around the air intakes. Lucky to have made it home. But I know of one other pilot went down in the vicinity of Tormentil, and son he ain't been found *yet*. The truth is, you can fly circles around the Tormentor but you can't fly over it. That air space is off limits.''

''Why?''

''I don't know. Airplane, hawk, turkey buzzard— nothin' crosses over the mountain. If there's a pilot left in the tri-state area don't know to avoid Tormentil, he can count on a specific warnin'—like a main bearing in the engine goes, or suddenly he gets flipped upside down. That happened to Bob Binford, Delta captain out of Atlanta. He was flyin' his own stagger-wing Beech at the time, not a Convair, so he lived to tell about it. I'll get you within one, two miles of the mountain, but I don't want to press my luck. Already squeezed it down to the last drop, maybe, flyin' spotter planes from the Eye-talian coast to Normandy.''

Whit reached for his wallet and counted out twenty-five dollars. Lon folded the cash into his shirt pocket, relieved himself of a cheekful of tobacco juice, hitting a one-gallon lard pail from six feet away.

While Lon was attending to his preflight checklist Terry stared at his father and then said, ''Do you think that's another tall tale?''

''About not being able to fly over Tormentil Mountain? I'm no pilot, but I know there are freakish air currents and headwinds, particularly in mountainous areas, that can push even a big plane, a C-47 or bomber, off course. I also know pilots are a superstitious bunch, and if you've had a close call or two in a particular area, you tend to stay away, blame it on gremlins or whatever. Has Lon got you spooked? You don't want to go up?"

"Sure I do. I'm not afraid."

When they were airborne Lon Bramlett picked up the course of the Cat Brier River and followed it north toward Tormentil on the North Carolina–Tennessee line. They could see it from a long way off. distinctive because it stood somewhat apart from the rest of the Balsams range, and because its summit came to a balding, half-scalped peak, different from the serenely rounded mountains to the west and north. A mountain with a specific and, from what Whit had been hearing, not particularly pleasant personality.

The Tormentor.

Lon and Whit were trying to carry on a conversation above the noise of the ninety-horsepower engine.

"How do you happen to know Faren Rutledge?" Lon asked.

"I just met her this morning. Served with her husband in the 82nd Airborne."

"Beautiful woman, and far as I know she's full-blooded `Kee. My daughter, Jen, she's workin' on her DCE down there at Holy Bible A&M in Greenville— that's what they call Bob Jones University—Jen was in school with her two years at East Tennessee State. Smart woman. Mind of her own. Not many Cherokee get college educated, particularly a foundling. Reckon I'm only tellin' you what ever'body knows already—it's a common occurrence on the Boundary. No idea who her father was. Mother died dead drunk early on, facedown in some filthy ditch water. Faren was took in by a Quaker family doing missionary service, and raised in Kingsport. They give her a good upbringin'. and a sense of mission. too, judgin' from the way she takes on the

Bureau of Indian Affairs. Sorriest bunch of bureaucrats ever assembled in Hog-Heaven, D.C. The Cherokee never have had much of a deal down in Qualla. Whole place used to stink to the skies, the infant mortality rate was a shame and a scandal. Now the Public Health Service is startin' to clean up the water supply and get rid of the mosquitos and rats; there's plans under way for better housing and a hospital. Faren, she must have that good Snowbird stock in her, them were the mountain Cherokee that defied the guv'mint when the rest of the tribe was removed to Oklahoma. Reckon you've heard about the Trail of Tears. She'll stand up to anybody, fight till she drops. But it finally did take a toll on her.''

"What do you mean?"

"Heard she had a nervous breakdown a year or so ago, they had to put her away for a while. Kind of a high-strung woman anyhow, and of course Arn—you know Arn. Can't imagine he's easy to get along with, although after they got married he managed to settle down for a couple years. Nobody can figure him marryin' a Indian in the first place—but there he was, past forty, no chick and no child, and here come along this young woman, who in my humble opinion is ever bit as good a looker as Miss Audrey Hepburn, and Arn had to have her. He was always a rake, but give him credit, he weren't no rounder. His entire life all he's needed to do is just look at a woman that certain way—Son, you got to be born with it, you can't learn it—and she'd be on her back with her knees drawed up, pantin' for him to get on with the lovin'. —Guess you didn't hear that back there, did you, Terry?''

"I heard you," he said, with a touch of scorn at being considered too childish to know about the commonplace lusts of adults. He lived in Paris. He knew a lot already.

"So that might have been what kept the relationship goin'," Lon continued. "But it's five years and there's no kids, and Arn I'm told is away from the house most of the time, won't give up none of his ideas—"

"What ideas?" Whit asked.

"Don't want to prejudice you agin' Arn. Expect if you be talkin' to him, ole army buddy, he'll open up and it'll all spill out. Sometimes he just don't care how crazy he sounds. He's got somethin' to prove, and that's all that matters to him anymore."

Whit was looking down, focusing his Hasselblad through a reasonably clean window. The hardwood wilderness beneath them shimmered, evanescent as a rainbow, not yet solidified to the choked density of high summer. Some very large oaks, slow to awaken to the more potent angle of the sun, were spiky with green but not full-leafed. You could see down through the tinted branches as if they were made of spun glass to a dark-floored limbo agitated by sparks of wildflowers. Here and there a dead tree, limbs blunted like those of a punished beggar standing out starkly in a well-dressed crowd. Then marshland, gilt willow and stinging sumac beside the lemony-green stains of sulfur-laden groundwater. Not so much as a single red-dog road, few clearings, no habitations or campgrounds. A view of a wide bend in the river, which he photographed; mossback boulders and the river falling deep and clear between them. The plane high above it all, black cross of shadow weightless, skimming treetops, undulating like a watery serpent.

"Take a look at the compass," Lon advised him. "It just went diddly-shit."

A slight, almost imperceptible shudder disturbed the airplane. A few moments later it was repeated. The air speed had dropped.

"What's going on?" Whit asked.

"Told you, it's the fuckin' mountain! This here's just a little sample of what we could run into."

Whit looked past his shoulder at the altimeter. They were at seven hundred fifty feet. Clear sky, and below, more woodland, some very tall trees now interspersed with evergreens in the foothills of the looming mountain. The wilderness surrounding Tormentil looked less inviting to him, harsher in color and texture, an area where they'd be unlikely to walk away from a forced landing.

"How close are we to the summit? About a mile?"

"And that's too close," Lon grumbled. "Gonna dog-leg it east toward Chiltoes, then head back home on the west perimeter. Tell you now, about all you'll see is some big heath balds—laurel hells, the old-time mountain men called 'em."

The red Stinson shook gently once more as Lon changed course.

"There used to be a spur line of the Shenandoah and Texas Railroad up to the mountain," Whit said.

"You won't see a' trace of it from the air," Lon assured him. "Probably couldn't even locate the road-bed on foot anymore."

They were now flying uneventfully on the altered course over the foothills of the Balsams. Whit was disappointed in his first assessment of Wildwood. Access to the mountain was going to be a major problem. At least twenty miles of all-weather road was the first requirement. Looking back, he caught a glimpse of the Cat Brier, or a tributary, what appeared to be a waterfall

in a vaporous glade. Build a road, build bridges, flood
several hundred acres—an expensive undertaking, perhaps
prohibitive, depending on the potential return. Not his
money—but it was up to him to make the recommendation, and he was already tense thinking about the project. He had what Blackie used to call ''a tiger in the
gut,'' a warning that it shouldn't happen, that they must
not disturb this enchanted place.

Enchanted? Faren Rutledge's term—and an image of
her solemn lovely face came to him with a vividness
that was more than memory; it was as if, witchlike, she
occupied his soul. He was startled from a reverie that
had begun to darken at the edges, as when in childhood
sleep would steal over him. Fanciful way to describe
Wildwood. All he saw, in the afterglow of Faren's
watchful eyes, was a spectacular woodland, grandeur he
hadn't been prepared for by the maps and old black-and-
white photos. A sanctuary.

The mountain was a different matter. He had felt the
trembling of the airplane in his bones. Clear air turbu-
lence, he reasoned. Not some invisible barrier turning
them away. But instinctively he disliked—no, *hated*—
Tormentil. He had observed the bulging set of Lon's
jaw, the way he worriedly drew a fist across his chin as,
for a couple of moments, Lon's reliable old bird had
failed to respond to the controls.

Whit tried to imagine what it would be like parachut-
ing onto the Tormentor. It would mean certain injury,
perhaps death. He had seen, from a mile away, only the
spires of mighty balsam and spruce and several shallow
depressions in all that shadowed greenery, freckled with
spring color. The heath balds Lon had mentioned, deceptive in their beauty. He knew they would be one vast
tangle of thorny little trees.

Nevertheless, in order to make a recommendation to at least bring in the survey crews, he needed to climb Tormentil. Arn Rutledge knew the best way to get there, if any man did. Faren had suggested that Wildwood was her husband's "private preserve." But he didn't own a square foot of the land, and no matter how much he resented the assumed encroachment, he might, like everyone else, have to take a step or two back out of the way of progress.

———— Chapter Six ————

Arn Rutledge heard Lon Bramlett's Stinson off to the west, felt a twinge of attraction but didn't trouble to look up from his place of concealment near the leafy glade he'd staked out for the past twenty hours. The intrusion of the slowly motoring plane was only a minor annoyance, and the sound of its engine had faded within thirty seconds as it flew toward Tormentil. Arn kept his eyes on the lightly misted bathing place which he knew the girl favored because of hot springs that fed the wide pool at the base of a waterfall.

His dogs had led him to a woodfern niche enclosed by boulders, where she'd made her toilet recently, fastidiously covering her droppings with a grasp of mint leaves before stepping down (probably, he speculated, able to go no deeper than her waist) into the water. He looked forward to seeing how she managed her bath. It had been a while since his first and only glimpse of her, as if through veils and the blazing red leaves of autumn's zenith. His body tended to stiffen too easily nowadays, there was a persistent ache in his left shoulder, but his eyes had never gone back on him.

Just a glimpse. Since then she had never been far from his mind, or out of his restless dreams.

Now the dogs were tied up more than a mile behind him, in the lee of an ocoee overhang, occupied with their day-old bones or catching forty winks in the cold shade. And he was alone with his gray-steel Winchester rifle, a razor-edged knife that his father had made from the broken blade of a crosscut saw, the net he'd knotted together from strong twine.

From the first glimmer of day he'd held his position, not moving as much as a foot in any direction even when he had to piss, accomplishing that with a minimum of movement, lying on his side, good strong flow and arc for a man of his years, who had had a wealth of pussy since he was thirteen and drunk his part of whatever was handed to him. Even while relieving himself he never took his eyes from the bathing place. He had at his back a ledge of rock overgrown with blueberry and sand myrtle so thickly intertwined a titmouse couldn't hop through it without his hearing. Profuse nettles made him invulnerable to attack from either side of the natural blind. Juncoes and sparrows twittered in and out, a red squirrel dug in the soft ground for hickory nuts, paying him no mind. He was perfectly at home in this scheme of things, just a little sore from waiting. He knew she would come eventually; but he did not know if she would come alone. If there was more than one of them, he had decided he would shoot quickly, to kill. Regrettably but necessarily the girl would die first, from a 30-'06 bullet dead-center of her fair and unlined brow.

He had considered the possibility that some would

call it murder. This deliberation ultimately made Arn smile.

Prove she was human first, he thought, taking a sip of water from a quart mason jar. Otherwise, if he had to do it rather than lose her again, then it wasn't murder any more than if he brought home a four-pronger or a brace of wild turkeys. What the Walkouts thought, that was a different matter. But they'd already judged him guilty of murder a long time ago.

For this season the temperature was high, at least seventy-five degrees, the air around him humid enough to wet up a sweat due to the proximity of the heated pool, which was turbulent from the impact of the fifteen-foot waterfall. The pool, in a glade that would soon be deeply shadowed for most of the day when the surrounding sycamores and beeches were fully leafed, was one of the anomalies of Wildwood. In his peregrinations, going back to boyhood, he had discovered two like it, and undoubtedly there were others, cozy hideaways sheltered by trees like the magnolia that didn't lose their leaves even in the bleakest winters. One more steambath undetectable in a landscape of cloud and mist and icy fogs.

It was close to noon, with the overhead sun flashing from the crest of the falls to the surface of the pool and up again to greening branches as if caught within a clash of mirrors that she appeared, coming down softly through the wavering planes of light and finely dashed spray to perch on a boulder near the waterfall.

For an instant he couldn't believe she was actually there. It was like being rudely nudged awake by Faren in a movie theater, having been bored to a cataleptic blankness by the triviality of story or the flat projected images that defied his willingness to engage them. And in that first staggered moment of wakefulness something powerful, uncanny, seemed to curve back at him from the screen with a focus that drilled him between the eyes, blazing through to the darkest reaches of the brain where all the perplexities of the universe were neatly linked and solved, liberating a tense, precious microsecond of joy.

He had not expected she would be totally naked, small yet enticingly formed. But how could she wear clothes, unless there was someone to dress her every day? She appeared to be five feet one or two inches tall, weighing perhaps ninety pounds. She was a strawberry blonde, sunlight bringing out a lot of red: her little pubic bush seemed to be on fire. Her straight hair looked well-brushed, and it was squarely trimmed where it fell below the undercurve of her young breasts. Who brushed her hair, and cared for her?

Now that he'd had the chance to view her objectively, he realized she would be unable to feed herself. Yet there was nothing starved, savage, or anxious in her appearance. Her fair face, on that sunstruck boulder, was blissfully turned toward the sky; her eyes savored the light behind closed lids.

Her wings, huge for such a delicately boned body, enhanced rather than detracted from her beauty. The fact of wings where arms should be seemed pleasingly natural. She spread them now, slowly, lively fans that quivered high above her smooth, rounded head and reached almost to the level of her knees. They were bordered in sable black, with dapples of orange and rust-red on a brownish background. Her wings, while not translucent, appeared too insubstantial to lift her in flight; but she *had* flown, or at least glided into his view with no show of effort.

Arn let out the breath he'd unconsciously been holding and wondered then if it might be possible to take her alive, without damage to the fragile-seeming wings. The net, a quick tap at the base of the skull to stun her—but he would have to be both silent and quick, she undoubtedly had the instincts and alertness of any other creature living in the woods.

Folding her wings behind her, the butterfly girl stepped carefully down to another level of the rocks beside the pool, fading into shadow. He guessed she was going to make her toilet, in the place where she would be unaware and literally trapped for the time it took him to creep up on her. And he was as good a man as any who had ever moved in perfect silence through woodland. His one potential pitfall was the stream he must cross. A slip, a tiny splash, and she could be gone instantly.

And there was always a chance the black goatman might be somewhere nearby. Her bodyguard, or servant; or so it seemed to Arn when he first glimpsed them months ago.

Arn feared no one. But he was practical about his chances of surviving a fight to the finish with the towering goatman, no matter how well he employed his knife. The goatman, he had observed, carried an archaic but reliable-looking handax.

She was still in sight, having hesitated, as if unsure of her footing. She bent over at the waist, peering into the dim recess between boulders. Sun illuminated the velvety crease down her back and glowingly described her upstart maidenly ass (disturbing to the equilibrium of the hunt he was trying to maintain, refuting his arbitrary assignment of her to the realm of the beast), the light shimmered as something alive and captive in the finely drawn web of a dusky wing. (Though she might fuck as familiarly as a woman, her element, inevitably, was air. Equilibrium restored.)

He knew he was not willing to go for months, another year perhaps, without his trophy. Without the vindication he craved, the awed silence of the skeptical and scoffing. Get right on to the business, Arn thought.

He sat up slowly, raising his rifle.

And heard, far back in the woods from the place where he had tied his hounds, an embattled uproar, a terrible howl of agony. He recognized instantly, from the timbre of the belling, which hound had been singled out for destruction.

Arn rose from concealment strangling on fury, and took his quick sighting on spread wings as she flickered aloft between the papery silver scrollwork of yellow birches.

The shot he fired was a fraction of a second late to bring her down; he couldn't tell before she vanished if he'd hit anything but the clipped branch that was now falling from the heights of a tree.

Gone.

He jammed on his campaign-style felt hat and gathered the few things he had with him, including his water jar and grimy canvas backpack, then retreated at a near lope down a twisting deer run only a few inches wide in places; he wore the Indian moccasins that he preferred while in the woods. In his passage Arn made few sounds, was unerring in his avoidance of obstacles or damp places where he might leave a footprint. Only an occasional flowering bough shuddered as he went by.

He slowed to a deliberate walk as he approached the alum-laden bluff where he had left his dogs sleeping yesterday.

Here there was a leaf-packed clearing with a diameter

roughly the height of the bluff, a trickle of water from the rock, rich black salt-filled humus in which no shrubs could take root. His remaining dogs, on their feet and straining at the leashes attached to their collars and snubbed around a windfall, had the blood of the dying dog in their nostrils and were unaware of Arn.

He took his time, motionless in concealment but with a good view of the clearing. He listened carefully, eyes on the fourth hound, a Blue Tick, still squirming weakly in a mess of guts; he had been cut from his balls to his sternum. Jim Dandy, the last of his trained coon dogs, a good semi-silent tracker. For Arn it was as bad as if he were a father seeing his child under the wheels of a bus. But he controlled his outrage, aware of potential danger if he rushed into that clearing.

There was a chance it had been a solitary old boar, in exile from the pack; but a "Rooshian" would have eaten the steaming guts, rooted in the carcass, then turned on the other dogs, ripping and tearing with his tusks in a fit of meanness until all were dead. Of his dogs only 'Chucky the Plott cur was an experienced boar hunter, but he would have been helpless on a leash.

A half hour passed before Arn was satisfied that whoever had killed Jim Dandy had not done it as a setup to trap him. It had been meant purely as a warning. Nonetheless, when he stepped into the clearing he carried his rifle cocked and against his side, his long thin-bladed knife in his other hand.

Jim Dandy was still now, the milky glaze of death in his eyes. The other hounds began to leap and howl; a curt word from Arn and they subsided to meek, uneasy whimpers. He walked around the dark ground where Jim Dandy lay, ignoring the too obvious message left for him. He could not tell without a closer examination of the flyblown remains if Jim Dandy had been disembowled with a knife, or a stroke of the goatman's ax.

The many bootprints he discerned tended to rule out the goatman, who, he suspected, wore nothing at all on his nigger's feet. The prints were all alike. A ripple-soled pattern. Big boots, at least a size fourteen.

He stuck his knife into the ground and picked up the croquet ball then, hard lacquered maple with a red stripe around it. He had found others in the woods during the past few years, along with oddities that defied the senses. Those that were portable he had taken home with him, shown them only to Faren.

Now he was satisfied it wasn't a Walkout who had killed his dog. He had a good idea of who had done the meanness, in a foolish attempt to scare him out of Wildwood. And one sorry son of a bitch the Jew would be, as soon as Arn got his hands on him.

He pitched the croquet ball into the sunlit trees atop the bluff, went down on his hands and knees and began digging in rank black humus with his knife and then his hands, until he had scooped out a grave two and a half feet deep. He rolled Jim Dandy into the hole, piled the trailing pulpy intestines on top of the body and replaced the dirt, tromping it down as hard as he could. From his pack he took a pint of corn squeezings, had a swallow for himself, sprinkled the rest of the lightning around the gravesite to nullify the telltale blood tang that a buzzard could put nose to from half a mile in the air. He didn't want scavengers digging up his departed hound.

Then he untied the remaining dogs and headed for home, hours away.

It was past four in the afternoon when he took a break in a deep draw, beside a spring where the dogs could lap up water while sprawled on their bellies. Arn let slip his pack and leaned his rifle within easy reach, sat on the ground chewing a handful of fresh sourwood leaves for his own thirst, not liking to burden his belly with water while there was still a ways to walk. Felt like it was going to be a good night to get likkered up anyway. He gazed up the draw at the quaint remains of the Rosebay trestle, its brick piers almost shapeless beneath masses of emerald kudzu. The gravel roadbed he had crossed and recrossed in youthful wanderings, the rusted rails and wood cross ties had slowly disappeared beneath layered tons of rotted leaves, tough rattan or luxuriant fern; trees stood tall in the former right of way, a broad avenue to the west slope of Tormentil.

Arn's father, when he came of working age, had felled trees for the railroad, assigned to the back-breaking ''misery whip,'' or crosscut saw. Sixty-five cents a day and found, not a bad living in nineteen ought three.

Trains had crossed this trestle every day and frequently late at night, carrying building materials and craftsmen, most of them fresh off the boats from countries Arn knew only as shelled scorched ruins, men selected for their genius in transforming stone and wood into works of art. The chateau had been under construction for more than twelve years. Long gone now, into a hell that had been described to him but still was far beyond his ken. It had vanished when Arn was just a toddler, and the distant nighttime whistle that had excited him in his bed shrieked no more.

He could hear it again, though, if he wanted to, in this shaded draw not many miles from the cabin on the Whippoorwill that was his birthplace. All he had to do was close his eyes and listen with a proper seriousness, the train would come; and he'd feel his father's hard arms tighten in tenderness and anticipation as they waited near the crossing, as the train thàt became first his breath, then his eyes, then his voice and thundering heart, jarred the earth and consumed him with its black velocity. Ah, yielding to the power of his minute self and the doomed flyer, wetting his pants a little in his father's whiskery embrace. Then the solitude that described the train's passing, the night closing around him like a heavy flower. Concealed again in childhood, yet touched, alight, miraculously aware his fate rode a black train traveling, somewhere, beneath a wild wood moon.

—— Chapter Seven ——

[The diary of Laurette "Sibby" Langford: entry for July 4, 1904]

Up quite late last night, my poor husband feverish from his mounting excitement and the pain that has been unrelenting since our wedding day just one week ago. I spared no effort to be a calming influence, but to little avail. Edgar's rash, specimens of which I have seen on the backs of his hands and the root of his throat, has made his skin everywhere sensitive to touch. I am not able to hold his hand, only to kiss him on his cheek, his forehead, while longing to take him in my arms. Even the light pressure of the silk sheikh's robe he adopted as a dressing gown when we boarded the train three days ago in Boston has been excruciating for him. The laudanum which the doctor has prescribed allows only for a fitful hour or two of relief. He has scarcely slept for the three nights of our journey, which now, thank the Lord, is nearing its end. To make matters worse, the weather along the eastern seaboard has been very hot and muggy. He does find a measure of relief in his icy bath. Because of the frequent and prolonged immersions, we have been obliged to proceed south at a snail's pace through the mountains so as not to agitate or spill his bathwater. But my husband's gallant spirits, his sense of humor, never falter. I have not heard a word of complaint pass his lips. Rather, he does his best to assure *me*, as if it is I who suffers so terribly, that the torment will subside. "It is the sting of the lash of Aŝŝur," he says: Aŝŝur, king of all the gods of Mesopotamia, the very sun of heaven; a master whose yoke he claims he willingly bears as a reminder that one must pay a price for the treasures which the ancient earth has yielded, the glory of discovering wonders the eyes of men have not beheld for thousands of years. I do suffer for my Edgar; but I know it would only worsen his trial if I revealed the true depths of my emotion, wept in his presence. I have been compelled to ponder anew *Maman*'s only words to me on the eve of our nuptials, as she sat clasping my hands within hers, a weary hint of tears in her eyes. "My darling Sibby, to be content in marriage you must always hold a part of yourself aloof, even in the act of submission to your husband." I am still unsure of why she said that, or precisely what she meant, for if so drastic a measure as opening my veins would somehow alleviate his pain, I would gladly do it. Is this not what it means to love a man with all of your heart and soul? I have taken my vows, after prayerful consideration of their meaning. I know that I will never hold back from my husband anything that may be of benefit to him. I am dedicated to his happiness. While he soaked in his bath of ice

water, with a sheet draped across the silver tub to spare
me the sight of his inflamed limbs and preserve deco-
rum, I read to him for hours. He has no fondness for
Henry James, and although Mark Twain makes me blush
at times, he also provokes Edgar to manic laughter. I
would prefer above all reading aloud the sonnets of Elizabeth Barrett Browning; perhaps in time I may en-
courage in him an appreciation of poetry. When my voice
became hoarse and it was all I could do to keep from
nodding, lulled by the swaying of the train, Edgar talked
to me. His voice, as always, was a tonic. Some say
(although not to my face!) that he is far from a handsome man; I have heard he is cruelly ridiculed for his
walk, never mind that it is only through a triumph of
the will that he lives at all, having accomplished more
in his lifetime of adventure and discovery than a score
of able-bodied men with fainter hearts and dull minds.
Pitiless gossip! I resented his nagging detractors when
first we met, I scorn them all now that we are man
and wife. If they could but look into his eyes when he
speaks of desert kingdoms, of Carchemish and Ugarit
and fabulous Nineveh—"dead civilizations" revived, for
me alone, by his knowledge, through the genius of
his descriptions. I am more at home in the court of King
Assurbanipal than I fear I shall ever be in Mrs. Astor's ballroom. Edgar's scholarship is equal to that of any
man's, yet he is still young—young in his heart, in his
enthusiasm for the adventures we will share together.

I am near exhaustion from the rigors of the wedding,
the travel, my worry about his condition; yet happier
than I have ever been. And still I anticipate the perfect
bliss of sleeping by his side.

We arrived past sunset of this day, and what a welcome!

As the train slowed, the dark brow of the mountain came to life from the booming of mortars casting aloft a pyrotechnical display that, while it did last, doomed to oblivion even the most familiar of our starry constellations. All around us, illuminated by the blossoming shellbursts, dwellings were in evidence beneath trees the likes of which I had not seen outside of the White Mountains of New Hampshire. Yet the setting was parklike, and I assumed the ranks of the mighty sentinel evergreens had been thinned to make room for construction of Edgar's woodland retreat. There were rows of homely cabins with screen doors and tarpaper roofs, even house-sized tents; a commissary, stores, a barber shop with a striped pole in front! I was reminded of the stereoptican slides I had recently viewed of Dawson City in the Yukon Territory during the great Klondike gold rush. From the platform of our car at the end of the train I saw (those moments when I could take my eyes off the shimmering, exploding sky), corrals for mules and horses, huge steam tractors, wagons, two sawmills, piles of squared white building stones, acres of dirt with nothing on them but little pools from a recent rain, and a gash in the side of the mountain where solid rock had been blasted away to widen this high plateau, where we were surrounded by wilderness seemingly without end. It was thrilling, but I shuddered in the crisp night air despite my shawl. I must admit I found it forbidding as well. A small city had been erected for the sole purpose of building the cottage, which when completed will put even "the Breakers" to shame. At that moment, however, I would have been far more content on the familiar strand of Newport, because not a soul was visible as we rolled to a stop. Where were all the workmen, their wives, the many hundreds Edgar

had employed? Ignoring great pain, he had come out
onto the platform of the observation car in his robe
and burnoose (looking uncannily to the desert born, a
true Arab prince!) to stand at my side as the last of
the mortars was stilled and, heavenward, the Bear and
the Hunter, ignobly dimmed by the rockets' red glare,
shone forth in their customary splendor.

Then, off in the trees, myriad flickering fires started;
we heard a chorus of voices rising to a shout and a
procession moved toward us, a long snaking line of lanterns and torches held aloft. Here they were at last,
and my heart was seized with joy as we were surrounded by the workmen offering cheers and felicita-
tions on this special day. Edgar raised a hand for silence.
"May I introduce to you Laurette, my wife," he said.
I could not have prevented my eyes from filling with
tears as they responded generously with more shouts
of welcome and wishes for my continued happiness. The
air is wonderfully fresh here, with a tang of resin, so
unlike the sea breezes at Prides Crossing, but, I am sure,
equally salubrious. Edgar will rest well these two
weeks, I will see to that, and I know he will be much
improved by the time we begin our homeward journey.

The architect, Mr. James B. Travers, came aboard before we retired for the night, and had a glass of wine
in the parlor car. He is a Virginian, of good family I
am told, yet he wore boots that were none too clean.
(I must remind myself that we are virtually on the fron-
tier: there is a red Indian reservation not ten miles
away!) Mr. Travers is tall, with a fine brown mustache, shoulders that could bear the weight of any re-
sponsibility. Although he is not a well-known architect
like Mr. Ogden Codman or Stanford White, he en-

joys Edgar's full confidence. They talked exclusively of the problems that would be encountered during construction of the cottage. It is to cover an area exceeding twenty acres. Imagine! I had nothing to say, and after a time I found it difficult, in my state of fatigue, to follow their discussion. Once, as Edgar was attending to a portfolio of the architect's plans with his reading glass, I turned my head to find Mr. Travers looking hard at me, perhaps severely. Although I have never encountered such rudeness from a gentleman, I smiled at him; he responded with a slight bow that was properly courteous and after that cast his eyes no more in my direction.

[The journal of James B. Travers: entry for July 5, 1904]

They have arrived, with an ostentatious complement of servants, and servants to wait on the servants. Mr. Langford, who I found reclining on Turkish pillows in an absurd getup, in one of his depressingly ornate parlor cars done in old-fashioned Pompeian reds and chocolates and olivines, did not appear to be in the best of health. Yet we fell to business right away. There are alterations he wishes to make in the plans: his vision changes by the hour now that he is on the site. So far he has proposed nothing that I find objectionable, or impractical, no furbelows borrowed from Second Empire or the Romanesque style I detest. Already I have spent the better part of two years designing the chateau (I cannot accept the current conceit of these damned men of great wealth who so coyly refer to their outlandish and elephantine vacation homes as "cottages"), and more than another twelve years will have passed before I see the chateau completed—my obsession conquered. There will be nothing like it on this continent, and few chateaux in all of Europe to compare. It will stand for a thousand years. Often I think it must be insanity to devote fully one-quarter of my life to such a project. But the challenge is enormous, my reputation will be ensured, and the fee will make me wealthy. Payment is guaranteed by an annuity whether whim or fortune fail my eccentric employer, and only with money can I hope to repair father's disgrace as I repay his crushing debts. Filial obligation, ambition, pride— all these chain me within a wilderness prison.

Mr. Langford's bride—I am told by the garrulous young doctor who has accompanied them on their wedding trip—is of a distinguished Brahmin family. Her father, even as mine, has had business reversals: a fire in one of his stores resulted in costly lawsuits. It cannot be to his disadvantage to claim Edgar Langford as his son-in-law. I thought perhaps it might be a marriage of convenience, her duty to her father outweighing reluctance to marry a man—even a very rich man—of his age, appearance, and reputation, but no: she seems much in love with her new husband. She is little more than nineteen years of age, with a slight presence, sometimes speaking barely above a whisper. She has a mixed sort of beauty, face perhaps too narrow, nose with a pronounced uptilt; but such imperfections fail to diminish her eyes. They are Delft blue, of a quality that transforms her earnest gaze into silent, saintly address. She is like a drawing promising in its early lines but with much to be finished. She is a naive, sentimental, sheltered child. She has been quite cunningly beguiled, I think, and exists for the moment in a febrile dream of romanticism. Perhaps she will never awaken to apprehend that her husband has all the trappings and inclinations of a despot. But life for the vast majority, as I have had ample time to appreciate, is not forgiving of our innocent dreams and capricious errors of judgment.

—— Chapter Eight ——

April 1958

Faren Rutledge was dozing in the bathtub, when she heard Arn outside the house putting his hounds into the kennel.

The cantankerous guinea hens that roosted around their property added to the homecoming uproar. She listened carefully, able to distinguish the individual voices of his dogs as well as Arn could. She heard Old Hob and Nolichucky and boisterous, aggressive Bocephus, and finally realized that only three dogs had returned with him. She let out part of the now tepid bathwater and filled the tub again from the hot tap. Arn came into the house by way of the kitchen. She wondered how late it was. She had read at least until midnight. She began to soap herself.

Presently he was leaning in the doorway of the bathroom looking at her. From seven feet away he still smelled strongly of woods and old sweat and recent liquor.

Not looking up at him, washing her slightly convex

belly with a cloth, her shoulders slumped, Faren said, "There's supper laid back on the stove for you."

"You didn't need to do that."

"I do every night when you're not here."

"I don't want to eat anyhow."

"Where's Jim Dandy? I didn't hear him."

"He was killed. Guts ripped out. I buried him in the woods."

The tightening in her throat made her lift her head and look at him as she continued washing. "Oh, Arn."

He had a three-day growth of roan beard, pale red flecked with white like grains of salt. His cheeks and high forehead were inflamed. He was smiling his fierce, tight-lipped smile of drunkenness and hostility.

"I know who it was."

"*Who?* Not a bear or—"

"It was the Jew. Jacob. Wantin' to take over my woods, afraid of what I'll find out. But by God, I found it out long before he did."

He watched as Faren raised her right leg, bar of soap moving slowly and circularly up the smooth inner flesh to her dark curly pudendum.

"Don't be washin' all the good smell off," Arn advised her. "I aim to have me some of that tonight."

She smiled, not encouragingly, but not emphasizing her doubts that he was up to it.

"What are you going to do about Jacob?"

"Time I'm through with him, he might get better but he'll never get well."

"Can you prove he killed Jim Dandy?"

"Proved it to my satisfaction already."

"You'll just get yourself locked up, Arn."

"It ain't your business, so why don't you shut your mouth?"

"Arn, we need money. More than I can bring in. If you don't pay attention to business around here, next thing it'll be the sheriff knocking on our door with a writ of attachment."

"It's almost tourist season. Hell, we always make up the shortfall by end of summer."

"Only if you stay out of the woods and get to work."

"You think I need advice from you tonight, Faren?"

"Are you so skunk-drunk you can't understand plain facts when you're hearing them?"

Arn rubbed his jaw and said with a twist of a grin, his eyes hazing over, "My daddy'd do a flipflop in his grave he knew I let a bastard squaw bitch talk to me that way."

She hurled the bar of soap at the center of his face; it was too slippery to catch even if his reflexes had been normal; he just batted the soap away and it slithered across the wood floor under the raised tub.

"Is it a fuck or a fight you want?" he said.

"I don't want a thing to do with you until you get yourself cleaned up."

"Well, haul ass out of that tub then, woman, and let me in there."

Faren stood up, dripping, crescents of soap film shining on top of her breasts. Her eyes deep, dark, brooding. "My name's Faren Hamilton, not Faren guess-who. And I'll outfuck and outfight you any night of the week. Because you know I'm not afraid to lift your scalp if I have to." She stepped over the side of the high tub and walked four steps to Arn and kissed him, leaning in toward his lips while one of his hands reached back to the patchy place on his head where there was a jagged ridge and his hair had never quite filled the scar gap, resulting from their most violent encounter two years ago. He let his mouth slip from hers gradually and lowered his hands, bringing them up under her soft handful of breasts and lifting the nipples to his chinline.

"Don't get to rubbing, you'll scratch me," she admonished, reaching out to take a pink towel from the peg beside the door. She wrapped it loosely around her and sidestepped past him into their bedroom.

Arn turned leisurely with a yawn and began to undress, leaving his clothes piled in a corner of the bathroom. He couldn't stand on one foot and had to sit on the rim of the tub to pull his socks off, got one off but couldn't continue to balance himself while sitting, fell back with a sudsy splash and lay with his head underwater, his knees up and his balls floating. He began to laugh, bubbles exploding to the surface. Came up choking.

When he could talk he called to Faren, "Who's that stayin' the night in the big cabin?"

"Staying the week," she replied, toweling herself slowly in front of the moonlit window that faced their backyard, aware of her dim reflection and feeling a lonesome twinge of separation, as if what she saw were the image of a twin sister, whose existence she felt in an ache of a sundered rib but whom she would never get to know. Little Faren guess-who. She had always yearned for brothers and sisters, lacking the company of other children on the block in Kingsport, where she had been strictly raised. And, without any actual playmates, like other lonely children she had made them up to keep her company. But this game that only children should play she still played too easily and Faren shuddered, feeling the eyes of the woman of the panes studying her astutely, filled with a morbid knowledge she wanted nothing to do with.

"Faren, you gone to sleep in there?"

"What? No, I heard you. Arn, it's Colonel Bowers from the Eighty-second Airborne, and his son."

"God a'mighty," Arn said after a lag of five seconds. The question that followed denied that he was pleased. "What's he doing here?"

"Oh—the company he works for owns Wildwood; he says he wants to look it over."

"Does he? You invite them to supper tonight, Faren?"

"Yes, they had supper with me. I told them I didn't know when you might get back."

"Why don't you come in here."

She went. He was lazing back with one foot out of the tub. He had long toes and longer fingers and, she assumed, a long dick for a man; at least it was longer by far than those of the two boys she had slept with in college. Arn wasn't a tall man, and he had begun to thicken at the waist despite a strenuous outdoors existence. A couple of ripples under the jawline, but his bones still stood out strongly in his face; his pale gray eyes were frank and fearless. With those eyes he could preach to women, as fine a sermon as any they could hope to hear in church. His message a sympathetic understanding of their eternal predicament, the desires of the flesh struggling against restrictions of chastity or fidelity. First he set them ablaze, then he quenched their fires, and never were they dissatisfied with his ministrations. Unfortunately there had been, after Faren's marriage to Arn, a few holdovers, women who just would not stop showing up on their doorstep or calling on the phone. It had amused Arn no end, even when she was obliged to run a couple of them off at the point of a gun.

"Soap's gone under the tub," Arn said. "Could you reach it for me?"

Faren obligingly went down on her hands and knees,

and while she groped for the bar of soap felt his spread hand sliding in a friendly way over her buttocks, and so she spent more time retrieving the soap than she strictly had to; when she stood up tall beside the tub and dropped in the soap, Arn had moved around enough so that his scratchy beard was at the level of her bearded pubes, and there she didn't mind the scratching.

"Today I saw a naked girl with the wings of a butterfly," Arn told her. "I took a shot, but I don't know that I hit her. At least I didn't bring her down."

"Shut up," Faren said, her expression anguished. "I don't want to hear about it "

"What do you want, then?"

"Do, do, do more with your tongue."

Her frilly cunt had lipped open like a dogwinkle shell he'd picked up a long time ago on a Carolina beach. And just the same color inside.

"Right here?"

"Oh God yes," she said. "But don't talk!"

"I'm going back after her," Arn vowed. "This time I'll get her, and no Jew, no Walkout'll stop me."

She pried his hands from her flanks and stared down at him for a long moment with eyes as full as lampblack moons, then turned and walked out of the bathroom.

"Where you going, Faren?"

"I want you to come after *me*!" she shouted. "Hurry up. Don't talk. Do you want me to go crazy again? Just give me some loving, Arn, and don't talk."

──── Chapter Nine ────

At the age of six he had mastered the art of the stage guillotine, also secret boxes within lacquered boxes. He rummaged in the air around him as if it were a closet: white doves fluttered from his clever hands. By then he was studying locks and cuffs, too, had made a few "slick" escapes. The magician taught him the principles, everything else was up to him. Although he was very young he had the energy to succeed, the ambition to astonish.

**(All of this contained in the dream.
So far so good)**

In Babylon certain of the adept practiced sorcery, as a part of their religion and for their amusement. Transforming themselves, with the aid of "cosmic" energy stored in machines, to birds and animals and back again. Or to punish their enemies by not bringing them back.

(The magician telling him this, also in the dream)

The magician's back was crooked, the boy's straight. He was straight and golden, and loved the magician, who was dark, like the lacquered boxes within boxes. Keeping all of himself to himself in boxes. In one box a diabolical eye, in another a giggle. The magician could put him to "sleep" (dreaming within a dream) by turning a gold coin around and around in his fingers until it fairly spun, flashing, pacifying. Prestidigitation. The magician worshipped lightning. He made lightning in a room that stood the boy's hair on end without harming him. The air sizzling, popping, singeing the nostrils. Sometimes the magician made himself invisible. They heard only his voice. Often when he wasn't speaking to anyone they knew he was there anyway, from the sounds of his breathing and by other signs.

(Coming to the "scary" part)

The magician studied plans he'd found in a buried library that was almost entirely shards and dust, and from the plans he constructed a "machine" using five miles of silver wire thinner than an eyelash. Humpbacked and visible in all of its crossings and recrossings, it filled a large room called "The Lantern," two stories high with glass sides between stone buttresses and a domed glass roof that opened mechanically. By then the magician had a helper, a tall thin man who wore dark suits and whose ears stuck out like a bat's. This man, the magician said, was a "genius." With the two halves of the dome rolled back, the "machine" digested stars night after night without a hum, an eerie thing to do; emptied the sky and gained strength like a storm. When it blew the boy away in a biting gasp of silverdust he fell headdown as a comet falls, framework intact but with liver brains and guts aglow, arms working furiously, screaming finally when it became clear the magician's black box would expand eternally to accommodate his terror.

(aren't you afraid of falling too)

——— Chapter Ten ———

At seven-fifteen in the morning Whit Bowers awoke in his bed with the sheet tangled around him like wet wash, the blankets on the floor. He heard Arn calling him from across the road to come to breakfast.

The dream had been bad enough, but not one of the all-time blood-curdlers: at least whatever disturbance he had made while in the throes of the dream hadn't been violent or vocal enough to awaken Terry. The boy was not visible beneath a mound of yellow blankets and big pillows. Late for him to be lying abed, but they had played chess until after midnight, and by then Terry was so drowsy he couldn't remember the correct sequence of the moves he was trying to establish.

Immediately after sitting up, Whit began to shudder uncontrollably; the air in the cabin was cold. The kerosene heater had run almost out of fuel and the flames sputtered bluishly in semi-darkness. Whit retrieved one of the blankets from the floor. His nose hurt and felt swollen: there was dried blood on his upper lip, he tasted old blood in his throat as if, instead of a pleasant supper, he'd feasted on raw meat in a cave last night. Probably, he thought, he'd accidentally assaulted himself while flailing away with his fists during the dream. Good God. Was Terry safe, sleeping in the same room with him? But it might be a long time between dreams. He could only hope.

Draping the blanket around him, he went to the door of the cabin and looked out. It was another rare and spacious country day.

"Good mornin', Colonel Bowers!" Arn said cheerily from the top step of his front porch. "A little too early for you?"

"Hello, Arn." He was hoarse as a rooster. He cleared his throat. "No, I need to be up and around."

"How do you find the accommodations?"

"Very comfortable. Ten minutes, Arn?"

"Be lookin' for you. Don't stand on ceremony, hie yourself straight to the kitchen."

Whit used the bathroom in the cedar-paneled cabin, scrubbing the stubborn blood from his unshaven face, then jostled Terry awake.

"Arn's home. Let's go have breakfast."

Faren was frying eggs and pork chops in two big iron skillets on her gas-fired Magic Chef range when Whit and Terry came in, Terry wearing the same clothes he'd had on for the past three days and with sleep still in his eyes. Faren gave him a kiss on the cheek, introduced him to Arn. "How about a dish of oatmeal to start you off, sleepyhead?" Arn rose with a hint of indulgence from his chair at the head of the oilcloth-covered table and shook hands with Whit.

"Keep yourself lookin' fit these days, Colonel. Terry, why don't you have a seat right there."

"Listen, Arn, I'm long out of uniform. Just plain Whit ought to do."

"What happened to your nose? You and the boy have a friendly little sparrin' match?"

Whit touched his nose gently as Terry stared at him. "Bumped a doorjamb in the dark last night."

"You better put some ice on that," Faren advised him.

"Doesn't bother me all that much."

"Two eggs or three, Whit? These are guinea hen eggs, you might find them a little strong to your taste."

"But they're good eatin'," Arn said. "First clutch I've come across this spring. Guineas hide their nests, it's a job to find 'em. But how they do lay."

"Three eggs will be fine," Whit said to Faren.

Arn smiled as he poured coffee into Whit's mug and refilled his own. His cheeks were freshly shaved and he wore an old blue plaid wool shirt tucked into faded jeans. He looked Terry over with friendly curiosity. Terry met his gaze for a second, then self-consciously studied Faren's parakeets in a hanging wicker cage.

"Favors you, don't he?" Arn said to Whit. "Just got the one boy?"

Whit nodded. "Millie and I were divorced right after the war. I'm single now."

"Kind of expected you'd be in command of the entire 82nd by now."

"I never was in Slim Jim Gavin's league, and I knew it. Besides, I had a potful after the Bulge."

"Same here. Maybe the Screamin' Eagles had it rough in Bastogne; but it wasn't no cinch where we were up there on the Salm. Goddamn snow and fog, never knew if we had Panzers in front of us or behind us. Remember how we crossed each other's lines once, both sides retreatin' at the same time? Plans, strategy, none of it meant a thing. That war came down to sluggin' it out, daylight and dark, till somebody knuckled under. I just couldn't believe God loved krauts so much he made so many of 'em."

"Did you kill a lot of Germans in the war?" Terry asked him.

"Never counted," Arn said, with a genuine and chilly lack of interest.

Faren began to serve them, and no more was said about the battles they had fought, as if Arn and Whit had reached a tacit agreement that neither of them cared for reminiscing. While they ate Arn talked sparingly, for the most part asking questions of Terry, whom he appeared to have taken a shine to. Did Terry enjoy hunting and fishing? Did he like guns? Terry owned up to never having fired a rifle. Arn shook his head in disbelief.

"Well, if you're stayin' long enough, maybe I'll get the chance to expose you to some of the finer things of life."

"Dad says you were the best shot in the 505."

"Don't know how true that is, but I never come near to bein' the marksman my daddy was. He could shoot the grease out of a biscuit and never break the crust." Arn smiled at Whit, but his folksy congeniality seemed cooled by watchfulness. "Faren tells me you're workin' now for the outfit that owns Wildwood."

"That's right."

"Got some big plans in mind. Golf courses. Maybe run a four-lane highway smack through it, put up a few of them roadside stands that sell peanut brittle and little statues of Bambi."

"I don't think so, Arn. All we're planning now is a

feasibility study. Any development, which would be on a strictly limited basis, is still years away."

"And maybe we'll both be old men before that happens."

"I wouldn't be surprised."

Arn turned his head to glance at his wife, who was standing by a window with tied-back curtains of dotted Swiss. She sipped coffee, looking across the table at Whit, in the filtered brightness her face as flat and brown and expressionless as a walnut plaque on the wall.

"What's on your mind for today?" Arn asked her.

"I need to go down to Qualla and shop some orders."

"Sutter handlin' your output this year?"

"No. I've had my fill of his cheating ways. He still owes me two hundred and fifty dollars from last season."

Arn's eyes glinted. "Tell him your old man's comin' down there to collect if he don't pay up."

"You won't, either. I'll take care of business on the reservation."

"Those white Cherokees are worse than Jews. And that reminds me."

"Arn," she said softly, "*no*."

"Like you said, you see to business on the Boundary. I'll take care of *my* business. I could stand another dose of pork chops to finish off these biscuits with."

Faren placed her coffee mug on the windowsill, took up the fry pan and placed it on the table. She said to Terry, "Maybe you'd like to come along with me this morning. I'll show you the reservation. Not just the part where the tourists go."

"It'll turn your stomach," Arn promised.

"Arn," Faren said with an edge of exasperation, "things aren't as bad as they used to be."

"I'd like to go," Terry said.

"Good. That'll give Arn and your dad plenty of time to talk about whatever it is they need to talk about. Whit, don't let him eat all those pork chops by himself."

"No, thanks, Faren, I've had enough." He passed his hand across his jaw; time for a shave. Arn had settled back in his chair chewing the last of a biscuit and some crisp pork fat with an air of contentment that might have been misleading; the fingers of one hand were drumming silently on the oilcloth. Whit recalled the first time he had seen Arn, when the regiment was formed at Benning in June of '42. He was a three-year veteran who had volunteered for the paratroops, hoping for some action. He looked as solid as a raw oak plank; you could read his grain like a road map. Now the grain was blurred, hidden. "Why don't you help Faren with the dishes?" Whit said to Terry. "I'll police the cabin and run a razor through this beard. What're your plans, Arn?"

"Nothin' much. Need to deliver one of my dogs to the vet's, he's rubbed a raw patch on his hind end and there's infection that's got to be cut out. So it you'll kindly leave me with the Pontiac, Faren, and take the coupe."

"All right, Arn."

"Whit, we'll meet down at the store in thirty minutes. That'll give me time to do inventory, go over the receipts, and make out a couple checks."

Whit was buttoning his shirt in the cabin, when he heard a horn outside, an impatient summons. He went out and got into the Pontiac station wagon. There was a big dewlapped cinnamon-colored hound in the back. Arn, behind the wheel, took off in a burnout and hail of gravel even before Whit shut the door. Arn had a look he'd seen before. Clamp-jawed anger, white spots glowing on his normally weather-reddened cheekbones, eyes like zinc washers.

"Something wrong?"

"There's this jackass I need to catch up to on the road. He went by me not two minutes ago, settin' on his motorbike just bigger'n shit."

"What's it about, Arn?" Whit asked, feeling his pulse quicken as they hit the blacktop road with a jolt at forty miles an hour, the back end of the wagon coming half around in a skid, the hound falling about in a tangle of long ears and bony baize legs.

"Crouch down back there, idjit!" Arn snarled at his yelping dog. He gunned the Pontiac through a bewildering latticework of sun and shadow on the hilly road, heedless of what might be in his way come the next bend. To Whit he said brusquely, "Got this score to settle, and it won't wait."

"Maybe you better take it a little easy," Whit suggested.

"Hell," Arn said with a weary contempt, hunched over the steering wheel. They had leaped to sixty miles an hour, tires screeching on every turn. "You don't let no man get away with butcherin' your dog."

"What man?" Whit asked, and then he saw, as the road straightened and the flowery woods thinned alongside the road, someone familiar on a black motorcycle half a mile ahead of them, riding into Tyree town. Arn made a low noise of satisfaction in his throat and stepped it up to seventy. They closed swiftly on the bike whose rider was Jacob, the French-speaking man from Fulcrum's Cafe.

Jacob couldn't have heard the Pontiac coming above the noise of his own machine. But he had a rearview mirror, and when the oncoming wagon filled it he looked back sharply, almost losing control of the bike. Then he turned and crouched lower and tried to kick his moderate speed higher; but a dirty cloud of smoke burst from the exhaust pipe and the bike wobbled again from either Jacob's anxiety or the strain he was putting on the engine.

"Yahhhhhh!" Arn shouted, and Whit braced himself, thinking that Arn intended to bash into the unprotected cyclist.

"Arn, slow down!"

But Arn had done some fast dangerous driving in his time; he could handle even the potentially unstable wagon as if it were modified for dirt track laps or hauling illegal alcohol. On the very edge of town he gave the wheel a twist to the left, passed the frightened Jacob, whose face was turned to them and so close to Whit he could see every pore in the man's nose, the sweat that had popped out on his brow, the electricity of fear in his wide blue eyes. Then Arn cut back in, skidding a little on some loose gravel spilled over from the driveway of the A&W root beer stand. To avoid colliding with the wagon, Jacob left the road. His motorcycle hurtled over a ditch into the sawmill yard, came down on both wheels, but so hard Jacob was bounced from the seat as if from a trampoline and went sailing, doing an ungainly hands-down turn in the air while his bike jumped and spun and crashed broadside into a stack of four by fours in front of the metal sawmill shed.

Arn hit the brakes gleefully, fishtailing to a dead stop five feet from the grill of a pickup truck coming the other way, slapped the stick into reverse, and went smoking straight back to the sawmill yard, raising dust. The hound he'd brought along was yapping its head off.

Arn was out of the wagon before Whit could react. One of the millhands standing in the wide shed doorway pointed to a mound of sawdust and wood shavings eight feet high, as big around at the base as a silo. Arn circled the mound and soon reappeared with Jacob in his clutches, pushing the stumbling stunned man along in front of him. Jacob was smothered head to foot in curly wood shavings and orange sawdust, only the whites of his eyes showing like partially eclipsed moons. If Arn had taken a match to him, he would have burned for three days.

"Let him go, Arn," Whit said, and when Arn showed no sign that he had heard, continuing to manhandle the wobbly Jacob, Whit repeated himself in a tone of voice he had learned from Blackie a long time ago, "*Sergeant, I said take your hands off that man!*"

Instinctively Arn released Jacob, who collapsed and then began, sobbing, to crawl aimlessly across the ground. Arn raised his head and looked at Whit, fists cocked, the look firing up to a belligerent glare.

"You don't know what he did!"

"For Christ's sake, Arn, you could have killed him."

Arn stood his ground as Whit approached him, no longer looking at Jacob, perhaps now considering Whit as his prime adversary. Whit gave him a wry, skeptical, half-annoyed look, and Arn's shoulders dropped a little; he dropped his hands too. Jacob continued on his disorganized way around the sawmill yard, moaning. Arn walked past the bike, lying bent out of shape beneath the pile of four by fours, some of which had been scattered around.

He said to the two millhands gawking in the doorway of the shed, " 'Mornin', Skeeter. Elb."

"Well, howdy do, Arn," the one named Elb replied.

He had a thin hatchet face, and his Adam's apple stuck out so far it looked as if he had swallowed the end of a broomstick. He was wearing a carpenter's apron and had a flat wide pencil behind one ear.

"Where's your waterhose, Skeeter?" Arn asked the other man.

"Right there by the corner spigot, Arn."

"Borrow it a minute?"

"You go right ahead, Arn."

Arn turned on the spigot and uncoiled the hose. Whit had kneeled beside Jacob, bracing him with both hands on his shoulders. He felt the man trembling, still buffeted by shock. There was a little blood from Jacob's nose mixed with the sawdust in his black beard.

"Just be still," Whit advised. "You might have cracked some ribs or done some damage internally."

"No. No. I'm—all right. But he—*he's* crazy! Why did he do that? My bike, my bike is wrecked!"

Arn came up behind them trailing hose.

"Stand aside and let's clean him up," he said dispassionately.

Whit moved just as Arn opened the nozzle of the hose and began spraying Jacob. The big man shuddered and cringed in the stream of cold water, began to cry hysterically.

Whit reached out and took the hose away from Arn, getting them all a little wetter.

"I've had just about enough of this, Arn!"

"Watch yourself," Arn said, in a voice more ominous for its lack of inflection. "I ain't lookin' at no courts martial now if I pound you into the ground."

Whit turned off the hose but held it in his right hand six inches from the brass nozzle.

"Your mouth's writing checks your ass can't cash, Arn. Now what the hell is this all about?"

Arn stared at Whit for a full ten seconds. coming to no conclusions about which of them might be the quickest in this situation. Then he disavowed any interest in scrapping with Whit and turned his attention to the soggy Jacob, who was sitting up sobbing helplessly while he tried to wipe wet sawdust from his face.

"I told you," Arn said. "He killed my best dog yesterday in the woods. Slit Jim Dandy from his asshole to his breastbone, left him on the ground with his guts dragged out and the flies a-crawlin'."

With a thrust of his big shaggy head toward the skies like a tenor dying in an opera, Jacob roared, "That's a lie! I could never do such a thing!"

"Let's just have us a look at those boots." Arn bent quickly to grab one of Jacob's feet, nearly upending him. Arn studied the rundown waffle pattern of the mud-caked boot heel and sole and a tic of unpleasant surprise grazed his lips.

"How many pairs of boots you own?" he demanded of Jacob.

"I have no more boots!"

Arn let go of Jacob's foot and stood back, scratching a cheekbone with one finger.

"Well, that ain't a-gonna get it," he said softly. "I figure you for a liar."

"You're the liar," Jacob retorted, his tone hurt, not accusatory.

He tried getting to his feet. He was nearly twice the size of Arn. He had fierce blue eyes but his awkwardness, his unshapely and babyish bulk, denied an inbred pugnacity or fighting skills. When Jacob spotted his twisted bike he coughed and sobbed, tears running freely down his cheeks, clearing away a little more of the sawdust. He limped toward the bike, moaning with each step.

The saddle bags had been thrown aside in the motorcycle's collision with the lumber pile. Whit retrieved them, began inserting some of the things that had fallen out. A learned tome on Assyriology, another thick book with ruins pictured on the jacket, this one printed in French. He found Jacob's dilapidated wallet, a U.S. passport, numerous letters dampened by water from the hose. The envelopes bore return addresses and imprimaturs of universities, museums, institutes of purposes unknown to Whit, in this country and in Europe. There were photographs. Whit picked them up patiently. All the photos were of relics; composite animals in crude clay, other figures that were half human, half animal. Bulls and dragons, lions and eagles.

"Give me those!" Jacob yelled, hobbling toward him. "You have no right to take my things!"

"Settle down," Whit advised. "I was just picking them up for you."

He handed over the water-spotted photos and correspondence. Then he glanced at Arn, who was standing with his thumbs hooked in his belt, looking skeptical but with the white spots of violence gone from his cheekbones. Looking as if he sensed he might have made a mistake, but was in no mood to apologize; a certain rancor persisted.

Whit walked over to Arn and said in a low voice, "When was your dog killed?"

"Yesterday."

"Where?"

"Wildwood."

"When?"

"Early afternoon." Each word came with reluctance, with a slight heave of his chest and shoulders, his lips coming together after each reply as if soldered.

"Terry and I were having breakfast in Fulcrum's Cafe about eight o'clock, eight-fifteen yesterday morning. He was there, too, on the stool next to Terry. They had a brief conversation, in French. Told Terry he studied at the Sorbonne."

"I know he's smart. Too goddamn smart for my liking."

"Pay attention, Arn. We saw him a little later at the gas station across the road there, making some adjustments on his bike. The point is, could he have got up there in the woods on his bike and killed your dog at the time you know he was killed?"

"You can't get back in there on a bike," Arn conceded. "Not that far, anyway."

"How long would it have taken him on foot, then? From the edge of Wildwood, where the road ends."

"It takes me six hours, without a break. From the looks of Jacob, he can't move half that quick."

"What about the boots? You found some prints where your dog was killed?"

"Yeah. If it was Jacob, he's not wearin' the same boots today."

"Anything else need to be said, Arn?"

"I ain't apologizin' to him. Rather talk to the sheriff instead. Which I'll be doing, once Jacob gets to a telephone."

"Maybe not." Whit returned to Jacob. "Arn made a mistake and he knows it."

"I'm going to prosecute this time! He almost killed me!"

"*This* time? What happened last time?"

"He's threatened me. Told me to stay out of Wildwood or I'll be sorry. But I won't put up with this harassment any longer."

"My name's Whit Bowers. I'd like to know your name."

"Jacob . . . Schwarzman."

"Jacob, I was a colonel in the 82nd Airborne Division. Arn served under me for three years, through some tough campaigns. I'm sorry all of this happened, and I'd like to try to make it right for both of you. I don't want to see Arn cooling his heels in jail for the next six months."

"It's where he belongs," Jacob replied, but he seemed less concerned now with Arn than the condition of his photographs and correspondence. He was still breathing hard, but not as if it gave him pain.

"How long have you been in this part of the country, Jacob?"

"Why do you want to know that?"

"If you've spent much time with mountain people, you know they tend to be wary of strangers, and they have their own code of justice. Arn lost a valuable dog yesterday. He mistakenly concluded that you were responsible—"

"I am not capable of doing such a terrible thing! I like animals—the four-legged variety, that is. Sir, I am a respected scholar in my field, though you may find that difficult to believe seeing me in this state. All that I desperately want is to be left alone. If his dog was killed, then he knows as well as I who must be responsible: let him take his anger out on the appropriate individual, if he dares."

"Who are you talking about, Jacob?"

"I have nothing more to say to you." He put a grimy

hand to his cheek. His tongue was working. He winced, then stuck his tongue out. There was a piece of bloody tooth on the tip. Jacob fingered the fragment of tooth. "I must have broken it when I fell. It's only a miracle I've survived this outrageous and unprovoked assault. And my motorcycle—how am I supposed to get around? I have no money to repair the damages!"

"Jacob, would three hundred dollars fix your bike up, and pay your dental bill?"

Jacob found nothing in Whit's face to kindle suspicion. "Is he going to pay me?"

"No, I'm good for it." Whit took out his wallet, extracted a business card. Jacob took the card in his shaking fingers and tried to focus on it. "You're employed by Langford Industries?"

"Yes, I am."

"But—they own Wildwood." His bright blue eyes opened a little wider. He stuffed the business card into a pocket of his overalls as if he were stifling alarm. "Why are you here, Colonel Bowers?"

"Just looking over the property, Jacob. That's part of my job."

"What does that mean, looking over the property? What does your company have in mind?"

"Future development, a resort area in the vicinity of Tormentil Mountain."

Jacob fell back a step. "You can't do that!"

"Why not?"

"You have no idea of the difficulty—the disturbances such a development might cause. Oh, no, no, this is very unfortunate—"

"Jacob, I know everyone around here is eager to preserve the—the unspoiled nature of wilderness areas. What's your interest in Wildwood?"

"I live there. I appreciate the peace and solitude. They're essential for my—my life's work."

"What work is that?"

"I'm writing a book. That's all."

"From the photos I saw, you appear to have an interest in archaeology. Didn't you tell my son you studied at the Sorbonne?"

"Yes. I'm an archaeologist. And I have lived and studied in Paris. Also Berlin, before the Nazis, and at the University of Chicago." Jacob Schwarzman now seemed more agitated than abused. His shock at nearly having been rubbed out in a vehicular homicide had faded. He looked more objectively at his bike, which was far from a total wreck. "I—I suppose it can be fixed. I have so little money right now, the last of my grants ran out months ago. No one believes that I—never mind. If you were sincere in your offer to make good my loss—"

Whit counted out five twenties and two fifties from his wallet.

"This is about all the cash I have on me. I have some traveler's checks I can exchange today. I'll leave another hundred in cash at the bank in an envelope with your name on it. Will that be satisfactory?"

Jacob accepted the crisp bills with a certain famished delicacy, like a starving aristocrat determined not to slaver at the sight of food. He folded them once and put them into his shirt pocket.

"Thank you, Colonel Bowers."

"Just call me Whit. I'd like to have the chance to visit with you before I go back to New York. Buy you a beer."

"Yes. Well, I—perhaps we'll be seeing each other," Jacob said with no pretence of enthusiasm. He glanced at Arn. "As for him—will you assure me that you will use your influence, see to it that I am not bothered again? It's very disrupting to my—my work, my train of thought. As I said before, I truly desire to be left alone."

"I'll see to it, Jacob. And thanks for your cooperation."

Whit walked back to Arn and said in passing, "Let's go." In the station wagon he unwrapped a stick of spearmint gum and watched Jacob setting his bike upright.

When Arn got in behind the wheel he said, "How much did you pay him?"

"Three hundred bucks."

"Shit, he could buy him one almost new for that."

"Maybe he will. I don't care what he does with the money. He could also have had you jailed and sued you besides. Aggravated assault, among other charges. You need that kind of grief, Sergeant Hardass?"

Arn grinned at this almost forgotten familiarity.

"What makes you think he won't anyway?"

"Because there's honor in the man. And because he's a stranger here, and you're not."

"So everythin's ducky," Arn said in a flat tone. His hound was whining. Arn started the Pontiac and drove out of the sawmill yard. At the blinking yellow light he paused before making a sedate left turn to go to the vet's and pulled another photo from the pocket of his jacket.

"Here's one ole Jacob missed. You want it for a souvenir?"

Whit looked at a well-lighted study of an elongated art object from a distant era, a composite animal. It had the long, arched neck, flattened head, and forked tongue of a serpent, yet it walked on four feet, two of which resembled the claws of an eagle. Its tail was long, with a tuft at the end. The body appeared to be covered with scales. It seemed more jaunty than threatening, a toy designed for the nursery of a long-ago elite child.

"Ever seen anything like that before?" Arn asked him.

"No."

"I have. About two years ago."

"What museum was that?"

"Never been inside a museum in my life," Arn said. He chuckled then, but there wasn't much amusement in his face. "The one I saw was alive."

⸺ Chapter Eleven ⸺

THE car in which Faren Rutledge and Terry Bowers drove to the Boundary, which was what the local people called the Qualla Cherokee Reservation, was a black '38 Ford coupe that needed paint, a new clutch, and a rear window. A piece of plywood cut with a coping saw to the dimension of the window space created a hazardous blind spot for the driver. Faren used a side mirror taken from a postwar wreck to see behind them, but there wasn't much traffic and those cars and trucks that Terry observed as they sputtered down the main street of the village of Cherokee didn't look much better than the twenty-year-old Ford. The big pastel showboats, most of them with trailer hitches that could pull a locomotive uphill, hadn't begun to arrive in great numbers as yet.

Cherokee, situated in a valley at the confluence of the Soco and Oconaluftee rivers, was a junky jumble five blocks long, a dismal amusement park in a splendid natural setting. There were a couple of respectable churches, clapboard and brick, but the rest of the town was geared to flotsam commerce, the quick dollar. Except for a grocery store and bank, Indian motifs dominated: all of them, Faren pointed out, inappropriate—from the Warbonnet Motel (the primitive Cherokee were good fighters, with a strict code of honor, but had never gone to war on horseback, with their chiefs in elaborate feathered headdresses), to the Wigwam Village (wigwams, or teepees, were characteristic of nomadic Plains Indians, not the settled Southeastern tribes). Their first stop was Wigwam Village, which had a gravel lot big enough to accommodate a few hundred cars with trailers. The facade consisted of a saw-toothed billboard representing a teepee cluster; a fourteen-foot plaster Apache with a tomahawk in his hand stood astride the main entrance. The fierce war paint on his brown face, the recently retouched whites of his eyes, made him appear crazed.

"I apologize for this," Faren said sadly as Terry gazed up at the grotesque statue. "The injustice is, my people don't make much, if anything, from the indignity, the insult, the rotten exploitation. All of the 'handicrafts' these stores sell are turned out in factories in Toledo or someplace. I think some of it comes from the Philippines now. And Mexico. Most of the businesses around here have absentee owners, with white Cherokees managing them."

"What's a white Cherokee?"

"Mixed blood. Often very mixed. A few of them can claim maybe a sixteenth of Cherokee blood, but how they do brag about their 'Indian heritage,' as if they had any idea of what it means." Faren hadn't brought any samples of her pottery with her, but she had a big zippered portfolio under one arm. She wore a denim skirt and fringed brown leather jacket, an apricot-colored

Ship 'n Shore blouse with a garotte-tied cream scarf. A gold barrette holding her hair back over one ear was like a hawk in flight, with enameled talons and beak. "Well," she said with a sigh, "I'd better get to haggling. You can just santer around town on your own if you want to."

"No, I'll stay here." He liked being near Faren. He liked her deep but thoughtful silences, and had begun to try to think of things to say that would coax from her depths a quick smile, like a small white animal making a dash from a burrow. And when she impulsively but needfully hugged him, the happiness he felt was astonishing. It flooded him to the roots of his hair.

While Faren was cornered with the Wigwam Village manager, a frizzy-haired, toothpick-chewing man with lips like the ass on an orangutan, Terry prowled the nearly deserted fluorescent-lighted aisles of the gift shop, keeping an eye on Faren's negotiations. The manager had an annoying (to Terry) habit of playing familiarly with the fringe on one sleeve of Faren's jacket and patting her on the shoulder while she went through her book of drawings and color photographs with him. When he wasn't keeping watch on Faren, Terry gazed with indifference at ineptly made bow and arrow sets, fake peace pipes, felt-and-feather headdresses, mildly naughty hillbilly postcards. There was music in the store, sourceless, the volume unchanging no matter where he went. Elvis Presley singing in a slush-filled voice, "Don't Be Cruel (to a Heart That's True)." He was succeeded by Pat Boone. And, Jesus, Rosemary Clooney. Terry was relieved when Faren called to him as she briskly headed for the door.

"How did you do?" he asked her outside in the parking lot. The day was warming up. He unzipped his jacket and took it off, carried it hooked on his thumb and over one shoulder like Johnny Halliday, the French Presley; Terry had Halliday's style down pretty well.

"He'll stock a few of my things, the signed pieces, if I agree to give him some 'authentic' Navajo and Pueblo *ollas* to sell along with them."

"Will you?"

"Sure. I need the money. People like the Southwest tribal stuff, it's colorful; all the thunderbirds and feathered serpents and Mimbres archetypes look more 'Indian' than what I do. I'll also be required to come in twice a week wearing a buckskin dress and one of those lazy-stitch beaded headbands, stand around for a couple of hours. I don't mind. As long as the shit sells." Terry didn't say anything. She nudged him with an elbow. "Don't you think I'd make a good Navajo princess? Or does my French bother you?"

"Mom swears all the time." He shrugged. "So do I."

"How do you say *shit* in French? I've forgotten. I was terrible in French."

"Merde."

"That's right. Why don't we leave the car here and walk? We're just going down the street."

"To the Totem Pole Craft Shop or the Cherokee Trading Company?"

"Both. Are you bored?"

"No."

A husky Indian driving a muddy Jeep honked as they started down the street, and Faren waved casually back at him.

"What's your mother like?" she asked Terry. "I know she writes."

Terry balanced his way along a whitewashed log for a

few moments, as if simultaneously trying to achieve balance in his feelings about his mother.

"Usually she's a lot of fun; we're always going places, having parties. She never leaves me home. She says she wants me to meet people who *do* things in life. Then, other times . . . she has problems. Gets stuck in her work, throws her typewriter across the room. Lies in bed for two or three days staring holes in the ceiling. Then if she talks to me at all, she criticizes everything I say or do. I guess it's because she's not happy with herself. Mom says when you have a creative mind sometimes it backs up on you like a sewer."

"I'll have to get one of her books and read it. Although I've never been much of a reader; can't seem to find the time. Of course, I won't let a day go by without dipping into the Bible. Force of habit. Mom and Dad Hamilton had me reading the Bible out loud before I was old enough to go to school."

At supper last night Faren had talked about her foster parents, the Quaker couple, who had been childless themselves and getting along in years when they adopted Faren. She had photographs of them in her parlor: two remarkably similar, somber people whose features were hard to distinguish, either from too little contrast or as if they dwelled the last years of their lives on a spiritual plane the camera had difficulty capturing. They had died when Faren was in college. A small inheritance had seen her through.

"Are you a Quaker?" Terry asked her now.

"No. Wouldn't be dressed like this if I were. I suppose the philosophy of the Friends was always alien to my nature. I don't exactly favor turning the other cheek. Gave them both fits when I'd come home from school bruised and bloody after slugging it out with a nitwit kid who called me red nigger or Pocahontas or something. When I joined a church a few years back, I guess you'd say I went as far in the other direction as I could."

"Why, are you a Buddhist?"

Faren laughed. "Lord, not *that* far. Begging bowls don't suit my style either. No, a Quaker meeting is kind of a quiet, private affair. I joined the Church of God, which is singing and shouting and getting the spirit any way you can. But I've kind of gotten away from them, too, lately. I don't go as regular as I ought to—that means at least three times a week, up to six hours on Sunday. Well, look here, the gallery's open. Come on in, maybe Hick's around."

They had paused in front of a narrow two-story building, with an art gallery below, a dentist's office upstairs. Faren bounded up two steps and into the gallery.

"Who's Hick?" Terry asked, following her in.

"Hickory Smith, my brother. Half brother, anyway. At least that's how we sorted it out when we met a few years ago. Hey, Hick! Anybody here?"

There was a series of photographs on one wall, artfully arranged under spotlights. Some were in black and white, some had a sepia overcast that reminded Terry of tinted daguerreotypes he had seen in Parisian antique shops. Terry studied a portrait of a Cherokee man about Faren's age. He wore a dark suit and an old-fashioned shirt without a collar. Thick mustache overhanging the angles of his jaw, arms folded, in appearance as stilted as if he had been stood up from his coffin to be photographed, the dark dark pupils of his eyes ghosting from the flashpan.

"That's Hick," Faren said. "A self-portrait. He took these other pictures too." A tumbledown barn, some elderly Indians gathered council-style on a porch, every man distinctively hatted. "He's got a big box camera on a tripod, goes way back: tries to get the old-timey look. Nowadays that's *art*, or so he tells me. Hick paints too; says he wants to do me and someday when I'm not so busy I'll sit for him."

A small unsmiling girl in jeans and soiled moccasins with little round bells on them came out of a back room and spoke to Faren in a language Terry assumed was Cherokee. The girl wore granny specs and had paint daubs on her blue workshirt, a long streak of white in her hair that also looked like paint, but probably she'd been born with the streak. There was a girl from Dublin in his school who had red hair and a white streak like that, the Irish called it "Veronica's veil," and it was supposed to mean something special, he didn't know what. Except for her eyes, which were black as watermelon seeds, the girl talking to Faren seemed more Caucasian than Indian; but she was fluent in Cherokee, a language that sounded Oriental to Terry's ears. Faren answered her, and asked a question. The girl shook her head a couple of times. Then she talked for nearly five minutes nonstop, explaining something, wringing her hands in a softly supplicating manner as if to overcome Faren's unvoiced resistance. Finally Faren nodded. Abruptly the girl turned and went jingling back to the room she had come out of and Faren just stood there, gazing at the floor, in a kind of reverie.

"Something wrong?" Terry asked her.

Faren's head came up, her face was animated again.

"Oh, no; Hick's not here. There's a meeting of some of the ministers of the Churches of God in this area. It'll last all day and half the night. That's where he is. Hick's a preacher too."

"Took her a long time to tell you that."

"It wasn't just about Hick. Trudy asked me would I do her a favor, and I guess I can't refuse. We'll go later, there's no hurry. Let's see if I can peddle some more pots before we knock off for lunch."

The Cherokee Trading Post already had a pottery glut; Faren was able to place a small order at the Totem Pole Craft Shop, which improved her mood.

"Doing better than last year," she told Terry. "I think you're lucky for me. There's still some places up around Gatlinburg I can hit early next week. Are you hungry? You didn't have much breakfast, and my stomach's rumbling. How about a picnic? I know a beautiful spot overlooking the Oconaluftee, south of the ranger station."

"Sure." He would go anywhere with Faren, anytime she asked.

At a grocery they loaded up with chips, fried pork rind, Velveeta cheese, white bread, bread-and-butter pickles, cold cuts, mayonnaise, and a carton of Dr Pepper.

"How about a moon pie?" Faren asked him.

"What's that?"

"You've never had a moon pie? I don't believe it." She was having a good time at his expense, but in a nice way. Faren bought a box of moon pies. "It's just kind of marshmallow and a little cake and chocolate on it, but tasty. Next you're going to tell me you've never eaten fried squirrel or hash meat."

"I like corned beef hash."

"Hash *meat*. Can't buy anything like it in a store. You cook the head, feet, and liver of a hog until they're tender. Then you take out the bones, grind the meat up kind of coarse. Grind some red peppers, sage, and salt. Serve it up with artichoke relish and baked pawpaws for dessert. That's eating."

Clouds were beginning to fatten like sheep in a spring pasture as they drove north on a winding road. The river was close on their right, sometimes glimpsed through the thick trees and high walls of rhododendron as a white tongue licking downhill. Faren hummed to herself, occasionally frowning as she nursed and humored the cranky old Ford up the grade.

The place she had chosen for their picnic was not far from but out of sight of the road, where the river rushed thinly over slabs of green bedrock. The banks were loaded with rhododendron, each bush weighted with tapered yellow buds as long as a man's index finger. Some of the buds had popped into pale pink bloom. Dogwoods were spread to infinity in the noontime shade. A split log footbridge crossed the Oconaluftee to a rocky hillside overlooking the river.

Faren said, "I knew a girl, she couldn't cross running water, even on a bridge like this one, unless she was chewing on something, broomstraw or leaf. She'd just lose her balance and go ker-plash." Faren herself was lightfooted and swift, even though she carried one of the bags of groceries and the logs were soaked with spray from the torrent six feet below. They were both well-wetted by the time they got across; tiny beads of water sparkled on Faren's russet forehead in a thin shaft of sunlight. She smiled, putting down the groceries. "Isn't this a good place? The bugs won't get bad for another month or so. Can you climb down there to the water without falling in?"

"Ha," Terry said derisively; she handed him the Dr Pepper carton.

"Put two or three of these bottles where the water'll wash over them; they'll be good and cold in no time."

When Terry clambered back up the slippery rocks, she

had already made a table on a flat ledge with a square of oilcloth and was putting sandwiches together: liverwurst, cheese, and baked ham. She used a wicked-looking pocket knife she had taken from her purse. It had a staghorn handle and one of the blades was five inches long. They feasted. Terry liked the crisp peppery pork rinds; even the gummy bread, totally lacking in texture, unlike the French loaves he was accustomed to, tasted okay with enough mayonnaise and pickles pasted between slices. After eating he went down to the river to retrieve a couple of bottles of Dr Pepper, looked up, and saw a black bear on the bank opposite him. The bear was shaking its head in a low arc and making grunting sounds. Terry scampered back up the rocks, bottles clinking together. Faren had seen the bear, too, and was unconcerned.

"He won't bother us," she said.

The bear had waded out into the river, and was looking up at them.

"Is he coming over here?" Terry asked, fascinated and a little scared.

"I'll just talk bear talk to him if he does." Faren used the bottle opener at the base of the smaller jackknife blade and handed him a Dr Pepper.

"Be serious."

"I am serious. All Cherokees are brothers to bears; because our legends tell us there was a time when they were human. And if you're *adawehi*—that means you have special powers of discernment and maybe the gift of tongues—you can talk to bears, other animals too. Wolves, Painters."

"Painters?"

"Mountain lions. But they're scarcer today than they used to be. You could spend a week in the woods and not see one. There's plenty bears, though, they get to be a nuisance some places. Just like tourists.''

Their particular bear was in the middle of the river, which flowed around him almost to his chin.

"Better talk some bear talk," Terry said urgently.

Faren sat up and faced the river, hands folded in her lap as if she were about to pray. After a few moments' contemplation she began grunting and chuckling gruffly, loud enough to be heard over the sound of the river pouring by. The bear lifted his head alertly, nose quivering. He answered back. Faren opened another Dr Pepper and put it in Terry's hand.

"Take this down and leave it where ole bear can get at it.''

"He wants a Dr Pepper?"

"He's probably never had one before; but he'll like it. All bears have sweet tooths.''

Terry went cautiously down the rocks to the river's edge, never taking his eyes off the wet bear; but the bear just looked at him, perhaps without ill will. At least he wasn't showing a lot of tooth, or looking as if he might suddenly come bounding at Terry in an explosion of spray. He left the Dr Pepper wedged upright between two rocks smothered in lichen, and returned to Faren.

She talked to the bear again. He came to their side of the bank, sat down in the shallows, gazed at the soda bottle, then took it in both paws, sniffing the contents. He began to drink, pink tongue the size of a baseball mitt catching every drop. When he was finished he put the bottle back and ambled off downstream.

Faren unbuttoned and removed her fringed leather jacket, folded it inside out to make a pillow for herself. "I've got some business to attend to in a little while," she said, "and I didn't get much sleep last night. Be-

lieve I'll catch a little nap." She covered a yawn with
the back of one hand, licked her lips, and smiled at
Terry. She settled back, almost lying down, cushioned
in a ferny cleft, and closed her eyes. "Don't go too far
if you decide to take a walk," she cautioned.

"I'll just stay here," Terry said, thinking about the
bear.

After he put the remains of their picnic back into the
brown paper bags so the scraps and greasy butcher paper
wouldn't draw flies, there was nothing much to do but
watch the currents of the river, butterflies in the undergrowth of rhododendron, cream-yellow clouds filling up
the spaces of blue sky visible above the treetops. And
Faren's composed, sleeping face. A little humidity in
the hollows of her eyes. She used only eyeliner and a
touch of lipstick. Her mouth was relaxed. There was a
little scar like a misplaced vaccination mark half under
her chin on the left side (slugging it out with a nitwit kid
who called me red nigger). A small steady pulse in her
throat.

When a mosquito alighted on her forehead he brushed
it off and her eyes opened halfway. She looked at him
as if in a dream, then put an arm around him and pulled
him gently to her. His head came to rest on her shoulder, warmed by a ray of sun. She was mildly fragrant, a
talcum of some kind. She didn't wear perfume. Hair
coarse and black over one ear, just the lobe showing.
Terry listened to her breath stirring faintly in her nostrils, soft exhalations, and studied the shape of her
breasts, rising, falling. He was stunned with desire but
of course she meant nothing by this, although he was
practically lying on top of her, aware of hip bones and
belly, but he didn't dare move the one cramped hand
which already was down there where he wanted to touch

her, the hem of her denim skirt at mid-thigh. Warm brown flesh there. Her legs spread, relaxed. Last summer in Cannes, french-kissing Paul Juilliard's sister Anne-Marie, who already was fifteen, they had simultaneously put their hands into each other's swim briefs. Oh, she had said, that's a nice one, but when he asked her if she wanted to, she shrugged and said, no, she liked him okay but she was in love with someone else. His first and only pussy, the fleetest of feels, a sleek little handful she let him hold and stroke for a few seconds longer as if it were a nervous lab animal out of its cage. Then, he couldn't remember, somebody had come in a door or up the stairs or something, they let go of each other just about the time he thought she was going to change her mind. Faren probably felt different between the legs because she was older, but he could only imagine what the difference would be. Darker, bushier, with a more provocative tang than the girlish, fishy essence of Anne-Marie that had lingered on his fingertips. God this was wonderful, but it was awful too. He tried to think about other things, but what else was there? The sun had disappeared like a thin coin in a cauldron of seething lead, the day finally darkening for good. Faren's faintly sighing breath, the river flowing strong as heartsblood through a green artery of the mountain, made him drowsy: and just in time; he hadn't shot off daydreaming about screwing her but he'd already leaked a little. He assimilated her close, airy, human rhythm, which quieted the pent-up beast of the groin and then his nerves; closing his eyes, he fell peacefully asleep.

Alerted by thunder a quarter of an hour later, they woke up together. There was a change in the air, ionic; a steady, high, drafty rustling of leaves. Faren pressed her cheek leisurely against his, smiled obscurely, still coming out of sleep: she ran a hand through his hair the way his mother sometimes did, plowing a furrow, exciting it in the wrong direction; at the same time she shifted her body slightly athwart his own so that they came together neatly but shockingly below the waist. He lit up all over except for his right hand, which had gone numb in the press of their bodies.

"It's going to storm," she said, and he wasn't at all sure she meant the clouding of the sky. There was weather in the blood to be reckoned with. They sat up, a common impulse drowsily managed, hands on each other for balance, her skirt wrinkled up past her knees, his right leg crooked inside hers, knee resting against a firm inner thigh, their faces inches apart and now giving off the last of their sleep like heat, clearing like mirrors that have been breathed on: they looked in each other's eyes, the light and the dark, no secrets unshared. What she saw was gratifying, but made her sad too.

"I know, I know," she murmured. "You're such a good-looking boy; and I do have a sweet tooth for you. We could get each other stirred up here and now. But Terry, what that does, believe me, just leaves good hearts full of trash. I want my heart to go on feeling kindly, with friendship for you that'll last forever. Understand?"

He nodded. More relieved than disappointed.

Faren pressed her lips against his for a moment, neutrally, drew back smiling again.

"You need a Cherokee name, for sure," she said, and thought about it, sizing him up. "What's your favorite sport?"

"Skiing."

"Hmm. I don't think there's an expression for that in Cherokee. What else do you like?"

"Swimming."

"Okay. You'll be Ayunini—the Swimmer."

"Is Faren a Cherokee name?"

"No. I'm Kálanu. Raven. You like that?"

"Yes," he said, and wished she would kiss him again. Instead she shook out her jacket and put it on. "Time to be leaving. I've got a chore to do. That little sleep cleared my head. Can you go fetch that empty bottle ole bear drunk out of? We don't want to leave anything behind that spoils the wilderness, get *utkena* riled at us."

"Who's *utkena*?"

"Lives in deep misty places like this. He's a monster. Kind of a serpent, but with horns. But if you've got a healthy spirit and nothing to fear, chances are you'll never meet up with *utkena*. And that's a good thing. Just to look him in the face means certain death, unless you're powerful too: *adawehi*."

"Like you."

"Like me. Reckon I'm a pretty handy sort to have around, don't you think?"

With sprinkles of pain in his right hand Terry went down the rocks once more and brought up the remaining bottles. He walked behind her across the footbridge, still hearing thunder but no closer. There was no rain yet. Just the spray from the river wetting them again. In the car they shared a handkerchief from her purse, odorous of lipstick and so many other things, exotic to him, that collected in women's purses. Faren looked at the sky, huge thunderheads dark as bruises. The trees were nearly motionless, the air still sharp and not hazy the way it would get just before rain fell in sheets.

"Hope all that stays up to the north," she said.

"Some of these old red-dog roads get to be like glass in a downpour. But—I promised Trudy."

"Where are we going?"

"Ways from here. Trudy's grandfather's house. She told me how to find it. He's lying in a coma, it's six days now. What they want to know, will he come around or is this the end." She started the car, backed down the road a little until she could get the clutch to engage, the balky gears to mesh. Then they went up the hill, in fits and starts. "Hate this ole Ford, wish we could be rid of it. But we can't roll up the price of another one right now, and there's times we need two, even though it's reached the point Arn takes off three weeks out of every four."

A short distance up the highway Faren turned left, began following a couple of ruts of clay and shattered rock, the car bouncing up and down. Woods pressed close on either side, branches of flowering trees and shrubs scraped the car body until the windshield was yellow with grains of pollen, pink and white petals fluttered in their dusty wake. There were no signs anywhere. The poor road branched and rebranched, they went south, then they went north again, past log cabins chinked with dried mud and where naked potbellied Indian children and piglets mingled in the putrid dooryard, past a trailer up on blocks, its metal sides peppered with rust in shotgun patterns, through a scary scrambling pack of dogs that came out from beneath a cabin as if they would chew the tires off the car, into deep, mysterious ravines, across flowing creeks and out again, laboriously, Faren saying at the sight of an immense dead tree or a skeletal auto sitting tireless near the road of a submarginal cornfield with last year's stalks hanging tough on a hillside, "That looks familiar," or, "Yeah, I know where I am now."

Suddenly she applied the brakes with an expression of disgust.

"*Merde!* Should have gone the other way at the Cohosh Fork. Get good and lost back here if we stay traveling in this direction. Well, let's stop awhile. I can't hold my water any longer and you must be perishing to go too."

They got out. The road space, like an alley between speckled white trees that made a living picket fence up to the turbid tin-colored sky, was only about ten feet wide. Gloomy sultry woods all around them. Birds shrill and musical, busy as bullets flying from tree to tree.

"I'll stay on this side of the car, and that's the boys' side," Faren said cheerfully, pointing. "Don't step off into the woods even if you need to squat."

"Why not?"

"Rattlers. Copperheads. That's two good reasons."

"Oh." Every word spoken, each breath they took in this walled place of closely packed cottony air, resounded magnified. His fly zipper opening. Faren working her skirt above her hips as if she were peeling herself, peeling long-stemmed cherry-swart fruit, slipping her silk-sounding underpants down to her ankles, then settling wide and spaciously bare-assed on her heels (Terry able to distinguish her movements out of the corner of his eye, not really seeing anything), holding the edge of the front bumper to steady herself. Pee coming almost at once, to her great relief and satisfaction. The unmistakable pressurized hissing of a woman in urination, intriguingly vulgar out-of-doors, so close to him in the road, strong acid-gold chemical change in the air he breathed, hot confusion of images in his head, he had his penis out but it swelled treacherously in his hand until he couldn't do anything himself, just stood there hurting and frustrated. So self-conscious, knowing she would hear him too. Jesus. It really hurt now, and not a drop.

Faren stood up, pulling her underpants snugly to her waist. She smoothed her skirt over her thighs, pushed hair off her damp forehead and glanced at his rigid back. She waited.

"Terry?"

"Huh?"

"Ready?"

"Uh . . . uh."

Faren grinned cheekily, leaned against the dusty hood of the Ford, chin in hands. After a few more seconds she said, "Want me to come over there and talk bear talk to it?"

He started to laugh. Doubled over, holding himself, laughing, still locked up tight and hurting like hell, three-quarters of a foot of stone hose in his hand.

"I'll just take a walk down the road for a couple of minutes," Faren said. "Holler when you want me."

When she was far enough away he relaxed and got going, at last, but kept laughing and seizing up and jerking all over the place, getting big wet spots on his wrinkled chinos. When he was through he climbed into the car and honked the horn. Faren came strolling out of an ethereal nimbus at a distant bend of the road. Terry felt very red in the face but Faren pretended not to notice when she joined him. She seemed solemn about something, backing the car up carefully until they reached the fork she felt she should have taken earlier.

"I wasn't poking fun," she told him then, patiently working the long gearshift and trampling the clutch until the obstinate transmission was out of reverse. "Trying to make you feel ridiculous. It's just good to have somebody to laugh with, a little joke that's nobody's but ours."

"I thought it was funny," he assured her. "I cracked up. 'Bear talk.' "

"If I can't laugh, then I get all sunk into myself. Maybe not so different from your mother, when she's upset her work's not going well. I don't know—maybe this wasn't such a good time for you and your dad to show up here. But I'm real glad you did. I wasn't feeling too great, just trying to get through each day, but sinking. Like the *utkena* was wrapped around me, and pulling me down into the deep pool where he lives. The last time it happened, I sunk so low they had to shock me out of it."

"How do you mean?"

"Electric shock, Terry. I had to have electroshock therapy to cure my depression. I was away for about six weeks. Arn came to visit me, one time. Then he just went back to his woods." Unexpectedly she began to cry. "It was pure . . . hell."

Terry was stricken, then angry. "You don't love him, do you?"

"Oh, yes, I do, Terry."

"Well—it sounds like—"

"I don't love some things about him. I don't love it when he leaves me alone, and I'm worried sick he'll never come back. But I love Arn."

Terry still felt angry but didn't know what to say, tried silently to phrase something rewarding, was upset by her weeping and hated Arn, *hated* him; and, helplessly, began to cry himself, each stifled, inadequate word of sympathy seemed to boil into a tear. He wiped at his cheeks, face averted.

When she could see where she was going Faren drove on; and when she could manage the wheel with one hand she put out the other hand to Terry, who held it tightly. Neither of them said anything for miles until they reached a settlement spread over low hills, farmland, half a dozen cabins and barns frail gray against a threatening sky with lightning inside the clouds like fireflies in dark bottles. Unshed rain scented the air, an old-fashioned tractor with iron lugs instead of tires was heading in across a sloping half-plowed field, dust devils kicking up behind it.

"This be the place," Faren said pensively.

Meadowlarks smote by the downdrafting wind careened across their path as Faren forced the car up the side of a hill blanketed with glossy yellow lespedeza flowers, no definite road to follow, just a welter of tracks worn through the ground cover to red earth. The house on the crest, its twin pitchfork lightning rods looking too fragile to absorb the power that gleamed in several places at once in the forbidding darkness overhead, was made of squared-off logs, with a swaybacked roof that was all hubcaps hammered into overlapping shingles. Children were flocking inside the house now, flat-featured girls in skimpy cotton dresses, toddlers wearing undershirts only, all of them barefoot. The old apple and pear trees on the hill were tortured to their roots by the wind, new leaves tearing off and flashing through the air with the velocity of thrown knives. The sky, a battlefield of dragons, crackling. Faren pulled up alongside the porch as raindrops, widely spaced but smacking down hard, starred the windshield.

"Just made it," she said. "Make a run for the porch, Terry."

The wind was nearly enough to knock him over; he had to force the car door shut. He picked his way up the steps to the porch almost on his hands and knees, aware of red animal eyes underneath, the stink of dogs and garbage thrown to the dogs. He waited for Faren and from the porch they watched as the rain came diagonally across the hill like a bright metallic theater curtain drawing swiftly to a close, blotting out their view of the valley down below. The house trembled in the torrent.

Faren said into his ear, "Terry, it's maybe going to smell inside like you're not used to, there's a whole lot of Trudy's people live in two, three rooms here, and an old man's dying besides; but you just can't let on that it bothers you."

"I won't."

Rain blew in their faces; they backed up and the door, which had been closed to a quarter-inch crack, opened for them.

—— Chapter Twelve ——

It was after six o'clock and Faren hadn't shown up to cook supper for them; Arn was acting peevish, although he'd drunk so much during the long, wet, frequently tedious afternoon, Whit didn't understand how he could have much desire for food.

They'd spent a not particularly comfortable day with each other following Arn's violent run-in with Jacob Schwarzman, so Whit had done some drinking, too, misjudging the potency of the white lightning Arn had vouched for and urged on him. His tongue was deadened, his head hurt, and his vision was fuzzy. He was a little worried about his son.

"If it's been rainin' this way down on the Boundary," Arn told him, "then those two are just holed up somewhere. Most likely with that Smith fella she calls her half brother. Roads down there ain't passable in a gullywasher. When she lets up, reckon they'll head on home. Pour you another shot, Whit?" He pointed to the two-quart mason jar on the polished floor beside his lounge chair. The jar had been brimful of hundred-proof liquor earlier in the afternoon. Now it was a quart low.

"Still working on this one."

Arn unscrewed the lid carefully and gave himself another generous splash. They were in the parlor. The electricity had failed an hour before, but Arn had set out a kerosene lamp once it got too dark for them to see each other except when lightning dusted off their opposing faces, somber as death masks stored in a reliquary. Arn's eyes screwed slot-tight and narrow as a Chinaman's, the only visible effect booze seemed to have on him.

There was a third party in the room with them, sitting off to one side on a horsehair sofa with hands folded obediently in its lap. Arn's Grudge.

Whit had first become aware of the Grudge a couple of hours ago after his fourth—fifth?—shot of squeezings, as a ghostly outline that appeared during silences and waned when they talked about things of interest to Arn, distracting him. Firearms and hunting, dogs and women. But as the day wore on, Arn was distracted less easily from the soreness that afflicted him like a bad tooth in his head, the matter of Whit Bowers standing up to him and humbling him in front of men who would flap about it, to Arn's detriment. No matter that Whit had been right to step in, and that Arn had gone off half-cocked and might have killed or seriously injured Jacob Schwarzman. Two wrongs didn't make a right in Arn's book (Whit knowing full well how his mind worked), and Whit, in wronging Arn, had done damage to his esteem that would remain long after Whit was gone from the valley of the Cat Brier. So the Grudge had appeared, slowly shaping up as if born of the frequent lightning, Arn breathing life into it until it was full-bodied, faceless but muscular, silent, intimidating.

The Grudge would follow everywhere they went until something powerful, perhaps violent, happened to satisfy it. Mere apology would not do. An offer to have it out, no holds barred, until one of them was unable to lift his head from bloodied ground? Maybe. Whit wasn't afraid of Arn, but he didn't want to fight him. The uniforms were packed away but the habit of command was ingrained; so was the assumption of superiority. He had his own pride to consider, and the liquor had made him stubborn. Fighting Arn and losing would be a disgrace. To Blackie's memory, if nothing else. But he also equated a beating with losing his son's respect. He kept looking over at Arn's Grudge, squinting to make it out there on the shadowy side of the parlor, stiffly wearing an old-fashioned garment that might have been a hair shirt. Fuck it, he thought. He wished Faren would come home. He wanted to see her more than he wanted to see Terry. She would recognize the Grudge right away, and banish it from the house. Send it out to live with the dogs.

This house needed Faren. It was a cheerless place without her, lackluster. Even Arn seemed to realize that, while he talked about other women, his prodigious sexual despoliation.

"Haven't you ever wanted children, Arn?"

"Wantin' ain't gettin'. Hell, I knew a long time before I got married I wasn't goin' to have none. It's not Faren. It's me."

"Oh. Sorry to hear it."

"Maybe it's best. Rowdy as I've been, by now I'd have bastards slung all over this end of creation; Ireland and England, too, since we spent all that time there gettin' ready to take Europe back from the Krauts. Maybe I wouldn't have been no good with kids, Lord must know what he's doin'." He chuckled. "Might have wound up married a whole lot sooner, like to that preacher's gal I had when I was about your boy's age. Kind of a washed-out pale little blond thing with big blueberry eyes, and her own notion of how to scourge the devil out of me, so I'd be a fit vessel to receive the spirit of Jesus Christ. She'd come along and drag me off in the woods and make me take my pants down. Make me! Huh. And there'd be my pecker standin' up big and red and I reckon ugly as sin to her. The devil. Oh, she'd talk to it. Stamp around and shake her fist, workin' herself up to a e-van-gel-i-cal frenzy. 'All right, devil, we're gonna whip you today. Whip you till you can't stand up no more.' I swear to you this is no lie. Then she'd get me down on the ground and squat-fuck me, little bubbies just a-bouncin', yellin' 'Praise Jesus!' And 'Hallelujah!' ever' time one of us would come, which was plenty often. So I learned a long time ago you never can tell about the pale shy ones, sometimes they burn the hottest. But she had the excuse in her head that it weren't no sin to be doin' that with me, because what she was really up to was helpin' me tame the devil. There was times we worked at it a whole afternoon and the ole pecker-devil still wouldn't bow down more than halfway. I'll say this for her, she never flagged in her devotion to the Lord's work. Wish I could think of her name now. Maybe it was Bonnie."

Whit finished the squeezings in his glass. A few drops too many, perhaps. Bitter as belladonna on the tongue, he was through the looking glass before he had swallowed it all. His head felt very large and roly-poly, his feet little and far away. He dimmed out, hearing Arn talk on and on but unable to make sense of the words. The rain would let up for a while, then thunder would come rolling back across the roof and shake the house, every window rattling, lightning like moments of pure blindness, needles dead-center through each eyelid and paralyzing the optic nerves.

Then Arn was leaning over him, holding the lamp in one hand, shaking him with the other.

"What? What's that, Arn?"

"Said I'll prove to you I'm no liar! Get up, if you can walk."

"I can walk," Whit said in a surly tone of voice; who was Arn Rutledge to pass judgment on his competence, he had a snootful himself, his breath was foul from liquor. All Whit really wanted to do was drink a gallon of cold water to awaken his numbed tongue and refresh his burned-out throat, then go to sleep. What had Arn been talking about, a preacher's daughter who—but that might have been hours ago. He'd totally lost track of time.

"Faren home?" he asked Arn.

"Not yet. On your feet, there you go." Arn was smiling at him, his head deformed by the nearness of the curved lamp chimney that contained a sooty orange flame. His eyes slits. Whit saw something of himself in the lamp and, between them, what might have been the ghostly outline of the Grudge. Was Arn lusting for satisfaction now? Whit couldn't think, much less throw a punch if he had to.

But Arn put a hand on his elbow to steady him. "This way," he said curtly.

"Where're we going?"

A big bolt of lightning, like a wave of the sea, came down on their heads. Rain gushed everywhere. Arn walked him slowly to the kitchen. He opened the pantry door. The pantry was long and narrow, with floor-to-

ceiling shelves on two sides. Strings of dried green and
red peppers, dark twists of sausage, and a couple of
cured hams dangled from ceiling hooks. There was an
unhinged trap door in the floor. Arn pried up the door
and leaned it against a shelf filled with old-style Ball
jars, the kind with rubber gaskets and clamp-on lids.
Dank air rose from below. Whit looked at wooden steps
going down into darkness.

"What's down there?"

"Root cellar. Watch your step."

Arn went first. He was able to stand erect on the dirt
floor with only inches of headroom to spare. He waited
with the lamp.

Whit descended with care, wishing he didn't have to
but having no will to resist. There were cobwebs between the joists. The walls of the root cellar were
crudely plastered; despite the heavy rain the floor was
dry. But he found it hard to breathe, air was scarce and
smelled of the grave, vaguely rotten.

In one corner were the corroded coils and green-
tinted thirty-five-gallon copper kettle of a long disused
still. "My daddy's works," Arn said. "He'd move
most of his corn down in South Carolina, where the
niggers paid him fifty cents a pint. Ain't a bad livin'
nowadays nuther, in spite of the ATU, but I just never
had the patience to sit around the woods tendin' mash."
The root cellar was crowded with other odds and ends of
mechanical junk, an old Jack Daniel's distillery barrel,
wooden boxes containing what was left of last year's
apple crop and some spoiling sprouted potatoes, which
accounted for the prevailing odor of rottenness. And
there was a big black steamer trunk that might have
been fifty years old. Arn set the lamp on the barrel top
and, crouching, opened the trunk. With two hands he

lifted something out and stood, turning to give Whit a
look. He was holding what appeared to be a crudely
fashioned loop of granite, not symmetrical, mounted on a
bronze pyramidal base. He set the object on the dirt
floor and stepped away from it.

"Ever seen anything like that before?"

Whit shook his head, wishing the fog would lift.

"No. What is it?"

"Buddy, I don't know what you'd call it. Found it
deep in the woods and lugged it home, this was two,
three years ago. I set it on the kitchen table and just
looked at it for a while, that's all, tryin' to figure out
what it meant or where it might've come from originally—
there ain't no words or markin's on it. Next thing I
knew flies in the kitchen was fallin' down on the table
next to it, buzzin' around on the oilcloth till they died.
Faren, when she come home, she took one look and
kinda drawed back like it was fixin' to bite her; she
knows about things that don't meet the eye, and she said
I had to pound it to pieces or throw it away where
nobody could look at it, or soon enough we'd die, too,
like the flies."

"What do you mean, Faren knows about things that
don't meet the eye?"

Arn tapped the middle of his forehead with one finger. "She's got what the old granny women 'round here
call 'the sight,' what some preachers mean by 'discernment.' Probably all the same thing, but she knew this
piece as a bad 'un right away, if you wasn't careful how
you handled it. She said it was four thousand years old,
but somebody not too long ago had been usin' it for the
wrong purposes, and it had a lot of energy left that
could harm us."

"How could she know all that?"

Arn said impatiently, "She just does. She *knows*. I
learned early on to respect her hunches. Before we got
married, when we was just gettin' acquainted, I borrowed Ralph Spivey's '53 Studebaker. which wasn't
two weeks out of the showroom, and drove all the way
to Hiwassee, Tennessee, where she was teachin' college
at the time. Yeah, I was slickered up and struttin' my
onions. Faren took one look at that red Studebaker and
wouldn't set foot in it. She said the brakes was bad. I
said, 'I just drove pret' near a hundred miles to take you
out, and you're not gonna go with me?' She said. 'Not
in that car.' I said, 'Well, good night, darlin'. and don't
you be lookin' for ole Arn around here anytime soon.'
Last thing I heard, 'Get those brakes checked!' But I
just drove off in a cuss-ed frame of mind, thinkin' that
she was the most contrary piece of pussy I ever met. But
I'm tellin' you, didn't travel half a dozen miles 'fore I
missed a curve, brakes just went completely, and I
would up rolled in a gully, the car pure-d totaled. Ralph
got himself twelve thousand damages plus a new
Studebaker from the car company; all I collected was a
busted spleen and a cracked shinbone that laid me up in
the hospital for a couple weeks. Faren come to see me
ever' day, and the same day they let me out of the
hospital I got married on crutches." He looked at the
object on the floor of the root cellar, and quickly away.
"To satisfy Faren I took my eight-pound sledge to that
thing. Couldn't chip the littlest piece off it. Looks like
it's sure 'nuff made of stone, but I reckon how it's
not."

"You found it in Wildwood?"

" 'Bout one third of the way up Tormentil, near the
Ookoonaka branch of the Cat Brier. Here's somethin' I
near forgot. There was dead birds lyin' around it, in all

directions. But I didn't connect the birds then with the—whatever it is, otherwise I never would have brung it home."

"You carried it, but you didn't suffer any ill effects?"

"Said I *brung* it, must weigh upwards of twenty pounds. Wrapped it in the ground tarp I had with me, tied a rope around it, and drug it behind me on a skid. Too heavy to handle any other way."

"Why do you keep the thing, Arn?"

"I reckon it's just steadily losin' power, locked up here in the dark. And it's proof, part of the proof that whatever I say I seen in Wildwood, I'm not just spinnin' yarns. And here's better proof."

This time, with the greatest of care, he removed from the big trunk a long oilcloth bundle tied at both ends with rugged twine. The bundle, in contrast to the solid, mysterious, slightly lopsided loop, seemed to weigh next to nothing. Arn hunkered down and untied the bundle with fingers that shook slightly; his face was reddening, almost a blush, as if he were a virgin bridegroom beside himself with the excitement of disrobing his wife on their wedding night. He laid the bundle open and revealed a nearly complete skeleton about five feet in length, the skull separate and staring vacantly up from the nest of bones formed by ribs and shieldlike pelvic structure. Or was it parts of two skeletons? Whit felt a twinge of dismay, trying painfully to distinguish the assortment through bleary eyes. Youthful-looking teeth in the skull. A powerful rib cage and breastbone sturdy as the keel of a whaling ship. One foot missing at the ankle—and where was the rest of it? The long arm bones, the tapering fingers, and complex joints. He saw instead kitelike frameworks as large as the body, attached to the shoulder blades. Not two skeletons as he'd thought, it was all of a piece—

"Oh, my God," Whit said, and Arn looked up, lips tight in a grimace of triumph.

"You see it, then, don't you? That skeleton ain't faked up nuther, like some claimed it to be. This is just how I found it, years after I shot him out of the sky."

"It—flew—?"

"Goddamn right *he* flew! The hawkman. Ten of us and a big pack of dogs saw him take off from a ledge high up Tormentil. Now, look here, you got to hunker down real close to see it. This little chip out of the breastbone? That tiny gray mark you see is lead from my 30-'06. I nailed him with the one shot from half a mile, got him clean through the heart, too, judgin' from the way that chip was taken out of the bone. Ten of us saw it, and I'm the only one left. Some of the others just tore to pieces while they was out huntin', by wild things with the minds of men. So how about it, Whit? When I tell you I seen a fire-breathin' animal in the woods no bigger'n a housecat but walkin' on eagle's claws, do you still believe I made it up? Wildwood is just what it sounds like—a wild place, and strange. You take your Alice in Wonderland, your Grimm fairy tales, *hell*, it's stranger than any of that. Wasn't always, not when my daddy was growin' up, but they hadn't built the big chateau up there then."

"Mad Edgar Langford's chateau?"

"The shit you think I'm talkin' about?"

"What's that got to do with—"

"Got ever'thing to do with what's transpired since, accordin' to Faren, and she's seen more'n I'll ever see in this life."

"Cover it up," Whit said of the skeleton, getting to

his feet and almost falling down. He went to sit on the root cellar steps, head in his hands. He heard Arn whistling a sour tune as he rewrapped the skeleton, put that and the stone loop that possibly wasn't stone back into the deep trunk.

"That thing—couldn't fly," Whit said. "No matter what the wingspread. The bones, the body weight—too much for it to leave the ground, but if it did, then it wouldn't be stable in the air. The whole idea's just a physical impossibility, like—twelve-foot grasshoppers walking around."

"That's funny," Arn said. "You know it's a scientific fact that bumblebees can't fly nuther, 'cause their bodies is too big for the size of their wings. So I reckon it can't be bumblebees I see all around the hollyhocks and trumpet vines in summertime. Now, I didn't say the hawkman flew good, that he was some kind of aerodynamic phe-nomenon headin' straight as an arrow or an angel for heaven. Truth is he wallered through the air like a goddamn wild turkey, probably didn't have no more range than a turkey does. If I hadn't shot him I think he'd of fell soon enough anyhow, and broke his neck. But still and all, he did get up there."

Arn imitated the screech of a hawk so uncannily, Whit's blood turned cold. The lid of the trunk slammed down, the brass catches all snapped into place.

"Still hanker to go up to the mountain, maybe get yourself killed in the bargain?"

"I'm going," Whit said. "It's my job."

He felt Arn standing over him silently; he sensed that Arn was glad. Whistling low again between his teeth, but a jauntier, old soldiers' marching tune. Whit felt afraid, fear he had never known facing an enemy he understood, men like himself.

"I give you this, Colonel. You never was one to shirk the tough jobs. I always respected you for that. So if you're wantin' to climb up Tormentil, reckon I can accommodate you and show the way. Better get along now to your bed and have you some shut-eye, I aim to leave at the crack of dawn. And I *garn-tee* it'll be a miserable few miles 'fore you walk off that shine hang-over you're gonna wake up with."

—— Chapter Thirteen ——

THE roof made of hammered metal hubcaps had leaked in a dozen places during the cloudburst, and a pot had been placed on the bed of the old man who was in a coma, to catch the drip there. Faren asked Terry to wait in the main room of the Indians' house, where it was crowded with children, dark (the only window, which was closed, faced the porch), and, as Faren had warned, smelled very bad. At one end of the long room there was a fireplace, the only source of heat in winter. A kitchen had been tacked on to that part of the house; it was barely large enough for a sink and a wood-burning cookstove, the biggest stove Terry had ever seen. The highly prized refrigerator stood out on the front porch. The house had electricity, a recent improvement according to Faren, but it had flickered off almost as soon as the storm began. Furniture was limited to a plank table with benches, a breakfront with warped doors, crackled varnish, and a brick where a leg had broken off, a chifforobe, a bunk-bed corner three tiers high, packed with pillows, ragged blankets, duckdown mattresses. Most of the children sat on the floor, where they could find a dry spot, and stared at Terry. One of them was trying to get something other than static from a portable radio. Two of the younger ones played roughly with a puppy, making it cry. After minutes had gone by with no one saying anything, the children would suddenly speak to one another in Cherokee, excited comments flying around the room; he imagined they were talking about him. (This is my friend Terry, Faren had said to them in their language. He lives in Paris, France. I have given him the name Ayunini.) After the chatter everyone settled down again, to giggles, sniffles, the yelping of the puppy, hail banging on the metal roof. Terry stood where he could see into the bedroom, the door having been left open slightly, wavering in a draft. They had given him something to drink in a jelly glass. It tasted like orange Kool-Aid. All he did was taste it; he didn't want a drink, he was having enough trouble just breathing. He felt awkward and uneasy, particularly since he didn't know what was going on there in the bedroom. But at the same time he was fascinated.

Several adults, most of them, like the children, of mixed blood, were crowded around the bed inside. The center of attention, the stricken man, had a deeply runneled face that reminded Terry of the accumulation of candlewaxes on the Chianti bottles you found on every table in cheap Italian restaurants. His mouth was open as if his jaw were out of joint. Terry couldn't tell if he was breathing or not, but he was drooling; a woman his age with a bird's-nest knot of gray hair at the back of her head wiped the spittle away with a cloth. The emaciated body was covered with a sheet. The fingers of his hands, outside the sheet, were hooked into claws.

The people muttered to themselves, sometimes in English. It sounded as if they might be praying. Since entering, Faren had been nearly motionless at the foot of the bed, her head bowed; occasionally she would bring her joined hands to the underside of her chin as if to steady herself, or formalize some conclusions she had reached. This went on for much too long as far as Terry was concerned.

A little girl with a shiny thatch of black hair tugged at his elbow to get his attention. Startled, Terry looked down at her. She wore ragged red shorts and a T-shirt.

"If you're not going to drink your Kool-Aid," she said, "can I have it?"

Terry handed her the glass.

"You speak English?"

"No, Chinese," someone else said, and a titter went around the room. "Big deal," a girl said indifferently. An infant pulled the puppy's tail; the puppy yelped.

A boy said, "Yellow school bus stop at bottom of hill every day. Indian children get-um on school bus, go to Consolidated school. Study hard. Learn white man's ways."

"No shit?" Terry said.

They loved that. They had shut him out while they looked him over; now they were letting him in, tentatively.

"How tall are you?" the oldest girl asked.

"Six feet one," Terry said, cheating a little.

"How old are you?" From another part of the room.

"I'll be fifteen in June."

"How come you live in Paris?"

"I live with my mom, and that's where she lives."

The little girl handed back the glass, her mouth rimmed

with orange that looked iridescent in the gloom. "I saved you some."

"Yeah, thanks," Terry said.

"Ayunini is a very important name to Cherokees," the oldest girl said severely. "He's one of our heroes."

"I didn't know that."

One of the kids turned from the window and said, "Look at the size of those hailstones." They all flocked to the window to have a look. Terry joined them.

"I'll bet it doesn't rain like this in Paris."

"Huh-uh. It mostly just drizzles a lot."

The oldest girl, who wore glasses and had Faren's features but somehow lacked her beauty, said, "I'm Sara Davidson. The Kool-Aid hog is my sister Edwina."

"I'm not a Kool-Aid hog!" Edwina pondered a put-down and came back with, "You're just jealous because I got a part in *Unto These Hills* and you didn't."

Sara said evenly, "I am not jealous. I don't want anything to do with the pageant. It's a distortion, full of lies about the Cherokee. When you're older, you'll know better."

After a while it got boring just looking at the rain and the hailstones that were strewn like moth balls on the perimeter of the porch and most of the kids drifted away from the misted window. Someone found a box of Hi-Ho crackers in the kitchen and it was passed around. One of the little kids crawled into a bunk to nap. Sara Davidson stayed at Terry's side.

"We live across the road. It's raining too hard, you can't make out the house now. Do you mind if I just call you Terry? None of us use our Cherokee names much. Mine's Two Doves. I think that's just a little bit precious. But it doesn't sound any better in Cherokee. What grade are you in?"

"Tenth."

"Me too. Faren's going to try to get me a full scholarship to Carson-Newman. That's a college near Knoxville. Do you want to come to supper? It'll be less crowded at our house."

"Thanks. I'll have to ask Faren what she wants to do."

They had supper with the Davidsons. William Davidson, Sara's father, was the man they had seen on the tractor when they drove up. He was co-owner with his brothers of the hundred acres he farmed. The Davidson house wasn't as poor-looking as the one they had spent most of the afternoon in. There were bright rag rugs on the polished floors, and the air was better. They had two bedrooms and an indoor toilet. The rain had slackened, but the electricity was still off. Mrs. Davidson made supper on the old wood-burning Wilson Patent stove in her kitchen. They had pork chops, hominy, light bread, and sweet milk by candlelight. Faren looked weary throughout the meal. He was dying to ask what she'd been up to in the sickroom, but he didn't feel right about saying anything until they were alone.

"Maybe you'll come and see us again," Sara Davidson said to Terry when it was time to go. She had done her hair differently before the meal, taken off her glasses. With her eyes unmasked, everything appearing equally vague to her, she seemed, shyly, not to know where to look. "If you want to send me a postcard from Paris, it's care of RFD one-twelve, Cherokee, North Carolina. Faren knows the address, if you forget it."

"Somebody else has a crush on you," Faren teased when they were in the car.

"She's nice," Terry said, a little full of himself. But

Sara was just a kid, unequal in appeal to Faren: her maturity, her densely interesting sex.

"Well, let's hope we've seen the last of this rain," Faren said as she ground the starter of the coupe. "These roads are going to be bad until we hit the highway south."

The car wouldn't start for a long time, then the engine coughed itself to life, but the effort had been hard on the battery. The road revealed in the feeble headlights looked more like a creek bed.

"It'll be easier leaving than it was getting here," Faren said a little nervously, driving down the hill. "We're only about four miles from town."

After a slow and slippery couple of minutes, Faren leaning over the wheel to wipe the misted windshield in front of her with the heel of her hand, Terry imposed on her concentration.

"You said you had to see the old man because they wanted to know if he was going to die, or what. But you're not a doctor, and it looked to me like he was almost dead already. I mean, how could you tell anything about him?"

"Well, Terry, I don't need to be a doctor, or even have the healing gift. Which I don't have, by the way. But I can usually tell from a person's aura what's happening to him."

"What's the aura?"

"Every one of us has a light around the body until we take our last breath on earth, then the light flickers real low and just disappears. Changes colors, too, depending on whether we're happy or sad or sick. Grandpap's aura was so faint and fuzzy I had trouble making it out. Spirit's still there in his body, but it's fixing to leave.

Trudy held the same opinion, but she hasn't been reading auras long as I have."

"His spirit? You mean his soul?"

"Whatever you want to call it."

"What does it look like?"

"Doesn't take a definite shape. It's a light, though, so pure and white you can't focus directly on it."

"Have you seen my aura?"

"So chockful of energy I couldn't hardly miss it. Today there on the Oconaluftee it was shooting out six feet in all directions from your head and hands. Red and orange flame."

"What does that mean?" Terry asked skeptically. All he could see when he looked at his side of the windshield was the same old face, metalized in reflection but nothing more.

She smiled. "Means you were excited about something. I wonder what?"

"Uh-huh. What color was *your* aura?"

"Now, don't be fresh with me. I can see mine only when I'm in a room that's nearly dark, and it helps if I don't have any clothes on. Then I just kind of sideways glance at a mirror to read the aura. Because I have to be careful about looking directly in mirrors or dark windows or even still water."

"Why?"

"Ofttimes I see things I don't want or shouldn't ought to see. And there's temptation, too, I can be charmed into going places I better not go, and may not be able to get out of."

Terry's mouth was dry. His heart gave a bump. "That sounds—"

"Crazy? Terry, you and me are part of a world we just don't know a whole lot about. There's so much more to it than we can see or hear or touch. Too many people have been visited by ghosts for it to be a lie. We think we're the smartest creatures there are, but so-called dumb animals know hours ahead of time when there's going to be an earthquake. Honeybees fly miles looking for pollen, and when they find it they go straight back to the hive and do a little dance that tells the other bees exactly where to find it too. Trees and plants and vines in the woods communicate with one another, science knows that. Call it supernatural, whatever. But I've seen—"

"Seen what?"

"Oh, I can't tell you any more," she said, giving him a wide-eyed, leery look. "I've got you bothered enough already."

"No, you haven't. I really want to know about this."

There was lightning, quick as the little jots of light he sometimes saw behind the lids when he rubbed his eyes hard. Then a boomer. Then rain fell again, heavily. The wipers couldn't keep the windshield clear. Faren frantically scrubbed circles on the misted glass trying to see where she was going. Her face yellow in the dashboard light.

"Maybe you'd better slow—"

The coupe skidded.

"*Merde!*"

They dropped suddenly on Terry's side and he tried, in a moment of stabbing fright, to brace himself, seeing trees too close in the lurching weak headlights. There was a nasty thump-screech beneath the car and they came to an abrupt stop before running into pillars of glistening bark. Terry lost his grip on the seat and sprawled facefirst onto the dashboard, his lower lip splitting like a ripe plum.

"Hey!"

"Are you hurt?" Faren was rubbing her chest where the scalloped steering wheel had dug in.

"I'm okay." He sat back, blood welling from his lip; he caught it on his fingers. "What happened?"

"Ran off the road." Faren pounded the steering wheel with a fist. The other hand still holding her chest.

"We're stuck," he advised, tasting blood on his tongue. "Better turn off the engine."

"Terry, God, is that blood?"

"I cut my lip, that's all."

"Oh, what's your daddy going to think of me?" She pulled her handkerchief from her purse and handed it, wadded, to him. "Press that against the cut. I'm sorry. I don't know *what* happened. All of a sudden I couldn't see." She turned the key in the ignition, and turned off the lights. They sat in a stifling silence in a flood, in the dark. Faren put her sweaty face in her hands.

"What are we going to do now?" he mumbled, the handkerchief sticking to his lower lip.

"I don't *know*! If the fuckin' rain would just *quit*."

"It will," he said, quietly authoritative. "We'll be okay."

She put her hands in her lap, twisting them together. "I didn't mean to yell at you, Terry. I get jittery sometimes, I don't like to drive at night. And now look. Is the bleeding stopped?"

"Yeah, almost."

Faren turned and, kneeling, reached over the back of the seat, felt blindly for a slicker and flashlight on the floor. She draped the slicker over her head and got out of the car. He could see her vaguely, moving around in the downpour, see the bright beam of the flash diffused through the streaming windshield. Then Faren and the light vanished long enough to alarm him—had she fallen, hurt herself?—before the driver's door was yanked open and Faren crawled in, half soaked despite the slicker.

"Hung up on a stump," she said tiredly. "Probably took the oil pan out, I could smell hot oil leaking all over the place. Even if the two of us could budge it off the stump it won't run. Need to get help."

"Around here?"

"While I was outside I thought I heard music—a hymn. We could be close to the church I go to. It's Wednesday night, regular service. Hick Smith ought to be there with the other Church of God ministers who've been meeting today."

"Which way do we go?"

"Well, it doesn't make sense to go anywhere until the rain slacks off, or lets up entirely. Then we'll locate the church. Sits high up on a hill, we can't miss it if we walk in the right direction." She dried her face on the sleeve of her blouse, looked at Terry. "We'll be late getting back, real late, if we make it at all tonight. I'll try to get to a telephone and call, but telephones are one of the things they don't have much of on the Boundary. Reckon Whit's going to worry about you."

Terry shrugged.

Still watching him, she said, "Some day we've had. Let's see that cut."

Terry carefully pulled the handkerchief loose from his lip. She aimed the flashlight across his face and down so as not to blind him. "Um-hmm. That's not so bad. Shouldn't need stitches."

"No."

"Hot in here. Can't crack the window even a little bit. We need all the rain, though. Been a dry spring so far, and that usually means bad fires."

Terry didn't say anything, and Faren stopped talking. There was a glimmer of lightning through the deluge; Terry saw her eyes closing, her mouth slack. He put a hand on her shoulder and tilted her his way. She nestled readily in his lap, knees drawn up. She took three deep, slow breaths and went to sleep. He gazed at her during the infrequent flickers of lightning, feeling competent, protective, worthy of her. The storm rumbles seemed farther off. When the rain slackened he rolled down the window halfway, letting musty cool air in. Faren slept on, obliviously. Because of the steady splashing from the drenched leaves of the trees hanging over them, it was hard to tell when the rain finally stopped. He wondered how his friends were getting along on their sail to Corsica. He was lost in a wilderness with a woman he found lovely, desirable, and perplexing, and he didn't regret not being aboard the boat.

When he thought they ought to try to do something about their situation, Terry awakened her by brushing her lips gently with his fingertips. Faren sat up with a deep sigh, rubbing her upper lip, which tingled from his touch.

"Reckon we can get on to the church now."

"I haven't heard any music or singing. Maybe the service is over and they went home."

"Somebody would've come by on the road and seen us stuck here. You shouldn't have let me sleep so long."

"It was still raining, and you looked really tired." Terry rolled the window up and stepped out of the car, aiming the flashlight so he could see where he was going in a wet tangle of high weeds. He helped her out.

"Which way?"

"Let me try to get my bearings," Faren said, taking

the flashlight. She switched it around. The narrow road-
way, dipping into a hollow that was as white as beer
foam in a glass, looked uninviting straight ahead. The
hill behind them was black with trees.

"Do you know where we are?"

"Can't say for certain, one hollow's like another, this
far back in the—listen!"

They heard muffled but lusty singing, so far away the
words were hard to make out. A hymn.

> When my time comes to go
> When my time comes to go
> I want to lay my head on Jesus' breast
> When *my* time comes to go!

"There they are," Faren murmured.

"Which way?" Terry asked. He couldn't tell where
the singing was coming from.

"Church has to be just up the next rise. We didn't
pass it yet, I know that."

The road was slippery and, in the hollow, awash.
They held on to each other in the fog, which diffused
the beam of the flashlight in Faren's hand until it was
nearly useless. The hill they had to climb, blindly, was
a steep one. But they were going in the right direction.
The singing was louder, instruments were distinguishable. First a rollicking piano, then guitars and tambourines. Handclapping. The brassy light of distant uncovered
windows became visible through mist and murk.

"Hallelujah," Faren said. "At last."

The second of two hymns ended. For a few moments
they heard only themselves, effortful breathing. They
were coldly doused by a quivering dogwood tree Terry
blundered into. Then voices began calling out randomly,

exulting. "Yea yea yea yea *yea*! Hallelujah!" "Thank you, Jesus!" "Spirit's moving here tonight." "Say it, say it." "Go devil, commmmme Jesus!" "All right!" The tambourines started again, a snaky, jangling, compelling rhythm. A small building surrounded by vehicles haphazardly parked took shape as they approached the top of the hill. The light in the windows was a low unsteady shining. No electricity here either, but lack of light hadn't dampened the enthusiasm of the worshippers in the backwoods church, which was made of unpainted concrete block, with a shingle roof, a metal awning over the doorway.

Terry saw dim jumping figures behind wet glass, shadows in collision with shadows. It looked like a riot in progress. "Are we going in there?" he asked, stumbling to a halt.

She tugged at his hand. "Sure. You're welcome. Nobody's going to bite you. It's like homecoming tonight. They're all moving with the Spirit. Just a'joyful in the Lord." A pulse of lightning was repeated in the windshield of a truck next to her face. Faren looked happy, eager. She was shivering. "Terry, Church of God's not like other old churches, dry as dust, where you sit in rows like waitin' on a bus and the preacher tells you what's good and what's bad for you and they pass the collection plate and nobody dares say boo. Here you *prove* your faith; anybody is welcome to get up and preach, testify, or pray when he feels called upon by the Lord. It's just a great feeling to know you're blessed by the Holy Ghost. Everybody moving with the spirit and indivisible—that's what this church is all about."

They went in. The one-room church building, about twenty by thirty feet and plain as a shoebox, was packed. Most of the worshippers were white or, Terry presumed,

White Cherokee; there were few obviously Indian faces. Benches lined three walls. There was a high flat-topped lectern near the back wall with a Bible as big as a scrapbook lying open on it. Strictly centered between two windows was a framed lithograph of Christ, twice life-size and with a well-trimmed beard, golden light of sanctity around his head. Kerosene lanterns hung from rafter hooks between the powerless, cone-shaded electric lights. Some casually dressed worshippers were sprawled on the benches, looking done-in but with a thin shine of ardency. A zinc pail of water with a dipper in it was passed around. A youngster, thumb in mouth, slept faceup in the hammock of his mother's dress as if drowned in tumult, his other hand outflung. In one corner two men and a hefty girl about Terry's age sat round-shouldered on stools beside the upright piano, acoustic guitars on their knees. Everyone else was circulating as freely as they could: weaving, shuffling, edging in random patterns from one side of the church to the other, as if to stand still were to deny the energy of the spirit that possessed them. Many hands writhed and waggled, dumbly magical, above their heads and in Christ's printed, patient line of sight. The windows at the back of the church were open, there were flowers in crocks and jars on the sills, furry iris and blood-red tulips. But the stilled cool air outside made little difference in the church. There the atmosphere was thick as gravy: oiled, humid, metallic with the salts of people's bodies, their sogged clothing and hair.

Few people paid attention to Faren and Terry. A woman she knew grasped her hand in welcome. A tall, severe-looking Indian who seemed unnervingly familiar to Terry stood in shirt-sleeves behind the lectern. His dark eyes were on Faren but he didn't smile. Terry remembered. The gallery in town, the artist's self-portrait. This was Hickory Smith, her half brother.

"Grab you a seat if you want," Faren said into Terry's ear.

"No, I'll stand."

A middle-aged woman in the forefront of the worshippers near the lectern was testifying. Terry leaned against a wall and paid attention. She was a little hard to understand, as if she had only a few teeth in her head.

"Ain't nobody on this earth worth nothin' 'less he be *used* of God. It ain't no good abusin' yourself with mankind, with the *o*-fenders and the *mal*efactors, you got to turn loose a that mess and give account to God *yourself*. Glory! For he sayeth unto you, 'Brethren, I would not have you ignorant.' What is ignorance if it ain't wickedness? Praise *God,* I quit my wicked ways, thank *Godddd* I'm saved! Fill me up, Jesus! And you know, if God looks down and picks you up, you got somethin' to praise upon. Hallelujah to God, I will enter my Father's house *justified*!" She began to mumble words like Terry had never heard before, which provoked ecstatic shouts from other worshippers. After a minute or two of gibberish and dancing rather stiffly up and down, as if she were standing barefoot on live coals, she resumed. "There is a *spirit* movin' between these yere walls tonight! I say if you're sane and holy, stay with the *old* way, 'cause if you get with the new way you ain't gonna sing and shout, no sir! And if you ain't got it, and you can't get it, what you oughter do is just go and stick your head in a hole and let somebody kick you till you say *yes* to the Lord. That's the way I feel, alla shabba shalla golem sabbeth wetum. *Yea!* I'm *saved* and sanctified and I'm *sooooo-o* glad!" She left off testifying and began to sing in a quavering voice,

"Devil can't do me no harm, nooo-o, devil can't do me
no harm—"

The piano player went wild, ripping at the keys,
tearing frenziedly into the hymn several bars ahead of
the crashing, shimmering tambourines and the guitars.
Thunder outside could barely be heard. Lightning flashed
on wheeling, dancing, shouting worshippers.

> When my soul is a' resting in
> the presence of the Lord—
> I'll be sat-is-fied.

Terry had lost track of Faren. She had edged away
from and into the melee, he caught a glimpse of her face
behind a bulky man whose shirt had ripped down the
back. Faren was singing, too, clapping her hands, thoroughly at home. She had forgotten about him, about the
fact that the hour was late and they were stranded. This
development turned him sullen. He wondered how long
the service, if that's what it could be called, would go
on. The music was a pulverizing force, he was picking
up vibrations from the paneled wall at his back. He'd
never seen people act like this; he was a little afraid of
them, of mob ecstasy that seemed, despite his resistance, to be working its way into his own blood; his face
tingled from the energy crashing wall to wall and his
mind began to feel bludgeoned. One rocking hymn se-
gued into another, it was as if there could be no end
until everyone passed out in a heap on the floor, the last
faint "Hallelujah!" whispered in the night.

Faren's half brother Hickory Smith was the next to
speak. With Bible in hand he rejoiced in the fellowship
of the preachers assembled there, the solidarity of their

belief in the church founded by Jesus on the rock of Peter.

" 'And Jesus answered and said unto him, Blessed art thou, Simon Barjona: for flesh and blood hath not revealed it unto thee, but my Father which is in heaven. And I say unto thee, that thou art Peter, and upon this rock I will build my church; and the gates of hell shall not prevail against it.' " Hickory Smith's voice was powerful, a match for thunder, the patter and then the slash of rain on the roof. His dark eyes had the off-center shine that Terry remembered from the photo in the gallery, as if more than one person occupied his body, and both were using his eyes simultaneously. Terry felt a creeping at the base of his spine but he couldn't look away from the preacher's face.

"WE BELIEVE THE WORD OF GOD!" Hickory Smith shouted. And they responded.

"HE THAT BELIEVETH AND IS BAPTIZED *SHALL* BE SAVED!"

"Praise God! Holly-holly-holly-hollylujah!"

"*GOD* HAS PUT THAT IN OUR HEARTS. AND WE BELIEVETH!

"IN HIS NAME AND IN HIS BLOOD HE PUR-CHASED THE CHURCH FOR SINNERS! DO YOU BELIEVE IT!"

"Thank you Jesus!"

"WE SHALL HAVE *VICTORY* IN HIS NAME!

"WE SHALL HAVE *POWER* IN JESUS'S NAME. *DO YOU BELIEVE IT!*"

"Praise God, praise God!"

"NOW IN JESUS'S NAME, *HALLELUJAH*, SHALL WE CAST OUT DEVILS OF SICKNESS AND DIS-EASE!

"NOW IN JESUS'S NAME, SHALL WE SPEAK IN TONGUES!

"NOW IN JESUS'S NAME, IF WE DRINK OF ANY DEADLY POISON, IT SHALL NOT HURT US!"

"Yea hallelujah!"

The tambourines began again, a metallic sizzling to Terry's numbed ears. And handclapping. Every face a beacon of faith.

"I *BELIEVE* IN THE WORD OF GOD! I *BELIEVE* IN HIS SIGNS. I *BELIEVE* IN WHATEVER TASK GOD PUTS FOR ME TO DO. BECAUSE I KNOW IF I'M FEELING WITH THE SPIRIT OF GOD IN MY HEART THEN NO HARM CAN COME TO ME, HALLELUJAH! DO YOU *SAYYYYYYY* HALLELUJAH?"

The "jah" bitten off and pronounced "yah" after the long, sung "say"; and they responded like a wave smashing in, country voices in blended adulation, with the grit and strength to burnish the high gates of heaven, they had stature in their ecstasy. Terry saw for a moment the gleam of Faren's teeth between parted, half-smiling lips, lips that had kissed him, he stood coldly alone in carnality amid the chaste and the cleansed. Her tousled dark head lolled. Her body was slumped and twisted downward as if something woeful at her feet exerted a pull, an influence: then she sprang erect in an excited, vital way: began to throb and swing to the rhythm of many spangled tambourines in palm-banging broadcast. The power that had enlivened her Terry found repellant, threatening. He yearned to rudely shove aside those who seemed clustered protectively around her, grab her by the arm and reclaim her from the unpleasantly indentured state she looked to be in, and, although it was storming outside, return them both to the solitude in which their affections had thrived. But once the impulse peaked and guttered, he felt less than bold, a prisoner outside the walls of rapture. He made no move.

The lanterns hung from rafters swayed in the spray-laden wind coming through the open windows; the unsteady flames nearly touching the sides of the chimneys gradually blackened the glass, lowering the level of light in the church. Faces failed in the duskier corners while preacher Smith, in the forefront of other preachers, gleamed like a fisherman from the wetting-down he had received.

"IF GOD *SAYS* FOR ME TO DO IT, I SHALL DRINK OF STRYCHNINE AND LYE, AND NO HARM SHALL COME TO ME, BECAUSE MY FAITH WILL SPARE ME!

"IF GOD *SAYS* TO TAKE UP POISONOUS SERPENTS, THEN I SHALL HAVE NO FEAR, BECAUSE THE LORD JESUS CHRIST HAS CAST AWAY *FEAR* FROM MY HEART. GLORY TO GOD IN THE NAME OF JESUS, THEM THINGS IS DEADLY BUT I SHALL HAVE-A BOLLA BUBLUM SHABETH WALLA COSHEM *NO FEAR!* PRAISE JE-SUSSSSS!"

Then they were singing.

> Well, some folks say a serpent
> is a man;
> There's a higher power.
> Those kind of people don't
> understand;
> 'Cause there's a higher power.

Hickory Smith resumed preaching; his cadence more staccato, voice rising thrilled while his face, always expressionless, settled into an even more trance-like mask, sweat or blown rain beaded on his skin, his

white shirt drenched and transparent on a hard brown
hairless torso that was webbed with vein and muscle, his
nipples hard, small and dark like another pair of eyes
long ago charred by fervor.

"I LOVE THE LORD! HE'S BEEN UH GOOD TO
ME! I KNOW I'VE GOT UH THE HOLY GHOST
TONIGHT! I KNOW WE ARE ALL WITH SWEET
JESUS TONIGHT! I'M NOT AFRAID UH WHEN
IT'S THE LORD TELLIN' ME WHAT TO DO!
PREACHERS, BRING 'EM ON OUT!"

A woman sang in a pure lilting voice, but the words
were gibberish; the musicians went their own way, wide-
eyed, bearing down brutally to harvest a hymn, big
holes worn in the soundboards of their old guitars;
every second child had a tambourine batting against
elbows or knees. Some of the preachers had knelt
behind Smith, but not to pray. They were opening flat
corrugated boxes with religious symbols painted on
them. And in a violet burst of lightning Terry saw
snakes.

Bunches of dappled diamondback pied snakes, some
nearly six feet in length and thick as a man's wrist.
Some earthy, some ashen, a few with the liquid darkness of eels, all heatless as death. Writhing snakes in the
hands of preachers, his stomach plunged to the level of
his knees and he gasped in shock. No one was paying
the slightest attention to him. No one could hear the
sounds the timber rattlers were making, either, but a
couple of them were vibrating their tails to a blur as
they were lifted aloft, pointedly positioned inches
from faces drowsily delighted in the opiate of yellow
eyes.

Snakes:

everywhere: mouths   their
open mouths like many kinds of wounds, deep-raw,
pink-healing, scarred scary white: snakes:
   limber clockworks winding tight the deathwatch
   hour   despised
but honored in the ritual:
handlers with no rational means of defense, moving to
   music
   and some fiery internal beat, heads also
   moving
   mimicking the staring lazy lethal motions of the toned
snake heads:

Bodies   pale
   underbellies   all drawn with a fine needle
cruising   flowing
snugly round flushed limbs   necks
bloodlines so near a bitten man
   might be dead in
   moments:
      (Will you say hallelujah?)
thrashing, vomiting up the fatally tainted blood.

                   (Thank you
Jesus)

But the guests of honor, to Terry's unbelieving eyes,
did not strike, even as they were passed hand over hand
to those who craved snakeflesh, the better to believe, to
certify their faith.

And not everyone took up serpents. Most of the
preachers did, and a few members of the congregation.
But one was (slowly) coming Terry's way, sinister tat-
tooed overlong arm with a head and not a fist foremost,
flat bald babyish head with flickering spirit tongue,

godsame but inimical eyes, he was nearly paralyzed until a preacher claimed it for his own, adding it to the one already worn casually down to his waist like an untied necktie.

Hickory Smith had a long rattlesnake on one arm. His outstretched steady hands held three more snakes.

Suddenly Faren was there, as if Smith had summoned her telepathically to his side.

Terry's mouth was open, but his throat had locked, he couldn't make a sound. Only his mind screamed at Faren.

Don't!

Thunder shook the little church. Lightning nearly blinded Terry.

When he focused on Faren again, he saw a snake's spade head, bent rigidly to the horizontal and less than an inch from the bridge of her nose. She was staring, tame to the wildness she withheld, into the snake's complex, radiantly burning, oil-green eyes. Terry almost fainted.

A copperhead was entwined around her other arm, its head lifted slightly away from the pulse in her wrist, tongue flicking at the bared palm of her hand.

Someone jostled against him in a frenzied jig. Terry caught a devastating whiff of bad teeth, grabbed his stomach, doubled over and projectile-vomited on the floor, something he hadn't done since he was a kid. His body was instantly cold and quivering, his mind filling with a dense blackness. He might have fallen in his own vomit, out cold, but lightning blasted a tree near the church, ripping off a heavy limb. The singing and shouting went on without pause. He recovered from the fainting spell, but the nausea hit him again, hemstitching his gut.

When he was able to look up, dreading what he might see, Faren wasn't there anymore.

His first thought was that she had been bitten and had fallen to the floor. But it was impossible for him to sort out exactly *what* was happening around the lectern.

He shoved his way through the crowd of worshippers. Someone seized him roughly by the arm before he reached the spot where he'd last seen Faren. He looked around at Hickory Smith, who had given her snakes to handle. There was a stifling musk, from serpentine anal glands, but his own hands were empty now. Smith nodded curtly to the floor, where Terry was about to put his feet.

A copperhead was inches from one shoe, masseteric muscles bulging ominously.

Before Terry could react, a preacher stooped and softly picked up the loose snake.

Terry looked around frantically, but Faren was gone.

Gone where? She would have had to leave through one of the open windows; she hadn't had time to lay down the long snakes or pass them on to someone else, then make her way through the entire congregation, nearly a hundred people, to the front door. The *only* door, near which Terry had been standing when he was briefly but violently taken sick. He was sure of that: Faren could not have left by the front door.

He turned on Smith. "SHE'S NOT HERE! WHERE DID SHE GO?"

Smith gestured with both hands toward the windows, and although Terry knew nothing about sign language, it was obvious the preacher was telling him she had "flown." *Like a bird, through an open window?* Terry's raw nerves seemed to be on the outside of his body, an excruciating version of the aura Faren had described;

he wanted to punch Smith for treating him like a child. The man was crazy. But Terry recognized, in spite of his distress, that Smith believed what he was signing, and seemed to be in shock. Terry looked again at the windows. They were small, narrow, only partway open. He thought of the width of Faren's shoulders, her pelvic girth—maybe, under stress, she could have squeezed through the available space with enough time to work at it. But the big jars of flowers on the sills had not been moved. And only about thirty seconds had passed since he'd lost sight of Faren and she had disappeared.

Disappeared.

The corona of Terry's nerves flared again; at the corner of one eye he saw a wide-mouthed snake and fangs. He turned and blundered to the door, stepping on toes, partly deaf from tambourines and the pounding piano.

Rain hit him in the face when he opened the door. He couldn't see a thing outside.

"FAREN!"

Lightning illuminated the humped bodies and heavily chromed front ends of the cars and trucks parked in the churchyard, the mercury-bright diagonals of windshields, the flogged high crowns of trees. Terry cleared and tried to shield his eyes, but saw no one moving in the glare. When the light faded it seemed twice as dark out there, even the dim outlines of vehicles receded from his view.

The door blew shut behind him; the hymning and ordeals of faith went on as before. Perhaps somebody would die tonight, grotesquely swollen and hemorrhaging from snake venom. Or perhaps they all led charmed lives, there *was* a God in heaven looking out for them. He cared only about Faren. And was terrified of the

unexplainable, her disappearance: the *utkena*, most terrifying of serpents, did he have her now?

He went around the churchyard in the driving rain,
calling hopelessly, falling down where it was slippery,
staggering from car to car, snatching open doors at
random to look inside.

"FARRRENNNNN!"

Then—

—there she was (Oh God oh God I believe!) standing
by the tailgate of a pickup truck, her back to him, head
moving slowly as if she were looking around for something. All this revealed to Terry in a forked gash of
lightning, a crack of thunder so near, he fell shaking to
his knees, certain he was about to die.

When he looked up she was walking slowly toward
him, head held high and still moving in that questing,
futile way, eyes in the afterglow wide with amazement.
He got up to meet her. She was ten feet away and hadn't
seen him. Dark again, the rain slashing his face, how
could he see her so well in the dark?

And how could she be perfectly dry when he was
soaking wet?

"Faren!"

She looked toward him quickly, as if she'd heard
him, all right, but couldn't make him out. And kept
walking straight at him.

Now six feet away. Staring. Listening. But not seeing
him.

"Faren, it's me!"

Lightning.

Rain all around her, but not a drop touching her. And
when the lightning died away she was still clearly visible, as if it were broad daylight. Slightly luminous, but

that might have been an effect of the lightning on his optic nerves.

She was turning her head again, cautiously, apprehensively, a look of pain in her face now, eyes suffering.

He took a step back, obeying some atavistic alarm system as she encroached on his space, slipped down painfully on one knee and braced himself, reaching up to stop her as, plain as the living day, Faren walked weightlessly into him and through him.

And disappeared even before he could whip his head around to track her. Nothing at all behind him but the watery glow of lantern light in the (closed) side windows of the church, beneath which the musicians sat at their instruments and the worshipful danced, the pure of heart played deftly with deadly serpents frozen in their wrath.

He was down in the mud for a long time, without the will to drag himself up. Not even lightning crookedly engaging a rod atop the church, heating it to a saintly glow, could disturb him.

After a while he crawled to the ribbed running board of a car, reached up to open the door, crept inside where it smelled of old engine oil, soiled diapers, and sweaty overalls. A blanket covered the springy, worn-out front seat. He wrapped himself in it, whining, his teeth chattering, and thought of Faren walking through him, his head right where it had been when they had napped by the river in the afternoon, this time she was oblivious and he realized that one of them must be dead, but who?

Whatever death was, it probably didn't smell like babyshit and feel like a spring digging into his behind in a 1940 Dodge sedan.

Walking around like that, well, he'd seen her and he

couldn't accept that Faren was dead either; it was as if she had been looking—looking—

Looking for a way back in, from somewhere.

Hadn't she heard him calling her? Hadn't she? *Fucking right she had!*

Wiping his leaking nose, crying a little but not whining anymore, Terry wondered.

Where was she walking now? And would she, could she, ever come back to him?

—— Chapter Fourteen ——

Wildwood, September 1906

For the first two years of her marriage, Laurette "Sibby" Langford lived like a monied adventuress, aboard a sumptuously appointed railroad train that went nowhere, while the French chateau her husband was building in the wilderness of the Great Smoky Mountains slowly took shape. It was, to a young woman of her sensibilities, an absurd, eccentric, demeaning way of life, and the experience, worsened by the ordeal of the bedchamber soon imposed upon her by Edgar Langford, nearly drove her insane. She had no more been prepared for marriage—even a conventional marriage of her time—than a blind, newborn kitten is prepared for the sack and the river. In her predicament she was, unfortunately, typical of the well-brought-up young women of the Gilded Age.

She was a Waring. The Warings of Boston, Massachusetts, had been decently rich for a hundred and fifty years. They were Brahmins, the elite of a society where genealogy was even more important than wealth, where the world was neatly divided into "us" and "not one of us." Oliver Waring III, Sibby's hard-working father, owned two of the largest department stores in the East and had an interest in woolen mills in Lawrence and Haverhill. The family lived, during the winter months, in a house on Commonwealth Avenue, Boston's best address. They also owned an eighteen-room manor house at Prides Crossing on the north shore, and a country estate of one hundred fifty-six acres near North Easton, to which they went each spring and fall. The Warings, like most other Bostonians in comparable circumstances, shunned ostentation and could be mean with a dollar. The manor house and the estate were always referred to as "our place by the sea," and "our place in the country." Mrs. Waring made do with only five live-in servants at the Commonwealth Avenue brownstone. She bought hers and Sibby's clothes in Italy, where the fashions were up-to-date but less expensive than those of Paris. When the family traveled abroad they stayed at good, but not the smartest, hotels, in Naples, Amalfi, Venice, and Florence, the favorite watering holes of touring Bostonians. At home they belonged to the Congregational Church, which was socially acceptable but not as fashionable as the Episcopal Church. Oliver Waring IV ("Boshie"), Sibby's older brother, attended Harvard and received a gentleman's grades; like his father, he wore the small gold pig that was the emblem of the Porcellian Club on his watch chain. Porcellian was not the preferred eating club; it was the *only* club at Harvard that would do.

Boshie joined his father in business at a time when good fortune seemed totally to desert them: the business, their very lives, hung in the balance after a terrible fire in one of the department stores. Oliver Waring III

had saved a little money where he felt it was destined
not to show; but the less than first-rate company he
chose to carry his insurance buckled under the weight of
large suits and took refuge in bankruptcy.

Sibby knew about the fire and knew there were problems connected with it that threatened to send her father
to an early grave, but she was spared the details. She
had been spared almost everything that could be interpreted as unseemly, or just none of her business, when
she was growing up. Unlike Boshie, and her two younger brothers who attended day school, Sibby was educated at home by tutors. She learned Latin and Greek,
and French from an elderly French governess. She read
the classics. She was permitted Elizabeth Barrett Browning as an escape from the drudgery of Milton. She
learned to do sums. Because the family owned a farm
where there were horses, she also was taught to ride.
She had acquaintances among a select group of girls,
but no real friends her own age. There were always boys
around, but she was not permitted to play with them.
Boys were a foreign nation to her, like Poland. She kept
a diary, recording events and superficial emotions, while
trying to equate the inevitable twinges and deeper long-
ings of puberty with Mrs. Browning's polished sonnets.
If she'd had sisters to talk to, or a mother who offered
more than twice-daily visits to inquire about her well-
being (always assuming she would hear no complaints),
Sibby might have learned a little something about life
before she was dashed into it almost without warning, a
well-mannered, nicely dressed girl so pathologically shy
she had to concentrate before speaking in order not to
stammer.

She met Edgar Langford aboard ship, sailing home
from Naples at the end of August 1903. After he had

taken notice of her and made the appropriate overtures to Sibby's mother and her mother's sisters, both spinsters, and chaperonage was arranged, she was allowed to stroll with Edgar around the decks of the spartan old steamship, one or both grizzled aunts a few paces behind. He was forty years old, and she was eighteen. He had never married. He had a crooked back, the crookedness becoming more pronounced as the day wore on. He walked, painfully, with an ebony cane around which silver vines twined upward to meet the handle, a large, gold-and-silver serpent's head with ruby eyes. It was a gift, he said, from the shah of Persia, a close and dear friend. Sibby trembled and pulled her cape closer around her; she had never seen anything quite so exotic.

Edgar was frequently flushed by the sea wind, by some internal combustion that also produced a torrent of words describing the beauties of unearthed civilizations and starry desert nights, nomads on camels, caliphs in their minaret kingdoms. She had read some of Herodotus, but she'd only vaguely grasped the fact that well beyond the eastern Mediterranean world of the Greeks, in the land between the Tigris and the Euphrates rivers, complex and inventive societies had flourished. Babylon had occupied the same site on the plain of Shenar for at least three thousand years—almost twenty-seven centuries longer than familiar, staid old Boston had been in existence. And Babylon had been much larger than Boston; fifteen square miles, the inner city surrounded by a water-filled moat.

Edgar Langford was easy to be with; although for three or four days she seldom dared to look at him, Sibby was not required to speak, only to listen, with a nod or exclamation when one seemed called for.

Mrs. Waring knew from the first day that Edgar

Langford would ask for her daughter's hand. This distressed her, not because she didn't like his looks (except for his twisted back and the waxed goatee he affected, he was rather a handsome man, with good features, pale but penetrating eyes, and a heroic width of jaw), but because instinctively she felt that one way or another, Sibby would be corrupted and ultimately destroyed by the marriage. There was something unholy about the man, which his paganistic cane symbolized. Her husband, however, was in trouble, despondent and perhaps suicidal. Edgar Langford was very rich. The meeting of Edgar and Sibby, at this crucial time, might have been ordered by fate. Sibby, to her credit, seemed to find him acceptable, even fascinating company. When Edgar, on their last day out, asked permission to call on Sibby at home in Boston, Mrs. Waring was able to agree with the semblance of a gracious smile.

Edgar Langford visited them several times during the winter. After the customary ten-course dinners, he entertained the family with tales of bizarre adventures in wild and hostile lands. He performed feats of magic. They applauded the Indian rope trick, and gasped when he drove sharp swords through a cabinet that contained the Warings' parlor maid. The girl emerged giggling and unscathed. He produced doves and bouquets of flowers, fresh flowers, in snowbound January, from beneath silk handkerchiefs. He was resourcefully charming. With a few strokes of his pen he rescued Oliver Waring III from certain financial collapse and, perhaps, prison. Sibby received, when Edgar was not in Boston, letters ornately romantic in style yet impersonal; she wrote to him every day, and at night often dreamed restlessly of the cane serpent's rubbed-down precious head and glaring ruby eyes. Their wedding day was announced. Time, for Sibby, passed in a blur of preparations and anticipation. At Edgar's request she had her portrait painted by John Singer Sargent. Her stammer had become virtually unnoticeable. There were two thousand two hundred sixty-eight pearls on her wedding dress, which weighed thirty-three pounds, exactly one third of her own body weight. On the day they were married it was 96 degrees in Boston. She got through the ceremony without fainting. Edgar Langford, whose skin disease had flared up, was in agony in a Savile Row morning coat with a stiff high collar, but he walked without his cane, and had a razor-thin smile for everyone. They had exchanged a single chaste kiss to seal their vows, but afterward he asked not to be touched by anyone, he was in too much pain. The two hundred fifty wedding guests, including his older brothers, who appeared not to like him, kept their distance at the reception. At eight o'clock that night Edgar and Sibby, serenaded by three dozen violinists, boarded the honeymoon express at Boston's North Station. He did not bother or even think to inform his bride that many years would pass before she saw any member of her family again, and that she would never return from what she had been told was to be a two-week wedding trip.

After four days rest at Wildwood, the cool herbal baths which Edgar took three times a day, and the various unguents he tried, began to have a healing effect. He felt well enough to consummate his marriage and, almost as soon as the thought crossed his mind, he went to Sibby's bedroom.

She put down the translation of *A Thousand and One Nights* she had been reading and smiled drowsily up at him from her chaise longue.

Edgar's sexual experience had been limited to numerous whores and Arab catamites, who had conditioned his expectations. Without saying a word he stripped off his toga and was naked in front of her. If he had been able to stand erect he would have been above average in height, with long straight legs. But his body was sadly awry, and he had scabs and scars from old breakouts everywhere from his lower chest to his thighs. His skin was still somewhat inflamed. Most unfortunately, his testicles were grotesquely large, his penis like an up-raised club. He was accustomed to this state of readiness eliciting fawning admiration, a mime of passion. Sibby's mouth just fell open.

He kneeled and seized her in a clumsy embrace, then opened her dressing gown. He went to work. In some ways he was as ignorant of human anatomy as Sibby herself. He didn't know what a virgin was. Her virginity ultimately defeated him, even as her cries of pain and terror excited him to a climax.

When he left her bedroom less than three minutes later Sibby lay sprawled on the chaise longue too stunned to cover herself. She was bleeding from a torn hymen, although not seriously. She felt as if she had been violated with a railroad spike and, since she was unac-quainted with semen, what he left behind on her skin felt as loathsome as if she'd been urinated on by a pig in a barnyard. And that was the end of wedded bliss for Sibby Langford.

In a fit of enthusiasm, oblivious of the fact that he had not achieved suitable penetration of his bride, Edgar the next day ordered a custom-made nursery car, in shades of blue, from the Pullman company.

Sibby considered throwing herself over a cliff. And her stammer returned with a vengeance.

Over the next few months she was raped sporadically

by Edgar, who was only angered by her reaction, her unconcealed distaste for his methods, the act itself. Sibby quickly understood what Mrs. Waring had been trying to tell her during their brief, and only, mother-daughter talk on the eve of the wedding.

There were days when she would not come out of her bedroom, when she sat and stared at the cold mountain rain streaming down the windows of the railroad car, and felt as if her soul had died while her body, sore and misused, wrongfully lived on. But she did not go mad, and she did not destroy herself in a frenzy of retribution and shame. She had a previously untested but strong will. Except for those periods when she isolated herself Sibby did not allow a ripple of discontent to show on the surface of the marriage. What was to be gained from that? More humiliation. Even if she had been living in a spacious mansion on Madison Avenue in New York, she could not have left her husband. Here it was both physically impossible and morally beyond the pale. She was married. For life. She belonged to Edgar Langford.

Edgar, enjoying a resurgence of good health, was kept very busy winter and summer with the construction of the chateau and his scholarly projects; he took frequent trips of two or three weeks' duration to visit universities and museums, always leaving her behind. Quite often, for months at a time, she saw her husband only at dinner and during his unannounced visits to her bedroom. She learned to endure his lust, and his eventual displeasure that no child had been conceived. The nursery car, with its cradle of gold mesh and ceiling murals of angelic cherubs at play on rosy clouds, arrived and sat disused on a siding. Sibby visited it only once. Stifled by boredom, she read, particularly romances by authors such as Richard Harding Davis, books she would

have denounced as trash if she happened to be exposed
to one before her marriage. She wrote long letters of
false good cheer to her family and confided nothing of
consequence to her diary, although scarcely a day went
by when she did not find a reason to mention the
architect, Mr. James B. Travers.

Her chief recreation, other than dinners with Travers
and occasional guests invited by Edgar, who invariably
spent the evening talking about archaeology in German
or some other language she didn't speak, was horseback riding. But the conventions of the day made it
difficult for her to go far on the mountain. Ladies, as
she had been taught, were expected to ride sidesaddle. It
was an acceptable if cumbersome method of getting
around on a placid horse where the paths were straight
and level. But that limited her to the vicinity of the
construction site, a hazardous course unless Mr. Travers
rode at her side, ready to take control of her mount
should he be frightened by the clattering appearance of a
steam wagon or the shrill whistle that preceded blasting.
Edgar could not sit a horse with any degree of comfort,
and never accompanied her.

Sibby's riding habits were heavy and uncomfortable,
with tight, padded shoulders. Under the full velvet skirt
she wore long trousers of covert-cloth, so that if she
took a tumble, not so much as a bare inch of her body
would be revealed. She also wore a padded derby with a
veil to filter the ever-present dust, and dogskin gloves.

She envied the grace and ease with which Mr. Travers,
a Virginian and lifelong equestrian, rode his fine chestnut gelding, Cyclops, up and down rugged slopes and
through the evergreen forests, where she surely would
be dislodged from her precarious seat by a shrub or
low-hanging tree limb.

She made a startling and bold resolution, but waited until Edgar was absent from Wildwood, presenting a paper to his peers at the only archaeological society that mattered to him. Then, on a morning's ride in September of 1906 with Travers, she made her radical proposal.

"I w-would like to be able to r-ride as w-well as you, Mr. Travers."

"Thank you for the compliment, Mrs. Langford." The architect turned his attention immediately to an overloaded mule-drawn wagon of lumber that was intruding on their path, and held both horses back.

"It w-was both a c-compliment and a request, M-Mr. Travers. I w-would like for you t-to teach me to ride a horse as a m-man rides."

Tall beside her, he looked down in astonishment, and Cyclops, sensing his master's uneasiness, did a little side jog.

"That is—unheard of, Mrs. Langford."

"I d-don't care."

"You—have you consulted Mr. Langford about this?"

"If it is s-something that will make me h-happy, Edgar will n-not seriously object."

"The problem is, of course, you cannot use the English saddle dressed as you are."

"I have designed an a-altogether d-different habit in which to ride," Sibby informed him, finishing breathless and so red in the face she was for once glad of the veil that covered her to the chinline.

"Do you mean—you will dress as a man?"

"That is an obvious r-requirement, Mr. Travers. W-when would it be c-convenient for you to c-commence with my lessons? I am sure you will agree that p-privacy is desirable, as I do not w-wish to m-make a spectacle of myself while learning proper eh-eh-eh—''

"Mrs. Langford, I *must* think about this."

"Equitation," she finished in a burst of exasperation, her eyes watering. "Are you a-f-fraid that my husband will b-be angry?"

"I am quite certain he will be angry. And have you considered carefully how others may interpret your desire for privacy?"

"No one n-needs to know what we are d-doing if we are discreet," she said rashly.

"My dear Mrs. Langford—" He didn't know whether to smile or be stern with her. His expression, under the circumstances, was comical. She was infuriated. She covered her mouth with one gloved hand, then blew it away in a gasp of desperation, no longer caring if she revealed to him the miserable state she was in.

"P-please. I be-beg you, Mr. Travers! Please do this for me, I m-must have this s-small degree of freedom, or—I think that I s-shall die!"

Four days later Travers led Sibby, still sitting properly sidesaddle in an appropriate, voluminous riding habit on her docile black mare, to a sunny clearing on the mountain, well away from the construction site. It was a roughly circular arena sixty feet in diameter, from which, with the help of a team of mules, he had personally removed all windfalls and boulders. The floor of the clearing was a well-trampled mat of spongy pine needles, a fair substitute for tanbark, adequate footing for the horses. He had left an extra English saddle there the day before.

He helped Sibby down, then changed saddles on the mare and attached a long lead while Sibby walked slowly to one side of the clearing, shuddering a little in the brisk air. She took off her gloves, then unbuttoned the wool habit. This she removed and hung on a stub of a fir tree. Underneath the habit she wore a long-sleeved linen shirt with a little velvet tie, and velvet jodhpurs her seamstress had made for her. They were of a burgundy shade that went well with her cordovan riding boots.

She walked back to Travers, derby in hand, eyes downcast, cheeks a dull red.

"Do you think this will d-do, Mr. Travers?"

He looked her over. He was not shocked; there was nothing indecorous about her appearance, although he'd never seen a woman in such attire before. He just knew that today would have repercussions. They both knew it. She raised her eyes to him before he could back down. And saw that he was not a man to back down, once he'd come to a decision.

"Yes," he said matter-of-factly. "I believe so."

She nodded. Thereafter she kept her chin up, and continued to look him in the eye with trust and growing confidence. His heart went to the bait like a fish in a pool.

"Very well. W-what must I do next?"

"First I will show you the proper way to mount. Here, please, on the left side of the mare."

That night Sibby Langford made a single entry in her diary.

I think I have fallen in love with Mr. Travers.

The setting down of these words was a revelation, perhaps the first time in her life she had dared to be completely honest with herself.

She added, *And he with me.*

But the nib pen made an uncharacteristic blot at the end of this line, and the tears of heartbreak she shed over the page for the next half hour nearly obliterated her words, while emphasizing the commitment.

── Chapter Fifteen ──

April 1958

"Hyar he is."

Terry was awakened in the front seat of the 1940 Dodge sedan by the gruff voice, by the sudden brilliance of lantern light in the space he occupied like a burrow. He gave a convulsive jerk which was followed by shudders and the onset of a headache like a mallet blow between the eyes. The greasy fumes of the burning wick stung his nostrils. Because of the pain in his head and the light near his eyes he couldn't keep them open long enough to see who was behind the lantern. Just had a whiff of him. Rose hair oil and sweat. The night air felt cold and damp but the rain had ended. The man holding the lantern backed out of the car, the light diminishing. Terry saw the April new moon repeated on the cracked windshield. Men were moving around outside, visible to him mostly as white shirts drifting like the sails of a midnight regatta, or laundry on a slowly revolving backyard carousel.

"In your car, William," a distant voice announced.

"Thank the good Lord," an equally unfamiliar voice responded quietly. Terry heard a child's sleepy complaint. "Reckon we'll get on now," a woman said through a yawn. Car doors opened and closed, an engine was started. Terry sat up on the lumpy seat, his forehead glancing off the rearview mirror. This he scarcely felt, but one hip was sore as a boil from a spring protruding through the worn fabric of the seat cover. Beneath the blanket he had wrapped around himself his clothing was sticking clammily to his body. His loafers were sodden, his toes freezing.

"Faren?" he said hoarsely.

Illuminated by the headlights of a passing car, the face of Hickory Smith, Faren's half brother, appeared in the door space.

"Better come into the church. Get you warmed up. We've got hot soup and coffee."

"You're crazy. I'm not going back in there!"

Hick Smith drew the back of one hand across his thick droopy mustache, as if it were a small animal that needed gentling. His deadpan expression didn't change. His eyes looked tired; that nearly hidden aspect of the sinister Terry had noticed earlier was missing, though he stared unwinkingly at the boy.

"Kid, ain't nothin' you need to be afraid of in God's house."

"*Snakes.*"

"The service is over," Smith said flatly, "and the snakes are gone."

"But where's Faren? I saw her! She was—" He gestured aimlessly; his throat swelled up at the thought of what he'd seen and he couldn't have spoken even if he had trusted Smith enough to attempt an explanation.

"I'm right here, Terry," Faren said.

He nearly knocked Smith over getting out of the car. She had come out of the church barefoot, like Terry wrapped in a blanket, mud on her face too. He threw his arms around her, needing to assure himself that she was solid flesh and bone.

"Terry, Terry," she murmured, unable to resist nuzzling him, nibbling at a cheek with her cold chapped lips. Coffee on her breath. As real as real. He couldn't help babbling once his throat unlocked.

"What happened? Where'd you go? I mean, where *were* you? I could see you! You walked right through me!"

"Did what? Terry, you're—I'm okay. Not hurt or anything. Nothing happened—"

"Nothing!"

"Shhh." Faren's arms were around him. She gave him a hard, perhaps a warning squeeze. It quieted him. She was damp and cold and began to shiver. He remembered how dry she had appeared to him, untouched by the downpour. Not seeing him, even as she walked casually through him as if he were a doorway. "We have things to talk about, but not now," she advised him. "Let's go in, lucky if we both don't take sick."

By the time Terry had swallowed a cup of chicken soup from a thermos, everyone but Smith and Faren had left the church building, and the yard. The windows were all closed and misted over. Smith had turned on the propane heaters; they hissed in a way that reminded Terry subtly but unpleasantly of the snakes he'd seen. He looked uneasily around him, imagining movement in shadowy places, his nerves expanding and contracting; he kept a close watch on the floor by his feet. Smith leaned against the wall near the front door reading his Bible while Terry finished his soup and Faren drank more coffee. They sat exhaustedly knee to knee on a bench, staring at each other, nodding, communicating by touch rather than with words. Terry was dazed by the lateness of the hour, by everything wonderful and harrowing they had shared that day, by mysteries he felt inadequate to explore. The food on his stomach had the effect of a knockout pill. Before long he couldn't keep his eyes open. Smith walked Terry out to his Hudson car, a bathtub on wheels, and Terry went to sleep in the backseat. Faren rode in front. When they reached Smith's house they woke him up and once again he was led as if in a trance, this time to a small second-floor bedroom. The room was clean and spare, with a narrow iron bedstead and an old-fashioned washstand that had a china bowl and pitcher on it. There was a chamberpot under the bed. Faren showed it to him.

"Guess you know what that's for."

Terry nodded, and looked longingly at the bed.

"Uh-uh, pull your clothes off first, then get under the covers. I'll be right back."

He was still on his feet when she returned from down the hall. She was wearing a robe and slippers. She had towels and a washcloth and pajamas with her. She poured water into the basin and cleaned his face.

"Need to talk to you."

"Morning's soon enough," Faren said.

"There's a funny smell in here."

"You're right over Hick's workshop. That's oil paint and turpentine and developer fluid you smell. Told you he was an artist. Are you going to get undressed or do I need to do it for you?"

"No."

"Pajamas are on the bed. Put your dirty clothes outside the door so I can wash and dry them first thing. 'Night, Terry.''

"Wait." But she was gone. With the hall door closed there was only moonlight coming in, beneath the shade drawn to within an inch of the windowsill. He shucked and pawed until his clothes were in an untidy pile on the floor. He forgot to put them in the hall. The pajamas were big on him. He was dropping off to sleep when the door opened, a spear of lamplight crossed the bed and Faren crept in to toss his soiled clothing in a basket.

And he heard her say: "I know now, Terry. Everything I didn't know before. Tonight I walked in marble halls, it's just there, waiting to come back. But those poor souls in their limbo, they can't ever make it back. Poor helpless people, they're lost forever."

He felt her sorrowing kiss on his forehead, reached up weakly to touch and keep her there, he felt lost himself. But she was gone, just as quickly as she had vanished in the churchyard. He saw and heard nothing more until long past daybreak.

——Chapter Sixteen——

Whit Bowers was awakened just before dawn by the somewhat hair-raising, gruff-throated sounds of milling hounds and Arn's impatient countryman's voice calling him out; time to be on the trail. Whit had the moonshine hangover Arn had prophesied, a cold sick feeling that the only place suitable for him just now was at graveside of his own funeral. He plunged into a cold shower that tasted of iron, but afterward still felt too inept to use a razor and decided not to shave. Lacing up his boots was a frustrating chore.

Arn grinned when Whit finally appeared, adjusting the straps of his backpack from Abercrombie and Fitch.

"Don't appear as how you've used that much."

"It's new."

"Now, that'd be *ideal* if you went to climb the Matterhorn with a gentleman friend. China service for two, maybe you got a portable pottie in there?"

"Arn, I'm not in the mood. Did you hear from Faren?"

"No. There ain't that many telephones on the Boundary, 'ceptin' in Cherokee town. But if she was in any real trouble, the woman would've found a way to let me know. So I reckon everythin's ducky."

"I don't feel right about going off for a couple of days without saying anything to Terry."

"Stay, then. Catch up to me when and if you can. Only thing is, one bear path looks like 'nother fifty yards into the tall trees. I could blaze a trail, reckon. Plant little flags along the way like it was a Boy Scout jamboree."

"When will we get back from Tormentil?"

"If we can just spend more time walkin' than jawin', late tomorrow night."

"Okay. I'll leave Terry a note."

"No need. I already woke Jewell up and told him where we'd be."

"God . . . I could use a cup of black coffee."

Arn just stared at him for a few moments, then relented with another grin. His own eyes looked a little redder than usual this morning, and he hadn't shaved either. "Believe you could at that. Pot's on the stove, Colonel. Turn the burner off when you've drunk your fill."

So they were back to rank, Arn putting a little distance between them for unknown reasons, although the Grudge wasn't in evidence. Yet.

A little after six-thirty they were on their way to Wildwood, following a path beside the flourishing creek that ran down through Arn's property. All three dogs went with them, including Bocephus, the hound which had been doctored at the vet's the day before, his hind end shaved in a crude iodined oval with stitching across it. For now Arn allowed the dogs to roam freely through the wet grasses and flowering weed, sniffing out rabbits that lived and fed securely in tangled undergrowth. He carried strong braided leather leashes wrapped around his right shoulder. His own frayed canvas pack, like a mailman's pouch but smaller, hung comfortably off the left shoulder. Arn traveled with few encumbrances. His rifle (a model 1895 lever action Winchester, the first rifle he'd owned and, other than the BAR he had lugged around for much of the war, his favorite), his sheath knife, a pocket knife, matches, some packets of toilet paper and two suppositories in foil, redbug repellant, a snakebite kit (more for the sake of the dogs than himself; he had never been bitten), fishing line and hooks, a tobacco tin full of coffee, a small battered pot to boil water in, a poncho to keep him dry in anything short of a flash flood, extra ammunition in a watertight case the size of a pack of cigarettes. He shot, fished, or dug for his dinners, and in late spring and summer there was abundant fruit wherever he went. In addition to his old grayish-brown felt hat with the turned-down brim, he wore a twill shirt and tan duck pants, a gabardine Ike jacket, grease-darkened moccasins that were molded to his feet like an extra layer of skin, and no socks. He moved with a stride that Whit admired but which gave him plenty of trouble from the start as he attempted to match Arn's pace. His own low-top hiking boots were broken in but they were heavy and a little clumsy on this gently sloping, rain-softened terrain; he felt subtly but irritatingly off-balance in both mind and body.

Last night Whit had dreamed of men who flew and a man who walked through walls, and of trying this trick himself although he had been told he wasn't ready yet. Getting into the wall with ease (it was limestone, blocks seven feet thick) but getting stuck halfway, suffocating from horror, screaming and screaming. The panic had awakened him, as it always did. And the coda to the nightmare was familiar if not reassuring. Released from the grip of the stone wall, not knowing how he had managed his escape, he found himself alone on a flat gray desert with dry folds of pinkish mountains rimming the horizon. The sun was blistering his naked back, his lips had swelled to twice normal size; he trudged westward, dying of thirst.

He was thirsty now, with a terrible taste in his mouth, kind of sour and chicken-crappy; but he knew if he gulped the water he wanted he would just make himself sicker, double up from cramps, and then he could count on Arn leaving him behind. (What was Arn after today, anyway? Why did he have the urge to go back so soon? Whit knew it wasn't for his sake.) Better to patiently sweat out the lightning, sweat until he smelled like a still. Then he could drink.

"Bring you somethin' to keep the wet off?"

"A slicker." So far it promised to be a fair, probably humid day following the hours-long storm of the night before. Whit looked for clouds, then asked Arn if he thought there was a prospect of rain.

"These are the Smokies," Arn told him. "We do have occasional dry spells, but ordinarily it rains up there five days out of seven, off and on all day. In between showers the sun'll come out, and that's what accounts for the smokes."

"Why did you bring your dogs?"

"You walk a bear trail, you run into bears. I'd ruther scare 'em off than shoot 'em, if I don't need the meat." Arn stopped suddenly, tired of talking over one shoulder. "Am I walkin' too fast for you, Colonel?"

"Yeah," Whit admitted, trying to catch his breath.

They paused beneath a red maple, twenty-foot garlands of wisteria with lilac bloom-clusters hanging from its branches.

Arn shrugged and said with a slightly exaggerated patience, "Well now, this here's the pussy part. Later on the goin' gets close to vertical."

"Later on I will have sweated out this goddamned hangover."

"Reckon you got a fair start on that already. I want you to know, I only give you the good stuff to drink. There's worse white lightnin' you can buy."

"What does the bad stuff do to you?" Whit asked, trying to imagine feeling worse than he did already.

"If it's bad enough, got a-plenty lye or lead salts or maybe fusel oil in it, it'll flat-dab kill you. Just a little bad, after a while you come up with a liver you could carve your initials on. You doin' some better, now that you've had a blow?"

"Yes. Give me another minute. Arn?"

"What's on your mind?"

"That skeleton you showed me last night. How could—any ideas how a man got to be like that?"

"Well, you know, there's plenty of peculiar things occur in nature. Ever been to a freak show at a carnival? Used to dote on those when I was a-younger. Sneaked under the tent one night to watch a red-haired stripteaser with balls and a dick like a blood sausage. She could get it up too. Or maybe it was a man with a woman's body and big jugs. Take your pick. Seen the alligator boy and the three-legged man. Now, that couldn't've been no fake. I'll swear to it on the Bible. He was settin' there in plain sight on a little stool and all but naked; and he could wiggle the toes of his three feet. Mountain woman my mama knew personally, lived a ways back up yonder of Blackhaw Ridge, she delivered herself of a babe with a two-foot tail hairy as a wolf's all wrapped around its little body; and they say it had wolf's eyes and ears too. The mister, he took it straight to the tanning trough and drowned it in lye water. Then he shot the lights out of his woman with an ole .44, 'cause he knew she'd had to have been with a werewolf to conceive such a child.''

"Sounds like one of those stories that gets better every time it's told. A werewolf? Now, you don't honestly believe in something like that.''

Arn didn't crack a smile. "Hereabouts a man's counted a fool if he *don't* believe, and takes measures to protect himself. I told you there's wild creatures, not three miles farther on from where we're standin' right now, that has the minds of men. Farfetched? Colonel, you and me fought in a war that seen men on both sides turn animal in ever' way but looks. What was the name of that dago boy grew up on the streets of Chicago, he was so good at slippin' behind the kraut lines at night with his knife? I seen him come back from patrols with blood on his mouth, he'd been drinkin' Kraut blood after he slit their throats. Call that human?''

"He was a psycho.''

"Maybe he had a cravin' to drink blood that he couldn't control. He *needed* it. 'Nother thing, there's still babies born with tails, more common than you might think. Doctor just snips 'em off like a rosebud and nothin' more's ever said about it.''

"Vestigial tails are one thing. Functional wings are another.''

Arn pushed his shabby hat back and rubbed his creased forehead below the hairline. He gazed thoughtfully at Nolichucky, his redbone hound, who was pursuing a feisty squirrel through Virginia sweetshrub and deer

laurel on the other side of the swiftly flowing creek. He
whistled sharply. " 'Chucky, leave off doin' that and
get your butt back over here!" He looked again at Whit.
"Well, no, I don't accept that the hawkman was born
that way. I think he was a hundred percent normal till he
got misused by some kind of black magic, a trick that
didn't come out right."

"What kind of trick puts wings on a human body?"

"Search me. But it *is* a fact that Edgar Langford was
a hell of a—what's the right word; Faren told it to me
once—kind of a male witch."

The appropriate term came readily to Whit's mind.
"Warlock. Necromancer. But necromancers were chiefly
known for raising spirits from the dead. No, he couldn't
do that."

Arn looked surprised. "Didn't know you was that
well-acquainted with the black arts. Or ole Mad Edgar
himself."

"I'm not," Whit said, feeling a curious, quick light-
headedness; the brilliance of the splashy creek obscured
Arn's presence momentarily, dimmed the barking of
the dogs and the warblers in pale greenwood. He felt
a tugging sensation, as if the waters of the creek had
shifted and he were standing deep in the foaming current. Easy to go with it should he so elect, floating to
where all currents converged in a dark backwash of
time—he resisted, afraid. At that moment his head pained
him as if it had been struck with an ax and cleaved in
two; with one disoriented eye he saw some people grouped
in a wild garden of thorn and lair, mistily observing
him: they were albino-foreign, with eyes like darkroom
bulbs, so close he might have reached them in a few
strides, if he dared. With the other eye he saw Arn's
sunfired puzzled face, sharp gaze of gunsight gray. This

split level of consciousness was fleeting; then the head-ache that had flared up excruciatingly began to fade, he found his tongue again.

"I don't know a thing about magic," he assured Arn. "But I—I've been reading a lot about Langford recently. When was it you shot the hawkman?"

"November of '38."

"Edgar Langford died in 1916."

"Yeah, maybe."

"Maybe?"

"Could be *died* ain't the right word for what happened to him."

Whit laughed; the conversation struck him as ridiculous. From hermaphrodites to werewolves to necromancers. He still felt a little clouded and bemused. He wanted to lie down in the softly sunned bed of lime green fern that overhung the creek until the feeling passed. Instead, he leaned against the maple's swayed trunk to take some of the stress off his already pack-sore backbone.

"What in hell are you talking about, Arn?"

Arn had faced north, the direction of the unseen mountain. Two of his hounds came leaping up the bank from the creek and shook themselves vigorously, sprinkling both men.

"Sayin' he might still be up there."

"Oh, Jesus," Whit muttered.

"Livin' in his fancy chateau like 1916 was yesterday . . . yesterday, hell. A fraction of a second ago. Faren's seen the chateau a time or two. Her last look was just before she got packed off to that mental ward. So—I don't know. Maybe it *is* there. But we can't locate it, see it with our own eyes no more."

Whit didn't say anything. After a minute or so Arn turned and asked him, "Remember screamin' meemies?"

"For the rest of my life I'll remember them."

"Those .88's traveled faster than sound, you didn't know one was comin' until *shitttttt*, there was dirt and vehicles and pieces of bodies flyin' all over the place. Just pure luck if you didn't happen to be in the way of one of them shells. Well—Faren says the chateau and most of the people in it somehow got to travelin' so fast, close to the speed of light, that normal eyes just can't pick it up. So to us it's just the same as if the chateau had disappeared."

"You're talking about a stone chateau, weighing as much as an Egyptian pyramid and covering twenty-four acres of land. And it, what was that you said, 'just got to traveling'?"

Arn looked disgruntled. "That's the way Faren described it to me. Reckon maybe there's a law of physics would explain how that could happen. Or else it's one of them black arts secrets that'll stay secret until somebody figures out the answer. Anyway, Faren knows and I believe that lookin' ain't always seein'; we need to make use of other senses we don't know we got."

Whit started to say something that Arn might have interpreted as a challenge to his wife's sanity, thought better of it, and also decided he wasn't in a mood to try to reconcile Arn's mystical speculations with his customary hardheadedness.

Arn didn't seem particularly interested in pursuing this most recent flight of fancy either. He picked up his own pack, and the rifle he had set aside.

"When you're feelin' froggy, we'll jump," he said.

They were soon at the borderland of the cove, broom corn pasture gone wild, the last of a succession of abandoned homesteads fallen to ruin, rail fences down in high weeds and brambles. The early morning sun slick on new leaves, faintly warming the backs of their necks. The dogs, having worked off their early exuberance, trotted along with tongues lolling, in front of and beside the deliberately walking men. Off to his left, at a distance, Whit could see a tall thin man in a porkpie hat and a woman wearing a calico bonnet hoeing in the garden behind their house. He caught the glint of a car moving south along the road that passed Arn's place a mile and a half away. Then the mouth of the big woods opened and took them in. Suddenly it was quite a bit darker, sunlight limited to pale freckles and blazes across their path, which was crossed and recrossed by the exposed sprawling roots of hickory, white oak, and poplar, roots grown so thickly together the path seemed nearly paved with them, like an antique corduroy road.

Arn stopped suddenly, looking around, taking a deep draft of the air that smelled, to Whit, only of humus and moldering logs, uprooted trees crushed against one another, the long strands of maypop and strangler vine that festooned their cracked bare limbs looking like a fright wig.

"Chestnuts," Arn pointed out. "Used to be a fine grove of them trees standin' in here; but the blight's killed 'em all off. Big as they be, these woods could die, make no mistake, if nobody takes care." He took another deep breath, frowned, went down on one knee to examine the dark ground between two gnarly roots. "Our friend Jacob's come through here already," he said. "Half hour ago, 'bout."

"On his bike?" Whit said, looking at the rough uphill path ahead.

"Yeah. I can still smell the tailpipe fumes."

"You've got some nose."

"Never ruined it with cheap tobacco. Didn't care to end up like my daddy, coughin' his lungs out bit by bit on his deathbed, but still cryin' for a smoke."

"How deep in the woods does Jacob live? He doesn't look like much of an outdoorsman to me."

"That's a fact. Well, I found the little lean-to where he leaves his bike, but I never thought to track him the rest of the way. I don't believe he's put up lodging of any kind. But I got a suspicion as to where he's holed up. He must have found a way in, so I reckon in that regard he's been sharper than me."

"A way in to what?"

"Mad Edgar's cave. You know about that?"

"He shipped so much artwork from the Middle East—at least two trainloads—that he had to have a place to store it all until his chateau was finished. So he blasted a huge cave in the side of Tormentil and ran a spur line into the cave."

"Yeah. You can still make out where that spur line was, but there's a hill of rock and dirt and near to full-grown trees in front of them old iron gates now, they dynamited a whole bluff down in that gorge. If you could get a couple bulldozers up there, which is just about impossible, it'd take a week to move all that fill. I doubt that it's worth it. I don't believe there's anythin' of value left in the cave. But I'll bet you there was 'nother entrance. Because ole Edgar, he was too clever not to have a secret way in and out, probably convenient to where he was buildin' his chateau."

Arn whistled up his dogs and leashed them; they walked on.

After a hundred yards or so the trail they were following, growing steeper and more complicated in its wanderings, divided, and Arn took the left-hand fork. It went around a hill and up another, very long hill that Arn described as a ridgeback. Limber sapling branches on either side grew almost to touching in the path's center, flicking at, fencing with them, whipping them smartly as they passed. The footing, of red clay mixed with mast and leaf marl and crumbling rock and decayed wood, sodden from all the rain, was treacherous. Arn, handling himself and his dogs as well, seldom paused and never faltered. Whit had sweat in his eyes and a fiery welt on one cheekbone. His headache had diminished. The trees overhead, immense shaggy vaults through which birds flickered lighter than air and without wingbeats, closed out all but precious fractions of the sky, the clear and cheering morning light. Around the walkers mist fumed, there were ghostly exhalations in choked groves. Whit caught sight of a doe's still-watching head, quickly withdrawn into shadow. The dogs panted as if exhausted but seemed to have spring steel in their haunches; their splayed heavy feet with claws like obsidian were dyed red to the dewclaws, stringy mud hung from their underbellies and wrinkled throats.

"Now, dogs," Arn said, "them three's all I got left, and they ain't nothin' too special, mostly good company. But for the best part of my life I've run with a pack of hounds thick as fiddlers in hell. Blue ticks and Plotts and redbones and a Catahoula hound I fetched back from Louisanner once upon a time; he didn't take to the mountains all that good, bein' a canebrake hunter, got a bad cough one December and perished of it. But sometimes the best dog you can have is just an ole cur. Had me a runty little wirebeard once that was the best tree dog I ever saw, it come natural to him. He'd follow a coon to torment, then he'd set a tree till he starved that coon down, and whip the stripes off 'im. Lord, I'm tellin' you. And boar dogs—you got to know it takes a nervy dog to fight a wild boar, and them weighin' upwards of three hundred fifty pounds, slip in just right and grip him by the ear so he can't use his tushes. Good boar hunters need more'n a dab of bulldog stock in 'em, that's a fact.''

They came to a stream too wide and full to cross, and had to make their way up along the crowded bank, using for handholds slippery branches of rhododendron and the washed-out roots of mighty trees soaked black in the flume. Breaking through elaborate spiderwebs, the frail light caught in them like the light of church windows. Arn reacted to every detour, every obstacle, with nonchalance, indifference; obviously he knew how to get where they were going, but was in no hurry, this was his church, his morning of communion. Whit's thirst had grown the more he sweated, the taste of spray on his lips was sweet and agonizing; he felt as if he had a mouthful of dirt in which his tongue, barely wetted, lay half dead. He was too thoroughly occupied by the act of climbing, reaching, straining, maintaining balance, to be awed by the prolific thickets with which he was immediately challenged, and the dark immensity of the woods to come. He didn't feel lost, exactly: he had a compass with him and good geological survey maps, and in a pinch he knew he could find his way out of Wildwood simply by following running water to the flatlands, but he was at a loss, humbled, a blinded man groping to be informed; he did not fit his skin well today, and his bones, like dry bones he had transported from the scorched desert of his dreams, were alien here in this fiercely greening, richly fecund, breathing, murmuring, terrifyingly beautiful and treacherous place. The

sensation he felt most penetratingly, as he struggled
toward Tormentil, was one of rebirth. But by daylight it
was not possible to recall the symbolic circumstances of
his dying, symbols so infallibly ordered on the stage-set
of sleep. So there was no meaning to be derived from
the sensation that was as pure and chastening as hunger
or sex; he had only the faint apprehension as he toiled
through tangles toward the hidden sky and the mountain
clouded by time and magic, that something crucial must
occur before he would be allowed, or enabled, to come
down again.

— Chapter Seventeen —

TERRY was just awake but with a lassitude that kept him motionless, staring at the ceiling and listening to birdsong outside the spare bedroom in Hickory Smith's house, when Faren came in, laid his washed and ironed clothes at the foot of the bed, then sat down beside him.

"Hi."

He turned his head, studying her, tongue worrying the sore lump where his lower lip had been split. She'd washed her own things. Her hair was clean and brushed and looked blue at the crown because of the light from the shaded window behind her; her lips were freshly colored. She looked well and at peace with herself. But a little shy with him, not knowing where to begin.

"You should have—" Terry said, and his throat tightened hostilely.

She nodded. "Oh, sure, you're right. I ought to have warned you, there might be snakes."

"But why—"

"Terry, it's a vital part of our religion, the taking up of poisonous serpents when you're moving just a-joyful with the spirit, loving the Lord, and there's no wavering in your faith. Because it says, right there in Mark 16, 'In my name shall they cast out devils; they shall speak with new tongues; they shall take up serpents; and if they drink any deadly thing, it shall not hurt them.' We believe every word of that."

"You mean because it's in the Bible nobody can get hurt?"

Faren lowered her head regretfully. "Can't say that hasn't happened, because it has, lots of times. And people have died or been brain-crippled from snakebite or swallowing poison. Those people just weren't ready; they felt the need but didn't have the victory."

"It just sounds weird to me. And I thought you were going to get bitten."

"No, I never have been. But I've handled snakes only a few times, and those were copperheads. A copperhead bite'll make you dog-sick, but the poison won't bust your heart the way rattler poison does."

"Where did you go? How did you get out of the church so fast?"

"Terry, I'm honestly not sure. I can only tell you, something did come over me that wasn't the true spirit of the Lord. And the snake I was holding turned into a wooden serpent with a gold and silver head, and ruby eyes that were spitting all over me like sparks from a stirred-up fire; I just went up and out in a flurry of sparks, right through the church roof." Terry winced slightly, wryly; she gripped his hand. "I'm not lying! Next thing I knew, I was walking down long hallways filled with statues and pieces of statues that must have been thousands of years old; and I could look right through closed doors three inches thick at people getting dressed up fancy. I can't begin to describe the gowns and wigs and getups for men, old-time silk breeches and embroidered waistcoats, it was like pictures I've seen of the Court of Versailles. But some of them were putting on costumes of feathers and fur, the skins and claws of animals. I realized I must be in Mad Edgar's chateau, on Midsummer Eve 1916, and his revels were about to commence. But nobody took notice of me; they couldn't tell I was among them. They didn't know something else was there, either: an evil force I could feel right away, it sapped my strength and drained my soul. I was just dwindling away, atom by atom.'' She tightened her hold on his hand, fearing an attempted withdrawal, rejection. "Oh, I was scared! I started to run, trying to find a way out before it was too late. And then I—"

Faren broke off, eyes going blank, and she slowly knuckled her mouth with her other hand, thinking, brooding.

"How did you get out?"

"I'm as baffled as you are. All I know is I found myself in the midst of a glaring cloud, like morning fog just before sunrise: that cloud took over the chateau, getting hotter and brighter until I almost couldn't stand the brightness, I felt as if I were all bones and teeth, like an X-ray picture. That's the only way I know how to say it. I couldn't make out a thing except for those ruby eyes, serpent's eyes, big and with hot blood spots in them, watching me. Then I might have gone dead asleep for a few seconds: When lighting woke me up I was lying on the ground fifty feet behind the church with a torrent from a drainspout washing over me. I heard in my mind the pitiful cries of some of the people who had been getting ready for the masquerade back there.''

Terry searched those vague moments when he had lain, at the end of a stressful day and close to oblivion, in the bed. "Last night you said—I thought I heard you say—they were lost forever. Are they dead?''

"No, Terry. I don't think so.''

"Wasn't there a fire? And then the chateau was buried in an avalanche?''

"That's what I told you when we met, because it's the explanation most people accept as logical. People will always believe what makes them comfortable, and doesn't overagitate their brains. But I've never really accepted the avalanche theory. You see, when I married Arn and moved in with him and he'd go off hunting for a few days and come back, I'd have little flashes of intuition, just from touching him; something he'd collected out there in Wildwood, not knowing about it himself, was all over his skin. I had glimpses of things that I'd prefer not to have seen; which is why I'll get a Bible and swear to it right now, the chateau is still *there*, and all of a piece. I had to pass through a tornado of fire, how and why I don't know, but last night I was meant to walk through those marble halls.''

Terry sat up and said with pained intensity, "No, listen, you were in the churchyard! In the rain, with me, but you weren't getting wet. I called you; I think you heard me. You came toward me like you couldn't tell where I was. Then you—walked right through me! I thought you must be dead; a ghost.''

She ran a hand obliquely from the back of his neck across the top of his blond head, leaving his hair in a wrong-way Mohawk ridge and his scalp a-tingle; beneath the sheet his own, impulsive serpent grew long through the buttonless fly of the pajama bottoms he wore.

"I'm no ghost, that's for sure." Her hand continued, fondly, down the side of his face, her slightly irregular, pinkish nails just grazing his cheek; she gripped and held his chin, froze his attention on her face while her eyes stared past him, at a corner of the room where sunlight was pale as a watermark on the plain off-white wall.

"Maybe," she said, "there's a fine line that can be walked, balanced on; and that's how I appeared to be two places at once."

Her own intensity caused him to tremble, negatively; she took her hand away and put it with the other in her lap.

"Well, Terry, whatever happened to us last night, let's hope it's over and done with."

That shocked him. "You mean something else that bad could happen?"

"No—I don't think so. I just wish I could make out more of the meaning of what—" Her gaze was lifelessly remote again, for a few seconds; then she came out of it and tapped him lightly on one shoulder. "Well, let's just try to put it out of our minds. Time for you to be up and around, your daddy must be near to frantic by now, and I'm in Arn's doghouse for sure."

Hickory Smith's wife had died of cancer two years before, leaving him childless and alone in his hilltop house. Smith was working in his studio when Terry sat down to the kitchen table for the breakfast Faren fixed for him: buttery buckwheat cakes, bacon, and eggs. She had eaten earlier, much earlier, done the wash, and cleaned house for her brother.

"I could spend the rest of the day digging him out,"

Faren grumbled; but the windows sparkled, the house was airy, it smelled keenly of fresh turpentine and artist's oils. She took in the rest of the laundry flapping on the clothesline outside and they drove into the town of Cherokee in Smith's pickup truck, where Faren used a pay phone at the Texaco station. By then it was almost noon.

She came away from the telephone with a frown.

"Couldn't raise Arn at the house, and the phone at the grocery's out of order," she said. "I'll arrange for the garage here to winch my Ford off that stump and tow it in, then we'll drive on home. Jewell can bring Hick's truck to him this evening and thumb a ride back."

Faren wasn't talkative the few miles up the road to Tyree. The pickup had a front-end shimmy and she had to grip the wheel hard with both hands to keep it riding true and steady, muscles bunched in her walnut forearms. They listened to Hank Williams, Kitty Wells and Lefty Frizzell on the radio. Terry had never heard real country music, and "It Wasn't God Who Made Honky-Tonk Angels" and "I Told a Lie to My Heart" appealed to him: hardship, disillusionment, misery, and sin. Faren's feathery sing-along voice raised goose bumps. Williams, she related, had died alone in the back of his Cadillac at the age of twenty-nine. Coronary, but he'd been a heavy boozer. "My age," Faren said, as if this fact implied a kinship of fate. She seemed sad to Terry, and not just from listening to sad songs on the radio. She was in mortal conflict with herself this morning. *Put it out of our minds*, she had counseled, but whenever he glanced at her face in profile against a window reddish with reservation-road dirt he saw her as if by forked lightning, striding perplexed and (he now knew) a little

frightened through last night's deluge; he had to keep
looking at her to reassure himself that a stitch in time
had sealed her safely in the present; she couldn't vanish
from his sight again, they would arrive together at the
conclusion of this bumpy journey in lambent April light.
For now all was well.

But when they reached home and found out that Arn
and the dogs were gone, and his father was gone, too, and
she had talked to dopey Jewell in the grocery store
and come out quickly, banging the screen door behind
her, the look on her face, an adult acrimony and displeasure he had not encountered in her before, caused him to
shrink a little, as if he had been smugly overinflated
from adolescence these past two days and was about to
be reminded of his true age and worth to Faren.

"They've gone to the mountain!" she said, raising a
fist, not purposefully but in a gesture of frustration, face
bathed in bad blood which, because her skin was already darkly toned, showed most startlingly in her eyes.

"What mountain?"

She used her fist, knocking in a northerly direction.
"Tormentil!"

"Why?"

Her fist moved to a spot near her breastbone, pressing
there.

"Arn's begging for trouble this time, that's all I
know."

Trouble—the word seemed as ugly as a psychic tumor
she had plucked from the center of her body; she seemed
not to know what to do with it, she stood stiff-legged
with unempowered energy, the noon sun streaming down
on her hot raven head, bold brows casting winged shadows like witchpaint to the corners of her unhappy mouth.
Then she whirled away from Terry, crunching through

the gravel of the lot past the high cab of the pickup truck she'd left near the store with the keys in it, her face flashing momentarily back at him out of the brightness of the sideview mirror. She reached in over the window-sill for her purse, continued on toward the house.

"Hey, where are you going?"

"After them! Before it's too late."

"I want to go with you, Faren!"

"No, you can't! Stay here, in the house, there's plenty to eat, you'll be safe here!"

"What's going to happen?"

She didn't answer him. She kept walking fast away from him, would've run but the denim skirt with the hem well below her knees didn't allow for running. He watched her cross the road in the shade of the trees near the house and hurry up the steps to her front porch, heard the faint clap of the screen door behind her. Jewell, attracted by the shouting back and forth, saun-tered out of the grocery, bottle of orange pop in one hand, his other hand shading his eyes. He looked at Terry, who explained nothing, and eventually went back in, where the light wasn't so bright.

When Faren came out of the house by the back door twenty minutes later, dressed for the woods and carrying a loaded backpack she'd had since her college years, Terry was waiting for her. He had his own well-used Alpine trail gear ready to go. He was sitting on a broad beechnut stump relacing a hiking boot that didn't feel right across the instep.

"Terry, I mean it. You stay put."

"No."

She walked slowly across the yard to him. Guinea hens roosting in a streamside sapling began an irritable squawling.

"One of those damn birds tried to bite me," he told her. "I don't think their eggs are worth it."

"They eat a lot of garden bugs, too, that's why we put up with their lousy dispositions. Look, your father's not here and that makes me responsible for you, and we've already been in one scrape too many, because I didn't use real good judgment. So I don't want to worry myself sick over you, you can't go."

He stared straight at her and it occurred to him, a major revelation in his young life, that women will always say no even when they don't mean it. Faren's face looked hard and stubborn but he wasn't fooled; when she knew he wasn't she stopped bluffing and dropped her eyes and that was that. Terry smiled briefly and finished tying his boot. He stood up then next to Faren, tall in thick-cleated soles. Feeling pretty good about the way he had handled himself so far. But worried.

"What kind of trouble?" he asked her.

"Terry, I just sense that something real bad is waiting for them up there on the Tormentor."

"Is something going to happen to my dad?"

"I don't know. But, more than Arn, he's the one should stay away from there."

Terry suppressed a shudder of nervousness. "Let's go find them, then. They're already way ahead of us, aren't they?"

She nodded. "Almost six hours. That doesn't mean much. Arn might turn the dogs loose on rabbits, or stop a while to fish."

"Should we take a gun? Arn has more guns in the house, hasn't he?"

"It's nothing we can shoot at, or I would."

"Don't you know *what* it is, Faren?"

"Yes. The chateau. It's dangerous. But I don't know any more about it than that, not yet."

"Do you know how to get up to the mountain?"

"I've never been in Wildwood. Never wanted to go. But all we need do is follow the creek here, which takes us to the headwaters of the Cat Brier up there on Tormentil." She gripped him by the upper arm and pressed her face against the right side of his neck for a few moments, gently, attentive to the fast pulse in his throat. "I guess I didn't really want to be alone in those woods, no matter what. We'll find them, Terry; everything'll be okay. Give me a boost with my pack, and let's be on our way."

── Chapter Eighteen ──

AFTER four hours of hard walking uphill Arn Rutledge and Whit Bowers came to an easier plateau, new wide-spaced growth of red and sugar maple with little underbrush, mainly dogwood and hobblebush, the creek meandering through it shallow, full of stepping-stones and tea-colored from the layers of leaves steeping on the bottom; the creek vanished in a broad swale filled with beaver lodges. A fire just after the war (Arn explained) had burned through several hundred of the acres they were now crossing. Arn, never at a loss for an opinion, thought that a good fire now and then was useful. It burned out choking thickets and helped break down the deadwood, giving younger trees room to thrive. There was a little too much emphasis nowadays on spotting fires early, jumping on them and putting them out before they could run their course as nature intended. But the U.S. Forestry Service hadn't yet put up any watchtowers on Wildwood land. The government, Arn said, was still pretty busy up at the park building new asphalt roads and campgrounds and hacking out trails in the wilderness that would make it just a hell of a lot easier for city people in their Bermuda shorts and Capezios to wander around admiring nature in the raw and maybe get themselves chomped on by a bear or a disgruntled coon in the bargain.

They paused before entering denser oak woods at the threshold of the mountains and had something to eat. Arn had brought along biscuits as big as quart jar lids and sausage, which they shared equally with his hounds. Whit had sore heels but no blisters, for which he was grateful. He sat with his back against a windfall comfortably padded with the big leathery leaves of mayflower. The sun was high and hot on the back of his neck and shoulders. The mountains he faced, wave after long wave in tones from burnished sunlit green to fadeaway blue that became indistinguishable from the distant sky, looked barely penetrable. Whit no longer found preposterous the notion that a chateau could be missing in this wilderness; an entire civilization, cities and pyramidal temples, had all but vanished for centuries in the jungles of the Yucatan. The spring wood they had passed through earlier, still weeks from a fullness of growth but already convolute and as mysterious in its depths as the windings of the inner ear, was close enough to jungle for Whit; and there were more rugged miles to go once they reached the hemlock forest that solidly rose from the shoulders of the mountains to their mile-high summits.

Nineteen sixteen: it had been forty-two years.

He could easily imagine large blocks of dressed stone tumbled into ravines up there on Tormentil, covered by rivers of mud and loose rock in the heavy rains that

followed a runaway fire, then by creeping wood sorrel
and the tough tangled mountain rhododendron. Conifers
grew quickly tall; there could be sixty-foot plumed pines
and spruces, big around as shaggy barrels near the
ground, where Sibby Langford had sat facing her several lives in a triptych of nighttime mirrors, languidly
brushing her hair before bed. . . .

Such sad, worried eyes.

His head was nodding, he was nearly falling asleep.
Daydreaming.

Her slight, pale hands, brushing. The back of the
hairbrush oval, luminous, inlaid mother-of-pearl. When
her hands were at rest, in her lap, the veins were ugly
and blue. With her hands raised to the crown of her
head, the veins all but disappeared, they seemed smooth
then, pleasingly childlike. But they were always cold.

She had been ill. She seldom left her rooms anymore.

She was looking at him in the mirrors with a wan,
inviting smile, the curve of her mouth pretty, like a
cowrie shell.

*Come, sit beside me, I've missed you. Such a busy
boy.*

(No:

I won't I don't know any of this

None of it is true   )

Whit snapped out of the reverie with a nervous jerking of his outstretched legs, having started to free-fall
but able to put on the airbrakes before it went too far.

Arn, watching him, said, a stitch of amusement at
one corner of his mouth, "Fall out of the plane without
your parachute on?"

Whit, dry-throated, said, "Yeah."

"Happens to me all the time."

Whit searched the sky for an afterimage of loving

blue eyes and shuddered again. The day was clear with noon at hand, he saw only a suggestion of clouds in the northeast, an area of the sky that looked as if it had been scoured to bone-dry whiteness by a wire brush. The dogs were lying down after their meal, drowsing slackly in the sun. Arn used a toothpick, tossed it away, took another from his shirt pocket. Whit saw a dragonfly with some of the luminosity of mother-of-pearl at the level of his eyes, and when it flicked away there was a red-tailed hawk soaring just above the pinnacles of the dead trees standing in vague still water in the marsh.

He was nodding off again when the hounds began to stir and whine and then to bark mournfully. Whit looked up, mildly startled. Nothing had changed, as far as he could make out, but the dogs were on their feet and bristling, uneasy, not oriented to anything visible, not all facing in the same direction.

He started to get up, but Arn reached out and pulled him down again.

"Hold it."

"What's wrong?"

"Don't know yet." He picked up his rifle and cocked it with a callused thumb, looking around carefully, maintaining a low profile below the windfall. They were on open ground with only a scattering of thin trees anywhere near them, no places of concealment within fifty yards.

"Bear?"

"That's not a bear alert they're givin'; nor hog. But tushers, unless they've gone off in the head, sleep days and forage nights."

"What, then?"

"Somethin' the dogs sense but we can't."

Arn seemed satisfied with this interpretation of their

behavior, and was motionless, without dropping his guard or taking his finger off the trigger of his Winchester. He watched his dogs, who also held their ground but with unnerved quiverings, glancing around at him with humid, unhappy eyes.

"How long are we going to wait?"

"I think I know what it is. We'll just wait till it happens, too dangerous to move now."

"Until what happens?"

Arn said testily, "You'll know for certain when you see it, and I won't have to waste words tryin' to half-ass describe it for you."

More time passed. The hounds whimpered and moaned. Whit was looking at a hawk, maybe the same one he'd seen earlier over the marshes, when everything in his field of vision moved. It was as if the sky and the mountains and the trees in the middle distance were all exacting reflections in a two-faced mirror mounted on a swivel, and the mirror had suddenly flipped 180 degrees to its magnifying twin, warping everything so hugely out of proportion that it seemed a nonsense blur of dark-hued elliptical shapes and flashing blueness turbulent as a monster-haunted sea. The eye could take in nothing but confusion, the mind balked; then the mirror reversed on the instant and the image regained its true, placid perspective, even as to the accurate placement of the low-flying raptor. And the mind balked again because from the clear sky a bolt of lightning carved its way earthward with the slow violence of a magical tree taking root.

The lightning filling the sky was too hot and close to look at for long. Whit lowered his head, unconsciously pressing back against the windfall, expecting a painful crack of thunder, like a tooth breaking in his clenched jaw, to accompany the bolt. But all he heard was the baying of the hounds. When they subsided he opened his eyes on pacified, unburnt blue and looked at Arn, who grinned tensely at him.

"Some place, huh?"

"What *was* that?"

Arn shrugged. "It's happened to me a couple of times before. Feels like you've took leave of your senses, don't it? But that's only the first part. There's more to come."

"What?"

"God only knows. Maybe we better get movin' now."

Within a quarter of an hour they were deep in the woods again, but the going was less rugged than Whit had anticipated. They made their way along a ridge above a deep wide ravine in which he could hear but only occasionally see, in a sear of light, the Cat Brier River pouring over ledges. The climb took them through a narrow parklike stand of butternut, oak, and rock elm; these were all nearly mature trees, at least forty years old, but smaller than many others nearby, limited in their growth by a lack of topsoil. There were large expanses of bare split rock on which nothing grew but scabby lichens. Whit saw evidence that the rock had been shaped and leveled by tools; pickax marks were everywhere, barely eroded by time.

"The spur line ran this way," he said.

Arn paused and pushed his hat back. "This is a natural grade through here. About three-quarters of a mile on up there was a nine-hundred-foot wooden trestle that carried the line across the river at Ellijay Gap. It's long gone. Dig down a couple feet anywhere beyond the treeline, you'll find roadbed and probably some rusted rails." He mopped his hot forehead with a handkerchief and stuffed it back into his hip pocket. "Let's make a little detour, want to show you somethin'."

His dogs stayed on the ridge; Arn led Whit partway down into the ravine, where it was shadier, leafier, flushed with violets; the trees were mostly beeches. In a little slanted cove crisscrossed by mossy windfalls rotting into the muggy earth and surrounded by ground cover of fern, ladyslipper, and goldenseal, Arn squatted near a patch of ground that looked recently and haphazardly dug up. Whit saw dried, dying leaves and odd-looking, immature roots. Arn smiled grimly as he picked through the ravaged plants.

"Good 'sang patch is hard to find anymore. I've been gettin' thirty-five, close to forty dollars a pound out of this patch year after year. Sold the 'sang to an old Greek who comes around in the fall. This is maybe twelve hundred bucks out of my pocket. You might say somebody's decided to take economic sanctions again' me."

"Jacob Schwarzman?"

"No. Don't believe so. He ain't good enough to spy on me in these woods. Hardly anybody is. That is, unless they got wings and roost in the tall trees."

Arn held up a knobby, twisted root with stubby appendages, pale and humanoid in appearance.

"Ginseng?" Whit asked him. He knew the powdered root was highly prized, particularly in the Orient, as a rejuvenator.

"Yeah. Used to be plenty of it growin' all over the Smokies, but the Indians dug it for trade and 'sang hunters gradually cleaned out these woods, until it got to the point where they were afraid to come here anymore. I had me this patch, and one not far from here I seeded myself. Takes about seven years for wild 'sang to grow good roots that the traders will pay top dollar for. And you can't be greedy. You got to leave the young plants alone and grub your roots only once a year, in the fall when the berries are ripe. Well—'' He stood up, throwing the dead plant aside. ''When I found this patch all tore up, few days ago, I made sure if anybody tried to do the same to my other patch, he'd have cause to regret it. Maybe it's time to get on over to the other side of the ridge and find out if—''

The hounds they had left behind began baying urgently, distress calls; even Whit, who hadn't been around dogs much in his life, could tell that they were frightened. Arn was already running, scrambling up the dark slope toward open ground. Whit followed.

By the time the men reached the stony ridge line the hounds had scattered. Arn took a fast look around, rifle cocked and held across his chest, but he saw and heard nothing except for an unusual number of birds flocking loudly out of the high branches of trees in their vicinity. He roared in displeasure at two of his hounds, who apparently had disappeared into the undergrowth. Only the black-and-tan, Bocephus, stood his ground nervously, sleek head aimed high, throat taut from baying. Arn walked slowly toward the dog, puzzled, talking to him. Whit stayed back to catch his breath, looking up the ridge. All the leaves were stirring, as if in a quickened breeze, the poplars flashing silver undersides, forecasting a storm. But he saw nothing threatening in the sky, which was still a calm, unclouded blue.

Whit turned to Arn, who was standing in front of his rigid dog, trying to understand what was bothering him. Bocephus, quivering from effort, looked apologetically at him but wouldn't stop his tight-throated hoarse baying.

''What do you think is—''

Arn couldn't have heard him; Whit's voice was covered by the screaming of a train whistle, the bellow of exhausts.

The ridge of granite on which they were standing trembled like a rickety boardwalk above heavy surf. Whit looked up and into the heart of the woods and saw a spouted tree of black smoke thick as lambswool at the top of its plume, saw a locomotive that hadn't been there two seconds ago, plunging at breakaway speed downhill, smashing large trees in its path, easily uprooting others with a cow-catcher like an outthrust angry iron jaw. It was a black Mikado locomotive with tender, one of the old coal-hauling behemoths, weighing well over one hundred tons. It had polished brass trim, a red-and-gold emblem of the Shenandoah and Texas Railroad mounted on the rivet-studded, circular boiler jacket beneath the headlamp. The cylinder cocks were open and jetting steam hot enough to melt flesh from bone. Trackless but carving a path through time, the Mikado, more than eighteen feet from the ground to the rim of its stack, remained upright but dragged its pilot, or cowcatcher, as it broke through the treeline. The big spoked driver wheels, eight of them, were locked and now luridly screeching on bedrock, throwing up the sparks of a volcano. It headed for certain destruction in the deep ravine. Whit stood squarely in its path, with the passivity of an awed child, of the fatally thunderstruck. His head cleaned out, brainless to the undercurve of naked skull. His blood had leapt once and frozen, his flesh was dumb as a mummy's. In wartime he had survived by virtue of his instinct for the unexpected. But he had no ingrained defense against the utterly absurd, the meaninglessly horrific.

Arn, who was better-conditioned emotionally to the surprises Wildwood had to offer, dropped his rifle and leapt up the ridge toward Whit, hitting him from behind and driving them both out of the way of the locomotive—which by then loomed in his line of sight as big as a house—and over the ridge's edge, horizontal steam surging at his thinly clad heels as he fell, an uncomfortably long way, through space.

Arn got his breath back and collected his scattered wits in a thicket, not in a hurry to move, attentive to his body as feeling returned, alert for steadily worsening, throbbing pain that would mean big trouble. He knew right away that he had not been scalded. He'd spilled and sprawled down the slope of the ravine, Whit falling away in a different direction, lying silently somewhere out of sight now. About all that Arn heard was the death wheezing of the huge locomotive, the slowing expiration of boiler steam. There was a stench of engine oil in the air, of brakeshoe and coal smoke that still hovered. If the firebox had ruptured, sowing the underbrush with glowing anthracite, a fire was probable; but he couldn't distinguish woodsmoke, or hear the crackle of flames eating through the ravine in his direction. The locomotive undoubtedly had chewed a broad path into the ravine to the river's edge. The birds had returned, squirrels chattered and scolded. No danger in that. He realized he must have lain stunned, legs tangled in briers, for two or three minutes.

He lifted bloodied hands (the blood welling slowly if at all, not pumping scarlet from a wrist broken and bone-slit) and felt himself as if he were a lover (no stob through the groin or gut, rib cage whole). His head pivoted grittily, he flexed the muscles of his back. Soreness, but not binding pain. That encouraged him to sit up, legs in a pinching and prick of branches, blackberry bramble. Could've been far worse luck, he might have gone in headfirst to have an eye extracted on a needle-tipped green thorn. He freed himself, trying not to rip his pants. More blood on his bare ankles, just scratches. He was still wearing both of his moccasins.

He began to feel almost cheerful about the narrow escape, and was further cheered to see lank-eared Bocephus poke his head over a windfall, whining at him.

"Bo, you good-lookin' bastard! Hie yourself over here."

With his dog he searched the area into which he'd fallen. He found his hat but did not see Whit Bowers anywhere. Was it possible he'd rebounded from a limber sapling or the ground itself into the path of the locomotive as it rolled over and over downhill? If that had been his fate, there might be so little left to find, even Bocephus would overlook the remains. There was a slashed trail broad as a highway from the top of the ridge, steamed and rolled so flat and slick he couldn't keep his footing while crossing it. He looked for a bit of clothing, a scatter of mincemeat and bone drawing tell-tale flies. But there was no sign of Whit, even in this reduced state. So he followed the trail downhill, around heaps of glittering coal spilled from the overturned tender; a good deal of scrap had been ripped loose from the locomotive, mostly piping and pumps. Leaves overhanging the path of destruction were gritty from soot or thickly dripped oil onto his hat and shirt.

The locomotive was lying on its side in a channel of the river, nearly damming the cold flow. Two saplings caught in the grate of the twisted cow-catcher waved gently in the breeze that had dissipated most of the steam from the exploded boiler. Water poured through the cab and a body bobbed inside: he saw a head, hairless, so well cooked and softened by steam, everything but the skullbone had turned to the consistency of calf's-foot jelly. Bright red handkerchief, trainman's brass-buttoned overalls, a shirt unstitched at the shoulder, sleeve and arm both gone, washed, he assumed, downstream. The dead man had been the hogger or maybe the fireman; but if there was another body sunk in the watery cab, Arn didn't care to see it now. He cleaned the blood off his hands in the river, made his way back uphill with Bocephus on the scent of somebody or something and forging ahead in scrabbling strides. Up on the ridge line he barked sharply, once, and Arn, hurrying, saw that Bo had located Colonel Bowers. Who, apparently, had crawled out of whatever cushioning thicket he'd fallen into and made his way up the slope, collapsing in the sun just where the wheels of the locomotive had deeply etched the granite.

Whit was conscious but slow in his movements. He reached for the hound's collar and tried to hold on. There was a gash on his forehead near the left temple, a bit of leaf stuck to the coagulating blood. His eyes, when Arn rolled him over on his back, were like milky agate.

"Hey, Colonel. *Whit*."

"What . . . happened?"

"Nearly got ourselves run over by a damned ole train."

Whit made a face of pain.

"By . . . what?"

Arn said sharply, "Where you at, Colonel? Normandy? Holland?"

"No. Wildwood."

"What year is it?"

"Nineteen . . . fifty-eight."

"Did you get drunk last night with yours truly?"

"Damned if I . . . didn't."

"Good so far. You remember stoppin' for lunch little while ago?"

"Uh-huh. Then the sky—Jesus! Billowing like a sail . . . and the lightning . . . that just came out of nowhere."

"Which it is apt to do, up close to the Tormentor. Reckon everythin's ducky. But let's get you on your feet, too hot lyin' here."

Whit tried, but he couldn't stand unaided. Arn let him slump to a sitting position.

"Let me have a look at your head." Arn carefully explored the area around the cut, but there wasn't much swelling, and the bone seemed intact underneath. Concussion, he thought. Maybe only a mild one, but there was no use asking the colonel to go anywhere under his own power for the time being. Give him a little water (his lips were dry to cracking), prop him in the shade. If blood was slowly leaking in Whit's brain, Arn would see signs of it before long. Maybe he should just try to pack him out now, better safe than sorry; but Arn knew he wasn't up to carrying a man for more than eight hours, retracing the difficult way they had come; and if Whit had a brain hemmorhage going, he'd be delivering a dead man to the hospital anyway.

"How're you feelin'?"

"Not too bad. A little woozy." His eyes seemed clearer; Arn was encouraged.

"You'll be okay by and by. Let's go sit in some shade now, just get your arm around my shoulder here, raise on up."

"Where are the rest of your dogs, Arn?"

"Aw, turned tail and run just before the locomotive came crashin' through here. They could be halfway home by now."

"There was a . . . locomotive . . . here."

"You remember?"

"I can smell it."

"Yeah, well, it's still here, down in the river. I'll show it to you later."

"Where did it come from?"

"Nineteen sixteen," Arn said. And he half-carried Whit into the woods, where it was pleasantly shadowed if no cooler, and softer to sit. He made Whit comfortable, with his back against a smoothly barked tree. Whit stared off into the distance, his body relaxed but his mind, behind his eyes, a block of granite. He accepted a drink from Arn's water jar. He licked his lips, moistening them.

"Nineteen sixteen?" he said with an uncomprehending grimace.

"I don't have no better explanation," Arn said reasonably. He hunkered down to look over his rifle, which he was afraid he'd damaged when he dropped it. He unloaded the Winchester, dry-snapped the hammer, and found the action to be in good working order. He sighted along the barrel to make sure it was straight. Then he loaded the rifle again.

"I'm gonna leave Bo here with you for company, go check on somethin' since we've got time to spare. I don't aim to be gone long, an hour at the most. You take it easy. Sip that water just a little bit at a time."

"Yeah," Whit said, still staring, puzzled, down the ridge. "I'll be all right. Let me get my bearings, try to . . . think about this."

Arn nodded. He left his pack but took his sheath knife and Winchester with him.

For fifteen minutes he walked steadily in a northwesterly direction, uphill, following an easy line of ascent where once there had been a wagon road from the spur line. The ridge he climbed was rounded and segmented, like a turtle's shell, into sparsely wooded middens. He came to a bluff where approximately a third of the ridge (limestone, a type of rock rare in the Smokies) had been quarried, leaving a pit partly filled with water sixty feet straight down. Nothing remained of the machinery that had lifted massive blocks to wagons drawn by a triple hitch of mules except a single big cogwheel, its rusted imprint on a vertical white slab just above the pool.

The quarry, with a shadowless squared emerald at its heart, looked pretty enough, and peaceful, but he knew it to be a hellhole of rattlers and, sometimes, an unidentifiable miasma that rose at night like the poisoned spirits of the betrayed and fitful dead, potent enough to knock nightfliers out of the sky overhead.

From the top of the bluff he heard the first weak, intermittent cries for help coming from a hidden vale north of the quarry.

There was fear in her voice. She sounded as if she had been strung up for a long time: maybe overnight. Arn took a deep breath and, unsmiling, his pulse rapid with anticipation, he continued on, rifle cocked in his right hand, left hand near the knife on his belt. The fact that it was a woman gave him no pleasure or sense of superiority in this matter. He walked down the other side of the ridge in golden light and abruptly entered into a ravine dark as a cellar, made his way cautiously tree to tree for several hundred yards, through deep shade of basswood and beech to the ginseng patch he'd booby-trapped.

Moving in this manner, it was more than a quarter of an hour before he could get a good look at her.

Better to be very very slow than quickly dead.

She was crying helplessly, pitying herself, probably in pain from having been hung headdown by one ankle: he wondered if this inversion had resulted in damaging stress on her lightweight butterfly's wings.

It had been easy for him to rig several snares, lengths of tough but supple vine snaking invisibly beneath the lush ground cover around his ginseng patch, the snares triggered like mousetraps. The thin long branches of the beech trees overhead looked much alike; there were hundreds of them, but only four had been carefully shaped to the maximum tension required to snatch a full-grown man several feet off the ground once he stepped into a noose and released the trigger. —Or, in this case, the butterfly girl, who (he had recently estimated) couldn't weigh more than ninety pounds. Little bitty thing, but womanly: her body, revealed in a spangled pattern of trembling mote-filled light and leaf-toothed shadow, glistening from perspiration, the beautiful wings, inky at the edges but thinning to a hot transparency like gauze about to blaze, drooping, useless to her now, a burden.

He felt a trifle sorry for her, but native caution held him back.

He watched her twist slowly beneath the noose, sobbing, moaning miserably, her hair, frazzled from humidity (it was rooster-comb red hair, with plaits of strawberry blond), falling straight down and half the length of her body, like a fiery wick dipped in a well of incendiary sunlight. The bull's-eye nipples of her breasts glowed, as if from the heat of her exertions. Her throat and brow were deeply flushed.

So there was his prize. To claim her, all he had to do was expose himself to the razor edge of the goatman's ax—because, the longer he studied the comely creature dangling over his 'sang patch like an especially well-drawn illustration from a children's book of faery, the more certain he felt that this was all too good to be true. She hadn't come here alone. She and her kind knew his Wildwood hangouts pretty thoroughly; he didn't doubt that he had been spotted earlier in the day with Whit Bowers. And he'd had a hunch all along that they were under surveillance, what had he said about having wings and roosting in tall trees? He'd been thinking then of the butterfly girl, who could fly impressively high, he knew that already . . . so they had rigged a trap of their own, difficult for her, as bait, but convincing. They had anticipated that he would be overeager and stupid at the sight of her, forgetting everything else in his hurry to cut her down and carry her off. Over one shoulder, because she wouldn't be able to walk very far in these woods without tearing her wings, no matter how carefully folded, to tatters.

Thus encumbered, he would be easy prey for the goatman.

He looked for likely hiding places, but that was a futile exercise: there were just too many. The goatman could be stretched out lean as a mantis in a shadowy tree overhead, blending fully with the darkness except for half-shut eyes. Or crouched deep in a thicket. Too bad he hadn't brought Bocephus along, Arn thought regretfully, to sniff the nigger out. But he still wasn't of a mind to just turn around and leave her, tantalizingly within reach again.

He coveted the butterfly girl. He was smitten with her uniqueness, her freakish beauty. Sex had something to do with it, but he most wanted what he'd never demanded of another woman—to own her. The hell with what anyone else might say, including Faren.

The way to work it, he reasoned, was to act almost as dumb as they expected, until he flushed the goatman from cover and killed him. He now had a good idea of how to accomplish that.

With his rifle ready and his knife in his left hand and resting against his chest where it couldn't be got at easily, he walked into the clearing, not moving his head much, hat brim pulled down so no one could see where he was looking at any given moment. Setting his feet down with care, most concerned about stepping into a trap like the one with which he'd grabbed the butterfly girl: they might have relocated his remaining snares, or fixed up a deadlier surprise of their own. His back was unprotected, which bothered him; but he just had to trust the sharpness of his ears. He needed a really firm grip on himself right now, but he was distracted by a tickle of the ludicrous, inspired by the winged girl hanging there, too much like a picture show for him to maintain his concentration as he damned well knew he ought to. Arn went to the movies with Faren only because he liked the cartoons, most of them anyway: he always called ahead to be sure they weren't going to show him some shit like singing mice or Casper the Friendly Ghost, but he'd stay over every time to see the Road Runner twice, and laugh all the way home recalling the tribulations of Wile E. Coyote, when one of his elaborate schemes to trap that hot-footed bird (bee-beeeeeep!) blew up in his crooked tufted face. Hell of a thing to be thinking about right now, that dumb fucking coyote . . .

He fully expected the girl to start screaming as soon as she became aware of him, to distract him and cover any slight noises the goatman might make as he readied himself to attack. But she was quiet, even after a frightened convulsive jerking of her body that set her to twirling almost full circle. It had to hurt: her right ankle, where the thong-tough vine gripped it, was skinned bloody raw. But she only sobbed weakly and gasped for breath.

Now Arn had her well covered with his rifle and could smile, though he didn't stop moving, circling sideways but changing direction unpredictably, the Winchester rifle barrel in the crook of his left arm, muzzle never more than eighteen inches from the perfectly round, taut bulge of her navel. Even if the goatman was so handy with his ax he could split Arn's skull from twenty feet with a whirling throw, the girl was sure to die as well, her belly blown out.

A stand-off, for now.

Her upside-down eyes were fixed on him.

"Will you cut the vine, sir?" she pleaded. Her accent was unmistakably mick, but he might have guessed, because of her overall rosy coloring and the tan freckles on the raised, slightly sharp bridge of her nose.

When he didn't speak or alter his smile she jerked again, frantically, hurting herself needlessly; her inflated nearly fleshless ribs looked fragile as paper lanterns.

"Would you be shooting me then? Have I no time to pray to the Virgin's Son?"

"Girl, I don't mean you no harm at all."

Her tears flowed, wetting her short sandy-red lashes and then her peaked hairline. Her free leg flexed at the knee. She had long toes for such a small girl. With prehensile strength they grasped the vine where it had crossed her right instep as she attempted to take some of the weight off her other, cramped leg.

"Then for pity's sake release me—let me go! It's suffering I am."

Arn stopped moving, perhaps slightly lulled by his fascination with her. He said, "I can see it ain't been much fun for you. What's your name, girl?"

"My name is—Josie Raftery."

"Where'd you come from?"

"Ireland. Dun Laoghaire."

"I mean today."

"I'm after thinking you already know."

"Yeah. Do you know who I am?"

"Indeed I do. *God and Sweet Mary, will you kindly cut me down?*"

"Where'd you get them pretty wings, Josie?"

"I tried them on—sir; the next thing I knew, they—were mine for keeps."

He nodded. "Do you know what I want, Josie?"

"Whatever it is—get on with it! But don't—leave me like this."

"I want you to call the goatman out. I want him where I can see him."

"Taharqa? But he's not here—I've not seen him all this day long."

"Josie Raftery, I'll bet you're sharp a-plenty, but you got to realize I ain't no dunce myself. You and that nigger're never far from each other; he looks after you, don't he?"

"I look after—meself," she said in a huskier voice and with a frown of indignation. Then she fell into despair again. "Oh, God. Sweet Jaysus! I cannot endure—much more of this."

"You won't call him out?"

"I swear to you, sir—I do not *know* where Taharqa is!"

Arn said in a low voice, "Then I reckon I got to do somethin' I'd as leave not do, just to make sure you're tellin' me the truth."

He reversed his rifle and placed the stock end against one of her hips, turned her in a circle. As her bare buttocks appeared he quickly slashed one cheek with the knife. Not cutting her deeply—he only wanted blood to flow, visible from a distance and inviting the goatman's rage, a sudden, fatally wrong move on his part. Josie gasped, but she hadn't seen the knife in his hand flicking toward her; and the blade was so sharp she scarcely felt the shallow diagonal cut, six inches long, where the cheek was fullest, didn't know what he'd done until blood began rolling down the middle of her back, and she smelled it.

"You said you wouldn't hurt me! You *are* a fearful villain! And why not cut me throat, too, have done with all your mayhem! Saints of glory preserve me!"

Arn ignored her; he was looking around the clearing, ready with his rifle and knife for the attack he was sure must now come. But nothing rustled in the bushes except some peeping birds and chipmunks; there was no sudden shaking of tree branches as the goatman plunged to the ground.

Nearly five minutes passed. Flies came to the blood, which slowly dried, darkening the streak; but the goatman did not appear. Either he owned better control than Arn had given him credit for, which made him all the more dangerous, or the girl simply hadn't been lying.

Arn felt grimmer, and shabby in his purpose.

Her eyes were closed now, her breathing had slowed,

there was a tinge of blue to her lips that worried him even as he wondered if a scar would be traceable where he had struck.

"Josie!"

Her wetted lashes fluttered, her lips parted, he saw her tongue and a little foam between not-quite-regular teeth, but she didn't utter a sound.

He let go of his rifle then, encircled her slippery waist with one arm, and hacked the vine in two. He lowered her carefully, setting her feet on the ground, but her ankles turned and she sagged against him, breathing in shallow gusts. The multicolored scales of her wings felt and looked like fine needlepoint; they were covered with a thin film of iridescent dust that stained the fingertips. He knew he had to be careful, the wings would rend easily, and might not heal as fast as flesh, if they healed at all. Eventually butterflies just wore out their wings, didn't they? As the blood drained rapidly from her head she fainted with a tremulous sigh.

Arn put Josie Raftery down on her side in a bed of birds' foot violets and phlox and, while staying alert for surprises, pondered what to do with her.

She came around after a few minutes and a nudge of his foot against the side of her throat, stirring with painful little noises, blinking her eyes until she was able to focus on him.

"It's dying of a demon thirst I am," she complained.

Arn knew there was a spring and a pool only a few minutes away. He sheathed his knife and kneeled, putting an arm around Josie's waist again, then tilted her forward over his left shoulder. He lifted her easily.

"Be still now, and don't give me no trouble," he cautioned; but Josie lay unresisting in his grasp on his wide shoulder. He adjusted her position until he had the balance just right, his left hand spread in the blood-tacky hollow of her back. Her wings were tamely folded, at a diagonal and resting against his hat brim. His peripheral vision was partially blocked, although a little of the sun's light filtered through the wings as if through loosely woven windowshades. The noose of vine remained around her sorely chafed ankle. He carried her out of the clearing to the west, rifle down along his right side, the worn stock in his armpit, finger on the trigger. Even so he was vulnerable as long as he carried the girl. But he lacked that well-honed sense of imminent danger, the instinct that he was observed. The farther he walked, the more secure he felt, convinced that he and Josie were alone.

"What were you doin' in my 'sang patch?" he asked her.

"There's so little of it to be found anymore, and we need the tonic. There has been a lot of sickness. It was a harsh winter, sir. Several of us died."

"Sorry to hear it," Arn muttered, moving as carefully as he knew how, but still rubbing her wings occasionally against low sharply pronged branches. She tensed in his grasp each time: the danger of torn wings alarmed her. He understood; what would she be without them? A doomed cripple.

"Oh, be right careful, won't you?"

"We're just about there, Josie."

Almost no sun leaked into the small glade where the spring bubbled from a cleft between stairstep levels of rock into a fern-bordered pool about twelve feet wide. He put her down at the pool's edge and told her to keep still, although she looked with longing at the clear flowing water.

"Hold it a minute."

Arn glanced up at the tenting of leaves on interlaced branches not far above their heads, glowing like a green-house roof. Nowhere she could go, he decided, if she took a notion to spread her wings.

He pulled his knife and cut the noose from her ankle. There were black specks of gnats like dirt in the still-suppurating wound.

"After you have your drink you better soak that ankle," he advised her. "Do you need any help?"

"No." Josie rolled quickly onto her stomach, tossed her long streaky hair back over her shoulders, wiggled a little through the fern until she could lower her mouth to the surface of the pool and drink. Then she bathed her heated face, holding her head half under the water for a very long time. When she lifted and shook her head vigorously her teeth sparkled, her sea-green eyes were magnified by waterdrops and almost blissful in their expression.

Arn wanted water himself, but he preferred keeping his eyes on her at all times. Josie lifted herself to a sitting position, wincing at the rub of fern on the cut cheek. She put her feet together and lowered them into the pool until the water was above her knees. She had spread her wings for balance; they wavered delicately, yielding glints of gold where the sun struck unsteadily through them. She sighed. Arn pulled his handkerchief from his back pocket and mopped his face; it was stuffy in this glade.

"And what will you do with me now?" Josie asked him.

"Take you home with me, girl."

"No!"

"What do you want to do, spend the rest of your life with a bunch of damned Walkouts?"

"Damned? Yes—through no fault of ours! Why should you hate us so? And want to kill us? We've done no harm; and our lives are difficult enough as it is."

"Look: the hawkman—well, that was a long time ago, I don't think I—if I had it to do over—"

He had no inkling she could move so quickly, almost with the speed of a hummingbird. One moment she was soaking her legs in the pool, the next she had flitted eight feet in the air, wings flung wide and clinging to the sultry, unmoving air; and of course (he realized too late), lacking arms and hands, she would have become expert in the use of her legs and, particularly, her long-boned feet and deft toes. He barely had a glimpse of the green smudgy waterrock she had fished from the bottom of the pool before she did a kind of sideways flip, one leg coming up in a ferociously well-aimed cross-kick, the rock chunking him with great force on the right side of his head between the eye and the ear. It knocked him down but not out, vision going as if a line to a lamp had been cut. He lost his grip on his rifle. As he was trying to pick it up she was on him again; in a dark flutter of rage she brought the rock down resoundingly on his forehead. White light burst behind his eyes, he bit his tongue as he thrashed on the ground. But he couldn't get up, and when he tried to grab her his clumsy hand slipped from a wet shinbone.

The sight of his good eye cleared long enough for him to glimpse the fierceness of her puckered brow, her jade glower, but he didn't see the rock coming as she rolled adroitly to one side again.

Arn barely heard the smack of the rock against thinly fleshed bone as he rolled toward the pool. And he was too far gone in weighted darkness to feel much distress as he sank into the pool, incapable of reacting even when water gushed down his throat.

Whit, dozing where Arn had left him on the ridge a brisk half hour's walk away from the spring in the glade, heard Bocephus growl at his side, and he opened his eyes as the hound got stiffly to its feet. Bo's eyes were hotly rimmed and glaring at something Whit couldn't see.

He put a steadying hand on Bo's flank and started to rise himself.

Something round, hard, and polished flashed out of the woods from a dozen yards away and struck the dog on the cleft bone between the eyes. Bocephus went down in a backward heap and lay motionless at Whit's feet.

Whit looked in disbelief at the orange-striped croquet ball that had rebounded into the root-crotch of a tree, then saw movement in dusky shade that claimed his full attention.

A tall and well-muscled creature walked toward him on two legs. He saw the curly head of a goat—thickly wrinkled devil horns, and unfriendly amber eyes. It could not be what he first wanted to believe, a realistically styled mask: the prim little chin and narrow mouth moved in a sideways, chewing motion; there was sinister life in the eyes. The rest of the creature was a man, with bitter-chocolate skin. It wore a deerskin loincloth and carried, in one hand, a short ax with a curved blade that glared in a sunspot.

In its other hand Whit saw Arn Rutledge's campaign-style hat, a part of the front brim darkly stained, as if dipped in ink.

Or:

Whit wasted no more time in speculation. The goatman had lengthened its stride as it approached, and Whit was defenseless against the ax it carried so purposefully.

Leaving his pack behind, Whit went running through the trees up the ridge, leaping windfalls, twisting through crinkly brush, putting as much distance between himself and the goatman as he could.

Stifling laughter as he ran, not fear.

He would get away, as he always had. The goatman could not catch him.

He was too quick, and he had too many hiding places, and as soon as the chase became tiring, the initial flush of exhilaration subsided, he would crawl into one of his woodsy sanctuaries—like the yellow birch tree with the hollow beneath its standing roots. The birch had first taken root on a decaying stump, the roots lengthening and creeping down into the earth as the stump beneath the tree slowly rotted away. Now the birch was full-grown but raised on its many broad roots three feet above the ground, forming a cozy boy-size cave no one knew about but him.

All he had to do, when Taharqa came near, searching for him, was be very still with his hands over his mouth, holding back nervous glee.

But he was just a little lost right now, he couldn't be sure where the birch was standing in these woods. Maybe it was higher up, where the park began. It had been a long time since their last outing. He knew he must continue to run, or the pretense of danger would fade. The game wouldn't be fun any-more. Run and run and run—but he was tireless today.

He had a small boy's stamina and a good lead on the Ethiopian.

And no matter how close Taharqa came, he always won the chase.

— Chapter Nineteen —

Wildwood, January 1909

THE architect James B. Travers, mounted on his fine chestnut gelding, Cyclops, paused on his return from a solitary morning ride, mustache iced to the root of his nose, and looked at the chateau revealed half formed to him within a chrysalis of frozen fog.

In his most depressed moods—and he was riding with one of them this morning, a creature of the spirit wearing a black executioner's mask—he was still capable of being aroused, astonished by the beauty of what he had created, beginning (could it be seven years ago?) with some penciled lines on a roll of draftsman's paper. The mountainous setting, the ice and fog and pale wintering sun, provided a touch of the fabulous, of unearthly romance, to what was solid, rational, well proportioned. Knowing that his vision had belonged from its inception to a man he had come to despise and at times wished to horse-whip scarcely clouded Travers's passion for the chateau. Some of the magnificent palaces of Europe had been commissioned and inhabited by royal fools and pasty-faced misfits, long vanished from the world and of interest only to scholars, while those masterpieces in which they had so fleetingly dwelled serenely survived the centuries, testifying to the genius of men like Jules Hardouin-Mansart and Philibert Delorme.

The same, he knew, would be true of Wildwood. If only his patience lasted, and the complications of his love for Sibby Langford did not destroy them both before the chateau could be completed.

For much of the summer and fall the lovers had enjoyed peace and contentment previously unavailable to them. Edgar Langford had been abroad during this time, on an arduous expedition to the Middle East which, his doctor had warned, might prove fatal to him. But Edgar was possessed by a desire for vindication. His bid to be recognized as the singular authority on the civilization of Mesopotamia had been rudely rejected by his peers, who now ignored him as a half-crazed dilettante, returned his lengthy papers unread, and jeered at his theories, his purported discoveries. A technologically advanced society, with cities illuminated by electricity, whose scientists could travel through time and space as casually as they might cross an alley? Who had the power to animate inorganic matter, even as God had made man from clay? He was a disgrace, not worthy of a serious archaeologist's time. Edgar festered with resentment, his back growing drastically more crooked with each snub, and spent increasingly impressive sums attempting to substantiate his earlier findings.

In spite of his doctor's misgivings, he had not returned from Iraq, shortly after Thanksgiving, in a worsened state of health. In fact he looked better than he had for some years: straighter, windburned, sharp of eye, and energetic. Success, or triumph, was a tonic for many lingering ailments: he had brought with him yet another trainload of antiquities, and, he confided to Sibby, secrets of life and death. He was not willing to elaborate. Sibby pressed him only halfheartedly, because she shared the view of the eminent archaeologists who scorned her husband that he was, if not mad, at least seriously deluded. And she was afraid, against all reason, that there just might be some ungodly truth in what he hinted at.

Edgar had little time for her, as usual. Through the Christmas season at Wildwood he spent long hours in his caverns beneath the mountain, translating dead languages from clay tablets, performing experiments with crude machines constructed from plans found in another monarch's tomb, a spagyrist's crushed cellar . . .

James Travers reluctantly turned his chilled horse toward the Wildwood stables, dreading his return to the chateau, and the dilemma which now only desperate, repugnant action might resolve. There was, of course, another way, if he were man enough: but Sibby had forbidden him to take that initiative.

"He will kill us both."

"Your husband is many things I find despicable, but surely he is not a murderer."

"Edgar will f-find a way to make us suffer, and suffer, until we t-take our own lives. *That* would be Eh-Edgar's way."

Oh God—the heartbreak he felt, hearing her stammer again. He grieved for the timid beauty of her youth, transmuted in the menace of their affair.

Last night, despite the difficulties increased by Langford's presence at Wildwood, they had met, in the architect's apartment, in his small study concealed behind bookcases. Only here did they feel completely safe in this massive building that when finally completed would contain four hundred rooms, seventy staircases, and three quarters of a mile of hallways.

Sibby had turned him remorsefully aside after a single kiss and told him that she was pregnant.

"Good God. Are you certain?"

She had the pallor of bone china, with lusterless blue crescents beneath her eyes. "A woman—knows. It has been two months since m-my last menses. And I have been ill in the m-mornings lately—Pamela has noticed. She smiles at me in a c-conspiratorial way, although I can be sure she will not s-say a word." Pamela was Sibby's personal maid, whom she counted as a friend if not a confidante.

"But—you have had these cyclical irregularities before. And, perhaps—it's been such a dismal winter, we've all been down with a touch of pleurisy or flu—"

"James—d-darling—the simple truth is, despite our precautions, I am g-going to have your b-baby." She sobbed then, in a blood-chilling way, and collapsed in his arms.

"Have you consulted Dr. Burrough?" he asked Sibby, when he could speak.

"No! I c-couldn't! Not yet."

"And what about Edgar?" Travers's throat closed; he felt a cringing vileness, having to consider the possibility. "Since he's been back, has he—have you—"

She pressed her lips against his ear, then straightened, keeping a hand on him as if restraining an unruly animal. Measuring his temper, his recklessness. Her smile was small and cold.

"Edgar has not—p-paid his respects to me, in that manner, since his return. He is f-far too busy, I am to understand—or f-finally disinterested, after so m-many unsuccessful attempts to f-father a child."

"Then we—we must—" Words failed him; the bitterness of their perceived fate was nightshade, shriveling his tongue.

Sibby wiped a last tear from her cheek. She was as plainly dressed as a schoolmistress: dark blue tubular skirt, high-necked blouse with a starched ruffled collar. She squinted slightly these days, having read too many novels late at night by gaslight; the chateau was not yet electrified. There was something severe in the way she regarded her lover then; she looked to be in a trance of calculation, a feminine schemer with whom he was unacquainted, who shocked him.

"What *I* must d-do is have the child—Edgar's child. There is no time to lose. The baby will be m-much too early as it is."

"Sibby, no—!"

Her throat was flushed, her eyes mildly inflamed as if she burned sacredly, martyr to their years-long affair.

"I will seduce Edgar tonight."

"You cannot!"

"Why c-can't I? After all, it was *I* who seduced you."

Travers flinched from this bold assertion as from the firecracker of a whip under his nose, unable to decide if it was true.

Her small fingers tightened on his arm imploringly.

"Don't you see? There is n-no other way. But once I have done it, I will have the excuse I n-need never to sleep with him again. And then I may go on h-having you, only you, my dearest."

Never to sleep with him again.

In the stable enclosure Travers gave his horse over to

a Negro groom and thawed himself with brandy in front of a fireplace in the slate-floored office. Enough blazing logs for a funeral pyre, or so it seemed to him in his morbid, downcast mood. Had she done it by now, or was she still awaiting Edgar's return from his caverns with the eminent guest Travers had yet to meet? It was now eleven o'clock in the morning. Why, he wondered, was he permitting this? The honorable thing to do was confront the man. *I have stolen your wife's affections. She is going to bear my child. We will go away at once.*

And leave the chateau unfinished. The bulk of his commission unpaid.

What did that matter? The chateau represented seven years of his life, but he was only forty-one. He was a gifted architect. He would find work.

On the other hand, it was foolish of him to expect a gentlemanly, even a sane reaction, from Edgar Langford.

There were men you could take a woman from. And men you could not. Who, if they had the means, would go to any lengths to exact revenge.

Edgar Langford had the means. And he was already pathologically frustrated in his desire to be recognized as a seminal archaeologist.

Travers was not afraid of Langford. Nor was he reckless as a child, deliberately poking a hornet's nest with a stick.

The sexual symbolism amused him dourly.

Just reckless enough.

And apparently *coitus interruptus* left something to be desired as a means of preventing conception.

He walked outside to where a sleigh waited to take him to the chateau.

Three quarters of the outer walls of the cubiform, three-story building were in place, and despite the brutal weather, work continued indoors, seven days a week; his close attention was required sixteen hours each day. He had already wasted too much of the morning.

He looked again through his vaporous breath at the superb facade exposed to him from the level of the outlying stables: the vertical alignment of bay windows, double moldings of native limestone marking the divisions between floors, classic pilasters flanking each window, the "pepperpot" turrets at each angle of the chateau now covered in blue slate. The power, the symmetry, the Renaissance grace of his rising masterwork totally absorbed him.

The child would have Edgar Langford's name; but the chateau would forever be attributed to James B. Travers. And that, finally, was what mattered most.

Leaving it now, uncompleted, under any circumstances, would be to snuff a vital force within him—his creativity. He would leave partially crippled, and resent it ever after; in time he might resent Sibby as well, his great love, his downfall.

She was still so very young. Edgar Langford was now past fifty, beginning his declining years in chronic ill health; his family was not noted for longevity. Mother and father long dead, a brother destroyed by a stroke at the age of forty-five.

How many years did Edgar have left? Or might it be a matter of months?

He regretted the thought, but it was clear that someday he and Sibby would be together, unstigmatized; there could be time for a child to call his own.

Sibby had been right; she must do it her way.

And pray to God her husband would be fooled.

* * *

In the middle of the afternoon Travers returned from his inspection of the massive open-work staircase rising in the *corps de logis* to the unfinished oval salon which served as the construction office for the chateau. There he was introduced by Edgar Langford to their dapper and celebrated guest, the inventor Nikola Tesla, who had been commissioned to provide electricity and heat for the chateau through a revolutionary new system. Already one of Tesla's polyphase generating systems was in place in the caverns, producing five hundred horsepower from a thirty-foot interior waterfall.

The chateau, however, was to be heated and illuminated by a different type of power, solar energy: a concept Travers found difficult to envision. Tesla, a native of Yugoslavia, was fifty-two, a man of prodigious discoveries and accomplishments (and some grandiose failures as well): he had perfected alternating current and designed huge dynamos to deliver it; he had been the first to demonstrate wireless voice and musical transmission. The word *genius* seemed inadequate to describe him. A drafting table already was littered with sketches of the machine Tesla had envisioned many years ago, but lacked the resources to build. He was chronically in debt despite the patronage, at various times in his career, of such men as J. P. Morgan, George Westinghouse, and Colonel Astor, hence his involvement now with Edgar Langford. Yet the two men seemed to have a genuine rapport; Tesla exuded a respect for his latest benefactor that was more than homage to the power of his wealth.

"I am inspired by your great work here," the inventor said graciously to Travers. "A truly magnificent undertaking."

"That is most kind of you. And how large will your

machine be?'' Travers said, pondering the sketches and diagrams.

''It is easily contained in a powerhouse the size of this salon. As you see, the central core, beneath a glass roof, is a cylinder, also of thick glass, some six feet in diameter and situated on a bed made of asbestos and stone. Mirrors covered with asbestos surround the cylinder, and refract the rays of the sun into it. The cylinder at all times is to be filled with water, treated with a chemical process I do not wish to describe. It is a somewhat complicated procedure. Chemical treatment makes it easier for the water to heat and provide the steam which will in turn operate the generators.''

''And if days pass without sun?''

Tesla smiled confidently, a tall lean man who wore a dark suit that was impeccable despite the dust of the construction site, as if he radiated some invisible barrier not only to dirt in the air but to noise and confusion.

''I shall soon perfect batteries capable of storing at least a year's supply of electricity—or it could last for a generation, if frugally dispensed. There you have it: clean, inexpensive power. My solar engine, the proto-type of which we will build here, will someday replace every other wasteful source of heat, light, and, I have no doubt, motive power.''

''How is heat to be disseminated?''

''Hot water will be pumped through valvular conduits of copper, controlled by flow meters of my design; the conduits will be surrounded by numerous wafer-thin vanes, also of copper, and covered by inconspicuous metal moldings at floor level. Radiated heat: smokeless, odorless, safe.''

''That is ingenious.''

"And installation will require almost no alteration of your existing plans, which already provide for the passage of interior plumbing."

They dressed for dinner that night, Travers and the inventor in white tie. Tesla also wore a sash with a starburst decoration upon it, the Order of St. Sava from the king of Serbia. Their host, seated where he would benefit most from the heat of the chimney piece that occupied all of one wall in the dining hall, wore a red silk toga trimmed in gold. Sibby had appeared in an unadorned aquamarine gown: she had been informed of one of their esteemed guest's many phobias. He disliked jewelry, particularly pearls, on the female form.

Tesla was a confirmed bachelor, although it was said many women, among them the daughter of J. P. Morgan, had been or were still in love with him. He had great personal attractiveness: six feet six inches in height, with a wedge-shaped, aristocratic face, high Slavic cheekbones, eyes that could be blue or a misted gray depending on the intensity of his thoughts. He was a man of such formidable intellect he sometimes appeared to be in a feverish drowse of contemplation, drifting away unexpectedly from the company he was keeping, steepling his abnormally long thumbs and fingers as some vision of technology absorbed him. In addition to Serbo-Croat he spoke eight languages with scarcely a trace of an accent, was an epicure and connoisseur of vintages; he was fascinating, even outrageous, in conversation, particularly when involved in explanations of his life's work and his fantastic predictions for the future: robots that would do the work of servants and common laborers; wireless communications with the inhabitants of

Mars. (Such inhabitants, Tesla asserted, were a "statistical certainty.")

Sibby had been quiet at first, and Travers recognized in her symptoms of great tension, although the glances she briefly directed to him gave no indication that anything sexual had recently occurred between her and her husband. Travers, overtired, felt out of sorts and imperiled by inaction. There was, across Sibby's bland face, a barely perceived but disturbing something, like a crack beginning in a priceless vase. Yet when she spoke, her stammer was reasonably under control; she was obviously charmed by the great Tesla.

"Is it true, as I h-have heard, that you once precipitated an earthquake, in the h-heart of New York City?"

"Quite true."

"And what m-monstrous machine was involved in your experiment?"

Tesla smiled ironically, and held up a pocket watch of modest size.

"The 'monstrous machine,' my dear Mrs. Langford, was an electromechanical oscillator no larger than my timepiece. I attached it to an iron pillar of my loft building, which, although I did not know it at the time, was based in the bedrock beneath the cellar. The tiny vibrations of the little oscillator, no one of which would awaken a sleeping baby, gradually built into a force that reverberated throughout the neighborhoods surrounding my loft. Entire buildings shook to their foundations, and windows were shattered; the poor Italians and Chinamen rushed into the streets, convinced their doom was at hand. By then I was aware of a dangerous vibration in the floor beneath my feet, and, although I was oblivious to the turmoil outside, promptly smashed the oscillator with a sledgehammer."

"And if you h-had not done so?"

Tesla replaced the watch with a flourish.

"Ah, then. I'm afraid I would have succeeded in destroying, utterly, the city I most love in all the world. The Waldorf-Astoria, my favorite hotel. The incomparable Delmonico's."

"I assume you have attempted no further experiments with your oscillator," Travers said.

"To the contrary. I have performed many controlled experiments, and gained valuable insight into the phenomena of earthly harmonics. There is a periodicity to the earth's own vibrations that may, of course, be positively exploited—or used unwisely, to our ultimate sorrow."

"Do you m-mean the earth itself could be destroyed, Mr. Tesla?"

"Why, yes. Split in half like an apple, through means that are mechanically sound. But it would take far greater power than that which one of my oscillators is capable of generating."

"Then we h-have nothing to fear," Sibby said; a woman, Travers was certain, nearly dying of fear at the moment.

"We must be afraid, not of the wonders of nature and the cosmos, but of the scientifically unscrupulous. Alas, there are far too many such men in my profession. At times I feel them surrounding me, slavering like feral dogs for whatever scraps of invention I may carelessly leave unprotected."

"Speaking of harmonics," Edgar Langford said, "the Kabalists and Hermetic students believe in other planes of existence that surround us, not available to our senses without the implementation of appropriate symbols, but quite wonderful to behold."

Tesla nodded, uncommitted to the notion, but interested.

"Ghosts?" Sibby inquired with a frown.

"Not implausible," said their guest, making a contemplative steeple of his hands, but not slipping into one of his monastic silences. "Life, I am convinced, continues despite the inevitable dissolution of the body, in the form of electrostatic or magnetic fields of energy and intelligence." He jumped without pause to another concept. "Electricity puts into the exhausted body so much of what it needs—life force, nerve force. The supreme physician. Through the proper application of electricity, we may all one day be immortal."

"As the gods," Langford murmured, unabashedly envious.

"Some of us may even be deserving," Travers said.

Following dinner, it was Edgar Langford's turn to be the center of attention. He had prepared a magic shòw. He had, in fact, been working obsessively on his show for many weeks. In the years since he had performed for Sibby and her family in the Warings' Boston parlor, his skills had grown, his illusions were more complex to perform. He required a stage built to his specifications, and assistants, one of whom was Pamela, Sibby's maid. The other was a black man, lightless as soot, an Ethiopian named Taharqa, obtained by Edgar during a stopover in Cairo on his most recent journey to the Middle East. Taharqa was an enormous, glowering, tongueless man with splayed feet sheathed in callus thick enough to withstand the cold of Wildwood's frozen ground; he obviously had never worn even the most rudimentary of sandals. His narrow but powerful torso was scarred from vicious beatings. Under what circumstances he had been deprived of his tongue and otherwise mistreated was unknown. He could not communicate with anyone but Edgar, through some occult language of the eyes elaborated on with gestures, and had no real duties except to be instantly available when Edgar wanted him. He wore, typically, an ankle-length blue robe of flimsy cotton cloth with a braided silk belt, darker blue, from which hung amulets and a holstered handax of curved black Damascus steel. Taharqa slept, slavelike, on the floor outside Edgar's apartment, on a small Turkish carpet, wearing thin in places from the sharpness of his elbows. Perhaps Edgar kept him close to hand because he felt the need of a bodyguard of unquestioned loyalty. Or perhaps he merely regarded Taharqa as a pet, was amused by the dismay and fear which the ever-silent Ethiopian inspired in other servants and the many workmen on the premises. Edgar doted on the foreign, the unusual, the inexplicable.

Pamela, who assisted him with props and played important roles in two of his newest illusions, was a sturdy auburn-haired Yorkshire girl, with a wide handsome face and eyes so brilliantly feline they shone in the dark. She had no education but was slick with her hands and worked in her spare time to perfect the elements of legerdemain she had been taught.

Edgar had wanted as large an audience as possible for his exhaustively rehearsed show: therefore by nine-thirty the as yet unfinished Great Drawing Room of the chateau was filled. Nearly five hundred spectators in all. Every servant and workman in residence at Wildwood (another three hundred commuted by railroad from outlying communities almost every day) were on hand, with their wives and awed children. Most of them were required to stand, for there were only a limited number of chairs and stools; all were wearing coats, gloves, and mufflers, because the two huge Renaissance ceramic stoves in the drawing room raised the temperature only about ten degrees above freezing.

The stage was a three-tiered affair, ringed below by footlights and above by theatrical lamps fixed to iron stanchions, all levels draped in folds of dark velvet that were decorated, in tingly silver, with symbols of the conjuror's art. Sibby, wearing a Russian sable coat, sat with her lover and Nikola Tesla in a small "royal" box on a diagonal thrust of the main stage and about four feet above the rough and dusty stone floor. It was also close to one of the antique stoves; their backs were warm, their noses numb. Travers felt rather foolish sitting there, waiting for rabbits to pop out of top hats: his store of childlike wonder had always been minuscule. They were attended by liveried footmen and drinking port, for which Sibby had developed a fondness—one of her trifling vices, and not nearly so dangerous as her need to chloroform herself to sleep in those intervals when they were not trysting. Tonight the port had inspired in her a rather pathetic vivaciousness, an ingenuous desire to be found appealing by the inventor whose air of aloof genius had piqued more than one woman of wealth and accomplishment to mount an assault on his publicized celibacy.

"It is beyond my c-comprehension, Mr. Tesla, how you have managed to remain unmarried all these years."

His smile was barely noticeable, his parry so accomplished he must have repeated it countless times in similar circumstances.

"An inventor has so intense a nature, with so much in it of wild, passionate quality, that in giving himself to a woman he might love, he would give everything, and so take everything from his chosen field."

Travers, who was getting slowly and sourly drunk and to the point of not caring what he said, commented, "I believe it was St. Jerome, who, desiring to live all of his earthly years in perfection of his soul, solved the problem of the disturbing flesh by unmanning himself."

Sibby gasped delicately, a hand to her throat, and looked at Travers with widening eyes, perhaps assuming his mood had turned pathologically to thoughts of self-mutilation as punishment for getting her with child.

Tesla smiled, this time more sincerely and with a hint of amusement.

"There is a source of energy which is, of course, uniquely masculine, that I think must not be tampered with, if one aspires to more than a lifetime of quiet contemplation—or the perfection of a pure bel canto voice."

Sibby gasped again and then began to giggle, rather out of control; fortunately her outburst was lost in a clashing of cymbals nearby as the temporary lights of the drawing room were abruptly lowered and the magician's helpers appeared onstage. The tall Taharqa in a scarlet robe and a rather absurd turban with a pale jewel as its centerpiece. And Pamela in a short pleated skirt and ballerina's leotards that revealed, fully, beautiful legs, although she was too short-waisted and too wide in the shoulders to have a truly outstanding figure.

Travers, as the lights went down, seized one of Sibby's hands and squeezed to stall her hysterical mirth; she gulped and breathed hard and stared at Pamela and whispered, "Look at h-her. She m-might as well be nude."

"Very fetching," Tesla said, steepling his hands, staring at Pamela, whose face was petrified in an expression that might have been stage fright, or deep concentration. Taharqa had much the same uplifted, starry daze in his yolk-yellow eyes, and Travers wondered if they were mesmerized—another, hitherto unknown talent of Edgar Langford's? Their breaths were luminously visible against the dark backdrop.

Travers did not release Sibby's hand until she tugged insistently. Then he reached for the glass of port that was kept filled to within an inch of the brim by one of the unseen footmen discreetly stationed outside their privileged enclosure. Unseen but all-seeing, and how much gossip would there be tomorrow, because he imprudently had taken Sibby's hand in his own? For that matter, did they have *any* secrets left? Had they been as simple as children, blissfully deluded in their passion for each other, believing they could conceal the brilliance of love fulfilled from eyes that were alert, in this hermetical society, for any enlivening spark of cynical entertainment?

To the accompaniment of gramophone music the magic show began.

Pamela clapped her hands and a footman approached with two crystal wineglasses and a bottle of port on a silver tray. Pamela unsealed and uncorked the bottle, poured one glass full of the dark amber spirits. She began to fill the second glass. Suddenly the port stopped flowing, as if the bottle had run dry. Puzzled, Pamela shook the bottle, then upended it: not another drop of wine appeared. She tapped one hand smartly on the bottom of the bottle, then quickly held it upright and aloft: a bouquet of red carnations blossomed from the neck. She gathered the bouquet and tossed it toward the

enclosure: fresh carnations fell across the table. Sibby
picked one up and smiled delightedly. "It's real!" she
called out. Applause and laughter; Sibby was popular at
Wildwood. As her husband was not. Travers, hearing
the applause, as much for Sibby as for clever Pamela,
felt his tension easing. Yes, there surely had been gossip; but perhaps not all of it was unkind.

Taharqa had wheeled out a tall lacquered Chinese
cabinet from behind the curtains. He opened the hinged
door of the topmost compartment. It was an empty
cube. Pamela handed the Ethiopian a cigar, and lighted
it for him. Taharqa drew on the cigar until it glowed,
then exhaled a cloud of smoke, thick and blue in the
spotlight. Turning to the open compartment of the cabinet, he puffed and blew smoke until it was cigar-foggy
inside, then closed the door. He walked away and stood,
out of the spotlight, with arms folded.

After a few graceful flourishes Pamela opened the
compartment once more and took out a snowy fluttering
dove, which she exhibited in her two hands. Then she
quickly replaced the dove inside the compartment. Almost immediately a loud knocking resounded through
the drawing room. Startled, Pamela looked into the
compartment. The dove was gone; in its place was the
head of Edgar Langford. He was smiling. The illusion
was unsettling, the applause it elicited nervous and
jerky.

"Good h-heavens!" Sibby exclaimed, and looked
away.

The knocking again. Langford rolled his disembodied
head, eyeing Pamela. He looked down, where the rest
of him should be. She nodded and opened the large
compartment below. But it was empty. Pamela demon-
strated just how empty with her hands, then stood back,

hands on hips, feigning perplexity. Edgar Langford looked disgruntled. There were nervous titters in the drawing room. Pamela turned the cabinet on small casters, and found more secretly hinged doors to open. Edgar Langford's head appeared again and again, once upside down, in newly discovered compartments.

Suddenly, unexpectedly, it was Taharqa's head they saw: and a second spotlight picked out the figure standing in near darkness at the far side of the stage, which everyone had all but forgotten about but assumed was the dour Ethiop. The figure turned slowly to the audience. It was Edgar Langford, wearing a robe and turban like Taharqa's.

There was an enthusiastic wave of applause, an outpouring of admiration; even Nikola Tesla joined in.

"How very clever. Worthy of my friend Houdini at his best."

"I h-had no idea he could d-do these things," Sibby said, more dismayed than entertained.

Edgar Langford could do many wonderful and baffling things, and proceeded to show them.

He levitated Pamela, tilted her this way and that on an invisible axis, then caused her to revolve in the air while passing hoops of steel from her feet to her head, proving beyond a doubt that she was not somehow suspended from the ceiling on thin wires.

He stood, weighted and shackled with forty pounds of chains, in a cabinet made of glass and steel that was filled with a rose-tinted water. To the tip of his broad stake-bearded chin. To the bridge of his nose. At last the water closed over his head. The top of the cabinet was then locked with a big padlock. Expressionless, further chilling an already cold crowd, Langford gazed out at them while a curtain was drawn completely around the cabinet.

Sibby grasped her throat with one hand.

A very long minute passed.

Pamela, trying to maintain a confident smile, began to fidget, looking around at the curtain.

Two minutes.

Sibby rose to her feet prepared to scream. At the same instant Taharqa sprang toward the curtains with ax in hand, as if he were about to smash the cabinet glass and attempt to rescue the unfortunate illusionist. But before he could touch them the curtains were whisked high and away and Edgar Langford was revealed, standing, still shackled, on the outside of the glass cabinet, glowing with a drowned pallor but obviously alive. Sibby swayed and Travers quickly lowered her into her seat. The level of the water in the cabinet had fallen appropriately but was motionless, not agitated as it should have been if Langford had just left the cabinet. Pamela seized the padlock and tugged. It was still in place, still locked.

He bowed slightly and gravely to their applause, then hobbled crookedly offstage to be unchained and change clothes while Pamela entertained with milder magic. Sibby made an attempt to recover her composure with another glass of port. It only made her slump, as if she had been robbed (more sleight of hand) of a vital bone or two. Travers had never seen her so demoralized.

"I must admit, I cannot devise an explanation," Tesla said after pondering the illusion.

But Edgar's finale was stranger still.

He reappeared in an unadorned black robe and cowl.

A circular stairway of glass eight feet high had been positioned onstage. It was brightly lit. There was, seemingly, no place for him to go as he mounted the staircase one slow step at a time like a monk on his way to the belfry to toll for Matins.

His audience, some shivering, others fatigued, were nevertheless riveted by his methodical progress. *What next?*

At the top of the glass stairs he slowly and reverently withdrew a single red rose from one voluminous sleeve of his robe and showed it to them. It was a fancy large rose, with a foot-long stem green as a garter snake, pronounced thorns like the wide-apart fangs of a deadlier specimen. He held the rose in both hands, high, higher, above his head; his eyes lifted in contemplation of its beauty. Then he turned his back on them and just as slowly brought the rose down until it could no longer be seen because of the spread of his cowl, and nothing of Edgar himself was visible inside the sacklike robe.

He shrugged, almost a convulsion. The robe fell away from his body, like a heavy cloud, fell all the way to the stage floor.

But they never saw his body. Because even as the robe was falling, Edgar Langford had disappeared, in a hot spotlight, a glare of glass at the top of a transparent flight of stairs.

Taharqa picked up the discarded robe. He and Pamela left the stage.

The spotlight on the staircase dimmed. The lights of the drawing room came up.

In the audience they looked around, a little dazed, disappointed, and began to murmur.

Travers heard Sibby breathing heavily through her mouth. She was trembling.

There was a sudden loud knocking that startled everyone. A child began to wail. Then the ten-foot double doors at the entrance to the drawing room were thrown open.

Edgar Langford stood in the broad doorway, casting a long shadow. He had put on one of his patrician togas.

"Thank you for coming, and good evening," he said. Then he turned and walked away as scattered applause built to an ovation.

A wineglass shattered on the table at which Travers was sitting with Sibby and Nikola Tesla. Sibby's left fist had done it, in an erratic swing, bursting harmlessly the frail bell, which contained only a dram or two of port. In her right hand she was holding, stiffly, a rose of the approximate size and shape as the one Edgar Langford had taken from his full sleeve at the top of the glass staircase.

The petals of this rose, however, were black from frost. The stem looked withered and long-dead. Only the thorns remained stubbornly sharp, and a bright drop of blood had appeared on the pricked ball of Sibby's thumb.

She stared at her lover.

"It w-w-w-was in my lap," she explained. "Eh-*Ed*gar put it there. I f-f-f-felt him w-when he w-walked b-b-b-b-b—"

Her lips curled upward in a funny, stunned smile. Her blue eyes quickly paled to the pustular whiteness of blisters. The blighted rose dropped from her hand, shedding petals, and her head fell stonily forward, facedown and with a little horrid thump against the lace-covered table.

The audience was milling, applauding, leaving. James B. Travers looked quickly from the stage to the doorway where Edgar Langford had dramatically reappeared for his brief good night, and then at the desolate rose, the remains of which lay on the table beside Sibby's still head; and he understood, with the particular clarity of the newly condemned, what he had this evening been carefully led to understand: it was not magic that Edgar Langford possessed, it was sorcery

—— Chapter Twenty ——

April 1958

IT was late in the afternoon when Faren and Terry, slowly making their way one behind the other up the gorge of the Cat Brier, found the locomotive that was lying on one side and half swamped by the silver river torrent.

For more than half an hour they hadn't spoken, because the downsurge of the forty-foot-wide river through its mountainous channel made normal conversation difficult, and because they were both tired from their long hike and needed all their breath just to keep moving, struggling, upward. When Faren stopped abruptly on a flat pitch of shale covered by the delicate evergreen walking fern called "sore eye," Terry, intent on his footing, bumped into her and nearly sent her headlong into the water—like a plume of sculpted glass—six feet below. He grabbed her in time. Faren recovered her balance and helped him up beside her; she pointed. The angled locomotive was about thirty yards upstream, blocky, blacker than the shadows that covered it except for a shaft of sun glancing off one silver-dollar-perfect rim of a forward driver wheel.

"How did *that* get there?"

"I don't know," she said. "Looks like a wreck."

"Yeah. But—didn't you say—"

"I know. The railroad up to Tormentil washed out more than forty years ago."

"Well, that engine doesn't look like it's been there forty years."

"Terry," Faren said, sounding cross, "it's just an old wreck, what else can it be?"

She cast aside the mattock they had been using alternately to cut tough rhododendron branches from their path along the slippery river bank and sank down into the dampened fern. The webbing of her right hand and thumb showed hot blisters; she bit and sucked at one of them.

"I just can't push on anymore. My legs ache."

"Okay." Terry set his pack down. "I'll be back in a few minutes. I want to take a look at that wreck."

"Don't go climbing on it, it's probably all but rusted through in places."

He said in a deliberately high voice, "I'll be real careful, Auntie Faren."

She soundly smacked the seat of his pants with her left hand, shrugged off her own backpack, and lay flat in driplocks of gorgeous fern, released from trekking as if from chains, gazing vacantly at some olive-sided flycatchers who flew like small arrows from a faint rainbow drawn across the river channel, nicking the metaled air with birdsound. Her eyes closed with the third deep breath she took. She was dozing when Terry came back and shook her.

"Faren!"

"What?"

"There's a body in the cab of the locomotive! It must be the engineer."

". . . You mean a skeleton?"

"No! A body. He hasn't been dead long. And you should see where that locomotive rolled down the hill. And—there's fresh oil on the rocks by the river. Coal, too, big chunks. The accident must have happened today. Come on."

Faren groaned and sat up. A glance at his eyes, his concerned puckered brow, convinced her he wasn't fibbing.

She followed Terry to the wrecked Mikado . . . saw all that he had seen . . . glanced into the cab at the waterlogged phantom. Horror in a twilight green wood. She backed away shakily, too conscious of the boneyard of her own body just beneath the temperate flesh. Looked up along the treeless line of devastation, roots showing unearthed and broken, sharp as stakes.

"I—don't—believe—this."

Terry had no reservations; he started uphill. "Let's go see if—"

Faren jerked him back. "I don't want to go up there!"

He scowled. She had pulled too hard, hurting his arm.

"Don't you want to find out what happened?"

Faren shook her head, staring, her mind on possibilities that frightened her even more.

They both heard, faintly, one of Arn's hounds crying.

Terry broke from her grip and scrambled away, following the slashed and flattened path the locomotive had made; a lump of coal, kicked away by one of his boots, shot through with glitter like a furtive cat's eye, bounded toward Faren. Dodging, she called to him.

"Wait, Terry! Don't go without me!"

He paused on the slope and looked back impatiently.

The light was fading fast, a tarnished silver, by the time they climbed to the ridgeback. The hound named Bocephus met them there, whimpering. It was obvious he was hurt. Faren kneeled and took him in her arms. The hound had a large lump between his eyes.

"Bo, Bo, what's happened to you? Where's Arn?"

Terry walked farther up the ridge, to the place where the trees were knocked down. The locomotive's path ended abruptly, some thirty yards back in the woods. He didn't know what to think. He took his flashlight from his pack and searched the torn-up ground. Saw a section of rusted rail attached to rotted cross ties, partially buried beneath tree roots. Buried for how long?

Faren summoned him with a wail of alarm and anguish that made the back of his neck feel spidery. He went running down to the open ridge.

Bocephus was standing at her feet, Arn's hat in his mouth.

"What's the matter?"

Faren took the soiled old hat from the hound, turned it around and around in her hands, sniffed at the stain on the brim. Her head came up sharply as Terry aimed the flashlight at the hat. Shocked, she stared at him in the bounce light, nostrils still flared.

"Blood," she said. "It's Arn's hat—and there's blood on it."

The dog trembled and lay down, whimpering quietly.

"Where is he, Bo, can you find him for me? *Where's Arn?*"

With an effort the dog raised his head, then lowered it between his paws again.

"Faren—"

She made a sound of pure terror in her throat.

"Faren, where did Bo get the hat?"

She gestured at the woods behind them.

"I'll go look," Terry said. But his teeth began to chatter. Only a streak of sun was left of the day. He didn't know if the air was getting colder. But he felt cold all over.

He walked into the woods and soon found his father's backpack. There were several bootprints nearby. And the single imprint of a bare foot, huge, in a soft shallow depression.

That was all he found, except for the croquet ball.

He picked it up, nearly in tears and as scared as Faren was. Because he remembered the airstream trailer and the man in the monk's robe who carried a croquet mallet, whose brother was a creature with the ears and horns of a stag. Who cried *geeeekkk!* as Terry ran away from them.

He began calling his father. Until he was hoarse and his throat closed. But there was no answer.

He picked up his father's pack and went stumbling back to Faren.

She was now sitting beside the injured dog, Arn's hat in her hands and her head against her knees, deep in grief. She didn't move when he shone the flashlight beam on her.

"Look, I found—"

He held the croquet ball in the light of the flash, but Faren didn't look around.

"Faren, there aren't any train tracks. Just some old rusted rails, maybe fifty years old. Dad was here; this is his pack. And I called him, but he . . . what . . . what's . . ." His voice broke finally. "Going *on*?"

She just sat there, spellbound. The curve of her back

rejecting him, his unanswerable questions. He heard the river, and the hound panting, and the cicadas starting up like an old watch being wound.

When he turned off the flashlight to save the batteries he was shocked to realize how dark it was.

Chapter
Twenty-one

AFTER Whit Bowers had run as far as he could run, then walked until he hobbled, heels aching, a severe stitch in his right side, he sat down to rest somewhere short of the summit of the mountain known as the Tormentor. The air at this altitude was so pure it had given him a savage headache.

His pursuer, the nearly naked goatman, was, he assumed (perhaps fatalistically), far behind him, having become bored with the chase. It was sunset. He was alone in the pungent coniferous wood, and lost, and, for now, uncaring, his mind thornily hedged, threatened by the sudden jabs of terrifying unreality he had too frequently blundered into while goading himself to his physical limits. Too weary to lift his head, he sat with his back against a very old fir tree, a tall shaggy column as big around as one of the pillars of Hercules, surrounded, seemingly to infinity, by similar trees. Wood sorrel on the ground. Quick starred shadows of birds on massive trunks illuminated by long rays of the sun. The sun, which he needed as he needed his own heart, a diminishing globe of light now, swiftly and surely drawing away from him. Night would fall, soon; he wasn't sure he could cope with darkness, stranded like this. But there wasn't time to make his way back to the ridge where he and Arn had parted company, where he'd left his bedroll and the matches he had to have to start a fire. It promised to be a cold night.

He knew he should be up and moving, to somewhere. Instead, he closed his eyes, slumping.

From nearby he heard what sounded like notes from a flute. He looked up, puzzled. The piping, bubbling sounds continued, along with more distant cries of towhees and Carolina parakeets, the rapid, hollow tapping of ivory-billed woodpeckers.

A very strange bird appeared from behind a spiky old windfall a hundred feet away. The bird had a head like a crow. The crown of its small head and ample upper breast were a gleaming oily-green shade. Its back was yellow, the wings and tail deep red. From the flanks and sides of the breast ivory plumes flared, becoming as delicate in texture as lace at the tips. The bird's bill was blue, the eyes a glowing amber.

His ex-wife had been an ardent amateur ornithologist and collector of bird prints, and Whit didn't have to look for more than a few seconds to realize he was seeing an Emperor of Germany Bird of Paradise, the male of the species. A great rarity outside its natural habitat, the highland jungles of New Guinea.

Some seven thousand miles away from Tyree, North Carolina, and the Great Smoky Mountains.

So what was it doing here?

The Bird of Paradise didn't seem to know, either.

From its agitated movements and cries, apparently it was in deep distress.

Whit got slowly to his feet. The bird saw him and took off in fright toward the heights of the dense dark-green trees.

Light in the woods had faded to a dusty brass. But there was a steadily brightening, heliographic glow in the distance, as if the last rays of the sun were striking glass or some other polished surface.

It acted as a beacon to draw him uphill, silently, trudging across the centuries of packed needle turf and flowing, blossoming vines beneath the mountain ever-greens.

He was almost unsurprised when he came across a couple of vivid pink flamingos. Either his appearance failed to startle them, or they were too stunned to react.

Someone he had known (not Millie) had admired and collected such exotic birds. But when and where had he seen them?

The source of the reflected light was a huge glass aviary, more than thirty feet high, covering perhaps two acres of ground. The steel-strutted dome was pierced by some of the tall fir and spruce trees, as if it had been carefully constructed around them.

A toucan with a red bill flew at him, then veered away, landing on a stubby branch of a tree to his left. The toucan tilted its head and fixed him, as if amused, with its shiny button eye.

Whit saw, through the translucent walls of the aviary, swift shadowy flights of parrots, macaws, and toucans. On the floor of the aviary there were egrets, blue herons, and more pretzel-neck flamingos. The dissonance was un-nerving, were was their violent, crazed movements. Birds flew headlong against the glass and the trunks of trees inside, fell stunned or dead to earth. Something had disturbed them. His presence? But he was too far away.

There was a shattered pane of glass near ground level, through which the birds he had seen in the woods must have escaped. He approached the opening in the aviary and looked inside. Warm feather-laden air and the perfume of subtropical shrubbery, blossoms bleeding scarlet into the deepening dusk. He saw a woman in a black and white nanny's uniform with a full, ankle-length skirt frantically wheeling a large wicker perambulator around the floor of the aviary, dodging out-of-control birds; from what he saw of her face she was propelled by terror, but the birds were making so much racket he couldn't hear her. She went up and over an arched bamboo bridge spanning a small lagoon, comically awkward in her panic, nearly overturning the perambulator. She stopped abruptly as a brightly colored bird with the wingspan of a condor flew predatorily close. The perambulator rolled a few feet away from her. She clutched at her head and then at her heart, stiffening. One black-booted foot kicked, heel down, at the ground; then she fell over backward in a motionless heap.

Whit Bowers had seen many men fall like that, but never a woman. He knew that she was dead.

He cracked out a heavy jagged piece of glass from the broken pane, his tortured reflection flying away from him, and stepped into the aviary. He ran through scattered squalling birds and through a shallow fountain to where the woman lay. More birds waddled aimlessly around her: bright, scarce, gruesomely beautiful birds, dazzling but stupid in their search for freedom, the open air.

He kneeled beside the nanny. Her eyes were open,

but sightless; and they were shockingly bloodred, turning her, in unpeaceful death, to an ogress. She was not a young woman. She'd always had problems with her blood pressure. He touched a grizzled cheek and cried. Too many grotesque surprises in one day, combat had never unnerved him so desperately. A runaway locomotive, out of the blue. The goatman, a playful, oddly familiar masquerade turned horrifyingly real. Now his beloved Jacqueline—

The baby was crying too. He got up dizzily and stared into the perambulator, at the clenched reddened face. A long-tailed bird with whirring wings dropped a nickel-sized chalky clot on the satin-edged pink bunting, near the embroidered initial *L*.

Whit was oblivious to the footfalls in mossy earth behind him.

A hand fell on his shoulder. He jerked around, saw the barbarously bearded face and harmless, close-together blue eyes of Jacob Schwarzman.

"Never mind," Jacob said. "She'll be taken care of."

"Is it—?" Whit looked again at the infant, and felt a fine thread of nearly forgotten jealousy running through him.

Jacob nodded impatiently. "We must get out of here. It's all happening too fast now."

"Jacqueline—"

"Yes, yes; a tragedy. But they'll see to her. She'll have a decent burial. Jacqueline isn't the first to drop dead just over the threshold. She might not be the last. But we don't want them to find us here. It violates conditions which—they believe—I have scrupulously observed."

"Who? Who are you talking about?"

"The Walkouts." Jacob nervously tightened his grip on Whit. "I'll explain everything," he promised. "You, of all people, have the right to know. But we can't talk here."

He pulled Whit away from the silver-trimmed perambulator. The light was all but gone from this outraged arcady. Some of the birds had begun to settle down, in high palmy places, but a few, spectral white or silver in the thick gray dusk, swooped around them, wingbeats chillingly close to the skin. Whit cringed, stumbling, his tears still flowing.

"Where are you taking me?" he asked Jacob, but not as if it really mattered.

"The caverns."

"We can't just leave the baby."

"She's safe in her perambulator. And with Pamela in the state she's in now—" He gave a world-weary shrug. "I haven't the means to care for an infant. But they'll manage. I'm sure some of the Walkouts will be here soon. They have what amounts to a psychic awareness of crossovers, like Jacqueline and—"

"Do you know—who the baby is?"

"Of course; now I do. She must be your sister Laurette. Please. Can we hurry? Or we may not make it at all."

Chapter
Twenty-two

In his dream Terry was married to Faren and they were living in Paris, in the Rodin Museum, at the intersection of the Boulevard des Invalides and the Rue de Varenne. There was a war going on. At night the sky flashed ominously: artillery fire. The neglected garden was crowded with strangers camped out among the famous sculptures: *The Thinker, Victor Hugo, Eve. The Gates of Hell*. In contrast to the full-bodied, larger-than-life statues, the garden dwellers had the wasted frames and death-bright eyes of concentration camp inmates. Terry was afraid to leave the house and go into the garden. For one thing, he was naked; his body sterile alabaster, a fearless white. His mother wanted her gadabout home. She had sent Terry's father, in full paratrooper gear, to look for him. Faren's hair had grown very long, it was nearly down to her ankles, wrapping coarsely, enticingly, around and around her own brown body, tailing off across a glistening shinbone. He was in love, but he was afraid of her too. If he looked for longer than a moment into her eyes, they turned an astral shade of yellow with vertical, ellipsoid pupils.

Without transition he and Faren were in the garden. They had taken the place of the man and woman of *The Kiss* on their pedestal. But they weren't just kissing, they were actually doing it. All around them, ghostfaces like a night stop on the metro. He was embarrassed to have an audience but he continued to heave himself into Faren time and again as if into a fleshly net, staggered by the blows of his heart, her tongue cold as bronze going up and down his smarting face. She gripped him frenziedly with her knees, the sky was exploding, *oh God—*

Terry ejaculated in his sleeping bag and woke up at once, distressed and faintly nauseated. He had taken off his jeans before bedding down, only his shorts were full of his sap. The sky was still flashing, exactly as in the dream. But he didn't have Faren in his arms. When he turned his head to look for her he saw that the other sleeping bag, two feet away, was empty.

He got up and, trembling in the chill night air, searched in his pack for a clean pair of jockey shorts. He took the soiled shorts off, changed, pulled on his jeans, and laced his hiking boots. The sky lit up again, soundlessly; was it going to rain? He didn't think so, the air was too still: and he felt resistance, a tension when he moved, as if he were pushing from the inside of an overblown balloon.

"Faren?"

Earlier they had built a fire, eaten hash from a can, gone exhaustedly to sleep. How long ago? He looked at the green face of his chronometer. It was only a few minutes after midnight. He picked up his flashlight. The fire was low, a few wispy flames. The eyes of Bocephus were burning red glass in the flashlight's beam. The hound was lying down, still looking poorly . . . as Faren would have put it.

Where could she have gone in the middle of the night without a flashlight of her own? But the sky was brightening every few seconds now, as much light where they had pitched their meager camp as a false dawn.

When he called again, Faren answered.

"I'm all right! Go back to sleep."

She sounded far away. "Where are you?"

"Terry, Arn isn't dead! And I know where they've taken him."

"Wait for me!" But he was rooted, not knowing which direction to take; her voice could have been coming from anywhere.

"No, no, Terry! Don't try to follow me. It can be dangerous. But I have to go *now*, the time is right."

Her voice sounded fainter; she was leaving him behind. Terry shuddered, biting his tongue to keep from sobbing.

"Faren—please come back!"

"I can help them, Terry—the Lost Ones. I'm real close to them now in time. Josie says if I help them, the others will let Arn live."

The next time he shouted there was no reply.

The sky was a bitter pale nightmare green; and he felt the ground tremble beneath his feet.

Terry moved through the resisting air as if he were rubbing against it, stretching it. First he tried to fight his way through the colorless membrane of the bubble that seemed to enclose their campsite; but panic only served to immobilize him more dreadfully, turning him to stone from the inside out. He quickly learned that slow, deliberate effort meant progress—he might stretch the resilient

air to infinity as long as he was careful. Breathing was
no problem. And while he could breathe, he would be
all right.

He pulled Bocephus to his feet. The hound whined in
pain but the loose folds of his skin in Terry's hands, the
sane sad eyes, reassured Terry that he wasn't losing his
mind.

"Go to Faren! Find her, Bo!"

Lightning lanced out of nowhere, turning a tree a
hundred yards away into a torch. Bocephus cowered in
Terry's embrace. He grasped the hound's collar, crouching, and urged him on.

"Which way, Bo? Where did Faren go?"

The hound began to move grudgingly. Terry crept
along beside him, keeping a tight grip on his studded
collar, the membrane expanding palpably with each step
he took, the blazing tree throwing red sparks into the
sky. Instead of winking out, the sparks fell into a circulating pattern, faster than hornets, thicker than the mountain stars. Faren had vanished, a farewell voice from a
lonely wood; his father, the death camp unfortunates,
had all vanished from the garden of his sexual dream.
Only the prehistoric war continued, and he was its lone
survivor.

The flaring light, as Terry and Bocephus moved uphill through thin smoke, was nearly continuous. Noctur-
nal birds and animals seemed confused, crossing their
path obliviously: all movement in the wood was slowed,
exaggerated. Shambling possum and gliding owl, paunchy
raccoons like old boxers retiring from the ring, larks by
the basketful. Bocephus, nose down to Faren's scent,
couldn't be distracted. The burning tree hadn't set anything else on fire, but the sparklers like little pops of
fireworks stayed sky-high, an angry tattoo. Terry saw a

black and gray tufted cat, twice the size of a domestic tabby but smaller than a panther, grimacing at them from atop the root clump of a windfall, its stiletto whiskers tipped glowingly as if drenched in radium. Then the membraneous air seemed to warp and expand, the bobcat grew enormously and out of proportion like a shape in a funhouse mirror until it was just a slippery image without definition; Terry and the hound slid on past this anomaly—or rather, he had the sensation of walking in place while everything else moved, slanting through his field of vision, the light accelerating to a mad velocity defined by the speed of sparks above his head, the streaming-by of smoke. It was too odd and unearthly to be truly frightening. He had only a jittery, awed, what-next feeling that was, surprisingly, almost enjoyable: because he knew he couldn't be fully awake, he was still half steeped in his absorbing dream.

Then the snakes started coming, big rolling hoops of them, black coachwhip racers and peppermint-striped ribbon snakes with their tails in their mouths, spokeless bicycle wheels descending streakily between shrubs and trees, rebounding with a cold rubbing sensation from his upflung hands and wavering off-course high in the air.

Terry yelled. He lost contact with Bocephus. He started to back away from the springy onslaught of hoopsnakes.

But when he turned around there was nothing behind him.

Literally nothing at all. A starless void. The end of the world.

He slogged on uphill. His heart lumpish and seeming to beat only when he paid attention to it. He called to Bo, to Faren, to anyone who might be listening, until his throat had shrunk and all he could do was croak.

The sky above the bluff he was climbing had changed

to a shade of gold in which the fiery sparks had come together like two ophidian eyes that regarded him hostilely.

In that glow he saw Faren standing, as if bewitched, at the edge of another abyss, hands by her sides, looking down. And all of their world had shrunk to the bright bubble that contained them: half a mile, perhaps, in diameter, and suspended in a grayish void of eternity.

Terry recovered his voice.

"Faren, where are we?"

She trembled slightly as if disturbed by his presence, but didn't look around.

"Faren . . . Faren . . ."

He wasn't the only one calling her. The other voices, a sorrowful chorus, rose from the depths of the well beneath her.

He caught up to Faren. She looked into his face, frowning, a quick hand going flat against his breastbone.

"But I asked you not to come. The bargain's made, there's nothing you can do here, Terry."

"What bargain?" He looked down into the old quarry, squarely sawn sides gleaming white, at a milkishly emerald pool. From where they stood it was nearly a vertical drop.

And in the pool—

My God.

"Who are *they*?"

"Oh, Terry." She caught his face between her hands, kissed him warmly but sadly on the lips. Then she stepped away. A long step, to the edge of the quarry. "We'll see each other again," she said with a heart-torn smile. "I know we will." She looked up then, dutifully, at the lowered, seething sky. Her smile faded as if by command.

Terry looked too. He saw the well-shaped, cloudlike, golden head of a serpent, savage ruby eyes in the fulminating cloud that filled nearly half of their earthly bubble. And from one of the eyes came crooked lightning that stunned and knocked him flat.

From where he lay he had only a glimpse of Faren going over the side of the quarry in a meek, sacrificial swan dive. Gliding like a leaf, and down. Harmlessly. Down.

The lightning crackled like a cage about Terry's head; his hair was standing raggedly on end. He decided that he couldn't stand up without being struck, perhaps lethally, again. But he could crawl forward on his belly; when he had gone far enough to look down at the strange green pool, he thought he saw Faren sliding deep into its swarming, heavily peopled heart.

The lightning was sullenly withdrawn; the eyes of the serpent came apart, sparks flying at random, brief atoms growing dim at aphelion.

He sat up in a fever, unlacing his boots. Intending to go after Faren. If she had jumped and survived, then he could too. No matter what was down there (the square pool appeared to be, not watery, but a mass grave in tumult) he would not let her face it alone.

"Oh no you don't!"

Terry looked over his shoulder, and was so startled he nearly toppled sideways into the quarry.

Josie Raftery reached out with one foot and grasped his sweater while continuing to hover more than three feet above the ground. The cyclical movements of her butterfly's wings fanned the air around them; she seemed to radiate body heat from the effort she was making to be aloft. She pulled him firmly away from the precipice.

"Can't follow after her, boy. You don't have the

protection, see." She smiled down at him a bit shyly, showing a gap between her front teeth. "You stay with me. I'm Josie. I'll look after you."

He was trying to assimilate what was absurd and incomprehensible: her melodious Irish tongue, the broad rowing wings that kept her airily on balance, only a waist-length shawl of strawberry blond hair to cover—not much. From the strong outthrust foot that still gripped him to an ivory hip and frankly revealed pudendum, she was naked.

"Sure and I must seem a bit strange to you," Josie said with a wider but embarrassed smile. "But we all do grow accustomed to one another, in the fullness of time and in the sight of God."

Everything seemed bleak to Terry then; his mind welcomed bleakness, oblivion. The unearthly sphere in which he was marooned with this creature now encompassed a bare half acre of rocky ground, a patch of starless night. The world at God's end, forgotten, a spit bubble. Faren was lost; he had no hope of sunrise. There was only a faint radiance from the butterfly girl, the sweet warm draft of her wings.

Terry shook her off and, with a last disbelieving sulky look, lay down again, cradling his head in his arms.

"*Merde*," he said, his tone irritable. "I'm going back to sleep."

Chapter Twenty-three

"FIRST a glass of brandy," Jacob Schwarzman proposed, his voice echoing as he held up a dusty bottle plucked from a scrapheap of archaelogica: "Napoleon brandy. At least eighty years old. But the finest brandy may well be ageless."

He looked to Whit for confirmation, not smiling, his troll-blue eyes alight as if from brainburn; his exhilaration seemed manic to Whit Bowers, who by contrast was immobile from weariness, reduced to childsize where he had slumped upon a monarch's throne of alabaster, chalcedony, and gold. But the throne itself seemed small, a plaything, when compared with the size of the man-made cavern in Tormentil Mountain that, Jacob claimed, had been home to him for more than three years.

This single oblong chamber, dynamited and chiseled from solid rock half a century ago, was big enough to contain a steel mill. The chamber was well-illuminated by bluish tubular lights that glowed like neon but had no connection with the whorls of electric wires high above them on the vaulted ceiling. The power source was, perhaps, dependent on a waterfall Whit could hear but had not seen, in a cavern distant from them.

After considerable manipulation on Jacob's part the cork popped from the dark bottle and a little brandy like insect's blood oozed down the hairy back of one hand. "Ah!" he cried, and reached for a vitreous, heavily ornamented goblet, the bowl held aloft by maidens in filigreed singlets. The goblets were from a trove on a long table, an eighteen-foot slab of solid pink marble that rested on the backs of winged lions. He poured several ounces of brandy for Whit, handed him the goblet, filled another for himself.

"I'm a poor fisherman and I can't bear to hunt; so I've seldom eaten well during my sojourn here. But thanks to our absent Caliban, who left forty cases of fine vintages stored in these chambers, I have drunk divinely."

"Caliban?"

"Absent for how long, I wonder?" Jacob mused, nose to the rim of the lucent goblet. His eyelids were half lowered. " 'How soon,' " he recited, " 'will time hide all things! How many a thing has it already hidden!' "

"Marcus Aurelius," Whit murmured, looking at the slightly dusty surface of the old brandy in his own goblet. He sniffed; the fumes hit him bracingly and freed an impulse that resembled laughter but didn't reach his lips. To hell with the dust, he thought. He drank.

"You've read the classics?" Jacob said, mildly delighted.

"Had to. They were Blackie's passion. He wanted me to know something besides engineering and soldiering."

"Blackie? Is that the name of your adoptive father?"

"Brigadier General Walter 'Blackie' Bowers. United States Army. Did I tell you I was adopted?"

"Is General Bowers living now?"

"No. And Ruth—my mother—died right after the war. Complications from pneumonia." Thinking of burials, he looked around, at sand-worn statues of partial men and maimed gods lining the wall behind him to heights of twenty feet or more. They scared Whit a little. But he'd had a fright as severe as cancer burning in his bones long before descending into this chamber.

"Would you mind describing the circumstances of your adoption?"

The brandy went to Whit's stomach like a saber cut. "Why?"

"It may be of some value as we try to figure out how you got from here"—Jacob lifted his goblet, indicating the world outside the cavern, the wild mountaintop—"to there." And he pointed, indefinitely, distantly, with a finger.

Now Whit laughed, but he was annoyed by Jacob's actorish behavior and the insinuation.

"I've never been here before."

"But you have! You were born here! Haven't you had sufficient proof of that already? You recognized Jacqueline, your old nursemaid. And the Ethiopian you encountered in the woods: you know his name, of course."

"That—goatman?" Whit had begun to shake from the omnivorous cancer. He spilled a little brandy, then gulped too much of it down, which made him choke and cough. In his mind there was a rainless bolt of lightning. His lips were parched, the soles of his feet blistered; his nearly naked child's body glowed from a remorseless sun. He bowed his head and recalled, hazily, horsemen on a gray desert floor. Texas: The Fort Bliss Military Reservation. All that was familiar from his early life, dependable in memory.

"The circumstances of your adoption?" Jacob prompted quietly, coming closer to the throne on which Whit squirmed uneasily, eyes closed.

"I was—abandoned, I suppose. In the West Texas desert, a few miles from El Paso. I wasn't a runaway. I didn't have any clothes with me, no keepsakes. They—they checked with the police in three states, but nobody ever reported me missing."

"How old were you?"

"Six, six and a half, maybe. A few months later I began to lose my baby teeth. I've always celebrated my birthday from the day that Blackie's cavalry troop found me wandering in the desert."

"Yes? And what day *was* that, Colonel Bowers?"

"June twenty-fourth. Nineteen hundred and sixteen."

"The time of day?"

"Late afternoon." Whit raised his head and looked hostilely at Jacob, who was standing a few feet from the throne, rubbing his brushy beard. "Does that prove anything?"

"Mmmm. What do you recall of your life, prior to being found in the desert on Midsummer Day?"

"I've never remembered a thing."

"Except for your name."

"No, I was—they named me Whitman, after Ruth's father."

Jacob paused, free hand going to his forehead as if he needed to check his temperature, having a tendency to overheat when he was excited. He drank deliberately, then took a deep breath to dilute the brandy fumes in his lungs.

"Your true name is Alexander Langford. Your mother was Laurette Langford, known as 'Sibby'; one of those rather meaningless, ridiculous nicknames children of the wealthy were given during the so-called Gilded Age. She was, of course, the wife of Edgar Langford."

"What is this—bullshit, Jacob? Are you trying to tell me that Mad Edgar Langford—*was my father*?"

"That is one possibility. But perhaps only your mother knew for sure. Unfortunately only some baby pictures of Edgar Langford exist. For most of his life he flatly refused to be photographed or to sit for his portrait. This was not due to mere shyness on his part; I suspect a hysterical obsession. He was sickly as a child, and possibly considered himself ugly. The diseases he contracted during his explorations would not have enhanced his self-image. Descriptions of Edgar as a grown man are sketchy; his enemies found him to have a rather malevolent countenance, with 'burning' or 'penetrating' eyes—only feverish, I'm sure. From what I have observed of you since we met, I think it's entirely likely that James B. Travers was your natural father."

"Who?"

"The architect of Mad Edgar's chateau, and Sibby's lover for the last decade of her life. I believe their affair may have begun as early as 1906. I have some photos of Mr. Travers: he was a tall, strapping fellow, like yourself—and your son. You bear only a passing resemblance to your mother, except for the lightness of your eyes. Travers's eyes were dark, dark brown perhaps, so I can't account for that anomaly, the dominant gene should be—"

"Jacob!"

"What is it?" Jacob asked irritably, digging into his beard again, disturbed in his speculations.

"I've had enough to drink, and—I'd like to get out of here. If you'll kindly show me the way, I don't remember just how we came in."

"Go? Now? You can't go!"

"Do you think you can stop me?"

"What I mean is—by tomorrow morning you will be lying in the woods as dead as"—Jacob retreated to the long table and picked up a beautifully feathered orange-and-blue bird with a crushed head that he had brought with him from the aviary—"as this Borneo kingfisher."

"I'm willing to take my chances out there," Whit said, getting down from the throne. "I need to locate Arn."

"But you don't understand—" Jacob let the gorgeous bird fall back to the table, and despairingly set his goblet down. "Oh, I see. You think I'm insane."

"No—but it may be you've lived down here by yourself a little too long, Jacob." Breathing the old breath of caves, that carried the spores of hallucination, of another man's lunacy.

"On the contrary, I'm perfectly lucid and I know exactly what I'm talking about. You're the one who is—quite naturally— confused."

"Yes. I'm damned confused. But I'm not staying here."

"Don't you want to know? Is it more than casual circumstance that brings you to Wildwood at this critical time? You've come full circle in your life, Alexander. You've come_ *home*."

"Whit. Whitman Bowers. I've never been anyone else. I'll find my own way out, Jacob. Good night."

"I warn you! It's dangerous to wander out there on the mountain at this time. The appearance of the aviary was only the beginning. You may suddenly find yourself buried beneath tons of stone when the chateau returns.''

Whit was walking toward the far end of the chamber, feeling a current of air against his face, hearing more loudly the sounds of the waterfall and a humming generator. Rusted railroad tracks bisected the floor between more of the monumental works of ancient artisans. The spoils of Edgar Langford.

Jacob's voice echoed. ''I can explain! What no one else can ever explain to you! How you came to be in the desert with no memory of your first six years! Just listen to me!''

The floor of the chamber by the rails seemed hot to Whit; he could almost feel it burning through the soles of his boots. There was a small sun blazing in the back of his mind. He was parched again. Not for drink, but for knowledge. Maybe even a crackbrained theory was better than a void.

''I'll listen,'' he said, ''while you show me the rest of this place.''

Jacob came on the run.

''I've dedicated my life to the mysteries, the phenomena. Others have come to Wildwood, hoping to discover what was hidden here. They all failed but I, I did meticulous research, *years* of research, before beginning my explorations. It took me less than a week to find the alternate entrance to the caverns—only a hundred yards from where the aviary reappeared this afternoon.''

Whit thought of the frantic nanny, blown dead in a bad squall of birds. And what had become of the infant in the perambulator? He knew it was wrong to have left her behind. But the light in his mind, the glowering sun, dissolved all images of the aviary as guilt sharpened to pain like a splinter of steel through his temples.

He was walking too fast. Jacob slowed him down by tugging at a sleeve of his sweater. He waved his other hand at the collection around them, a jigsaw city of dust-shrouded relics: steles and tombs, sections of frescoed walls, stylized faces in profile regarding them dimly from within massive packing crates.

"I'm sure you have no idea of the significance, the immense value of these artifacts. They were left in the caverns because of their sheer size: Edgar Langford simply couldn't fit them into the scheme of his chateau, huge as it was."

They had come to a series of passageways the size of subway tunnels, spread like fingers from the square palm of the cavern they were in. The rails continued far back into the mountain, beneath receding vertical tubes some of which had dimmed to shades of purple or indigo, creating shadowy spaces along the way. From one of the tunnels a draft of moist air flowed strongly. The waterfall.

"Would you like to see the generator first? It's been operating down here continuously for half a century, unattended; it was designed, by a genius named Tesla, to need no attention for at least a hundred years."

While he was talking, Jacob had managed to place himself, as unobtrusively as possible, between Whit and the dark entrance to the passage on their extreme left.

"Where does that lead?" Whit asked, pointing behind Jacob.

"A small chamber. It was used as a workroom by Langford or perhaps Tesla, the wizard of the lamps; but they left nothing of importance there. I've turned it into my library, stored thousands upon thousands of cuneiform fragments that I someday hope to find the time to translate."

"Are you sure that isn't the way we came in?"

Jacob stared at him with wounded blue eyes.

"You said you wouldn't leave. You promised to listen to me."

"Only if you could explain a few things. The aviary, for one."

"Just give me—"

A sound came chillingly to them from far down one of the passages; it was something like the screech of a jungle cat. Jacob's lips trembled; he bit them.

"What was that?" Whit said. "Are there animals down here?"

"No, certainly not! Sometimes the wind at night— blows a certain way through the natural chimneys that ventilate these caverns. That's all you heard." He took hold of Whit's sleeve again, obsequiously. "If you'll follow me—the generator is a marvel, you must see it. It creates an ambient force field, just how, no one has ever been able to discover. I keep some food in a larder nearby—nuts, cheeses, wild fruit—and a few bottles of chilled white wine. I know you must be hungry. If you'd like to bathe before we eat, the temperature of the pool below the generator is precisely that of the human body—amniotic, you might say."

The catlike yowling was repeated. Or was the sound more human than animal this time? Whit couldn't be sure. Jacob's attempt at a smile was that of a man suddenly frozen in ice.

"It isn't so difficult to get used to—once you've been down here for a while. Come; there's nothing to be afraid of."

They walked together down the gently sloping passage toward the cavern that contained the waterfall; a slight wetness in the air glistened on chiseled stone but the spaced tubes of light were unaffected, so many of them mysteriously, coldly alight after countless thousands of hours; they composed a parade of Whit's and Jacob's mismatched bodies, a crisscross of spectral shadows surging, then receding, along the walls and the floor.

"How did you become so obsessed with Edgar Langford, Jacob?"

"Obsessed?" Jacob turned his head as if to spit out the word, but thought again. "Yes, I suppose that's accurate. Since I've come to know him, as well as the man can be known by sifting through his published works and the impressions of his contemporaries, he has never been out of my thoughts for long. I've even dreamed about him; unpleasant dreams at times. A genius, but paradoxical, as are all great and ambitious men: consider his brilliant scholarship, his foolish intrusions into magick, his dark vendettas, his romance with old and dangerous gods."

"You called him Caliban, didn't you?"

Jacob chuckled too loudly; the sound rang from the stone enclosing them.

"An apt comparison. He was—is—cunning, classically paranoid, a notorious misanthrope, a warlock by inclination and in practice. Always leagues ahead of his competitors in the science of Assyriology, which is, as you know, my field as well. It was common knowledge that Edgar Langford looted the sites he discovered, that a treasure-house lay buried beneath this mountain, and was likely to remain buried for all time. But as I researched the last years of his life, studied the architect's plans for the chateau, read accounts of extensive excavations inside Tormentil, I was convinced that many of his unique discoveries were still intact, waiting to be rediscovered. I was right. But I never imagined that I would find so much else in Wildwood; that the—the *horror* of Midsummer Eve, 1916, would be revealed to me."

"The night the chateau was destroyed."

The waterfall was near; Jacob raised his voice.

"The very night Mad Edgar's most elaborately conceived illusion became a dreadful reality for all of his five hundred guests—when he at last went too far, and has yet to return. No one returned alive, unaltered—except for his beloved son."

Whit said wearily, "Jacob, I don't want to go into that again."

To Whit's relief (a mild claustrophobia almost unnoticed when they first entered the tunnel had become stifling, traumatic) the passageway widened and descended gradually; they were in the cavern that contained the waterfall, the generator, and several other machines that looked dead, entombed, perhaps never used; their design and purpose were a mystery to Whit, although he had a degree in engineering. The cavern was rugged, natural, with stalactites. The waterfall poured from a rift in the face of the rock thirty feet high and opposite the ledge on which they were standing. The ledge had been shaped, leveled, enclosed by a pipe railing still thickly protected against rust by gray paint. There was a resonance in the rock on which they stood, from the turbines. A mist hovered above the pool where heated water was gushingly discharged from the machine.

"Have you heard of Nikola Tesla?" Jacob asked.

"No."

"He was Serbian. Even before he left his native land, as a very young man, he had already conceived his plan for this simple induction motor, which has almost no parts that will wear or break down. His invention made alternating current possible and practical, so that electricity could be cheaply transmitted over long distances. Unfortunately he surrendered his claims to future royalties to the Westinghouse Company when that company was threatened with bankruptcy before the turn of the century. As a consequence, he was always desperately in need of funds to further his research. And that is how his distressing alliance with Edgar Langford came about.''

''Why was it distressing?''

''Each man was a genius with visionary qualities. But Nikola Tesla's inventions, his pioneer work in radio and robotics, were important and useful. Edgar Langford's great contribution to science, adapted from the Babylonian sorcerers he revered, ultimately became so dangerous it was a threat to every living thing. Tesla has alluded to this in his diaries, which I saw for the first time three years ago in Yugoslavia. He remorsefully accepted blame for the disaster that took place here. But I'm certain Tesla had divorced himself from Mad Edgar's schemes just before Midsummer Eve; otherwise he would have vanished with the others. He also made note of the fact that Edgar's machine, which had *no* working parts to wear out, may be even more powerful now than it was in 1916.''

Whit looked around. ''Which machine is that?''

''No, no, those are just some of Tesla's playthings—smaller polyphase motors and a primitive atom smasher. The first workable cyclotron, constructed long before the Manhattan Project.''

''Cyclotron? Could it have had something to do with the disappearance of the chateau?''

''I'm telling you it was *Edgar's* machine that must

have drastically altered the electromagnetic field surrounding Tormentil! It has no name—in English; but the Mesopotamian adepts called it "Star-eater." Which is another way of saying its energy came from cosmic rays. All of which are invisible, just as the machine can no longer be discerned, though it continues to exist, and grows, as Tesla feared, ever more greedy and powerful, an extension of the lethal mind of Edgar Langford."

Staring at the waterfall, Whit felt something horrible in his own mind, a humped and hairy tarantula of disbelief, freezing reason with each tetchy, fingering step it took. He leaned against a railing and gave his head a hard shake.

Jacob said, "I think you should bathe now. It will relax you. The stairs to your right go down to the pool. You need only to be careful of the current; there is an outlet deep in the rock on the other side, and you could be sucked underground for miles. I'll be gone for only a few minutes."

Whit looked up. "Where are you going, Jacob?"

"I told you. I have food. And there are photographs I think you must see."

Jacob picked up one of the wireless tubes from a rock shelf; it began immediately to glow in his hand. He went quickly back the way they had come. Whit wondered if he should follow him; he doubted the man's sanity and didn't trust him; but his own mind, knocked sidewise and senseless in time, was not reliable. It was pleasant in the rainy cavern, in this closed weather without death in it, away from the strict stone gazes of warrior deities. He walked to the steps and looked down into the green and foaming pool, mist rising to the level of his face, wetting his eyelashes. Inviting. An antidote for depression. The resonance carried through the ledge of rock from the generator had begun to lull him.

He stripped off his clothes and walked naked down the steps cut into the side of the ledge to where the pool lapped over stone. He sat down, submerged to his chest. Ah. Better than Jacob had described it. There was room to lay back and he closed his eyes, hearing underwater the downpour of the waterfall and the thrum of the generator like a primeval heartbeat.

But, distantly, a baby cried unattended in an expensive perambulator. Why had he been so furiously jealous? Nanny staring red-eyed in a fouled birdcage, blasphemously transformed into a dead thing. Dead from—an army surgeon once had explained to him what killed soldiers who otherwise appeared unscathed. Something called the vagus nerve became paralyzed at moments of extreme terror. Jacqueline, who in the words of Jacob Schwarzman had "crossed over." *But from where?*

Yes, he knew her. Her Parisian scent, her dressy rustlings, her lullabies, her handclap and stern wordless rebuke when he was up to something she didn't approve of. Those hands, so white with a tint of purple in the nails, firm without fondling as she washed him in his flotilla-laden tub, buttoned him into pajamas, tucked him in his princeling's bed.

Mother often came then, into the nursery, almost too late, to say good night and kiss his cheek as he was nodding off to song or story. . . .

He had loved her in the beginning. Then love had come apart like a straw boat in a torrent. Mother: yet despised, flaxen, fading, yellow as a pear, delicately bleeding primrose into the deepening night from which

he had escaped, to wander in a dusty trance through low
cacti and greasewood.

When he trudged up the steps from the pool, his head
heavy from the weight of despair, there was a grayish,
nearly worn-out towel draped over a pipe railing. Jacob
had returned. Whit had no idea how much time had
passed. Jacob's back was to him, discreetly. He had
brought a large rush basket with him, a couple of folding canvas campstools. Whit pulled on skivvies and
joined him. On one of the canvas stools Jacob had
spread a spartan dinner: nuts, dried fruit, mushrooms.
Whit felt an off-balance yearning for damask cloths and
canapés, cold unblemished silver. He was handed an
opened bottle of white wine.

Jacob pointed to the vacant stool. "Please. You sit
there. You're my guest. I don't mind standing."

"What are we eating?"

"The fruit is crabapple, persimmon, and peach. Those
are walnuts and pecans, very nourishing." He was chewing with his mouth full; little white bits of nutmeat
sprinkled his black beard. "The mushrooms are excellent with that wine, you must try them."

Whit looked suspiciously at the mushroom sections.
Some, spongelike, looked familiar and edible. Others
did not.

Jacob shrugged. "I know what you're thinking. But
I'm an expert mycologist. My hobby for years. I know
what is deadly, and what isn't." He picked up a whole
mushroom and plunged it into his mouth. "These are
morels. Common and harmless. The oyster mushrooms
are also exceptionally tasty."

"What about the brown ones?"

Jacob swallowed, and reached for another morel. "An

ordinary boletus, you find them everywhere in Wildwood. Enjoy your wine."

Whit sipped. It was delicious. He reached for a handful of nuts and chewed them, then sampled the fruit and mushrooms.

"Are you feeling better now? The water has mineral properties I find rejuvenating."

"I have a lot of questions, Jacob."

"First, why don't you examine some photographs? They could be more revelatory than any explanations I have to offer."

From a rucksack he removed several fiberboard folders and began looking through the first one, which contained a loose assortment of old pictures. He mulled over certain ones.

"I own the most complete collection of photographs pertaining to the development of Wildwood, also biographies of nearly everyone who came here, who built and staffed the chateau. Literally hundreds of them. But, as I told you, there are no photographs of Caliban. There exist scores of wedding pictures of your—" He glanced at Whit's face, then amended what he had been about to say. "Of Sibby Langford, her family and bridesmaids, even the groom's attendants. But Langford is conspicuously absent from all of them."

"His phobia."

"Exactly." Jacob began handing the photographs, some cracked and peeling, to Whit.

"There you have the house on Commonwealth Avenue in Boston, where Sibby Waring Langford grew up. That is her mother and father. The young man with the derby in the crook of his arm is her older brother, nicknamed 'Boshie.' The other boy, wearing a Fauntleroy suit, is Sibby's younger brother, age three at this time. He was known as 'Peevie,' perhaps because of a temperamental disposition."

"Why should I be interested in them?"

"All of Sibby's family were guests for the Mid-summer Eve gala which Mad Edgar conceived to celebrate your sixth birthday and the completion of his chateau. The gala that went so catastrophically wrong. It was the fall of the house of Usher and the masque of the red death all in one grisly moment. And this is Sibby Langford on her wedding day. Looking, despite her best efforts, somewhat pensive."

Whit took the large stiff-backed photo from Jacob and gazed at the young woman he had been assured was his mother. He felt, for a staggered moment, that he was going to fall off the campstool.

"Of course you recognize her," Jacob said quietly.

"No. No, you're wrong. It's just that—"

"What?"

"You said that he was—a monster of some kind. And she's—"

"Frail but lovely. Certainly she was not blind."

"Then how could she marry him?"

"A madman? A monster? It came to that. But when Sibby met Edgar Langford he was, in addition to being indecently wealthy, renowned for his travels, his scholarship, his discoveries. And no one who knew him ever denied that he could be a fascinating conversationalist; a spellbinder. Sibby, who was just nineteen, resourcefully sheltered and very immature, was simply talked into believing she loved him. Or perhaps her love was real; her diaries vanished with her and I have only copies of the reams of letters she wrote to her family assuring them of her deep happiness. It may well be that she *was* happy with Edgar for a short time, until the less attractive aspects of his personality became dominant. There are strong hints of sexual perversions practiced in the Eastern brothels he frequented during his expeditions. If Sibby soon fell out of love with her husband, well, there was Mr. Travers. He seldom left Wildwood for the thirteen years required to complete the chateau. He was a lifelong bachelor, never linked with another woman.''

Jacob produced a photo of the architect, on horseback, hat brim pulled low as if he were looking into the sun. A full mustache, a good chinline, were apparent. He sat his horse with an ease Whit himself had never achieved; although he had grown up with the U.S. cavalry, he had been unable to develop any fondness for the animals.

Whit held the photos of Sibby and Travers side by side.

''They were lovers?''

He had bitten his tongue, an unexplainable spasm. Love, envy, hatred—but whom did he hate, and why? The doomed girl in the heavy wedding dress with the soft, chastened eyes of a saint committed to the stake, or the tall architect in his highwayman's slouch hat, poised for a getaway on his high-headed horse?

''I have proof,'' Jacob said smugly.

''A letter? A diary?''

''An eyewitness to their affair.''

Whit swallowed more wine from the bottle. Jacob, busy sorting through dozens of photos, pausing to look at labels he had pasted on the backs, had stopped nibbling. Whit reached for a remaining section of mushroom and ate it. A good woodsy astringent taste he hadn't appreciated in his other samplings; it cleared his palate, heightening the effect of the wine which he craved, for its silvery lightness, the tranquility it bequeathed in the darkness that was most troublesome, those depths where the heart lay stunned. He picked up the photos of the bride and the architect, only to put them down again. His heartbeat, now, was rapid, he had begun to breathe unconsciously through his teeth, drawing down cold that shook his spread and luminous rib bones. Jacob stopped what he was doing and gazed thoughtfully at him. Sweat rolled like rivulets down Whit's forehead and cheeks.

"How could you have an eyewitness?" he asked the archaeologist.

Another photo was thrust at Whit. He took it with numbed fingers. He had to look closely to see anything. The light in the cavern was brighter, auroral, but the face of the woman emerged slowly from the murky background of the photograph like something elusive floating beneath him in a pond. He sensed beauty behind the pleated wing of a black Spanish fan, all that was alluring canceled except for one keen cheekbone, a hot and forward eye, a flash of bared white temple above which, in her massed locks, a rich comb perched egotistically as a peacock.

"Who is she?"

When Jacob didn't reply immediately Whit looked up. His face above the black cataract of beard was changed, shy and drained, yokel-looking; temporarily he was reduced to the vaporous state of the lovelorn.

"Her name is Pamela; Pamela Belford. She is—was— Sibby Langford's personal maid." He drew a breath and pleaded, "Lovely, don't you think?"

"Is? Was?"

"Pamela is living here, with me. The Walkouts don't know. It's a violation of our agreement. If they should find out, well—not only would they take Pamela from me, they might also sentence me to death. So you see, I must be very careful. I hardly ever leave her, except when I need to go into town for mail, or other necessities. The medicine she needs.''

"Then she made it through the—what you call the Crossover."

"Yes. Her mind, unfortunately, was affected by the experience. But slowly—I know if I am patient—'' Jacob's eyes were watering; he wiped them. "She's had some good days so far," he said optimistically. "I think I have been in love with Pamela from the moment I first came across that photograph, more than eight years ago. I never dreamed we would meet."

"How old—?"

"Pamela's twenty-one. She came to me only a few months ago, and of course time is frozen where they— the rest of them—are detained. Imprisoned."

Whit was a long time raising the bottle of wine to his lips, and although he was careful, some of it dribbled down his naked chest.

"Pamela's the one—told you about—"

"The lovers. But she never betrayed Sibby. She refused to spy on her despite Edgar's bribes and finally his threats; when at last he discovered for himself that Sibby had deceived him, he tried in a fit of rage to strangle poor Pamela."

"She isn't—dressed like a maid in the photograph."

"No, that was one of her stage costumes. She assisted Caliban in the magic shows he staged for visitors and staff. She became quite accomplished herself at prestidigitation."

"What else—did she do for him?"

Jacob was furious at Whit's allegation.

"She didn't go to bed with him! She has never belonged to any man but me!"

"Where's—Pamela now?"

"Sleeping. She hasn't been well lately, the reason I was forced to go into town two days ago. When that maniac Rutledge nearly succeeded in running over me."

The bottle fell from Whit's hand, but failed to break on the stone ledge. He looked stupidly at it. Wine was leaking out, precious wine. He looked apprehensively at Jacob, who from this low angle was transformed, his head blown out of proportion to his body. His beard resembling a thicket sprouting thorns.

"Jacob—I feel—something is—I think I—"

"You're now feeling the effects of that last piece of mushroom you ate." Jacob's voice sounded as if it were coming from the bottom of a well, even as his head floated ragged as a storm cloud over Whit. "Which I selected especially for you, because it has distinctly powerful hallucinogenic qualities."

"What the hell—you mean you—trying to kill—"

"No, no, you won't be harmed! You'll have only a slight headache when the drug wears off in a few hours. In the meantime it will lay bare your subconscious, stimulate your memory, help to illuminate those six crucial years of utter blankness. Perhaps, if you think back now, you will be able to describe to me, minute by minute, what you saw on the night of Mad Edgar's Revels."

"Crock of shit, Jacob. Telling you—*I don't know*. Never was here."

"Come now, you *are* Alexander. Tormentil was your home."

Photos fell from Whit's lap. Jacob hastened to retrieve them before they might become soaked in the puddle of spilled wine. He held up Sibby Langford's likeness.

"Concentrate. Remember. This is the woman who gave birth to you. You suckled at her breast. Think of that warm and nourishing breast, let your memories flow, like the milk of your mother."

Whit stood, a jointless flaccid exercise as if he were made of gum rubber, and tried to push Jacob aside. But he had no more push than a reflection, no elemental force. The waterfall tumbled huge and heavy, beat heavily on the mind. But through the lagoon of the inner ear it was a ripple, a spiritual sibilance. The photograph he wanted to deny preempted most of his field of vision. He tried to move his tongue, denouncing what the eye would not. His tongue felt dead as a stump. Brackish saliva flowed down his chin. A shadow had set upon her profound countenance, besmirching the time-golded forehead. He felt a corresponding jagged crack down his breastbone, through which his heart squirmed sick and full. He pressed it back with both hands and slumped, a martyred pose, on the campstool, nearly overturning it.

Jacob, excited, steadied him.

"Who are you?"

His body flowed, thinner than any mist, through Jacob's hands, though the cavern walls and then a wall of morticed stone. He laughed at the conceit that occurred to him. *Who am I?*

"Imaginary," he answered.

"Do you see her? Listen! Do you hear her voice as she sits and rocks you?"

"She's imaginary, too; doesn't exist." But the waterfall spoke differently; her phantom sang to him, plaintive song that shivered the fragile reality he clung to. He turned his face aside, seeing on the wall a tubular sun with a fiery corona. The light of this sun made silver a huge and brainy mass of wire; there were flashes of electric blue beneath a deaf and dumb eternity, black as the inside of the magician's box.

(No   I'll fall
  help me
              father, help)

The mercurial magician folded his box, then folded it again until it was small enough to slip into a pocket, and harmless. But the great machine kept on. And on, at its sacred work.

It's only a machine that I have made for us, little Alex.

(But what is it for? What does it do?)

Tricks.

(What kind of tricks?)

The metaphysical magician, laughing. Embracing him. And the ghostboy felt, at last, an emotion that fit true, unfalsified by archivists or the invective of tall-tellers.

We can turn ourselves into birds and animals, and back again. Wouldn't that be fun?

(I guess so)

Or punish our enemies, my delightful Alex—by not bringing them back.

Now the magician, Messianic, had frightened him a little. He seemed to understand this. He stroked the ghostboy's head: so like his own, or at least he was willing to think so when his mood was right. The boy stared at the linked and wiry machine, through which he could study starmaps near and far, aureoles and obelisks afire.

(What are enemies?)

Those who would do harm to us. Lie and cheat, and try to trick the trickster.

(Do you have enemies?)

I have profound and diligent enemies, sanctimonious conspirators who would take everything from me. My inheritance. My treasures! that I alone had the ingenuity to unearth, that rightfully belong only to me. They would take all that, and more. My wife, my life, my son.

(No!)

But you mustn't let them frighten you. Here, let me wipe your eyes, sweet Alex. My soul, my heartsblood. No one can ever take you from me. Because you see, I know my enemies. I know the worm in every bud, and its name is greed. And when they are all gathered here, in my house, I will deal with them before that worm can begin to devour me. What is a lowly worm to the celestial serpent? We will deal with them, my dearest son.

All the fierceness that was in the ghostboy went into his embrace.

(Yes! We will!)

But he shouted it to an idea, an unnumbered star, a vanishing ray, a cold and ticking brain, that buried lode in empyrean ether.

"Whom are you talking to?" Jacob demanded, shaking him. He had lit a brash cigarillo. The smoke was rank and choking. The waterfall behind him crashing, then leaping up in splayed rainbows. "Who is it you see?"

"Leave me alone! I want my father, I want him!"

"But Mad Edgar is gone—he made you all disappear from the mountain, through his miscalculations. Is that the truth, or isn't it?"

Whit struck at Jacob's face but drew only stinging fire from the end of the cigarillo, sparks that Jacob hastily brushed from his beard.

"Don't call him *Mad Edgar*! It's time for the parade! My father and I are going to ride on my birthday float."

"And your mother—"

"I don't want to talk about her! I hate her!"

"Alex—"

Whit shook his head sharply; he put a hand to his throat. He was numb there, and choked by the smoke from Jacob's cigarillo.

"Are you my enemy?" he mumbled.

"No, no, I'm Jacob! Your friend. I'm everyone's friend. Even your father's. And there are many, many questions I want to ask him."

"He's—" A sob. "I can't find him now."

"Why don't you look for him again? Just go back a little further in time, Alex, I'm sure he'll be there."

"The machine won't let me. I can't go back before the machine was."

Jacob waggled his virile cigarillo, blue smoke circles in the air, tainting the rainbows. Whit squeezed his eyes shut but there was no place else to go, except into a black box of cosmic dimension.

"Machine?" Jacob said eagerly. "Describe it to me."

"Brain."

"It looks like a brain?"

"It *is*. A brain made out of silver wire. Stars flashing all over it."

"Where is this brain, Alex?"

"Oh, it's in the lantern."

"And the lantern is open?"

"Yes, yes, open!"

"What's the matter?"

"Storm!"

"Lightning too?"

"Yes, yes, lots of lightning! Oh, I don't *want* it to rain! Then there won't be a parade."

"My God, my God," Jacob said, tugging ecstatically at his beard, "they did it, they put it together! But only Tesla had the genius to make it work. If he had been there that night, he might have prevented the great tragedy that—"

"Where's my father!"

"Try to understand, Alex. The chateau, everything inside or within a hundred yards of it—Jacqueline, rocking little Laurette to sleep in the aviary—was part of a harmonic pattern, sympathetic to the harmonies of our earthly sphere, but capable of being disturbed, susceptible to a certain electromagnetic slippage—"

"I don't understand you!" Whit howled; held by Jacob, he was terrified of the beard and the close-together, fanatical blue eyes of a stranger; by definition, an "enemy." "I don't know you, let me go!"

"Wait! He—he taught you magic tricks, didn't he? Tricks with scarves. Think of the chateau, the mountain on which it was built, as nothing more than a trick knot in a stage magician's scarf, a knot which he can slide with ease from one end to the other. You've done that trick yourself, haven't you? I thought so. All right, I want you to think of the chateau as another kind of knot, slipping just far enough along this harmonic scarf so that it suddenly seems to vanish—like the stars after sunrise. The stars are still there, but even the keenest eye can't find them in daylight. If we don't see them, why, we can easily believe they've gone, somewhere. Vanished magically from the cosmos. Now imagine this: all of the people in or near the chateau, all of the birds and floats and carriages and members of the band with their big brass instruments, picture them standing very, very still for a long time, just out of sight like stars in the noon sky, while we grow old. But they don't change or grow older by even as much as a full second of *their* time. Because for them, nothing has changed at all. They don't realize that anything has happened, that where they were just a moment ago on the magician's scarf, time has continued at its normal velocity, the world has gone on without them: babies have been born, the aged have died. Wars have been fought, inventions have been invented. Then the knot in the scarf is shifted again, just a fraction, and a few of them, one after another, along with croquet balls and perambulators and what have you, are literally dashed back into *our* stream of time. They feel as dazed as if they had been struck by lightning. Some go insane from the scare. And nearly all of them are changed—in horrible, unalterable ways. Because your birthday party, the Revels, was to be a masquerade. Remember? Everyone was fitted for costumes that were made in the chateau's workrooms—costumes of feather and fur, of beasts and birds both mythical and real. Even you had a costume ready, Alex.''

"I don't know what you're talking about!"

"But you know there was an aviary in the park, already stocked with exotic birds—not so many birds, however, that there wouldn't be room for more. And the animal park your father built was nearly empty: cage after shadowy cage ready to be occupied. At the end of Mad Edgar's Revels, all of his invited guests, those whom he unreasonably despised or feared, were to be, by means of his sorcery, transformed into the beasts they had innocently impersonated while dancing through the night—"

It was not a man holding him, it was a vulturine bird with tough claws and the head of an old blue-eyed lion, the dark mane acrawl with licelike screaming creatures. Whit flailed with both hands, smashing Jacob full in the mouth, sending the bloodied blob of cigarillo flying into the pool. He stepped forward to hit Jacob again, and silence him for good. He stepped on the wine bottle and his feet went out from under him.

—And there he went, plunging again, headfirst through space, naked except for his underwear, he'd had no time to put on his soft and furry Pooh Bear costume. And the glare of the Texas sun on hardpan blinded him up to the moment his head smacked down. His lungs filled, then hardened with a weight of stone that sank him into an even more remote corner of eternity—hushed, vast, and lightless: without the hope of a tear to relieve its lonely monotony.

Chapter
Twenty-four

TERRY awoke at the edge of the wood near the quarry pool, wrapped in a blanket that didn't belong to him. Already the morning was bright on his bare shoulders; even before opening his eyes he felt as if it just might be a good day. At any rate, nothing could be worse than the night before.

"Hello," Josie Raftery said as soon as she saw him stir. "You slept right through the crack of dawn, begod."

She was standing between him and the sun. The great scallops of her wings were spread, absorbing warmth. Terry sat up quickly, the blanket falling around his feet, and only then he discovered that he didn't have a stitch on. Mortified, he tried to gather the blanket around him, having awakened, as always, tumescent; but Josie, with a laugh, snatched it away from him with her toes.

"Hey, what are you doing? What happened to my—" He sat hunched on the ground with his knees up and his arms wrapped around them, afraid to look closely at his surroundings. All the earth, it seemed, had been put right, but there was no telling how quickly it might be shaken again, tumbled into chaos.

"You will not need clothing. I never wear any. Divil your shyness, then, and don't be making strange with me. Can't give you a pair of wings, boy; but in other ways we're equal now, like the first man and woman in Paradise." She laughed again. "You might as well stand up; it's pathetic you're looking, huddled there on the ground like a whipped cur."

Terry filled his lungs and got to his feet, hands at his sides unprotectively; but blood was thick in his cheeks. Josie reefed her wings, then walked a circle around him. Unclothed and condemned to earth like a derelict goddess, she was hale but with a lewdness that was a pestering sore in his eye, her sex blunt and fox-furred. But then, all women were foreign to him between the legs, where he was proudly shaped and elongated and not so hairy yet. Her breasts, however, were pretty, and worth dwelling on: orbs within tresses, twin sunrises.

"What's your name?" Josie asked, stopping again in front of him, muting the light on his face. He liked the crook of an ivory-mellow tooth when she smiled, the weather on her cheeks. Her wings thickened when folded. They were not as flimsy as he had first thought, seeing light filter through them, but appeared to be composed sturdily of scales, like a fish's but translucently fine.

"I'm Terry. And you're—"

"Josie."

"Y-yeah." He was trying to be nonchalant, but his teeth had chattered and he gulped air. Then he was slowly reassured by the rustling breezes and plain-positive birdsong of a customary dawn, orchid and arc-light through simmering trees. He looked down at himself. "Well, how did you—how could—"

"Wasn't me that undressed you; was himself over there."

She fanned her wings toward Terry, barely skimming, tickling him: a spiritual, not a sensual touching. *Are we friends?* She meant to be touched in return, and he reached out timidly to stroke a leading edge of one wing. Nappiness; pleasant, mildly provoking. Then he looked behind him, where Josie also was looking. His heart chilled like a stone in a creek.

The goatman was hunkered nearby, tending a fire in a circle of stones, slicing with a wicked handax strips from a side of cured boar meat.

Josie touched his cheek again; Terry shivered.

"No, it's not a mask he's wearing. Name's Taharqa. He's my friend, and he'll be *your* friend as well, if only you will allow him to be."

Terry, dubious, studied the tough dark body, the skeleton so thinly contained that bones shone fiercely in gleams beneath the skin whenever the goatman moved. He was tall and scarred and looked powerful. He worked with the ax as if it were a paring knife, until he had filled a big frying pan with bacon. He placed this pan over the crackling fire of fragrant balsam wood, began breaking a handful of little speckled eggs into another pan.

Not far from where the goatman was cooking Terry saw, gratefully, Bocephus the hound chewing on a bone. The goatman had tied him to a tree, but he seemed to have adapted placidly to his circumstances, and his odd captors. Both Terry's and Faren's backpacks were hanging from stobs of that same tree.

Terry shuddered, as if the hung pack symbolized her death.

"Where's Faren?" he demanded.

"No way for me to know that." Josie frowned, her wings fretting. "Somewhere in time she'll be, between here and there."

"There?"

"The back beyond the vale," Josie said vaguely, her wings more agitated. "She's under the guidance of the serpent Erim now, for good or ill. I believe you made his acquaintance, in the upheaval of the night we've just been through."

He was breaking out in goose bumps and bit his lip futilely, trying to keep his body precariously under control.

"I need—I have to take a—"

"Anywhere in the woods you like," she said. The perfect hostess. "Mind you don't step on something sharp, if your feet are as tender as the rest of you looks."

"Thanks," Terry said sardonically. The goatman had turned his horny head to look at him: was that a smile? He didn't know one goaty expression from another. Jesus, and he could have gone sailing!

He went back into the woods where the pines were packed like a quiver of arrows, where he had some privacy to relieve himself. But still he had trouble, standing there in the new morning in unfamiliar surroundings, pee simply wouldn't come. And he thought of Faren grinning at him across the hood of her car, *Want me to talk bear talk to it?* That broke him, he gave a great hoohaw of a sob that probably could have been heard for miles and dropped shakily to his knees. While the tears streamed down his face he managed, in that position, to empty his bladder too. After a while he got up, wondering which way was home. Naked or not, he was getting out of here. . . .

The good smells of bacon and eggs cooking came to him through the green wood. He walked numbly back to the open space on the bluff, only stubbing his toe once, and limped toward Josie, who was now sitting cross-legged with the blanket he had slept in spread before her. She was eating, a heaped plate on the blanket, long-handled spoon grasped in one foot. Terry was appalled and fascinated. Freaks. He wiped at a tear-striped cheek. She looked up neutrally at him. The hell of it was, he couldn't help liking her while he was feeling sorry for her. At least, except for taking his clothes away, they didn't mean him any harm; the worst that could happen, he might catch cold. But that was being a hell of a baby, even thinking such a thing.

"Sit," Josie said between mouthfuls.

The blackamoor brought him a plate of bacon and eggs and some kind of fruity beverage in a metal cup. Up close he smelled decidedly of goat, and Terry stiffened involuntarily. Josie noticed, with a touchy smile. Holding her metal plate at a slight angle with one foot, she scraped it clean with the spoon.

Terry picked up his own spoon, wondering when he would be able to stop looking at her pussy, when it would merely *be* there, unremarkably, like the nose on her face. It was just that every time she lifted her foot to her mouth—

"Those are quail eggs you're eating," Josie told him, to be making conversation. "Ever tasted quail eggs?"

"No. Uh, how did you—learn to—"

"Feed meself? Brush me hair? Wash me face when it's darty? Well, now, it's more than three years by that I crossed over, wearing wings instead of the arms I was barn with. Real wings, not pretty sequins stitched on silk. That's the sacred wonder of it all. Me first thought was, if it is I have died and gone to heaven, then where are the pearly gates? And all the saints gathered beneath their golden halos? Before long I *was* welcomed, by

some others who had crossed over long before me.
Saints they were not. Creatures from a brimstone pit,
more like. Aye, and I nearly went daft from grief and
fright. A common reaction among Walkouts.''

"Wait a minute. What's a Walkout?"

"Those of us who have slipped through the vale of
time, to our sorrow, from the night of Mad Edgar's
Revels into this day and age.''

"How did that happen?"

"Best fill your stomach while you have the chance.
We've a few miles yet to go this morning.''

"But how did you—?"

The goatman brought Josie another heaping plate of
bacon and eggs and also some dried fruit, which she
nibbled first.

"There are others who can explain 'crossing over'
better than me. You'll have the opportunity of talking to
them once you reach Walkout Town.''

He stared at her, perplexed.

Josie swallowed and paused before digging into her
mound of steaming scrambled eggs.

"The truth is there's naught but theories of black
magick or witchcraft to argue, endlessly it seems. Me, I
try not to think about it so much anymore. What happened to us was strange and tragic. Why God would
permit such a thing is a mystery. But I have to keep
me faith, though it has been very hard. Many's the time
I've wished for a priest to talk to. Ah, well. I'll not
question His divine wisdom in giving me wings on this
earth, and that's all there is to it. Because, Terry, I have
the wits to know I've gained more than I ever lost.''

She was silent for a while, eating with a gusto Terry
couldn't match, although he managed to put away a few

mouthfuls himself. The goatman sat on his heels beside the fire, with his own plate.

"Well, I eat a great deal, as you see," Josie said as if apologizing. "Six large meals a day, but gluttony it is not. That is barely enough food to keep the meat on me bones. I use *e-nahr-mous* amounts of energy when I fly."

"Do you like flying?"

"Do I like it, says he? I would soar with the sweeping wind day and night, sleep in the lofty clouds if I could."

"How do you fly? Is it easy to do?"

"Ha! Easy? And have you ever rowed a boat?"

"Yes."

"Sure and wasn't it hard work, then, after a few minutes. Well, that's how I fly—by rowing through the air. Sounds simple—but I can tell you, I was many a week catching on. Because I was afraid at first, you see, deathly afraid. Of falling, and tearing me wings to tatters. Then what would I be? At last I screwed up me courage. Scolded meself: 'Josie, if you won't use your wings, then it's dead you might as well be; for what sart of life will you have, stranded on the ground?' Then I took meself to this high place. It was to fly, or drown in the pool. But that day, with God's help and a generous wind, I flew—no, I soared! I may not describe the ecstasy of it. No longer was I a self-pitying coward, but blessed. So many crossed over as hopeless, blinded, bumbling creatures. But Josie Raftery, a nobody, had the gift of flight."

"How old are you, Josie?"

"I would be twenty years of age now surely. I was not yet seventeen when I crossed over. I was a seamstress, me sister a scullery maid, and us both nurse-child—arphans, you would say.''

"What happened to your sister?''

"I have not seen nor heard of Patricia to this day. She may never cross. Or perhaps she's among those misfortunate souls, trapped between there and here in what we call the Well of Sorrow.''

"Do you mean the pool down there in the quarry?''

Josie nodded. "Aye. 'Tis the way in. But so far there has been no way out for the likes of them.''

"Or Faren?'' he said, such fear in his voice that Josie prudently looked away.

"Your friend has a magic caul about her, a way with the Serpent, an understanding of the nether world such as few possess. That is all I know of the matter, and all I care to know. I pray to God she will be successful in that she was sent to do.''

"Where do you live? In the woods? What about winter, don't they have blizzards here?''

"Blizzards we have surely. But where we are the winters are not so harsh, and often they are mercifully brief. And I do live in me own snug hut in Walkout Town, with a bubbling spring for bathing and warmth.''

"Do you live with anybody? I mean—'' He looked at Taharqa. "With him?''

"I do not!'' Her wings fanned out in a show of indignation; but her lips twitched amusedly. "Not that it would matter. He is a eunucher.''

"A—he doesn't have any—''

"Hmm. Just so. Our arrangement is a simple one. Taharqa gathers food for the both of us, and prepares it. In return, I read to him.''

"Read?''

"Do you take me for an ignoramus? I have me own Bible. And there is a library in Walkout Town."

"A library? Where do the books come from?"

"Why, they are bought in bookstores," she said dryly. "There are those courageous souls among us who have decided to go outside, to earn money for those things we cannot make or gather in Wildwood. Tools and radios and the batteries needed to operate them. Medical supplies."

"You mean they—do they work in sideshows, in carnivals?"

"Yes. What else is there for them to do? They close their minds to those who would make a jeer of them, and are paid handsomely in the bargain."

"*That's* what I saw! It was a trailer with a flat tire outside the motel where we were staying in Asheville. There was an old man who looked like he was wearing a deerhead and another one in a monk's robe, with a croquet mallet. Maybe you know who—"

Josie nodded. "I know them. They are brothers. One is dying but we have an infirmary, morphine to ease his suffering. Before Midsummer Eve they were men of quality; they lived with their families in fine houses, in the city of Boston."

"I'll be damned!" Terry said excitedly. "Listen, those two really scared the—I couldn't even explain to Dad—"

He fell abruptly silent; it had been a while since he had thought about his father.

"What is it, Terry?"

"My father's in Wildwood somewhere. He was going up to the mountain. But something must have happened to him. I need to find him, Josie."

"Was he in the company of a man named Arn Rutledge?"

"That's right! Do you know where they are?"

"I know where Mr. Rutledge is." She put out her right foot. The vine burn around her ankle had scabbed over. "Do you see this?"

"Yeah; how did it happen?"

"I was bait in a trap, for the clever Mr. Rutledge."

"You were trying to trap Arn? Why?"

"Self-preservation."

"What happened to him?"

"Beat him good-looking, I did," Josie said with grim satisfaction. "I told you. I know how to take care of meself."

She stood up then, with a slow unfolding of her wings. Stared down at Terry, a harsh angel, someone altogether new to him.

"Mr. Rutledge was not badly hurt; he will recover. Taharqa fished him from a spring not far from here, once I had done knocking him in the head with a stone."

"But what about my dad?" Terry looked reluctantly at Taharqa, his mouth open in shock, thinking of the black man's ease with his handax.

"I truly do not know where your father went, nor what has become of him," Josie said. "I will try to find that out for you."

"Where's Arn now?"

"Walkout Town. In a few days we will decide, by council, what should be done with him. He may be let loose, with a severe warning. On the other hand—" She turned, showing Terry her slashed buttock. "He did this to me, so I'm not in a forgiving mood. I think the man would stuff and mount me like a trophy if he could. But I'll be no man's trophy, or plaything, ever. If the deciding vote is left to me, I will vote for him to die."

She flew then, straight up from the ground. Bocephus rose lumberingly and barked as Josie glided in a graceful, sunny figure eight above the quarry pool. A line of birds in flight broke sharply from her path, skimming past the radiance of an extended wing, her flowing hair. Terry, feeling dull and earthbound, could only stare, amazed by her virtuosity.

Josie called to him.

"You may pull on your trousers now, if it's more comfortable you are that way. Follow Taharqa—he will take you to our Walkout Town. Meantime I will just have a gander up the mountain, to see if there is any sign of your da."

Chapter ——— Twenty-five

ARN Rutledge reckoned he was lucky to be alive, but the circumstances didn't please him.

Some of the sight of his right eye had returned, although his head was still swollen and aching below the temple from the thumping Josie Raftery had given him. Never saw it coming, that was what galled Arn so bad. She'd been just too clever and quick for him. More wasp than butterfly, that Josie. Maybe if he was so lacking in wits he couldn't stay one jump ahead of a shanty-Irish kid (no matter that she could fly better than a goddamned helicopter), then it was time he quit the woods. But, more than likely, the decision was no longer his to make.

He was tied up, his hands down in front so he could take a leak when he had to, but he couldn't reach up and back far enough to adjust the knot of the heavy noose around his neck. A vengeful snare at the end of a slack rope that gave him some freedom of movement so he could sit outside the hut in diffused sunlight, but still the threat was always there, rough hemp rubbing under his jaw, reminding him of the fact that he could just as easily be vertical and dangling in air, neckbones loose as unstrung beads in his cooling flesh. Since worry never cured a thing, he didn't dwell on the possibility that when the Walkouts finished disposing of their late, lamented dead they would get around to him. Meantime he just stayed quiet in the dooryard of the conical hut covered in split-oak shingles which served as his jail, wished for a drink of whiskey, and observed all that he could see of Walkout Town.

It was no longer a mystery to Arn how he'd never found it during all the years he'd rambled freely through Wildwood. The town site had been chosen and then laid out by a man with a talent for camouflage and misdirection. From the angle of this morning's sun he had judged the location to be midway up the southeast slope of Tormentil, an area so thick with conifers standing seventy feet in height or more that even the pilot of a low-flying plane (if one had the nerve to approach this close to the notoriously jinxed mountain) would see nothing but familiar monotonous patterns of bough and bark, rock and rill, shadow and shifting light and frequent mist on the floor of the evergreen wood. But even a daredevil pilot couldn't fly directly over Walkout Town. It lay, in a neat pentagonal pattern, in the cleft of a three-sided bluff of nearly vertical naked rock that looked pale, almost glacial, from a distance. This apparent translucence was due to numerous shallow waterfalls winding down the rock. All year long, Arn was sure, the angles of the bluff had maximum exposure to the sun wherever it traveled in the sky, sunlight that was reflected down and through the trees and the swirling mists, the smokes, from the many hot springs bubbling up through shale earth. There was one inside his hut, and maybe all the huts were built around such springs. Most days, then, the odd, disarranged citizens of Walkout Town must go about their business in a warm and glowing fog. Even deep in winter, Arn suspected, temperatures might not fall below freezing here.

Anyone who attempted to climb the mountain from the south, on a trail that eventually would take him close to Walkout Town, would be faced with a series of ravines after negotiating some of the most treacherous terrain Wildwood had to offer, filled with bog and bramble and bear wallow, home to painters and packs of wild European boar. From sinkholes vapors rose that were less than healthful, that in fact would kill a man who breathed too deeply the bad air. Arn had, in his younger days, pushed his way through a part of this hard uphill country, more from stubbornness than from curiosity. At some time or other he might well have stopped (a Walkout had informed him) less than a quarter of a mile below their town, surveyed a ravine across which poison oak and ivy grew in tangled strands, never realizing that beneath the forbidding ivy they had concealed a suspension bridge strong enough to support the weight of an army halftrack.

He would like to meet the man who had engineered all this, Arn thought. Because Arn admired his style, his practical nature, his sense of proportion. He was pretty sure he and Travers would get along, up to the moment the Walkouts found it necessary to hang him.

Today they were holding a funeral service, which didn't go very far toward cheering him up; the mourners were out of sight somewhere in the scintillating grove, all he could hear was the hymning. Late last night they had brought the victims in. He was still plenty groggy but could see everything because the mountain was acting up, and the sky was bright with bolts of lightning. He made out one of the victims to be the engineer of the locomotive that had rumbled trackless through a gap in time and wound up in the gorge of the Cat Brier. The other was an old lady in a long black dress, a frilly cap. Nursemaid, he decided, because one of the Walkouts was wheeling an old-style wicker baby carriage, and he heard the squawling of the hungry child. The two bodies lay atop a cart pulled by the big nigger with the goat's head. He wondered what the baby looked like, but wasn't eager to find out. He did think about his wife, and the child they'd never had, before he crept back into the hut and passed out again.

After the proprieties of burial had been observed Walkouts drifted back from the gravesites, crossing an open rectangular area that was neat as a pool table and almost as green. Moss, he figured; grass couldn't grow beneath the needle-shedding pines and other evergreens. He wondered what they used the space for. On the far side of the rectangle stood a building similar in design to the huts in which they all lived. But it was much larger, a meeting place or storehouse.

The woman who appeared out of the shining mist to his left startled him and he swore under his breath. But then he recognized her; she'd come the night before. All she wanted was to give him a drink from the pail she carried. Except for birds and hymns, the creaking of the wheels of the funeral cart last night, and the baby's famished wail, Walkout Town had been nearly a soundless place since his arrival. Arn was accustomed to woodland quiet and solitude, but the noose had him jumpy, and the Walkouts—well, the nigger goatman was a prize beauty compared to some he'd had glimpses of. The woman who held a dipper to his lips had a plain but serene face and a slight, sad, unvarying smile. Her long hair was graying. A few age spots showed on her slim hands. There didn't seem to be anything wrong with her; but either she was mute or didn't want to talk to him. The drink, as before, was a cool herbal tea sweetened with honey.

"Send the boss man around," Arn said to her when he had slaked his thirst. "I think we've got a few things to talk about."

The woman replaced the dipper in the pail and turned to go. The hem of the long dress she wore caught on a twig of a low shrub and pulled just enough to reveal a flash of a stemlike leg, the rock-hard toe of an ostrich. Arn's stomach lurched but he didn't throw his tea up. He just sat there with his tied hands between his knees watching as she slowly returned down the misted path, wondering if the bustle of her dress concealed a bulbous, feather-duster behind.

About half an hour later a man wearing a russet monk's robe and hood came hobbling on a deformed foot to Arn's hut. He wore a dirty sock on the foot and carried a croquet mallet, either for defense or balance. His mismatched eyes were wide of Arn's direct and inquiring gaze. He had a troublesome wheeze.

Arn smiled pleasantly, raising his hands a few inches in greeting.

"Why didn't you let me drown and have done with it?"

"No, sir; then your death would have been on Josie's conscience."

"But you do aim to hang me."

"That has not been decided, Mr. Rutledge."

"You know me, but I don't know you."

"My name is Oliver Waring the Fourth."

"You can just call me Arn, never could get used to any 'mister.' "

Oliver Waring the Fourth nodded slightly. "Boshie will do for me. I've answered to that silly name since I was a toddler."

"I asked for the boss man, and here you are. What I'd like to know—"

"We are a community. No one of us is 'the boss.' I shall try to answer whatever questions you may have."

"Just one question. Who killed my best tracker dog, Boshie?"

"I did."

"I'm surprised you could pull a boot on over that foot. What is it, anyway, a split hoof?"

"I'm not the devil. And not all of us are part animal. My deformation is due to an accident sustained years ago during the construction of Walkout Town."

"If you're so-called normal, what's kept you here?"

"For one thing, I am needed. For another, I have never doubted the day would come when I would have the opportunity to redress the unspeakable evil done to members of my family."

"You expect to somehow get your hands on ole Mad Edgar, is that it?"

Another stiff nod. "Yes. The time may be nearer than we have calculated. There has been so much activity during the past forty-eight hours . . . do you have another question, Arn?"

"No. Just a statement of fact. It ain't a-gonna be that easy to hang me, no matter how it looks to you right now."

"We all do what we must to survive. It may be of some comfort for you to know that your fate is in your wife's hands. As much as we despise you, we revere Faren for her spiritual support. We can only pray that she is a match for the evil she must soon encounter, on a plane of existence where the sorcerer undoubtedly will have the advantage over her."

"Jesus," Arn said, the blood draining from his face. He lunged against the noose that held him powerless. "What have you freaks done with my wife?" he croaked.

"She has been influenced, naturally, by her concern for your well-being, but also by her desire to find a solution to the terror that has possessed us these many years. She is much too good a woman for you, Arn. There is nothing more I can tell you now. All any of us can do is wait, and prepare as best we can for the final crossing."

Chapter Twenty-six

BELLY-UP from mushroom, he was nudged awake by drops of water beading coherently from spindrift apart from the brouhaha of the water-wall, along the underside of the gray pipe railing—drops falling thriftily, measuredly, on the bridge of his nose, wetting cheeks and dry-blooded lip. He awoke in a shaking of cramped and scattered limbs as if in a grave-fit, his brain twinkling glumly in the old, odd twilight of mushroom dreams. He was deaf to the balmy thunder of the water-wall. Where he looked, light rocketed or pinwheeled, the goldenrod and chromed magentas of cavelight. He faced, upside down and in free-fall, as weightless as his shadow skimming clouds, a jagged bowl of mountains.

Hallucination.

Stalactites in a cave, Whit thought, ears peeping open to the languors of the water-wall. He was pleased to be making sense at last, having been marooned on his ledge of rock for at least a month. He felt at his fingertips the hum of a wizardly generator. Other, furtive

fingertips touched his face. Stubble. A bump on the
forehead, soreness ear to ear. His tongue dry and sour.
Another drop of water fell: he blinked, flinching as if it
might be buckshot.

The images in his mind—birds and corpses. Black-
bearded Jacob.

Eat.

Where *was* Jacob?

He accomplished the chore of sitting up. Nausea smote
him.

Drinking with Jacob; and the seductive mushroom.
His undoing.

Whit leaned against the pipe railing, engaged in
thought, aging from the effort. He licked a line of
waterbeads from the railing. The front of his brain
glowed from the ferment of the water-wall—the primeval water-wall.

Now he remembered something of importance. He
had looked at photographs of virgins, dark and light; the
lightness of the one too pure for longevity, the other's
dark sex boasting and virtuoso: *where was she now?*

With Jacob.

There was an emptied bottle of wine on the ledge
with him, two campstools with remnants of dried fruit
and nuts on one of them.

His clothing was there too, strewn carelessly. But he
was not one to fling his clothes any which way while
undressing. Military upbringing. Neatness a necessity.

He found his chronometer. Smashed. It told less of
the passing of time than the stubble on his jaw. Only a
day's growth of beard, to his surprise.

Time to get going. Somewhere; anywhere else.
Starflash, sunrise, a wind coursing through tall pines.

But no more of carious rock, the hot and misting pool, this underworld.

He began to put on his damp clothing.

When he picked up his tan twill pants he saw, unmistakably, most of a handprint in blood. The blood on the material was still tacky, it adhered to his fingertips when he touched it.

He had no wounds. His own hands, when he looked again to be sure, were clean except for the just-smudged fingers.

But his hands were too large to have left this print. And so, he was sure, were the hands of Jacob Schwarzman—a scholarly man too squeamish to kill.

But someone, steeped in blood, reeking of a slaughter, had prowled this cavern while he lay so profoundly unconscious he might well have passed for dead, someone had examined his clothing like a curious animal. And left.

He felt ineradicably marked, a pariah, beyond redemption. He shook from dread. At the same time he cast around for a weapon. But there was nothing more substantial than one of the dull tubes of some glasslike mineral, that took on a wan glow as soon as he picked it up, absorbing ambient energy from the whorls of wire that, he had been told, ran overhead through almost every passageway of the caverns.

He called to Jacob, but heard only his own voice ghosting back through corridors to drown in the splashing of the water-wall.

Only Jacob could get him out of here.

He went out through the passage with the lightweight tube raised, its extra light welcome, his shadow bending tall above him.

The giant's cavern with artifacts from a dead country,

iron gates at one end shut and barricaded by tons of mountainside, gave no hint that Jacob had been there recently.

Something had been said about a library. Jacob had seemed eager to bar the way.

Perhaps that was where he lived as well, with Pamela. *"Jacob! Pamela!"*

There were two connected rooms. Stacks of clay tablets in one. Scrolls and books and manuscripts in Jacob's hand. A magnifying glass. Tools, including a hefty chisel more than a foot long. Whit picked up the chisel in his other hand. Fortified, he entered their living quarters.

Jacob had constructed a sizable bed from packing crates and straps of iron and leather, furnished it with pillows and patchwork quilts he'd bought or perhaps lifted from the clothesline of an isolated cabin somewhere. He'd made a chair that looked comfortable. There were stoneware basins to wash or urinate in, a clothestree from which hung a workshirt, overalls, an old-fashioned-looking calico dress. In a leather casket Whit found bottles of pills and two hypodermic needles.

A third hypo was crushed on the stone floor, which had also absorbed a considerable amount of darkened blood.

Someone was dying—or dead.

But where?

He took care examining the floor with the light in his hand, found an easily followed line of blood that tapered to intermittent splotches in the passage winding uphill from the death chamber.

He was afraid to keep going that way; but he had no-where else to go.

The only light here was the light he held in his hand.

He hadn't gone far when he heard the shuffling, snorting, laboring sounds of someone dragging a sacklike weight over the rough floor of the tight passage.

Whit stopped, listening, nerves prickling.

Heavy, rasping breathing echoed through the passage.

Then, abruptly, it was quiet.

The silence was worse than anything he'd heard so far.

With the light thrust ahead of him, he resumed.

But the light seemed to be fading. Looking up, he saw that the loops of wire did not extend through this passage. With each step he was moving farther away from the field of energy that empowered the mysterious tube.

How soon would he be in total darkness?

The passage branched; he hesitated. Then she was on him almost before he realized anyone was there.

Her lovely, dark-eyed face emerging from the taupe background. She was wearing a long skirt of a grayish shade like the rock, a black cape with a high collar. Her heart-shaped pale face took on a slight amber tint from the waning light.

"Pamela—good God."

She didn't respond to his voice, just stared at him with an almost phantasmal absorption.

"I'm Whit—Jacob must have told you about me."

Nothing came back to him from the locked and isolated brown eyes, the stiff pout of her red lips. There was a streak like rust on one cheek. He realized she was holding a hand behind her back. The other was seated deep beneath the cape; a balmy Napoleonic pose.

"Where's Jacob?" he asked her.

She began, slowly, to back away from him. The mildest apprehension revealed in her tentative movements.

"Is he hurt? Are *you* hurt?"

Whit followed, pressing her. She moved faster. Watchfully. Not taking her eyes from his face.

So little light now, he was opposite Jacob and only three feet away before he noticed him, and then he might not have seen a thing except that Jacob was shanky naked and quite pale; he was jammed into a cleft of rock, almost as flat as a fresco except for a bulge of belly eaten into, lusciously bitten but some time ago, only a stagnant ooze of blood continued. The right side of his head was torn away to the bone. One eye gone, and the other a dreamlike blue. The black beard shellacked hard with blood.

Pamela pulled her hand from behind her back and threw down what she had been concealing, Jacob's overalls. She bared bloodied teeth and from her throat came a yellow yowling, that betrayed a carnivore's passion for another kill.

Tossing off her cape, she came at Whit, quick and cunning.

The swipe of her short-haired massive paw, equipped with needle-pointed claws two inches long, missed his face; but he smelled the tarry old blood caked between claws. The instinct to kill or be killed, fortified on battlefields nearly as bizarre as this one, saved him. With the chisel he struck deep where Pamela was exposed and most vulnerable, in the hollow of her throat between her collarbones. The chisel broke her neck, impaling her; she died at his feet.

He dragged her down the passage, far from Jacob Schwarzman's blue and deathly lugubrious gaze.

He couldn't help himself, he had to undress her.

Everywhere she was woman, except for the hard

black pads of the tufted paw, striped tangerine and old gold of a tiger's powerful forearm.

Yet her face was lovely, unmarred now except for a trickling of blood from one corner of her mouth; he could understand Jacob's infatuation with felinity, his valiant attempt to salvage her mind.

He covered Pamela up again, and closed her long-lashed clouded eyes. Sat grieving on his heels for all of them.

Chapter
Twenty-seven

Wildwood, June 19, 1916

THE inventor Nikola Tesla, who had not slept for forty hours, yet was customarily and impeccably attired in a dark suit, the knot of his tie as perfectly formed as a rosebud, had nearly completed the last of his three laps along his chosen path at the ragged edge of the parkland which surrounded Edgar Langford's chateau. Here the down-drafting winds of mountain forest were inflamed with resin, a tonic for the mind. He was less than a month away from his sixtieth birthday and although he had been crushed and crushed again by disappointments, detractors, and thieves, he still possessed the energy of a stevedore. It was a summer night of waltzes and whippoorwills and the thrilling whistle of the evening train as it rushed across the long trestle through Ellijay Gap. The chateau, its outbuildings and large gazebos, were uniformly lambent, beauty which Tesla, the lightbringer, had created in painterly fashion. The lawns, beneath a frequently sulking moon, were bathed in dew; garden hedgework green as Guatemala lined the serpentine walks and coaching paths of crushed marble stelliform in their high brilliance. But his mind, as he walked, was not on what he considered to be a trifling chore effortlessly brought off. He could have illuminated the entire range of the Smoky Mountains like a diadem had he possessed sufficient funds and the desire to do so; the resultant lightshow would have been visible as far away in space as the planet Mars. It was a subtly frightening enigma that absorbed him, a great rarity in his prolific career: a machine, a dynamo which had no proprietor, and thus could not be under any man's control. It was his inability to manipulate what he had wrought that Tesla found perplexing, and chastening.

He was aware of something huddled, dark, on the path ahead, outlined in a dying-down light like the pallid fire around a nearly consumed coal; he slowed his pace, then realized, after taking a few more steps, that it was a human form, kneeling face to the ground, either in pain or prayer. He heard a sighing, thanksgiving sound. Abruptly the person rose and faltered, footloose, lurching; he suspected drunkenness, and at the same time realized that it was a woman, although she wore close-fitting trousers and hiking boots. She was a stranger to Tesla. He kept some distance between them.

"Have you injured yourself?" he asked, giving her the benefit of the doubt.

Regaining her balance, she shook her head, throwing off a few luminous droplets of light, as if she had been bathing in an ethereal, incandescent pool. He was fascinated; there was no indication of St. Elmo's fire in their immediate vicinity. Her hair was short. From her features, the savage duskiness of her skin, he surmised that she was of the Cherokee. They were not forbidden on

Tormentil Mountain, but few of them had ever come
this far seeking work.

The woman took a couple of deep breaths and, with
hands on hips, stood staunchly in his way, staring at
him. It was annoying to be interrupted, but Tesla was
unfailingly gracious to all women, particularly those
with Slavic cheekbones the equal of his own. He was
taken with her strict and niggerish beauty, and he was
curious. He bowed slightly. She smiled in return, white-
toothed, but her expression quickly was grave again,
inscrutable.

"I haven't seen you here before," he said. "Do you
speak English? What is your name?"

"I'm Kálanu: the Raven," Faren Rutledge told him.

"My name is Nikola Tesla."

"I thought so. You're very tall." She gestured
toward the round towers of the chateau, the soaring lantern of the central facade aglow beneath the night sky.
"Is that your work? It's almost as bright as noon."

The great inventor smiled. "If you know who I am,
then you know I am the master of light." Now that he
had been diverted, he indulged a whim to startle, or
perhaps amuse her, if she had any degree of sophistica-
tion. Tesla snapped his fingers, and a ball of red flame
appeared almost under his long nose. She flinched,
awed, but resisted stepping back. He balanced the ball
of fire on the back of one hand, rolled it up his arm,
passed it around the back of his neck. There was no
smoke from the fireball; only a faintly acrid odor in the
air.

"Hold out your hands," he said, as the fireball lolled
on his left shoulder like a tamed cockatiel. He demon-
strated. "In this manner."

She hesitated, then smiled, trusting him. He plucked

the fireball from his shoulder and placed it gently in her cupped hands. Her eyes widened, she tensed as if she were about to drop it. But she wasn't burned, there was no pain.

Faren swallowed, dazzled, dark eyes avid, pondering the phenomenon she held in her hands.

"What do you want me to do with it?"

Tesla shrugged, then leaned over and blew on the fireball. It disappeared without a trace. Slowly Faren rubbed her hot but unsinged palms together.

"That was brave of you," he acknowledged. "But now, if you will pardon me—"

"No, don't go!"

"I have much to think about, and I think best when I am alone."

"But I've come a long way, and I need your help," she said, an uncontrived note of desperation in her voice.

"Well. If only I could spare the time. But I am fully occupied for now. There must be someone else who—"

Faren glanced again at the distant chateau, at the lantern with its dome of glass that occupied the highest point above the many spires and chimneypots. A nerve center glowing with a different, more ominous light, galactic in its coldness, silvery cerise, pulsating rhythmically.

"Can you destroy his machine, the way you blew out the ball of fire?"

Tesla was shocked, as if he'd felt, just then, her quick thoughts in his own sacrosanct mind; her fear.

"Who *are* you? What do you know about—and why should you say such a terrible thing?"

"I know about the machine. I know it eats the stars like a toad feeding on flies; and if you can't stop it, then we're probably all doomed. Because I can't go back now, either, to where I come from. Not unless that damned machine is dismantled, or blown up. If it isn't, then I'll be like the others: a Walkout. If I live at all.''

She was emotional, irrational; she distressed him profoundly. He shivered slightly at the whistling of the train, nearer.

"You are not making sense to me."

"You helped him build it. And you're too smart not to appreciate how dangerous it can be."

"Within defined limits, there is no danger."

"Oh, bullshit."

"I beg your—"

Faren held out her hands to Tesla, palms up. She was trembling too.

"Your ball of fire couldn't hurt me. But that web will soon have power enough to turn men into creatures that are part bird, part animal—I've seen them! I know he hasn't told you, but that's what Edgar Langford plans to do; he hates everybody, *hates* them—"

"Preposterous!"

"Maybe even you. Listen. That beautiful chateau, the gardens, the birdcage, the zoo—on Midsummer Eve everything will just vanish; it'll all be whisked away by his machine, unless you do something *now*."

Tesla scoffed, but his throat felt tight and dry. "Nothing as solid as stone may simply vanish."

Faren shook her head despairingly. "It will pass into a kind of vale where our senses can't locate it. I've always known what happened to the chateau; but that's because I have the Gift."

"Young woman, I must ask you to please step out of my way."

"You have the Gift too, although it doesn't work the

same. But you can visualize marvelous machines in your mind; the most wonderful inventions come to you in a flash, out of nowhere. When you were younger, and had that nervous breakdown—"

"How could you possibly know about *that*?"

"It's part of your pattern—what I see. Never mind. But your senses went completely out of control, for more than a year. You could distinguish objects in the dark by the images they made on your skin. You suffered from roaring noises in your head; and a train whistle twenty miles away made your body vibrate uncontrollably. You were in touch with other places, other worlds—"

There was a cruel flash of light behind Tesla's eyes; he covered them with one hand. His precise and brilliantly focused mind failed him then, like the light of a match in a storm on the sun. He felt naked to this woman who seemed made from darkness and called herself "Raven."

"Don't go on," he murmured. "There's nothing I can, or will, do."

"But you've been thinking about it, haven't you? And you're afraid of Edgar's machine."

"I know it to be an almost perfect source of limitless power. Night after night, its energy expands exponentially."

"Get rid of it!" Her fear and anger clouded around him, bitter as plague. "You know how."

"It would be necessary to destroy the entire chateau! Millions of dollars worth of his property. How can I betray my benefactor? He's made so much of my research possible."

"He's nothing but a crazy man. You must have realized that by now."

They heard the celebratory whistle of the inbound train, a blowsy chuffing; the lightening of the windy woods around them brought her eyes into bold relief. Faren looked around.

"Lord, here they come! More of his innocent guests, headed straight for Mad Edgar's web." She pressed closer to Tesla. "I'm telling you the truth—he'll turn half of them into monsters with his wicked machine."

"It was only meant as an experiment—a—a plaything."

"You can't lie to me. You're afraid of it—and afraid of him too."

Faren lowered one shoulder and threw herself against Tesla, knocked him down, sprawled on top of him. She went quickly through the silk-lined pockets of his coat, and found what she was looking for. He tried to hold her back. His hands were large but slipped from taut denim and she ran, toward the headlamp of the locomotive, homing in on the Wildwood depot.

Gilded coaches whimsically shaped like pumpkins, drawn by teams of matched black horses, were drawn up alongside the gaslit cedarwood platform to receive each visitor as he stepped down from a private car. Dray horses hitched to massive wagons awaited the unloading of tons of luggage. The chateau's overdressed band, sixty members wrapped in full-volume brass, saluted the train hulking forward and dead slow now but with a clangorous bell, unmusical violence.

Tesla, on his knees, went unheard as he shouted, "Catch that Indian woman! She's stolen something valuable from me! You must get it back from her!"

The Mikado locomotive, black and red and trimmed in slender, reedy brass, stopped in flaring skirts of steam as Faren dashed across the tracks in front of it, for a moment wildly luminous and observed by many of the welcomers. It was obvious, to one man at least, that she'd been up to no good.

He reined his big but aging horse around and crossed the tracks in pursuit of the hard-running woman.

Faren was nearly out of breath and the horse took long strides, easily clearing a split-rail fence she had to clamber over; she was toppled in mid-air, sent crashing to the soft ground on the other side.

Before she could drag herself to her feet and take off in another direction, into the deep, safe woods, James B. Travers had dismounted and seized her. He was a fit big man but with sagging pouches under his eyes and winter in the full sideburns. She glared at him.

"You'd better let me go!"

"What are you doing this far from the reservation? What's that in your hand?"

She kicked at him, to no effect. Nikola Tesla leaned against the rail fence, catching his breath. Travers glanced at the inventor, then twisted Faren's wrist. Her clenched hand opened as she grimaced in pain. The thing she had stolen from Tesla, small as the works of a music box, fell to the needle-matted ground.

"There it is, thank God!" Tesla cried.

Travers, keeping a firm grip on Faren, stooped to pick it up.

"That's all she took from you?" he inquired of Tesla. "What is it?"

"An oscillator, sir. Obviously she knows of its potential. I judge her to be out of her mind. Obsessed by some obscure vendetta that may have to do with her tribal origins. Somehow she has gained the knowledge that the small oscillator you hold in your hand, attached to a wall of the chateau, would in a matter of hours cause it to crash into a heap of rubble."

Travers blanched, and looked again at the little machine; so much destruction from such tiny vibrations. He felt movement along his spine, as if the oscillator were already operating, stealthily, in the palm of his hand. He looked up at Faren.

"Good God. Who are you, and why should you want to destroy my life's work?" He spoke softly, as if to a crazed animal, or to the devil.

His softness set her to weeping.

"Mr. Travers—I know who *you* are. And believe me, something terrible is going to happen if you don't— won't give me the chance to talk to you, to explain, while there's still time."

Two men in fedoras who were part of the security force that protected the chateau pulled up in a closed automobile. Without replying to Faren, Travers turned her over to them.

"Lock her up until the sheriff arrives to take her off our hands."

"Fuck you!" Faren shouted. Travers winced, then looked contemptuously amused. He turned his back on her as she ranted, "How can you be so stupid? I'm the only one who can save any of you, and you won't listen!"

"Such language from a woman," Tesla said regretfully, pocketing the oscillator that Travers returned to him.

Travers swung up into the saddle and sat looking at Faren, who was being forcibly placed in the back of the automobile. Of Edgar Langford's arriving guests, few seemed aware there had been a disturbance. The band was playing a Sousa march, and Faren's continuing protests and appeals attracted little attention.

"She's not like any woman I've ever met," Travers

said, wondering if he was correct in so quickly dismissing her as a lunatic. Agitated, yes; and something perilous, preternatural, had flared in her eyes: *I know who you are.* The old, dull saddle creaking between his thighs even as Sibby withered on voluminous cushions in her constant twilight. He carried within him, like a burnt gallows, the charred skeleton of their tragedy. *While there's still time.* But if you truly know me, thought Travers, you know then how I have used my time, and there is so little left—with no prospect for absolution. There is only stone and mortar that must endure. *Give me the chance to talk to you, to explain.* He took a last look at the automobile careening off to the accompaniment of toot and flute and buffooning brass, and imagined his beautiful chateau in ruins. Skyrockets were expanding overhead, painting the nearly full moon in corpselike colors. The lines around Travers's mouth deepened, hardened. No, he would not speak further to her, whatever she might be: salvor, destroyer, dark messenger of the unfriendly gods whose only passion was for torment.

"Mr. Travers?"

"Yes, sir?"

"At what time will the train be departing for the East?"

"Promptly at half-past twelve, Mr. Tesla."

"I would like a car prepared. I'm afraid I must leave on short notice—I have urgent business that will require my presence in New York for the next fortnight at least."

There was so much going on, twenty-four hours a day, in preparation for the Revels: and Alexander wanted to be in on everything. Thus he was most often at his

father's side, napping where he happened to sprawl
when too exhausted to stand anymore, whether it was at
three in the afternoon or quite late at night. He rarely
visited his mother, lying so seriously ill in her apartment. And he no longer had Jacqueline to himself: she
was busy with the baby girl born just two months ago,
an event he had reason to associate with his mother's
present condition. When Edgar was unavailable to him,
then Taharqa or any one of numerous maids attended to
his needs.

They were having a late supper in Edgar's apartment,
when the train arrived. Alex was given permission to
leave the table (he was just picking at the meat course
anyway), and go to the windows, where he trained his
father's large brassbound telescope on the depot.

"How many coaches tonight, Alex?" his father asked
him.

Alex counted to ten and stopped; he couldn't see them
all.

"I believe your uncles are due to arrive tonight from
Boston."

"What's an uncle?"

"In this instance, they are your mother's brothers.
Mr. Oliver Waring the Fourth and Mr. Robert Westerfield
Waring."

"When is Charlie Chaplin coming?" No one else on
the guest list interested him half as much. The twiddling
cane; the nervous mustache and tipsy bowler hat. He
frequently slid out of his chair chirping laughter at the
antics that flickered in the screening room Edgar had
recently installed. He loved Charlie Chaplin almost as
much as he loved his father.

"Perhaps tomorrow night," Edgar informed him.

"Come and sit down now, and you may have your dessert."

"Is it chocolate mousse?"

"Yes, it's chocolate mousse."

"Yum." Alex returned to his chair, and was seated by a footman. He put his head into his hands, thinking. Edgar sipped wine and looked at the boy's downturned face, glimpsing a slightly sullen expression.

"Something is on your mind."

"Well—it's only four more days. And nothing's ready! The floats don't look like anything yet, they're just chickenwire."

"They will be quite beautiful once the papier-mâché and paint are applied."

"I heard Mrs. Carmody say she needed *ten* more seamstresses to finish all the costumes—"

"They are arriving this very minute, and will be at work within the hour."

"Oh."

"Is anything else bothering you?"

"There're only a few animals. But you promised—"

"I promised you strange and glamorous pets for your zoo. You shall have them. Don't I *always* keep my promises to you, Alex?"

A large quivering mousse was brought to their table, and the boy was served. He plunged in a gold Tiffany spoon and sucked on it.

When he could speak he looked his father in the eye and said, "Yes."

"All right, then. If I have satisfied all of your concerns, when may I see a smile?"

The boy shrugged instead, stirring the mousse on his plate but not eating any more of it.

"I heard one of the maids say—"

"Dear, gossipy Adelaide?" Edgar interrupted with an edge of malice and irritation in his voice.

Alex already knew better than to say anything that might get a servant into trouble.

"I dunno. Just one of the maids. I don't know all of their names yet."

"Yes, and?"

"She said that Mother—" He shook his head, bewildered. He was a clever boy, a prodigy. In a few days he would be six years old. He understood already that life was a series of puzzle boxes, illusions. The workings of some could be grasped right away; others must be exhaustively studied, and frequently they still made no sense to him. "—that Mother will soon die." (What sort of illusion was death?) "*Why* will she die?" (Not all illusions were entertaining.) "Where will she go? Into the ground, like Dombey?" He was referring to a favorite pet, a Springer spaniel which, let loose' in the stable yard, had been kicked in the head by a nervous hunter-jumper.

"You must never, *never,* pay the slightest attention to the idle chatter of servants. They are common people, peasant immigrants, less than dirt under our feet. Is that understood? Come to me if you have questions."

"Well—"

Edgar took a few moments to cut into his own dessert, a spotless and glowing *beurré* from his hothouse orchard.

"It *is* true that your mother has been very ill with a fever since the birth of Laurette. We all must have hope that she will soon recover."

"Was it the baby's fault?"

"Your mother had a difficult period of labor," Edgar conceded.

"Does that mean lying down like a mare when a colt is going to come out?"

"Yes."

"Did Laurette come out between mother's legs? All wet and slippery?"

"Aren't you going to eat your mousse?"

"It's too sweet tonight," Alex said indifferently, having no appetite except for information. "Well, *tell* me."

"You always want to know too much for your age."

"I want to know as much as you do."

"In time you certainly will."

Edgar Langford's secretary, a young man with a mop of yellow curls and pince-nez glasses, was beckoned from a doorway, where he had been waiting. He placed a red leather folder on the table beside Edgar's place setting. Edgar didn't open it.

"Tonight's arrivals, sir. The Warings have requested a few moments with Mrs. Langford."

"She is too ill to be disturbed at this hour, Standish. Tomorrow."

"Yes, sir. Mr. Tesla regrets that he must leave tonight on urgent business, and would like to pay his respects."

A grimace of surprise and disapproval was followed by a deepening of the flush on Edgar's pocked cheeks.

"Very well. Tell him I will meet him in the lantern, at half-past the hour."

"Where is Mr. Tesla going?" Alex said, and he smothered a yawn. His head had been drooping toward the tablecloth.

"Perhaps he may be persuaded to postpone his hasty departure." Edgar looked up at his secretary, who seemed uncertain about the next item of business.

"Anything else, Standish?"

"It seems that Mr. Tesla was assaulted near the depot by an Indian woman, who is now being detained for the sheriff."

"A Cherokee? Here? Was Tesla injured?"

"Fortunately he was not."

"Where did she come from? Is she some outcast from the Reservation, looking to steal whiskey or a watch?"

"No, I don't think so. She was dressed as a man and obviously deranged, babbling some nonsense. She said she was of the serpent Erim. She seemed convinced you would know what that meant, and demanded to be allowed to speak to you."

Edgar Langford stared down at the table for a few moments. If his complexion had been red before, he now appeared near to combust. But his eyes, as always, were ashen, cool in cognizance and speculation. He reached out to fondle the head of his walking stick, gold flowing through his hand, faded fangs but undimmed ruby eyes like gloating Acheron.

"Continue to detain the woman. The sheriff will not be notified until I have so decided."

"Very good, sir."

Now Edgar Langford looked across the table at Alexander. The boy's head was resting on his arms. He was asleep.

"Have Taharqa come and put my son to bed," he said to Standish. "I'm afraid the pace we've set these past few days has been too much for him. I don't want him to take sick . . . and miss all the fun we're going to have."

Nikola Tesla waited on the floor of the lantern in the haunt of the rare machine, hands clasped behind his back, gazing up through welder's goggles at the drizzled lacework of silver. Months had gone into the assembly of the machine, which now carried on its mysterious work autodynamically, extracting from the dry and ancient cosmos droplets of mirrorforce light that spun and rayed within brainy convolutions, busy as the wasps of God, in damned eternal silence, foretelling of a wild season. He no longer believed these myriad impulses occurred at random, but he had no clue as to the meaning of their restless foraging; the cold dreaming clusters they sometimes formed. The machine was tolerant of his presence, but too bright for endurance, powerfully competitive. In Tesla's opinion the halves of the dome had remained open too long. For rainless weeks, through temperate nights, the corpulent machine had been fully exposed to the deep empyrean. Almost nightly, electrical storms flickered over the Smoky Mountains; it would be only a matter of time until a boiling tempest appeared directly above Tormentil, loosing terrific bolts of energy, gratifying the theomorphic machine.

Bronze doors opened and Edgar Langford entered, crumpled over his walking stick with the bane head and brackish red eyes. Light lent by the servile machine swelled glamorously around his head, a suave lavender aura.

"I regret your precipitous decision to leave Wildwood. Might an additional two hundred thousand dollars in compensation persuade you to reconsider?"

"It would not, sir."

"Go, then. I shall carry on without your counsel."

"To which you lately have given so little of your attention. I feel that I must urge you, for the last time, to halt all experimentation, and dismantle your machine."

Edgar Langford laughed incredulously, and aimed his

walking stick at the center of the radiant machine. "I've never had a toy half so entertaining."

"Toy? Why are you trifling with me? We both know it to be a huge and insatiable malignancy."

"Are you afraid of it, Tesla?" A wasp of light, rapacious, was poised above one dark brow.

"I am afraid of what I do not know—all that you may well have held back from me. I have had no choice but to be guided by your translations of the Babylonian tablets."

"I am the only man alive who could have translated them," Edgar acknowledged boastfully. "No copies exist in any museum. None will ever be made available to those who might have been my colleagues."

"I suggest, Mr. Langford, that you dismantle this ungodly web at once. It feeds, so voraciously, on sources of power I scarcely comprehend."

Edgar Langford limped past the inventor to another area of the lantern, where he placed himself between two small, chimerical objects made of some rustless unalloyed metal and mounted on identical pedestals. Almost imperceptibly at first, then with a scary, twinkling velocity, he began to dissolve before Tesla's melancholy eyes.

"We are both geniuses," Edgar asserted. "I have the greater knowledge; naturally you are jealous of me. Do you know how I achieve invisibility? You do not have an inkling. Because I am no mere illusionist, my dear Tesla—I am Marduk himself, king of sorcerers. If you have patience, then I will share all of my knowledge with you. Stay, be privileged."

"I cannot, sir; your motives appall me."

Langford was rabid at this impertinence. *"And what do you know of my motives?"*

Tesla, wearied from exposure to the overweening machine, spoke before he thought.

"The Cherokee woman said you would destroy everything. Now I think I believe in her strange clairvoyance. Your web may be harmless at this moment, though I doubt it; but a reckoning is very near. More power, gathered from the cataclysmic surge of an electrical storm, may have untold effects—distinctly unpleasant effects—on anyone within range of the web. They might dissipate in a puff of flame. Or, God forbid, suffer"—he lowered his voice—"even as I believe you have suffered, debilitating molecular changes."

When he turned from his last appraisal of the aloof machine Tesla was talking to apparently empty air—Edgar Langford had altogether disappeared. From sight. But his cranky laughter resounded in the lantern. Then the head of the walking stick appeared, thrust beyond the electromagnetic field between the chimerae. The head of the Sumerian serpent was tiny in comparison to the shapely machine, but impressive in its store of undiluted evil. Tesla quaked, and wished again he had not spoken of the woman.

"*She* said? I must pay a visit to this Cherokee who claims to be of Erim—who seems to know so much of my affairs. The train is waiting, Tesla. I bear you no ill will. Your fate is to be slighted and obscure, while I am reverenced by all of mankind. Farewell."

Chapter ——
Twenty-eight

By early afternoon the sun had passed on, leaving a trace of light like a thin radium bone as the sky piled on more sultry, funereal gray. But the air was charged, as if a storm might be in the offing. Arn, weatherwise, knowledgeable when it came to changes in the atmosphere of Wildwood, was sure it wouldn't rain. Not from the way his skin prickled. Something else was suggested, more spectacular, perhaps, than a locomotive screaming hellishly out of thin air.

The Walkouts, at least those who had been around for a few years, must have sensed it, too; but they went on with their games of croquet on the broad rectangle down by the meeting house. It looked as if everybody played: something they had in common, he reckoned, besides disfigurement. Maybe they liked the game because they were reminded of the good old days. Or it might mean more to them than that. The way they went at it, croquet looked to be more of a ritual than a social event, because the Walkouts didn't just hang around jawing the day away like loafers on a whittling bench. In fact, they talked very little. If he was one of them, Arn thought— and the more he thought about it, the uneasier he became, sensing a madhouse in their seclusion, lunacy thinly under control. Arn's cousin Jewell was on the simple side, always had been, but he could make out all right as long as someone clearly explained what was expected of him and showed him how to do things. But these people, the Walkouts, most of them (he assumed) had been rich, educated, and important. Now they were quasi-beasts on this stamping ground, freakish even to one another. How many, he wondered, had climbed up to the top of the bluffs behind the town and jumped in despair? What was the cost to the survivors merely to go on surviving, what did they have to live for? Croquet and other games; rules to be taken seriously, rituals to observe. The ablest minds concerned with trajectories, lines of force, winning and losing. Could be it came down to just that: win or lose, against whatever nemesis happened your way. His own experience told him something. Momentarily idled on a battlefield, sunk in mire and nearly subhuman from exhaustion, the emotional toll of bloodletting, he would aim and re-aim his rifle, totally concentrated, thinking of nothing but sightlines and windage and the perfect, fatal shot. His version of croquet.

Along with the cracking-together of hardwood balls he heard someone walking up the path to his hut. Arn felt seriously cast down when he glimpsed the thickset curlecue horns of the goatman brushing aside dark boughs of balsam. Maybe they had decided hanging was too good for him and were handing him over to the goatman to be drawn and quartered with the slick handax. Then he recognized Terry Bowers trailing after the nigger, and Terry had Bocephus, panting and scrabbling, on a short leash. Arn broke into a smile and got up a little stiffly.

"Hey, Terry! What you doin' here, son?"

Terry looked shocked to see the noose around Arn's neck. He wet his lips and glanced at the goatman.

"They said I could come talk to you."

Bo was whining ecstatically, standing up to pound Arn on the chest with his muddy front paws.

"Easy, Bo! Get down. Terry, make yourself at home, such as it is."

The goatman leaned against a tree nearby, his arms folded, yellow eyes on them. Arn wondered if he had a goat-sized brain to go with his horned head. As far as he knew, Josie Raftery did the thinking for the two of them.

The sky took on a midnight look of lightning, or voiceless gunfire; treetops turned a more flagrant green, like shining combers of the sea before a hurricane. But the air was stifling, and didn't move. Only the light moved, flickering through the caves of cloud. Arn sat down again, trying to keep his back to the goatman. It put quite a strain on his already raw neck. He could better appreciate just how much that little butterfly girl had been willing to put up with in order to ensure he would not escape *her* trap. The girl had sand; he admired her almost as much as he admired his own wife. Whom he probably wouldn't be seeing again. But then, he hadn't anticipated seeing any friendly face, and here was Terry looking him in the eye while he rubbed Bocephus behind his ears. Plain mother luck: although Terry might not have the run of the place without an escort, he certainly wasn't tied down, which could prove to be useful.

"Reckon you wonder how I got myself into this predicament."

"I already know," Terry said. "Josie told me."

"Josie, huh? And where did you meet up with our little flygirl?"

"Last night, a few miles from here. I'm not sure just where I was. I came with Faren."

That raised Arn's pulse. "When was the last time you saw Faren? These Walkouts, they've talked her into somethin', could be dangerous for her."

Terry did his best to describe the sequence of events that had taken place at the brink of the quarry; Arn listened to a description of the serpent's head in the clouds and the Well of Sorrow without apparent skepticism. The serpent reminded Terry of what had happened in the parking lot of the Church of God, and he told Arn about that too.

"That's a hell of a tale," Arn said carefully when Terry was finished.

Terry, not looking at Arn anymore, scuffed in the dirt with the heel of his boot.

"I wasn't dreaming. And I'm not lying."

"Never figured you for a liar. Seen a few things myself in these woods that would qualify me for a straitjacket if I let on to anybody. All that counts is, Faren's missin', and I—*we* got to find her and help her out. You agree?"

Terry nodded.

"But I'm not goin' nowhere trussed up thisaway."

Terry raised his head. "Dad's missing too. Josie went to see if she could locate him, but she hasn't come back yet."

"Forget about Josie," Arn said in a harsh low tone, hoping the goatman wouldn't overhear. "I'm depend-in' on you, Terry, to get me out of this noose. Right now I don't have another friend in the world. It's just you and me, son—against all of them."

Terry looked anxious. "I can't—"

"That's okay; I know you're watched close now. But you're a smart boy, you'll find an opportunity to slip away, come back with a knife or ax I can use."

Firelight in the clouds accentuated silence, except for the tock, tock of maple balls emulating pendulums, gaunt clocks of the weather that measured erratic seconds, the untimed distortion of all their lives.

"Josie showed me where you cut her," Terry said to Arn. "Why did you do that?"

Josie again; what was wrong with this boy, was he hypnotized by her pretty wings? Or maybe it was her pretty red pussy that had got to him. Arn smiled culpably.

"I played a little rough with her; and you can see where she nailed me in the head with that rock. I might never get the normal sight of my eye back. I'll call it evens with little Josie. But she ain't the reason they got this noose around my neck. In '38, when I wasn't much more than a kid, I hunted one of the Walkouts down. He had the wings of a hawk. I shot him out of the sky."

"What for?" Terry said, horrified.

"Terry, I'd never seen nothin' like that hawk boy, and—well—I just didn't have good sense at the time. If I had it to do over, I wouldn't shoot, but they ain't in no mood to accept apologies. It's blood for blood where these Walkouts are concerned. And Terry"—Arn risked cutting off the oxygen to his brain, leaning closer to whisper—"don't get to thinkin' you're in a better spot than me."

"I haven't done anything to them," Terry said, not as sure of himself as he tried to sound.

"You *know* about them. And you know where their town is." Arn paused, looking into Terry's eyes until he saw a swarming of doubt, then concluded, "That could be your death sentence too."

Taharqa had come up silently behind them, but Arn smelled him even before Bocephus got his back up. Terry looked past Arn, then rose stiffly, a hand on Bo's leash. Light hunted in the clouds, like a pack of ghosthounds, a fox of fear.

"I need to go now."

"That's okay," Arn said hoarsely. "You think it over, Terry. I know you've got plenty of savvy for your age, and you'll do what's right. For both of us. By the way. The last time I saw your old man, he was in good shape. Little bump on his noggin. Hell, him and me went through a war. I know he can take care of himself. And what I always admired about him, he took care of his men first."

Terry seemed to get the message; at least Arn thought he saw the boy give a little nod as he walked away, tugging at the reluctant and whimpering hound, who turned despondent eyes on his master.

Arn crept in the direction of the hut to give himself slack rope, and breathed easier.

It wasn't quite as good as having a knife in his hands, Arn thought. But at least he had something to hope for now: that young Terry was half as resourceful as Whitman Bowers, a Medal of Honor nominee, had been in wartime.

There was a different mood in the clouds, bristling circlets of orange fire steadier than lightning, rings within rings. And the Walkouts played on without comment, *tock-tock*. Arn felt soft in the head, puzzled, morose. Something big coming 'round this time for sure. Unless

Faren figured out a way to stop it, if she'd managed to fetch up all of a piece, wherever that damned serpent had dropped her off in time.

Faren and snakes: she could never bring herself to kill one, even the streaking black racers that frequently found their way into the chickenyard.

There'd always be something about her he would never get to know, never be a part of. Maybe that was one reason the marriage had worked out, although admittedly he'd done a lot less than his share. Like the elements she surrounded him, sometimes cool, sometimes blazing; she preyed enticingly on his mind like the thin moon of severest night.

Well, if they all lived through this—

But he didn't want to dwell on it. Just bide his time, try to stay alert. First things first.

"Terry," Josie said, "would you mind bringing the lamp closer?"

He put down the woodwhistle, cut from a spring-green elm branch, that he'd been softly amusing himself with. The kerosene lamp stood on a cedar stump table that had been shellacked to a high gloss by Taharqa. He carried it near the curious bed, part hammock, part saddle, where she reclined. Suspended like a swing from the roof beam, the bed was furnished with many small cushions fluffed with tiny bird feathers. Josie had passed through the torture of a megrim, but she still lay pale from exhaustion, and madder-eyed.

"Not too close," she cautioned. "You might singe me."

With great effort she lifted the wings drooping on either side of the hammock.

"Will you look for me? It's a poor state I'm in."

She had flown widely for most of the day, in search of his father. Had returned too drained of energy to feed or bathe herself.

"What am I looking for?"

"Wear and tear," Josie told him. "Me wings can't last forever, I'm saying."

It was a new thought, and a shock to Terry; Josie without her wings? He looked carefully at them, holding the lamp high and low. She watched him.

"What do you see? You saw *something*. Out with it."

He had discovered a small hole, like a cigarette burn in fabric. But he turned away with the lamp and said casually, "No, they're okay."

Josie sighed, dark eyelids closing. "Praise all the saints."

"Don't you want something to eat now?"

"No. But I'll trouble you for another drink of the honeyed tea. I need sugar in me blood. Too little sugar and I commence to shaking in an anguished fit. Once I frayed a wing as I was tossing about."

There was a pottery jar of dark yellow tea on the table. He replaced the lamp and took the jar to Josie. She raised her head and he supported her with one hand, holding the jar so she could sip the sweet drink.

"Aye. That's much better. Me headache's almost gone. And is it clammy to your touch I'm feeling?"

"No." He continued to hold her in the crook of his arm. "You didn't have to wear yourself out like this."

"Many a day it's not such hard going. But today the air was heavy, fiercely charged. Not twenty-four hours by there was a crossover: the birdcage."

"The what?"

Josie described the aviary, and its origins, to him.

"Today I saw fine feathers, lovely birds of the tropics that put me to shame."

"Drink more tea," he urged her, noticing a tremor.

She smiled gratefully, eyes on his face. Tired and troubled eyes, but showing less red than before. She had a few sips from the jar.

"We will all perish, of course. The sky-blue cocka-tiels. The snowy egret. The blushing flamingo. And Josie, the butterfly girl."

"Don't say that!"

"But better off she is than Josie the little seamstress could ever have hoped to be. We sewed day and night, until our fingers dripped blood, to the very hour the Revels were beginning. When me work was done I went out for a bit of air, beneath a sky I shall never forget. There was nothing familiar of heaven, nor stars in their saintly distance. All was fire-slaught and hideous, rainy hues of blood in boiling cloud. But no comets fell to earth; they merely grazed us, shooting into the radiance of the lantern."

"What lantern?"

Josie frowned, concentrating, wanting to describe it precisely.

"It was a cupola of sorts, but vaster, and all of glass. The dome could be opened. The lantern was at the very top and center of the chateau. None of us were told what it contained; no one dared to trespass. There was said to be a machine inside, spun entirely from silver wire fine as the webs of spiders. This machine made no sound, but it shed a fabulous light—in the black of night outdoors all green and human things glistered like corpses in sea-wrack. When I looked at the tips of me poor worn-out fingers silver light was twirling there, forming into clusters brilliant as olden treasure. I could not account for it—thought I must be hallucinating surely, so destroyed was I from me labors. I had finished the costume some woman of great worth would be wearing that same night. I sewed a thousand spangles on silken wings. I only wished to know the luxury, to have them on for a minute or two, and dream of handsome men who would quarrel over a dance with me. These wings sat lightly on me shoulders then, as they were meant to do.''

"What happened? Your wings aren't silk, they're real.''

"I cannot explain the sorcery of it; nor can any who were worse afflicted than meself.''

She closed her eyes again, and began to breathe deeply. Terry decided she was sleeping, but when he removed his arm gently and got up to return the jar of tea and honey to the table, Josie spoke to him.

"I don't wish to fall asleep yet. Meanwhile, if you would sit next to me, it's easier I'll be. I've missed having someone close to me own age to talk to. But I know I'll not be having you for very long.''

Terry came silently back to sit on the rush-matted floor of the hut beside the suspended bed. He ran a finger over the leading edge of a fallen wing, and found it rough.

"I know; they are fraying faster. Next may come a lengthy tear, and then—'' She returned to the theme that haunted her. "The life of a butterfly, so I have read, is but little more than a week. It's borrowed time I'm living on.''

"Josie—''

She shifted her weight on the bed, facing him. "Lay your head against me breast. There's a comfort.''

He did, and was aware of the flighty beating of her

heart, the dampish fragrance of strawberry hair, a timid nipple, a charge in her body.

"I'm wanting pity like a cat wants the mange. Just saying what is true: for we must all pass on in old God's time. I do have more than a groundling's death to think about, Terry. Because if Mr. Travers and the Jewman are correct in their calculations, us Walkouts may have the opportunity to return."

"Back to the chateau? But—it's not there."

"Oh, yes 'tis. Exactly as we left it. Now, that again is sorcery, but twice at the ending of summer, when I had the desire to up and fly by the light of the full moon, I saw it meself surely, from afar—because no bird nor butterfly nor dumb beast of the wood may pass over that perch of mountain where the chateau stands. D'you follow me, Terry?"

"I don't know how you could see it if I can't."

"Maybe you will, and soon. Providence and Mary, and didn't you see for yourself a divilish serpent come down from clouds, bolts of lightning crackling from its supernatural eye?"

"Yes."

"Well, mister honey, on the brightest of nights, when the air is still and the light is rare and sparkling, the chateau appears in its own firmament, but heavily veiled. Faith, I heard music. I knew beyond a doubt, gliding high on wings I sewed meself, that I had been gone but a moment, and no one missed me. But I could find no way back in. The veils are purest electricity. So powerful they were, they tumbled me right away from there, head over heels in the sky."

Josie was quiet for a few moments, content, mulling the phenomenon she had described. Terry stroked a wing, which left his fingertips faintly iridescent. He touched them to his lips. Her wing quivered lightly, ecstatically, her heart was loud in his ear. Her breast had warmed beneath his cheek.

"Travers and the Jewman—"

"Who are they?" Terry interrupted.

"Mr. James B. Travers is the architect who designed the chateau. He was one of the first Walkouts; also it was himself who built this town for us, so that we might be something more than half-daft creatures living in caves and treetops. He saw to it that we had a community. And he has always given us hope that someday the travail will end. The Jewman is Mr. Schwarzman, an archaeologist. He is large and blue-eyed, with a wild black beard—"

"Hey, I know him! My dad and I talked to him at Fulcrum's Cafe. He studied at the Sorbonne, he said. He spoke good French."

"Yes, Schwarzman. He knows more than Mr. Travers about the sorcery. Once he rashly predicted a time when the chateau would retarn, but it did not happen then. Because of the bitterness his failed prophecy engendered, he was no longer welcome in Walkout Town. But I believe he sincerely wished to help us, and that someday his theories will be proven. The chateau *will* retarn."

"What'll happen then?"

"We have all talked and talked about the prospect. But no one knows. There are some who believe the sorcery will be reversed and all will regain their human shapes, and it will be as if these years in the wild wood did not happen. We will remember nothing."

Her eyelids closed heavily again; but again she rejected sleep.

"Yes, and it might happen just that way. But things that seem too good to be true, they say, usually are."

Terry sat up slowly, troubled by the import of this remark.

"You mean you won't go back? Even if you can?"

Josie smiled. "Once I met an eagle in the air, white-capped, with an eye as bright as God's evening star, and forever fierce. He might have ripped me with his talons but instead we soared together, companions, down the gildered day. Terry . . . I have known such heavenly silence, and the grace of eagles."

Terry said nothing. She continued to smile at him, comfortingly.

"The only thing I have lacked that I truly long for is the love of a fine lad, as much like yourself as ever I could imagine."

Terry lowered his eyes, then raised them, more boldly, to stare at her.

"This morning I admired the purity of your body. And I'm after thinking, you can at least stand the sight of mine."

He nodded.

"Do you know what to do?" she asked him, mildly apprehensive. "There's so very much of you, in a manly way. And have you done it ever?"

"I know what to do," he said.

"Would you be after calling it a shameful wickedness, and meself a hoor?"

"No!"

"Well, may God forgive me, I know that I ought to fear the flames of hell, but I do not. As there's no priest to advise or wed us, then must we advise each other, plight our vows in this time and place according to our truest feelings. What is the meaning of sin, once we are all taken to the heartless peace of our graves? Could an hour of making sweetest love do such terrible injury to our souls?''

Terry couldn't speak, but he shook his head.

"And would you be thinking it unseemly should I wish to keep me eyes on you, whilst you are taking off your clothes again?''

Her wing trembled against his cheek. He rubbed it lightly, up and down, then rose and stripped off his sweater, unbuttoned his shirt.

For a long time after he was naked he didn't make a move toward her.

"I don't promise," he said shyly, "that it'll be better than flying.''

"Oh, Terry, me cupidon. I'm dry as death. Water me with your rain.''

He lay down with her in the hammock. Her wings rose to form a tent over them, dimming the light of the lantern in the hut.

Chapter
Twenty-nine

Through trial and error Whit Bowers found his way out of the caverns, emerging from a hideaway gate within a ravine of what appeared to be natural stone, but wasn't. It was night. Within a sky of black glass deep flaws, linked like organisms in a primordial sea, glowed intermittently—shades of rouge and spectral yellow, nickled blue and blooded lime. Walking through a windy drift of evergreen, he stumbled across a lax conquistador beneath a fir tree. The figure in garish pewter stirred, losing his grip on a halberd: the helmeted head turned, revealing a jackal's snout.

The voice, in contrast to the glittering animal eyes, was youthful; meek.

"Did I go to sleep?"

Before Whit could say anything, the armored creature rose in an awkward clashing of metal against the tree trunk.

"I'm sorry, Mr. Travers. I didn't mean to fall asleep.

I'll get right back to where I belong. You are Mr. Travers, aren't you?''

"No," Whit said. Watching, but only half-listening to him: he also heard an orchestra, distant as the susurrus of the sea, like sad tidings.

The jackal looked around in total confusion, then gaping alarm, prominent nostrils flaring.

"I thought you were. Everything's hazy. What's the matter with the sky? Which way is the chateau?"

"I don't know."

"But I have to get back!"

"You can't," Whit told him, feeling a cramp of pity. He was little more than a costumed boy, a servant. Soon he would go mad. Whit turned away.

The aviary was nearby, its glass repeating the colors of the sky. He walked toward it, hearing the conquistador sob as he blundered off in a different direction. He went into the stinking aviary and looked around. Scores of live birds remained, huddled in nervous sleep. He was relieved to find that Jacqueline and the baby in the perambulator were gone. Someone must have come for them, as Jacob had predicted.

But where were they now? And where was he? He wasn't much better off than the young conquistador with the jackal's countenance, lit up in swashy metal, tracing a leftover line of melody to an unearthed orchestra, demesne of the ghost chateau.

There was someone Whit knew he had to find, if he existed in this wood: the architect he had been mistaken for. They must be living somewhere nearby, he thought. The Walkouts Jacob had described.

The queerly illuminated night sky was bright enough so that he could have a look around. But if any of the Walkouts were as dangerous as Pamela or (perhaps) the black goatman, then he wanted to be armed before he went any farther. His choices seemed severely limited: a stone, a club. Then he remembered the halberd which the jackal-faced young man had left behind, and wondered if it was real.

Whit found his way back to the place where he had stumbled across the armor-suited Walkout and saw the halberd gleaming on the ground. He picked it up. The weapon was authentic, not a costume prop. It consisted of a straight shaft of some hard wood that was six and a half feet long, topped by a sharp ax blade and a steel spear point. It would be somewhat heavy and awkward to carry on a sortie through thick and unfamiliar woods, but he felt better having it in his hands.

Circling the aviary for a sign of those who had taken away the body and the child, he discovered a track that seemed to have been trampled recently, by many pairs of feet, and the ruts from a wagon or cart. He followed this track downhill, coming to a waterfall suspended from a jagged cliff like a chandelier of brilliant, prinking, columnar crystal; where it rilled, light riffled over the surface, resembling candleflame on glazed red oil. He was reminded of a shelled cathedral, or a wake. He wondered what had happened to Arn. He was thirsty but afraid to drink here. He crossed the rill on stepping-stones, holding the halberd horizontally for balance, and entered an estate of evergreens so steeply massed and silent and bitter in its darkness that he felt abruptly grim, and death-bound. Yet he believed, or was afraid, that he could hear the distant orchestra behind him, weaving in and out of consciousness: a fadeaway trombone, a wanderlost rhythm. He pressed on, breathing hard, twisting the halberd this way and that as it hung on tough springy boughs.

Somehow he lost the track, and almost immediately tumbled over a low cliff into a pit.

The fall knocked the breath out of his lungs, the music from his mind. He saw glints of red in pitch blackness. His ribs pained him.

When he could breathe again he rolled slowly onto his back, gasping. The sound of labored breathing, echoing from rock walls, was louder, grunting, bestial.

He saw, as his vision cleared, shapes moving around him, and he heard guttural threatening voices. Above him the obsidian sky, crazy-cracked with lurid light. Next to his head, a stinking bone. Six feet away a lowered tapering head, the curved razor tusks of a wild boar, four feet high at the shoulders.

He was surrounded by them. He had fallen into their den or feeding ground. He knew only one thing about them, that they were dangerous.

Where was the halberd?

They were coming closer: muttering, muttering murder.

If he continued to lay there, then they would be all over him, rooting, tearing him to pieces. He'd seen what domestic hogs, roaming around a ravaged countryside in Belgium, could do to the corpses of soldiers.

If he moved, then he must move the right way, and fast; but which way was that?

He felt around him with his hands, keeping his eyes on the boar who appeared to be closest. A miracle that he hadn't fallen on the blade of the halberd, and cut himself seriously. But if he had been bleeding, the boars would have smelled it; already they would be eating him.

His groping right hand touched the haft of the halberd. Closed on it.

A chance.

He was so numbed by terror he wasn't sure he could move quickly enough, find some high ground in the dark, keep them at bay. The lean and hot-tempered boars. How fast could *they* move? And how many were there?

Whit decided it would be a fatal mistake to try to run. He must hold this piece of ground, or else.

Screaming to release adrenaline, hoping to startle or panic them momentarily, he rose to his knees and pulled the halberd to him, gripping it with both hands. Then he jumped to his feet, screamed again, swung the ax blade at the nearest boar, cleaved a haunch to the bones.

God, they were monsters!

As the wounded animal went down he sensed a charge from another direction, wheeled and drew blood from a snout with the point of the halberd. Hauled it back and slashed at another swiftly moving shape. Sent it bowling away and shrieking in blood throes, the din a Hadean nightmare. Even as he whirled and feinted and slashed, sobbing, everywhere that pig eyes flared, he fought with a sense of dread and hopelessness, knowing he must be overrun, brought down beneath their keen little hooves.

"This way, sir!"

He was so shocked to hear a human voice he almost gave up his life.

There was a gunshot, or at least it sounded like a shot; and a boar that had leaped for his exposed side as he half-turned to look around was seized in mid-air and snatched away just as its tusks grazed him.

"I'm behind you; stand them off and continue to back up. No, don't look for me; I'll try to protect your flanks—there, to your right!"

Whit pivoted and slashed, the blade of the halberd jarring deep against a haggish skull; blood sprayed him.

He jerked the halberd from the fallen boar and retreated. Some of the boars had become interested in the flesh of their wounded companions, milling around as if they were part of a blood carousel, romping and storming. But the rest were pressing to the perimeter of his jabbing staff, too many, too many—

He slipped and went down with a cry of despair, his arms aching, too tired to lift the cumbersome weapon anymore.

Something huge flew over his head and landed in the midst of the boar pack. The body of a horse, hooves flailing and raising dust, blocked access to Whit. There was another shot.

"Get up! Climb the cliff! You're almost there!"

Whit stumbled to his feet, dragging the halberd, and scrambled to the base of the cliff, looking back at the vicious melee, unable to believe what he was seeing through the haze of dust.

The glimpse he had of the rider showed him to be a gray-bearded man, with muscular arms and a bare torso. He was well forward, leaning across the horse's head, with what appeared to be a blacksnake whip raised in one hand. But, no, that wasn't right, because the horse he rode had no head. And the man wasn't astride the horse at all—great God almighty, he *was* the horse!

Squealing and snorting, most of the wild boars were routed, sprays of their blood imparting a pinkish tinge to the dust boiling sky-high. As he wheeled to crack his whip the centaur lost his footing and lurched to his front knees. Another boar attacked, where the body of the man joined the body of the horse. Whit charged from the ledge on which he had found breathing room and speared the boar in its side; grunting from strain, he hurled the kicking animal to the ground but this time could not unstick the point of his halberd from rib and gristle.

The centaur, getting to his feet, loomed over him.

"Quick, on my back! I'll get us out of here."

His flowing hair was as long as his beard. Whit grabbed a handful and mounted the centaur, was thrown forward and almost unseated as the centaur galloped away, roughshod over the boars that remained in his way, sparks flashing from iron shoes on stone beneath the mast that covered the floor of the ravine.

The centaur's back was slippery from blood. But if he had been injured, he seemed not to notice, or care: he was hollering for joy, arms raised exultantly, the sleek whip flashing in the night. They were headed downhill, and Whit had to grip the coarse long hair of the centaur's head with both hands to keep from being jarred to the ground.

"Where are we going?"

"What do you care? A minute ago you were pigmeat."

But they stopped soon enough, the graybeard winded and trembling, showing a limp when he broke stride. His torso streamed blood and sweat. Whit slid down from his back.

"Are you hurt?"

"They chewed on me a time or two, but they couldn't hobble me. I like my bacon, sir, but that is getting it—the hard way."

There was a gleam of swift water in the vale where they had paused. The centaur kneeled ponderously, sighing, on the moss bank. He laid down his coiled whip and bathed vigorously, throwing up handfuls of water, drenching his locks and beard, coughing and muttering to himself. Whit washed the boar blood from his hands, drank from the cold clear stream. They looked at each other frankly, man and manbeast, strangers but comrades thrown together by ordeal. The sky above them shimmered, ghostly and vaporous; there was foxfire all around. Their eyes glowed from it.

"You're one hell of a fighter," the centaur said. "I've taken on Rooshians before, but I'm afraid I lack the stamina to handle a large pack of them. I was already getting old before I was born, if you know what I mean."

"No," Whit said, still feeling a little numb and shaky from his escape, and strangely childlike in the presence of the centaur. "What's a Rooshian?"

"European wild boars, imported and set loose in these mountains by so-called sportsmen in the twenties." He shook his grayed head angrily at this murderous violation of a wild sanctuary. "As if we didn't have enough problems surviving."

"You're—a Walkout."

"What else?" the centaur said with an ironic smile. "Call me Jim."

Stunned, Whit ventured, "James—Travers?"

His smile vanished, the aging face hardened. "That was someone else, in a time beyond recall. Jim will do. And what do you know of Travers?"

"He—Jacob seemed to think that you—may be my father."

The gelded centaur limped closer, eyes narrowed to see Whit better.

"It can't be. Not *you*. You're no Walkout."

"I'm not sure. Maybe—I am. They found me wandering in the desert. Texas, late afternoon, 21 June 1916. That's the first memory I have, although I was at least six years old at the time. But all my life I've dreamed—"

"Of what? Of whom?" the centaur demanded. The large equine body, cold with scars and fresh wounds, trembled impatiently.

"I dream of a man who was a great magician. And a woman, dying. Calling for me. But for some reason, I—hate her. I don't know why."

"God help us!" In his excitement the centaur reared, and Whit backed away from the threat of hooves, the coiled blacksnake in a knotted fist. But the centaur settled down with a windy sigh, eyes watering from strain. "No, don't be afraid. Let me look at you! If it's there, if you haven't had it removed—"

"What are you talking about?"

The centaur leaned forward, a trifle unsteadily, from the waist, his large ungroomed prophet's head coming within inches of Whit's face. He had two very different eyes, one intelligent and sharply appraising, the other blooded and blurred as if by madness, adrift in its socket. He stared at Whit, then withdrew to a height of contemplation, muttering to himself.

"What did you see?" Whit asked crossly.

"Yes, it *is* there. Edgar's mark. You had it as a child. No, this may not be a coincidence. But how, in the name of the almighty—"

Whit touched the small mole on his jaw near the left earlobe.

"This? My son has one too."

"The lightness of your eyes—" The centaur's trembling became unendurable. He wheeled and began to run in circles, galloping across the creek in a brutal ecstasy, crying out incomprehensibly. It was like a running fit, a terrible seizure. The power of wild horses had always unnerved Whit. Again he was afraid of being trampled; he looked for an outlet, a way to escape the runaway creature. But before he could move to safer ground the centaur stumbled and fell hard, lay shaking and blowing on his side.

"Alex!" he shouted; and Whit heeded the call.

"Are you all right?" he asked the centaur, looking for trouble, the jagged edges of a smashed leg bone. But there was no apparent damage.

"Old—too old for such—nonsense. Losing control. But nothing—in the past thirty-one years has prepared me for this night. You must be Alex. I'm sure of it."

"*His* son? Not yours?"

"We will speak—if you please—of a man named Travers. Who, for all practical purposes, died on Midsummer Eve, 1916. I knew him well, his genius, his flaws; but my period of mourning is long over."

Staring at the centaur's form, the seamless conjoining of man and animal, a tragic prison for both, Whit nodded.

"You've talked to Jacob," the centaur said. "Then you must know something of the history of Wildwood; and the inevitability of the love of James Travers for Sibby Langford. Your mother."

"He showed me pictures of her. Jim—I have to tell you. Jacob is dead." Whit explained everything that had happened in the caverns. The centaur listened quietly, his sentient eye upturned, chestnut flanks quivering intermittently.

"There have been two hundred and sixty-three Walk-outs," the centaur said. "We will count you as number two hundred sixty-four, but your case is unique in my experience. All of the others appeared in these woods, in one form or another, within a few miles of the chateau. The first was in 1921; the last may have been

Jacqueline, your nursemaid, whom we buried only a few hours ago.''

"I met another near the aviary tonight. And I—I had the feeling that the chateau was close by. I only needed to look hard enough, in the right direction, to see it. But I was afraid to.''

"There has been so much activity in the past three weeks. The veils of time are disappearing one by one. The Revelation is at hand, I'm convinced of it. But you are most interested in the matter of your paternity. For my part, I would like very much to know how you survived almost certain death, that deadly Midsummer Eve.''

—— Chapter Thirty ——

Wildwood, June 23, 1916, Midsummer Eve

An hour of daylight remained when Edgar Langford ascended to the lantern to pay his last respects to Faren Rutledge, whose metamorphosis he had been observing, despite the many distractions of the past few days, with ever-increasing excitement and fascination.

As it had been for the past several weeks, the lantern was open to the sky, a sky half-filled by turbulent, purpling cloud shot through with the rays of the sun. No storm yet; but thunder mumbled in a promising way, and the air around the lantern was agitated, prickly from cosmic energy. The speed of the supernatural machine had increased in this vividly charged atmosphere. Its countless synapses composed a red starfield in a universe of quick shimmering silver. Looking into it was like looking into the mind of a god; to be close to the machine for any length of time was to be transformed, even deified (should the magician choose). Yet she was still resisting, although, he saw at once, with a gratifying shock of the pulse, her resistance had weakened since his last visit.

Kálanu, the Raven: deservedly she belonged in a cage, a stout one; this he had provided. Not a cage made of steel bars bolted to the floor of the lantern, but a field of his own energy, which emanated from the walking stick with the serpent's head. He had left it floating a few feet above her. From its influence her only escape was into the mind of the machine, which already had begun to do that wondrous work for which it had been designed. Although she stubbornly clung to human form, Kálanu was inevitably changing: he saw a sleek black wingtip materialize before she gathered her waning force and willed the return of flesh and fingerbones. He looked into the sternly beautiful Cherokee face, so wearied from the ceaseless struggle as she pitted her own will, her nearly useless magick, against the will of the machine.

He smiled, drawing forth her hatred, and her fear. The bones beneath her taut russet skin seemed to be moving, reshaping themselves inhumanly.

"Let . . . me . . . go," Faren said, naked. on her knees, but still able to demand. not to plead.

His smile thinned; he gestured in a manner that emphasized her essential powerlessness, and his control.

"Why should I? I think you are lacking in gratitude. You came across time for the purpose of causing me harm, to disrupt my valuable work. I might have had you strangled and thrown into the woods, to become a shack of bones for the lowest of creatures. Instead, I give you the opportunity to seize immortality; you need only humble yourself, and accept the transformation that is inevitable."

"And when I do . . . your serpent . . . will eat me,"

she said, glaring momentarily at the hovering walking stick, the avid ruby eyes.

"The strength of the Serpent versus the speed and cunning of the Raven. It should be an interesting contest."

Momentarily he saw riffling feathers, an awesome dark wingspan, before she denied, again, the metamorphosis. The gold head of Edgar Langford's walking stick, having expanded to meet the challenge, shrank back to its normal size.

"Ah, well," he said, disappointed by her temporary return to equilibrium. "We shall have to wait a little longer. But I'm sure before the night is over . . ." He looked up, at the darkening clouds, at a flash of lightning barely brighter than the aura of the silver machine. He gazed again at her tormented, glistening body, the heaving breasts, and felt something rare for him: sexual stimulation. The impulse was distracting. To couple with her would have been dangerous, he had realized that on their first meeting. She could diminish his magick. Even now the involuntary twinge of lust was clouding his clear vision of triumph over those poor specimens of humanity who had come flocking to his Revels. Leave her to her losing battle, he thought, as she groaned at his feet and shook her head, trying to rise from the floor of the lantern, her hands splayed, the tendons of wrists and shoulders standing out like the cables of a suspension bridge.

The doors of the lantern closed solidly on her despair, a strangled cry. Edgar Langford turned to find Taharqa waiting for him.

The Ethiopian, already wearing the goat's-head mask assigned to him for the Revels, began signing rapidly; Edgar frowned, interrupting him.

"I have no time for Sibby now."

Taharqa put a hand urgently to his throat. Edgar's frown deepened.

"She cannot be dying?"

Taharqa nodded, then made the sign for "doctor."

"He is with her? Very well, then, perhaps it is a crisis; I'll go at once." He dismissed Taharqa with a nod and proceeded, as quickly as he could without his walking stick, to the apartment where his wife had been bedfast since giving birth to a daughter several months ago. For the convenience of their guests, the slick marble floors and stairs of the chateau had been overlaid with thick plum-colored runners loomed in Turkestan, but still he was afraid of a misstep, a fall that would be disastrous for his brittle back. How inconvenient of his dear wife to die at this time, he thought dispassionately. He had already resolved to keep the unpleasant news from her brothers and other revelers until they were past caring what had become of her.

But, to his dismay, he found Sibby fully conscious when he entered her bedchamber. Dr. Burrough was not there; only Pamela attended her.

"Edgar, I must speak with you."

"How deceitful of you, Sibby, to imply a crisis."

"In order to gain your attention."

"Taharqa was most convincing. Who else have you enlisted in this conspiracy to waste my time today?"

"Please, Edgar. Don't leave yet! All I am asking of you is your permission to go home."

"Home?" Edgar replied, genuinely perplexed. "Wildwood is your home."

"I wish to return to Boston, my birthplace, so that I may be with my family when—" She began to cough, wanly pressing a pale yellow handkerchief, darkly flecked, to her dry, earthworm-colored lips.

"I will not discuss this," Edgar said, ruthlessly ignoring the state she was in.

"I would like—for my children to accompany me. But I realize—Alexander will choose to remain with you."

Edgar turned to Pamela and said in a soft frightening tone, "Leave us alone."

Pamela, reluctant, glanced at Sibby, then lowered her head and hurried past Edgar Langford.

As she was closing the thick bedroom door, Edgar said, "Pamela, go and change now. *Everyone* is required to be in costume by sunset."

"Yes, sir."

Sibby was coughing again. Edgar waited, patiently enough, for her attention.

"You are far too ill to travel. Even if I thought you could survive the journey, I would not allow you to leave Wildwood. Nor will anyone else leave. All of my guests are to be permanent guests."

"What—do you mean?"

"It is only a matter of a few hours until the Transformation takes effect, so you may well live to see what I mean."

"Why—would you wish to keep anyone here—against his will? My brothers—"

"You will never see them again, dear Sibby . . . in a form that you might recognize. But perhaps they will recognize *you*, and cry out in the voices of exotic beasts as you are driven through the animal park under glass, on the way to your tomb."

"What are you going to do?" Sibby sat up, swayed, fell back against a silk pillow, eyelids drooping. She gasped for breath.

"I have devised an entertainment for my son's birthday, far more ingenious than anything that has been seen on earth during the past five thousand years. My guests will participate, with drunken delight and wonder; but then, when they realize what is happening to them, there will be screams and frenzy. For years I have heard them screaming in my sleep, all of my detractors and betrayers; I have never forgotten a single one of their sneers and slights. Nor have I forgotten your infidelity of long standing."

"What difference—can that make to you n-now?"

"The fact is, I have every reason to be grateful. Because of your affair with Travers, I have a son whom I love, and who worships me."

"He is—*your* son. I c-carried him—a full nine months. So I—I m-must have been mistaken when I thought—"

"When you thought you had become pregnant by your lover and hastened to seduce me, after so many months of neglect."

"B-but Laurette—I f-feel so confused. I do not know—which of you—"

Edgar Langford shrugged his sloping shoulder and limped to the windows. He had heard a meaningful crack of thunder.

"I am indifferent. Only Alex matters to me."

He pulled back a heavy brocade drape, looked at a massive storm cloud, veined with lightning, that was almost directly above the chateau. He relished the display of lightning for a few moments, then limped to her bedside.

"Because I have a reason to feel gratitude, instead of hatred, I decided weeks ago not to subject you to the animal park or the aviary. Instead, I offer you a quiet release from this life."

He looked into Sibby's eyes for a few moments, then reached for one of the oversize pillows on her bed.

Ill as she was, he was surprised to learn that she had the strength to scream so loudly.

When James B. Travers rode into the stable courtyard on Cyclops, Pamela was waiting for him, half dressed in her costume for the Revels; she pulled off the tiger's mask, glittery with sequins, identifying herself in the morbid twilight.

"Mr. Travers, thank God!"

"Pamela, what is it?" But he felt a shock of fear in his heart for Sibby.

"You must come! Mr. Langford, sir, he—he—" She began to cry.

Sharp thunder caused Cyclops to shy and wheel about, flinging up damp tanbark from his hooves.

"Get hold of yourself, Pamela! What is wrong?"

"I am sure that—he means to take her life tonight."

Travers grimly reined in his skittish horse and reached down for Pamela.

"Ride behind me," he commanded. She was wearing tights and had no trouble mounting the horse. She held him around the waist with arms gloved past the elbows; the gloves were of thick velvet and, like her mask for the Revels, tiger-striped. Travers galloped his chestnut gelding toward the chateau, luminous in the threatening night. On the grounds a parade with floats outlined in tiny twinkling lights had begun to form. But he was most aware of the brilliantly silvered lantern, around which a terrifying web of lightning crackled almost continuously from the depths of one of the blackest clouds he had ever seen.

"Tell me what happened!" Travers shouted.

"Mr. Langford came to visit not a quarter of an hour ago. You know that she wishes to return to the East with her brothers—"

"Yes. I should have taken her myself, weeks ago, no matter what the consequences."

"He was angered by her request, and said that he would not discuss it. He then ordered me to leave the bedchamber. I was apprehensive, sir, and so stayed by her door; but as they spoke in low tones I heard nothing of what was said. Then she screamed. At that I flung the door open. And saw him, sir, s-saw him—"

"Pamela!"

"I'm sorry, Mr. Travers. Could we not go more slowly, I am afraid I will lose my seat."

"Just hold on tightly, you can't fall. Now tell me what you saw."

"Mr. Langford was standing over the bed, a large pillow in his hands. He was holding it only a few inches from her face. When he turned and looked at me, I swear to you there was—murder in his eyes."

"What did he do?"

"He threw the pillow down and came toward me, holding out his hands as if he meant to seize me by the throat. He is a strong man, as you know, for all of his ills. I was numb with fright and could not move. But instead of strangling me, he pushed me aside and left the apartment at once—surely you do not intend riding through the gardens, sir!"

"Like hell I don't. Was Sibby conscious? Had he—"

"Oh, yes, she called to me and I went immediately to her side. She was struggling for breath, and asked for a sip of water. When I had given it to her she seemed—almost calm, peaceful-like, though her fever was high. It was she who soothed me, with a pat of her hand.

'Now, Pamela,' she said, 'you must go at once and find Mr. Travers.' I was mortally afraid to leave her alone, but she insisted. 'Never mind. I will be all right for now. My husband will not dare come back tonight. We have a little time, Pamela; and we must use our time well, for all of our lives depend on that.' Her exact words to me, sir and I—*oh, lud!*''

Travers had jumped Cyclops over a low privet on their way to the chateau. The horse then forded a gold-fish pond and galloped past a lighted jewelbox gazebo exhibiting a number of startled houseguests in animal costumes. Pamela pressed her cheek hard against Travers's broad back, closing her eyes as they neared the chateau.

''Pamela, I want you to prepare Mrs. Langford to leave here immediately. I will be back for the two of you as soon as I am able. Have you ever fired a pistol?''

''No, sir, only a fowling piece of my brother's.''

''It is quite easy to do. You must steady the pistol in both hands, point it, and pull the trigger slowly. When it goes off you may be confident you have blown a devil into the hell which he so patently deserves.''

''But—I have no pistol, sir.''

''I will give you mine.''

''And where are you going?''

''To find the boy,'' Travers said, urging Cyclops carefully up the steps to the front entrance of the cha-teau, then through the open doors of the *corps du logis,* scattering the members of a strolling string orchestra and more guests who were mingling at the base of the massive circular staircase.

If it hadn't been for the plush runners of carpeting, Travers's horse would have slipped on the marble floor as if it were a sheet of ice. As it was, the architect was able to ride Cyclops up the wide spiral stairs to the second floor of the chateau, and straight to the apartment of his mistress.

The doors to the sitting room of the apartment were standing open. There was no sign of Edgar Langford. From the bedroom they heard Sibby Langford calling feebly for her maid.

"Thank God," Travers said, and turned to Pamela. She was so frightened her teeth were chattering. "Get down!" He drew the Colt's revolver he always carried beneath his coat while riding in Wildwood. Pamela slid off the back of the horse. Travers handed the cocked pistol down to her. "Don't dawdle," he said.

"Sir, you mustn't leave us—!"

"I'll be back in a few minutes." There was no faster way to get around the chateau than on horseback; he turned Cyclops and galloped him down the hall toward Alex's apartment. It was a two-minute ride. Servants and guests in the brightly lighted hallways again went to the walls as the horse appeared. There was a tremendous crack of thunder above the chateau.

At the doors to the boy's apartment Travers leaned down and depressed one of the bronze handles with the butt end of his whip. The door swung open. Cyclops balked momentarily, then squeezed inside.

They were face to face with Taharqa, wearing a goat's-head mask for the Revels, his loincloth, and his handax.

Alex Langford, hearing the horse in his playroom, came out of the bath wearing only underwear shorts, a piece of his costume in his hands.

Travers said to the boy, "Your father has gone mad. He tried to kill your mother. For your own good, you must come with me."

Lightning outside the playroom windows turned all

their faces to chalk. The windows were open. A strong but rainless wind had twisted the drapes.

Alex shook his head and backed away

Taharqa drew his handax.

Travers's blacksnake whip hissed and cracked The ax flew from Taharqa's hand and rang off a stone wall. The black man sprang toward it and was lashed around one ankle, held fast. He fell hard on one shoulder, rolled. clawed off the binding whip, crawled in pain toward the gleaming ax a dozen feet away, able to use only one arm.

Travers cut off Alex before he could dart into his bedroom. He leaned out of the saddle, scooped the wiry boy off the floor, and pinned him facedown across the gelding's shoulders, holding him there with one hand. Then he reined Cyclops around in the doorway, Alex screaming lustily for his father.

Taharqa had reached the handax. And Edgar Langford was standing in the doorway with a face of rage.

"Cut the horse's throat!" he said to the Ethiopian; with all of his strength he turned and slammed shut the big door.

Travers's whip hand also held the reins. He had all he could do to keep Alex from wriggling off the horse.

When Cyclops saw the crippled black man coming at him with the ax, he snorted in fear and backed away.

Taharqa swung his ax, but the curved blade missed the long throat of the horse by less than an inch. Cyclops reared in panic and Travers was nearly unseated. His horse fell rump-first against a wall, staggered, but kept his footing. And then there was nothing behind them but the open window. black cloud, bleak lightning.

"Kill Travers." Langford demanded.

Taharqa had recovered his balance from the nearly

lethal swing of the ax and was crouched, wary of the horse's hooves. The room was beginning to fill with a magnetically blue and sparkling light. Edgar Langford seemed to dissolve in the light until nothing was left of him but the wise alert pupils of his eyes, the snakelike, eroded skeleton of his defective spine.

The last thing the architect heard before the Crack of Doom was Langford saying, "You will never have my son!"

Despite the pressure of his hand in the small of Alex's bare back, the boy suddenly flew away from him. Travers saw Alex for a moment, levitated just inside a window, screaming, small hands scrabbling in the charmed air for purchase. But the cloud behind the boy was agitated, as if by the screw of an enormous ship, or a twisted backbone with numinous power. He reached for Alex and saw his hand disappear mildly to the wrist in a blue whirligig, then the boy vanished like a blip of water on a scalding stove top. The dissolvent energy of the light spiraling into the room continued to take him painlessly and remorselessly, even as the horse beneath him swooned and the stone walls evanesced, and he felt as a trumpet's blare inside his mind the vile amusement of the man he hated most in the life he now appeared to be leaving.

Chapter Thirty-one

Wildwood, April 1958

"And that's all there was. A quiet death, followed, within a moment or two, by a nightmare, rebirth as something quite outside the realm of humanity."

They were moving at a slow pace through the woods beneath a sky of scary galaxies, meteors big as fish in a blood-soaked sea. Whit Bowers mounted on the centaur who wanted to be called Jim.

"When was that?"

"The year of Jim's rebirth? It was 1927." He breathed audibly, wheezing at times along the ill-defined path, but otherwise he gave no indication that he considered Whit a burden. He seemed to be more comfortable, even now, referring to himself in the third person while recalling his crude metamorphosis. "Already there were Walkouts in Wildwood, like a stranded sideshow. They were unable to form any sort of coherent community. A few quickly died; their hybrid selves functioned badly, or their minds failed, or the weather—" Whit's palm rested where the spines of man and animal were fused, and he felt a tremor there. Jim's voice was deep, his tone elegiac. "He was very sick himself, that winter. You can imagine the difficulty he had in accepting his fate, the wicked adversity visited on him by the demon Langford. Jim was horseflesh; he was human. A bereaved human being. But there are minds that break all too easily, and others that wear like steel. The pragmatic mind maketh a lesson of hardship, and seeketh solutions. Jim put his mind to work in the service of those more cruelly used than he."

"Could you tell me where we're—"

Without pausing the centaur lifted his tail and broke wind resoundingly, groaning all the while.

"Stomach trouble," he explained. "I've always had it. The problem is food. What my tastebuds find agreeable disturbs my digestive tract. I'm certain I have an ulcer. And I've nearly worn my teeth to the gumlines from chewing, chewing, the coarse oats and grains I must depend upon to live. But on my rebirthday and on the New Year I allow myself a jug of whiskey." Jim reached up with his whip hand to courteously hold aside a large bough that might have swept Whit off his back. He laughed. "The truth is, I allow myself a jug whenever I feel like it. I learned to make my own whiskey by observing a small band of moonshiners who once plied their trade in these woods. That was, perhaps, fifteen years ago. When I was well-versed in the process of distilling spirits I showed myself to them and made application to purchase their works, when I might well have seized everything through the power of eminent domain. Their reaction was most interesting. The eldest of the three men fell down clutching his chest. His son, an individual of submarginal intelligence, attempted to fire a rifle at me. I appropriated it with my whip. He fled with his red-haired cousin, who subsequently fractured his pelvis in what must have been a nasty fall; the cracked bones and his overalls were discovered long after at the foot of Painter Leap. Before I could be of assistance, the old man died of heart failure. We buried him. No one ever showed up to look for him or claim the abandoned still. I wonder why?'' His shod feet rang briefly on stone as they took another course downhill.

"How far—"

"Have patience," Jim snapped. "You're fortunate to be alive. And you have a strong body, you're in your prime. I don't drink when I'm in the woods, otherwise I might have been lolling by my pool, deaf to the world, while those boars eviscerated you."

"The last time you saw me, I was falling through the window of a room in the chateau."

"There was nothing I could do to resist the power that was attracting you."

"But—if the other Walkouts appeared in Wildwood, how did I wind up in West Texas?"

"I don't know the fate of all the Walkouts. There may be a few others, like yourself normal in appearance, scattered throughout the world. Perhaps, because you were in free-fall at the time, you were simply deflected, a displaced mote, to the desert. You might as easily have reappeared in Malabar, or the South Atlantic ocean. There is no explanation."

"Do you think it's coming back?"

"What do *you* think, Alex?"

Whit began to shudder, as if the ghost of a child alien to him were awakening, dreadfully, like a long-dead nerve.

"Yes. I think it's coming back. But I don't want to see it."

"Odds are your father is still there." Jim added, sardonically, "You must surely want to see *him*."

"I don't—I still can't accept—"

For a few moments the centaur stood still at an overlook; below them smoke rose from the dim lights of the fires of Walkout Town. It obscured part of the distempered but silent sky, a catastrophe eons old threatening anew.

"Make no mistake. He *is* your father. And it would be fitting if he is there, waiting for you, Alex."

"Oh, Jesus."

"For me as well," the centaur said.

"And you—want to kill him."

The centaur ambled to a nearby tree and began to rub one shabby, balding flank against the trunk, sighing pleasurably. Then they continued downhill.

"For the last three years, since Jacob and I began to talk, and I came to believe in his theories of Wildwood's disappearance, I've thought about little else. It may be that the potential opportunity for revenge, however remote, has kept me alive well past my time."

"We were in the same room, you said. And now we're all here, except my—except for Edgar Langford. Why isn't he a Walkout too?"

"Remember. It was *his* magic."

"I don't believe in magic."

"Nor centaurs, I suppose," Jim said. And he lashed Whit's back with a sweep of his wiry tail. A meteor flamed in the smoke and stuffy mist, illuminating them, too brightly. Whit closed his eyes, reeling from icy remembrance, and the sheer drunkenness of fantastical night. He nearly lost his balance, like a child on a cock-horse.

"Hold on," Jim said sharply, "and try not to shift

your weight. We're almost home now. We'll have a drink at my place, and talk. If the appearance of the sky these last few nights is significant, then all of our questions may soon be answered."

Terry got up from the bearskin beside Josie Raftery's suspension bed and, after carefully moving aside one of her protective wings, went outside still half asleep to relieve himself. Through the blur of trees in a saffron mist he saw, passing at a distance of no more than a hundred feet, what appeared to be two men on horseback. Then his scalp crawled a little and his testicles shriveled like prunes; he wished for a closer look but was afraid to follow, and whatever had been there vanished so abruptly he couldn't be certain it was real. He heard a voice he recognized, was about to call out, shuddered and thought better of it. He crept back onto the bearskin in the hut beneath a warm wing, which quivered in response to his agitation. He was goose-bumpy all over.

Josie murmured, "Are you all right?"

"Uh-huh. I thought I heard my dad outside. He was riding a—but it couldn't have been a horse." Still trembling, he curled up more tightly on the thick nap of claw-edged fur.

"What you saw is called a centaur. Half man, half horse. His name is Jim."

Terry giggled nervously.

"He may be the oldest Walkout; certainly he is the wisest, on his good days."

"What about his b-bad d-days?"

"Ah, well, poor thing, he does no harm. Look here, mister honey, if neither of us is going to sleep again this night, perhaps you wish to lie down with me again."

"Maybe I should go look for my dad."

"If he is here, you will see him come the dawning. *Please*, Terry?"

Her beryl eyes were vivid as catsgleam in the primitive dark; all else he knew by heart: her pretty breast, the masquerade elegance of her repose.

"Move over," Terry said.

In the darkness of his nightmare, Faren came to Arn Rutledge bearing light.

She held a lantern in an outstretched hand. It was scintillating, scathing, his eyes watered and ached to look at it. He preferred looking at his wife, who was tautly naked, her skin the color of copper and slicked-on old blood. Aroused, he wanted to embrace her, hands conforming to those familiar and comfortable contours of hip, pelvis and tarbabe pussy. But the noose the Walkouts had put around his neck still held him back; and, even if his hands had not been tied, the lantern was between them, an obstacle that seemed more formidable with each passing second.

"Faren, put that damned thing down and untie me!"

Look at it, she told him telepathically. Her eyes were wide, her Cherokee face so stern it seemed cruel.

Something fluttered in the brilliance of the rayed light, and strove to acquire an ominous shape: it was a black bird, a raven. He closed his eyes against the pressure of the light and the struggling bird. But the light burned through his dry lids as if they were onionskin.

"Faren—" he pleaded. Disturbing dreams made him meek, as nothing in life could ever do.

When he looked for her again all that remained was the caustic lantern suspended inches from his face. He saw, where Faren had been standing, a lifting of enormous wings saturated with fire at the tips. He tried to reach and hold her, but was choking at the end of the rope, fainting from lack of blood to his brain. The raven shrieked and flew, night-fierce; but something, not his own bound hands, dragged it fighting back to earth. The raven's talons were caught in the coils of a serpent of such size it had no head and no tail: it existed, endlessly, a colossus of the harrowing void between earth and sky.

Arn heard his wife scream, in a human voice, but the vision disintegrated grayly and he found himself facedown, gagging and trembling uncontrollably, on the burlap-covered dirt floor of the hut. The rope had become twisted around his body during his bouts of possessed sleep. Getting untangled in the dark was a demeaning, frustrating chore. His fury mounted with each failure. At last he was able to crawl outside into the witching misty night and wake all the sleepers, the oblivious ones.

"Walkouts! You sorry sons of bitches! Let me out of here! It's got my wife! You hear me, freaks? Cut this rope!"

Arn paused for breath. But he was prepared to go on yelling for the rest of his life, or until someone came.

In the stall-like hut where the centaur lived with loaded shelves of books and his yeasty still, Whit Bowers heard the sergeant-major. He had been drinking the centaur's potent mash whiskey, and had dozed off along with the garrulous Jim. When he started awake he was disoriented and shaken, certain that he was in yet another foreign country during a lull in a ghastly battle.

As he got up from the floor he heard what could have been a dud shell going off just outside. He flinched, but the explosion was mild, even festive, as if a champagne cork had been ejected from a jeroboam. The noise was followed by an instant of blue-toned light, blinding as a photoflash. He was fixed in his tracks before he could reach the wide gate across the entrance to the centaur's hut.

Jim, who had drunk a great deal more than Whit, was stretched out on the floor, Chiron fallen, a living myth though sourly breathing, wearing a patchy scarred hide. With his retinas dazzled Whit stumbled against him. The centaur raised his head slowly.

"What was that? Where are you going?"

"Outside. I heard Arn, he's in some kind of trouble."

Jim groaned and farted. Whit edged around the squalid equine body and pushed the gate open. Outside a stream of sparkling light dense as a river flowed, with many sharp bends and against gravity, through the mist and thick trees that stood around the oblong park of Walkout Town. Whit cupped his hands around his mouth and called.

"Arn!"

The sergeant-major's hoarse voice came back to him as Whit heard the centaur getting to his feet in the hut.

"Colonel Bowers!" His delight and relief were plain despite the distance between them. "Where you at? Get me some help up here, ole buddy, can't hold this hill much longer—all by myself."

Jim clumped outside, his breath preceding him like a flush of gasoline. Nearby other Walkouts, wraithlike in the mist, appeared from their lodgings, attracted more by the fluent river of light than by Arn's distress calls. They made sounds of ecstasy, of tribulation.

"Hold on, Arn, I'm coming!" Whit turned to the centaur, whose bloodshot eyes contemplated the wending

light. It shed thickets of crystals like ice that glittered
alluringly but quickly melted in the warmer mist.

"Where's Arn?"

"Never mind. He is not in jeopardy. Do you hear
that?"

"Hear what?"

"*Music*. You must hear it. Music from the chateau!"

Whit nodded. It was the same faint orchestra he had
heard on leaving the aviary hours ago. Melody still
missing, but the notes of a clarinet were needle-sharp
and unerring as they flew across time. The Walkouts
were agitated by the tantalizing reed, like bees in a
hungry hive.

"Colonel Bowers! Hey, Whit! Get me out of this
noose, Faren's in bad trouble!"

"What's he talking about?" Whit demanded. "What
noose?"

"The man is a murderer," Jim said indifferently, his
attention concentrated on the faded music. "We've merely
given him a taste of our justice after all these years."

"You're going to hang him? For Christ's sake—"

Something remarkable had appeared, mildly dark but
sharper than the sprightly transparence of the light stream,
a few hundred yards from where they stood. It was
weaving in and out with the swirling flow through the
trees, acquiring a shadowy substance, coalescing. It
was, perhaps, a lookalike centaur, galloping blankly
but inexorably in their direction. Then Whit realized it
was not one creature but a bluesy horse, another dark
figure distinguishable behind its rider.

"Dear God," Jim said in a quiet voice; but he sidestepped ponderously against Whit, nearly knocking him
down.

"What *is* it?"

The running horse, each stride suspenseful, precise in its purpose as a ticking clock, was closer. The man in the saddle wore a broad-brimmed hat, and carried a coiled whip in one hand. He raised an empty face, glittery as days-old death, to the watchers. The other silent rider was a woman in tights. She clung to the man's back, hair floating slowly around her head like the hair of the newly drowned.

The centaur screamed, inflating Whit's pulse, provoking an uproar from the other Walkouts.

"It's Travers!"

More Walkouts appeared, surreptitiously, in the clearing near the motive light as the horse of nightshade blue and dream momentum passed by and began to vanish upstream, where the now-diffluent stream poured toward the crest of Tormentil Mountain, rising, like a dissipated spell, toward the sky. And then the wind hit them, a torrential blast clearing out the light and the mist and the failed music, sweeping trees toward the ground, bowling over those Walkouts who had nothing to cling to. Whit fell back against the centaur, reached up to anchor himself with a handful of gritty scalplocks.

As the wind subsided, a sparse exhalation, the night sky, for the first time in hours, was visible—the old eyes of eternity fire-flecked, a three-quarter moon glistening like the belly of a pregnant angel.

The teasing music returned through the steadying pines, and they heard the laughter of friends and lovers long unseen.

Whit thought he had become accustomed to the funereal and the bizarre, but as he stared at the sky, momentarily forgetting Arn, he saw a butterfly glide enormously from the dark treetops.

"Josie! Josie!"

The Walkouts were looking up, pointing. The butterfly soared higher.

"Tell us, Josie!"

For half a minute the butterfly hovered above Walkout Town, a ruddy shadow on the moon like a blood tattoo. Then it began a graceful descent.

"Dad?"

Whit turned and gaped at his son, who smiled assuredly, pleased to be a surprise. Then he stared, like almost everyone else, at Josie the butterfly, something secret of his own in his excitement, his admiration of her godlike skill.

"Terry—what the hell—where did *you* come from?"

Terry just shrugged, looked again at his father, then belatedly hugged him, his heart ripe with the affections of youth, the pride of a new-found manhood.

"You okay?" Terry asked him. "I thought you were lost."

"I was. But tell me—"

"Oh, I came with Faren. But I don't know what happened to her." He lowered his voice, casting an awed glance at the nearby centaur, very like a god himself but in his cups, and unsteady. "Arn's here, though. They—"

"*Josie!*"

More voices were calling now, anxious to be relieved of the horror of doubts.

"*Is it there, Josie?*"

As the butterfly flew toward open ground and the Walkouts converged on her, Terry pulled eagerly at his father's sleeve.

"Come on, I want you to meet Josie. She's—hey, she's just so *neat*."

The centaur broke into a clod-flinging gallop, the man-

third of him thrust forward acutely, like the prow of an
unseaworthy ship.

"Did you see it?" His intrusive bulk and his bellow
momentarily silenced the other Walkouts.

Josie Raftery hovered a few feet above his uplifted
face, splendid wings rowing slowly in the moonlight,
her body severely straight and angled a few degrees
from the vertical.

"Yes," she said, with obvious reluctance. "It's
there."

The uproar from the Walkouts was like a sudden
squall that disturbed her airy balance; she nearly fell,
head-down, but righted herself with a frantic leg-scissors
and dashing of wings; she sought elevation, detachment
from their delirium.

"Wait!" she warned them, but they were in full cry,
rushing off the croquet pitch and into the woods, the
centaur in front, then in their spectral midst, then lag-
ging badly.

Josie came to vacant earth and folded her wings,
covering in a gesture of dark chagrin her nakedness
before the stranger, Terry's father.

"Josie, this is my dad."

"Yes, I thought so," she murmured, downcast, finding in Whit's presence a reminder that Terry had a life
in some distant elsewhere that they, as lovers, had
failed to acknowledge. "And how do you do, sir?" She
looked up and away from him to the shadowy windbroke
centaur. They heard the sobs and shouts of the Walkouts
surging uphill, climbing over and around each other in
their frenzy to reach the promised chateau.

"Jim!" she called. "Can you not stop them?"

"Why should I?"

"I'm afraid! Do you recall Jacob's words—"

"It doesn't matter what Jacob said! He was no saner than any of us. No less subjugated."

"Are you going too, then?"

"Yes! Yes, Lord give me strength, I'll be the first to return!"

Brandishing his whip, the centaur took up the shrill cry of the disenfranchised, vaulting after those who had left him behind. Whit observed him with a shudder of anxiety until he had no more substance than smoke, a shadow blending into the mountainous dark.

When he glanced at Josie he saw tears shining like silver coins on her fair cheeks and Terry standing intimately close, under the protection of a sable-bordered wing.

She said bitterly, "And what welcome do they think awaits them in the demonarchy? Not a welcoming, nor relief from their affliction. Only more torment, I'm thinking. Oh, God save them, I'm so sorry."

"What did Jacob tell you?" Whit asked her. "Josie!"

"He said—it might someday reappear, poised upon the earth but not locked into it, and truly this is what I did see, dead low shining like a ghost bound in chains of horrid lightning. Fearful! And he said—though we might go back, and mingle with its haunting, still none of us—could become what once we were. It is no house at all but an engine that awaits them, familiar to the trusting eye but diabolical, an engine that will convey them straight to a hell deeper and more forbidding than anything the mind conjectures."

Arn's voice echoed through the nearly deserted town; and they heard the mournful howling of Bocephus the hound.

"Colonel Bowers! Can you get me out of here?"

"Where is he, Josie?"

She put her head wearily against Terry's; her breast heaved, her tears flowed. He wiped them awkwardly, and kissed a wettened cheek.

"Ah, well. What difference now? You might as well turn the damned rogue loose. Come on, then. I will lead you to him."

Terry released her and Josie sprang into the air. They followed her at a jog to the hut where Arn was crouched just outside the door. Josie remained on high, aloofly, her back to the deed as Whit loosened the rugged slip-knot and freed Arn.

"You okay, sergeant-major?"

"Hell, yes, everythin's ducky. What was all that hooraw?"

Terry had disappeared into the trees behind the hut. He returned with Bocephus laboring at the end of a rope.

"The chateau is back," Josie said above their heads.

Arn looked up and met her eyes. "Wouldn't be funnin' with me?"

Josie made a wordless sound of contempt.

"Then—that could be where Faren is. In trouble." A spate of coughing caused him pain, and brought blood to his lips. "Don't know what—I can do, except raise plenty hell long as I'm able. Colonel, I—I could use a good man."

"I'll come, Arn."

"Me too," Terry said.

Josie flew at him, angrily and protectively, backing him away from the men.

"Terry, no! It's dangerous there."

"Why?"

"Have you not heard a word I've said? When it goes, in the flash of a second, all who are inside or around the chateau will be lost, perhaps forever."

"I only want to see it. Don't you?"

"I told you, *no*, I would not go."

"Listen, Josie," Arn said, needing to clear his throat often to get words out, "you and me—have had our little differences. But—I want my wife back, hear? If she's in the chateau I'll find her, only you got to—show me the way. Just get me up there, and I'll take my chances."

She seemed coldly pleased by his insistence; but her enamored, worried eyes were full of Terry.

"So be it," she said. "Follow me, then—all of you."

And suddenly
here was yesterday; the sharp thin air
of mountain April had thickened languorously
where the dark wood ended, it was odorous
of a heavier, rose-reeking June night.
Across the emerald esplanade, bedecked
with striped pavilions and garlands
of electric lights, teeming caravans
formed to outbursts of jocularity
and rollicking music. There were
fractious camels, lofty giraffes,
silver-garbed parade horses, dawn-pink
flamingos, doves in wicker cages on long
poles. And all those revelers unadvised
of a wild and deplorable magick that
crackled invisibly a cunning distance
from human apprehension: spear carriers,
musketeers, mummers, beasties vivants.
Death, the old ragpicker, was not in
sight among them. But the Walkouts,
assuming the reality of what they sought,
frantic or numbed by amazement, searched
the mobs for husbands, wives, friends.

"Sweet merciful Jesus," Arn said in a hushed, hoarse voice.

Whit and Terry couldn't say anything. But Whit's chin was trembling like a very young child's.

Nearby, the shattered aviary, a relic in real time, stood dark and silent.

Josie, at treetop height, faced resolutely away from the chateau, but she couldn't stop her ears, and thus was unable to keep from weeping.

Arn slowly fixed his attention on the center of the chateau, a light outshining the ground firewheels, coruscations trivial and immense; it was as if a small sun lived there.

Something struck his forehead, a single warm droplet, not rain. He looked up.

"What is it, Josie? That light? Where's it comin' from?"

"A room they call—the lantern. Dunno why. Mr. Langford, they say, built a divilish machine inside, made all of silver wire. It is—the working of his machine that gives off the fell light."

"Lantern?" Arn rubbed his raw neck, recalling the dream, or vision, in which Faren had appeared to him. "That's where she is! Bet my life on it. Colonel, you comin' with me?"

He had to repeat himself. Then Whit turned to him with a stricken look, a small shrug of apology.

"No. I—have to find my father."

"General Blackie? He ain't here. He's been dead for—you still a little off from that crack on the head?"

"I can't explain now."

Arn said angrily, "Well, I ain't got time for you to explain. Terry, take care of Bocephus for me, I'll be back soon as I can."

"It looks—different over there," Terry said. "Like a mirage. Dad? Doesn't it?"

"See how it shimmers," Josie called. "Isn't only the lantern. That is a force, not a thing, under a bad spell and all unstuck in time. Aye, none but a fool would go inside."

"No," Whit said, his light-impacted eyes like glass wells in his skull, his voice so strange Terry almost didn't recognize who was speaking. "It hasn't changed. Everything's the same."

"Enough bullshit. My wife's comin' out of there, and right now."

Arn took off at a run, prompting an outcry from Bocephus. Terry had to use both hands to keep the loyal dog from flying after Arn. He found a tree small enough to snub the rope around. Bocephus crouched down with a whimper of dismay.

Whit turned to his son in the outreaching light. His brow had caught, his mind seemed eerily aflame.

"Stay here with Josie," he said.

"Dad!"

"Maybe she's right. But—my mother and father are in there."

"Granpa—"

"No, no." Whit shook his head impatiently. "Somebody different. You never knew him. Maybe I didn't know him very well, either. I have to find out for myself who he was, what he was like."

Josie said urgently, "If you have a mind to go there, do it *now*, for pity's sake. And do not linger!"

Whit walked rapidly away from the woods. Terry hesitated a couple of seconds, then started after him. But Josie plunged down in front of Terry, her wings spread forbiddingly.

"You said he'd be a fool to—"

"Terry, did you not see your da's face? He is driven to go. There is some mystery in this we do not understand. But it is coming to an end now, for better or warse."

"All of you are acting crazy!"

"Yes, I do feel a touch of madness meself." She looked back at the chateau, face suddenly incandescent with horror; hair-raising. Terry trembled and Bocephus moaned. "I am tempted to retarn. It's an agony. I wish to see me dear sister's face again." Her wings fell. Terry had his chance but made no move to go around her. "I am too afraid."

"Of losing your wings?"

"To lose them might not be so tragic. Yet I cannot know if arms will be restored to me, once I cross the threshold of Langford's magic. Is there any save himself who truly understands it? Or is it forever out of control?" She grieved there in the outland of her destiny, fixed by the glare of the perilous, about-to-blaze ether surrounding the chateau. "No, I would rather feel safe, for just a little longer. Safe, and with you, Terry—although I know that when you leave Wildwood, I may not go."

As Whit crossed the park of equatorial green, dapper in dew and smoke-blue curlicues, mind and memory oscillated wildly between light and dark, beginning and ending, the bitter and the sweet. Each long stride diminished those he had left behind, his blond son and the faery butterfly; he felt years younger, fresher, eager—all that mattered was home, the many graceful windows and the realness of stones. He paid little attention to the stunning light of the lantern, the glints of disorder in all that brilliance. He passed tableaux of festival, brisk orchestras, tumblers and fire-swallowers and dog-clowns, swanboats on a glossed plane of lake; he arrived out of breath at the flight of alabaster steps beneath the central facade. There he paused, shrugged off more years like a heavy packload and went inside.

Jongeleurs strolled through the *corps du logis*, mock-mandarins and highborns posed famously for the flashpan. He wasn't included, but felt tolerant; this was *fun*. The huge helical staircase, made entirely of marble, was a familiar playground. Elated, he thought of games of hide-and-seek: the staircase was designed so that those who ascended could hear but not see others coming down from the upper floors.

"Do you know where my father is?"

The servant he addressed looked at his soiled clothes and then his unshaven face, seemed puzzled and a little afraid of him. He drew away with a hasty head-shake of apology, as if Whit had spoken in an obscure language.

Oh, well . . . But he felt a vague sense of distrust of the carefree moment, and, looking at the runners of carpet crossing the *corps du logis*, which showed the deep imprints of horse's hooves, his wishbone hurt him, he imagined his father missing or dead: sealed forever in the perfection of one of his ingenious mazes, swallowed up by a thick stone wall of this house.

No, that couldn't be right. He was immortal, by right of his magick. He was waiting now, in the boy's rooms, perhaps having brought some simple new illusion with which to amuse them both. Whit/Alex made his way to the crowded stairs, hurrying, as usual: he ran everywhere in the vast chateau, never a spare ounce of flesh on his body. His father, of course, could will himself from one distant room to another, instantaneously.

He found a long upper hallway deserted, glaring, the

ceaseless grinding of the lantern-light hard as carborundum to the senses; he seemed to use only a fraction of the interminable hallway with each dogged, running step as he followed the big horseshoe prints in the carpet. Intaglios in stone between narrow mullioned windows, the faces of philosophers and tyrants, looked down with cored eyes as if from crypts. His too-strong shadow was a menace, an unwelcome harbinger. *Something bad was happening in his rooms . . .*

But when he stopped outside the open door, blood pounding in his ears so that he couldn't hear well, and peaked cautiously inside, he saw no one. He advanced into the playroom, aware of odors, horsehair and piss. His bear costume for the Revels lay in a cinnamon heap on the floor; his shelves of toys and magic props were undisturbed.

"Father?"

The bedroom and bath were empty. He came slowly out of his bedroom, yawning, looked at the open windows, the maculate, gossamer accretion of light there, sharp green and spewing fireworks beyond. Idly he picked up his bearmask and sought a mirror, annoyed that the mask had shrunk and didn't fit him.

The eyes, even the unkempt face, were his father's, but when he whirled no one was standing behind him. It was yet another illusion, he realized, thankful but a little shaken. His father teasing him. But where had he gone? He dropped the bearmask, yawning again. The intelligent, proprietary light willed him to fall into a doze on the corner couch, accept the permanence of homecoming.

He shook off this powerful suggestion, throwing down the bearmask. He was irritable and uneasy; he didn't want to sleep, he wanted to talk to his father. He looked around the room and saw, past the windows, not green-

sward but rusty barren mountains in a yellow sky, heat
waves rising from a crackled desert floor. The desolate
vision thoroughly frightened him. He backed out of his
playroom into the lonely hall, seeking comfort, wanting
his father but thinking, unexpectedly, of his bedridden
mother . . .

Arn Rutledge released his grip on the servant girl,
dressed in multi-eyed peacock blues, who had reluctantly guided him to the lantern. Another time, he would
have admired to pluck her. She ran away, less afraid of
him than of what might be inside, behind the sculpted
bronze doors that stood sixteen feet high. Arn found no
conventional means of access—the doors were without
handles and apparent locks. Their hinged tonnage responded, perhaps, to occult suggestion. Or brute force.
Of that he was capable. He put a shoulder to one door
and strained like a big mule in harness.

The door moved, a few inches, and he was assaulted
by the blade of a cosmic dagger; a heatless inferno raved
him blind. He stumbled against this fury into the lantern, calling Faren.

"Helllpppp meeeee!"

All he could see was the bird, wings beating frantically against the stones of the floor. And then, shielding
his eyes as best he could, he looked up and made out the
form of a serpent suspended above the writhing, feathery blackness. He was transfixed by the poisoned ruby of
a jealous eye. There was a dry spittle of venom like
cyclone dust around its toothy, ancient head.

With the serpent's attention transferred to Arn, Faren
slipped momentarily into human shape, although she
had talons instead of feet.

Arn took one step toward her and then his power to

move was nullified; he barely had the strength to breathe. The serpent's head angled again toward its principal victim, and Faren's tormented wail became the corbel's croak of mourning. Arn's eyes streamed tears from the ferocity of the light, at the center of which was a blue void. Weakened, hands hanging at his sides, he dropped to his knees.

Josie, too fidgety to do anything but fly, carried a stick in one foot to ward off the ruffian owl and other nightwingers that came near where she hovered, so attractive a morsel, just outside a dark wall of hemlock. Through the fizzle and smoke of low pyrotechnics she was quicker than Terry to grasp the changes taking place within the sphere of the chateau: the blooming dahlia in the heart of the lantern-light, a lovely, complex, fatalistic blue with the vitality to wrench and wrap solid stone. And the airy frost now descending overall, like the ice-notes of a seductive music, stilling merriment, glazing time to perpetual zero. Her heart stuck in her throat, she faltered clumsily as Bocephus bayed and Terry called anxiously from below.

"Josie! What's happening?"

"I dunno—it may be that—"

"Do you see dad? *Is he coming?*"

"I cannot—see him anywhere," she said. There was a haze like snowfall across the slowed, appalled landscape. The figures of revelers were dimming to her eyes, with little upstart flickers of their magnetically charged bones like the blissful dead in a shallow cemetery. Or the harrowing undead.

Sickened, distraught, she tried to keep her eyes closed to the inevitable dissolution of the restless chateau. As she had feared and predicted, all were lost. She felt, not righteous, but lost herself.

"Josie, can't you do something? *It's going away!*"

Josie shuddered, and looked back despairingly at the wild wood, emptied now of Walkouts. She glanced at Terry's pale upturned face and impulsively went spiraling down, dangled lamely in air face to face with him, covetous, afire, sensitive to his distress.

"Ah, Terry."

He was shaking, he couldn't speak. She said it for them.

"It was so unexpected, and so sweet. And if that is all there is, surely I may be content. I will try to send him back to you, my dearest Terry—if only I have time."

She kissed him, and he covered her breasts, a tender laying-on of hands. Only then did she feel brave enough to part with him. She vaulted straight up with a mighty surge of hard wingbeats, spiraling once, twice; then she turned to frigid music and flew, in a rainbow arc, toward the ganglia of the lantern, the blazing blue imperium; hearing Terry, and smiling to herself, aloft and in her element, and in a state of everlasting peace.

"You'll come back too! Josie, you come back!"

The doors to Sibby Langford's apartment were open.

He was stopped by an emanation of sickroom, and brooding perfumes. But the light of the hallway was in a brackish mood; his bones felt as fragile as a skeleton of sand shaped by the blue tide, and the stones of the chateau seemed less than solid: they were subtly adrift in his field of vision, loosely packed dunes on their way to a formless chaos; they might easily bury him if he was motionless for too long.

He heard his mother's voice, a far-off plaining.

He felt, where his heart must be, a slackening of attitude, a thin cracking of obdurate emotion like the shell of a walnut.

How could he not have loved her? Or been restrained from loving?

"Pamela? Where are you?"

Where *was* Pamela?

His throat convulsed. He had killed her, not many hours ago, with a chisel that broke her spine. But how could he tell that to his mother, if he went in there?

He must go. Not to see her, now, was to fail them both in some eternally disgraceful, unforgivable way.

In the sitting room, her Singer Sargent portrait overlooked richly stuffed furniture in tones of wistful magenta and sunny rum. But only a single small lamp illuminated the large bedchamber; it was difficult for him to make out his mother's still form, the meager flax of her hair on the slanted pillows.

"Mother."

"Who's there?"

That wasn't easy to explain; and as he hesitated in the doorway, with the dreamland blue of magnetically-charged lantern light shimmering behind him, he was aware of a malevolent other, a watchful third presence. He looked around uneasily. The air was bluest, direst, where the ceiling curved like a loaded bow above the ship-shape ruffling of the bed canopy. A brute eye, composed of black and silver lines of force, existing to electrify, floated there potently, full of itself, examining him. Fear muddled Alex's resolve to make amends, and kiss his mother's cheek, a kiss he had so long denied her.

She tried to lift her head from the pillow, then abandoned the attempt with a dry sob.

The eye shot toward him from the bow of the warping continuum. Sibby Langford's small lamp spun a web of intricate light from which came forth, dark as a spider, the ambitious sorcerer, his father.

As his feet lightly touched the floor Edgar Langford appropriated the floating eye and popped it back into the cavernous socket, where it glistened like a morbid wound. He stared at the intimidated man in the bedchamber doorway, but it was Langford who suffered the greater shock.

"I'm—Alex. I've come back, father."

Langford wryly turned his head, accentuating his strained posture, the misaligned backbone. In Sibby's triptych mirrors the magician revealed three smiles at once: astounded, suspicious, inimical.

"Take it off!" he demanded.

Alex just shook his head, not understanding.

Langford raised a hand to his own, saturnine face, in which the unassimilated eye glared supernaturally.

"Your mask! Take it off! No one else can be me! I won't allow it!"

Alex slumped, rubbing the stubble of his chin, his unfeeling jaw, which was paralyzed by tension. Tears of despair flooded his burning eyes.

"There's no masquerade. Your Revels are ending, father. And I—I only wanted to say goodbye to both of you."

His father shrieked in outrage, and plucked a hair from his head. He placed the hair in an outstretched palm, and blew coaxingly on it. Alex watched dully, no longer eager to be inflamed by even the most novel show of magick. He felt the tug of real time, and the collapsing of the sphere around them.

The hair lifted from his father's hand, and assumed a

more substantial, sinister shape: it was now a barbed black weed, turning with tornadic fury, an auger in the air. Alex straightened, alarmed, and raised his hands as he began backing away. But the deadly thing his father had created pursued him, punched through his left shoulder in a quick spouting of blood and ground-up muscle. It had the power of a high-velocity bullet ripping into him, and he was knocked down on the parlor floor.

His mother, unable to discern what had happened, but recognizing the form of her husband, cried out in terror.

Edgar Langford limped after Whit and crouched over him, hands extended, fingers spread.

"No one else can be me!"

Alex looked at the face of the man he had once loved unquestioningly. There was no remnant of this demanding affection, only sorrow. And, finally, loathing, for the perversion of genius that had ruined them all. But he had to try once more.

"Father—I'm Alex. When I explain I know you'll understand how—"

Edgar Langford's fingernails sprouted, sharp as sabers, two of them stabbing toward Alex's eyes.

There was a sharp crack, almost a pistol shot. Langford's head jerked up, his eyes bulged. Alex saw a thin black line, like old blood, across the throat. His father was staring at something behind Alex, who already knew what was back there, he had smelled it.

Langford's hands trembled ineffectually in the blue air above Alex's face, the growth of nails stopped: they withered. He was jerked aside by the blacksnake whip that was strangling him, fell heavily. Sibby Langford gazed aloofly down from her ornate frame. And her lover, iron shoes ringing on stone, came slowly into Alex's view.

Alex sat up holding his bloodied shoulder, unnerved by the sight of his father in convulsions as he tried to breathe.

"Let him go!" he begged the centaur.

"He was a moment away from murdering you. Do you care so little for your own life?" The centaur gave another, furious tug at the whip; Edgar Langford writhed across the floor, a posture of obeisance, dribbling red from a bitten tongue. His head swelled fat with congested blood. His eyes were on the centaur. He raised his hands again as if to summon magick; but his magick was nil. His rasping breath made the noise of an overstressed machine, of a drain in the earth. "I can't go back to what I was. None of us can. Oh, well. This hour is for the weary, our dancing is done." The centaur cast aside his whip and stood trembling, alight, intoxicated. Then he reared to a nightmare height and came plunging down, mashing Mad Edgar's ripened head against the starry marble.

Alex tasted vomit, and spat it out. The centaur stood brooding above the body, head lowered, his spirit drained. The light of the lantern, comely indigo, was as pacific as the balm of afterlife. But there were crucial voids in its darkness.

"Is she alive?" the centaur asked Alex.

"Yes."

"You had better get out of here," the centaur advised, squinting at the charged light. He pattered around Alex and entered the bedchamber. After a few seconds Alex followed him, through a stiffened haze that might have been from his own pain, or something imminently fatal.

The centaur had knelt, awkwardly, on his forelegs, beside the bed.

"Sibby."

She didn't acknowledge him, and Alex wondered if she had died too. Then her head turned on the pillow.

"James?"

"Yes, darling."

"I can't see you very well. What is it you're wearing, a beard? And your hair—"

"It's only my costume. For the Revels."

"But what an ugly costume."

"I'll take it off in a little while," he said.

"James—I'm so glad you came. Edgar was here. I'm afraid—"

"You don't have to be afraid anymore. I'll stay with you now, forever."

Alex moved clumsily in the doorway, and they both looked at him, Sibby seeing only a hunched form, a familiarly shaped head.

"James—who is that?" Sibby said, alarmed.

"Only a friend. A very good friend. Don't worry."

"The children—"

"They are in no danger, I assure you. They will always be—in good hands."

"Thank God. James, would you hold me for a little while? I've missed you so."

The centaur took her in his arms. When he bent to kiss her forehead she was motionless, unbreathing.

"Sibby?" he said.

In the doorway Alex sobbed.

After a few moments the centaur raised his head. But the electromagnetic haze had all but wiped him out, Alex saw only the hard glitter of his eyes.

"Leave quickly."

"You'll die too!"

"At last. But there is no need for you to go with us. You have your son. And your sister, who needs you."

The notion of a son meant nothing to Alex, but mention of his sister excited, for the first time, sympathy. But how could he find her now? He was faint from shock and pain. Turning in the doorway, he bumped his injured shoulder, and groaned.

"Not that way," the centaur said calmly. "You have no time to run. Out the window."

"Jump?" Alex said, confused. There was a mild wind in his face, grit, the dispulverated stones of the chateau flying around him in the vast slipstream of time. A skyey roaring clogged his ears, the roar of a hundred unbridled aircraft engines. Unsure of just where he was going, his back bent as if he carried an unnameable burden, he fought the billion-moted wind, and came to a sill, an opening on pure space in which raged a jungle of electricity, not unlike the sullen flares of concealed guns. His guts roiled. He would have to jump into *that*—but he had done it before, and survived. Instinctive courage guided him now. He clambered onto the wide sill, rocking, stung by the keening wind, nearly blinded. He waited for the signal.

"Go! Go!" shouted Chiron, the jumpmaster. And, despite his crippling shoulder injury, he was able to push himself hard away from the door of the C-47, tumble thrillingly into the abyss of whistling flak and fireflies, down and down. He felt a slight popping at the base of his spine, at long last detached from the cumbersome past. But where was earth, serener pasture for the nakedly fallen? Into what deranged universe had he flung himself, in which direction did he travel now?

*   *   *

Josie Raftery flew to the storming light, to the opened dome of the lantern. It occurred to her, dimly, that her wings, when exposed to all that energy, the crucible of magnetized, dreamtime blue, might vanish in a puff, leaving her to plummet at breakneck speed. But she was in a state of morbid excitement that was close to a trance. Although she had seen lightning from a distance, she drew none as she approached the glass clamshells, slowed to a circle and beheld the machine responsible for her transformation. It was not the horror she had sometimes tried to imagine. Rather the skein seemed almost frigid in its effulgence, burning, as ice burns, from the refraction of a hidden sun, hum-drum, with a power beyond mere potency. Josie felt awe, but she could not be afraid of it.

But something fearful was taking place below, away from the strapping machine.

The big raven with a woman's shapely head, stubbornly but futilely beating its wings in an attempt to break a silken spell; Arn Rutledge, nearly prostrate, oppressed by the might of the magician's walking stick—an airborne serpent, rounding into scaly coils, its own head rhythmic as a metronome in a hellfire haze.

Josie acted without consideration, flying down to seize the serpent with her strong feet. One near the tail, the other behind its head, so that it could not strike with gilded fangs and rend a wing.

The serpent reacted with such rippling strength it nearly dislocated her hipbones. She knew it would destroy her before she could fly up and out of the lantern, carry it far away from the chateau.

"Get out!" she screamed at Arn. And with desperate force, her body on fire from pain, she rowed with a strength equal to the serpent's toward the machine.

It now seemed more green than blue in its appealing deeps, lusher than Ireland, a sight for sore eyes and a wanderdone soul. The head of the serpent whipped loose, she felt it climbing swiftly toward her heart, but now the machine, the blessed machine, was taking hold of them . . .

Arn awoke as if he were in a picture-show and looked up, into the lustrous air. He saw Josie and the dangling serpent superimposed on the hair-thin wires of the machine. There was a moment of writhing, a silvery pop, a thousand tiny Josies and insignificant serpents, then nothing but buoyant impulses of light, all going their separate ways, sizzling faster than his eyes could follow, in interesting trajectories, pathways to blue oblivion. He arose stupidly, weak at the knees, and stared at the unsightly mess of dark feathers strewn across the floor. A wind was blowing, lightly stinging his exposed flesh. His life seemed to be going by, he was numb with recognitions, but felt a yearning not to be finished so soon. It could have been due to vertigo, yet the walls of the lantern seemed to be loose, affecting a vague shilly-shally as if they were immersed in a clear, subtropical sea.

He became aware of tentative movement in the heap of feathers and saw Faren's hand, wedding band glinting, grope across the stone. He pulled her, naked, coated with something slippery like afterbirth, from a pile of wispy corbin-bones that dematerialized almost as soon as she was clear of them.

She looked at him and smiled with a flimsy, trembling mouth. Then her eyes rolled back in her head, and she fainted.

Arn threw her over one shoulder and carried her from the insubstantial lantern, finding the zigs and zags of bright impulses in the deep blue light confusing, inconsistency in his bones, his heart and brains just floating. There was a sound as if one of the faraway revelers had popped a particularly big champagne cork. It was a meaningful sound, last call, he remembered a refrain from pub-crawls in England: *Hurry up please it's time*. Burdened with Faren in the hospitable, grasping light of the lantern, he turned down a dimming flight of stairs, not sure of the way out. If there still was one.

The wind was a lash, a beast, a wailing, a remonstrance, an outpouring from the deep-set caverns of time and space. Terry and Bocephus huddled together, tied to a wildly swaying tree by the length of rope attached to the hound's collar.

When the wind stopped, as abruptly as it had begun, the end of the night was mild, sweet, clear and cold.

The chateau was gone.

Josie, his father, Arn, Faren—gone too.

Terry got slowly to his feet, still holding on to Bocephus, who trembled nervously, his nose in the air.

"Where are they, Bo?" Terry whispered. "Did they get out? Can you find them?"

With clumsy fingers he untied the dog. Bocephus just stood there for a few moments. Then he began an exploratory circuit of the sunrise woods, flushing birds and small game, but nothing that interested him. Terry, with a glow of fever, anxiety gnawing dully at his breastbone, followed as best he could, sometimes losing sight of the tracker dog in hefty stands of hemlock and blue spruce, thickets of flesh-pink rhododendron.

Then Bocephus barked and Terry ran, stumbling, where it was still shadow-dark. Up a rise with the trees close together like very tight doorways, then a sudden brightening, a space through which Faren Rutledge stepped sideways. He nearly ran over her. She was wearing Arn's Ike jacket and nothing else.

"Terry!"

She held him to her breast, hugging him almost hard enough to pop a couple of ribs. Arn came up grinning behind her, Bocephus leaping all around him.

"Arn, what happened?"

Arn shrugged. "Well—it ain't all that clear in my mind, but we're okay. Did you see your dad anywhere?"

"No! And Josie—she flew to the chateau just before—" He stopped, thinking of his last glimpse of her, as little as a moth among the distressed stars above the shining lantern.

"Saw her," Arn said, his face so unexpectedly grim that Terry cringed.

"Well, is she—did she—"

"I don't know exactly what happened to her, Terry. But she won't be comin' back."

Terry turned and walked away from them, stunned and angered.

"What about dad?"

"I don't know," Arn told him. "Hell, I just don't know. Bo, take off!"

They searched the wood for two hours, until Arn called it off. He sat down to have a talk with Terry. The exhausted boy, who shivered in fits and starts, was beset by panic. Arn talked to him as if he were a young soldier under fire for the first time. His hand was on Terry's shoulder, squeezing hard.

"It looks like we ain't gonna find him."

"But if you g-got out, he m-must have got out too!"

"Now, I'm not sayin' he didn't. But it's plain he ain't around here. Terry, I'll be back to look for him, with all my dogs, and I'll stay in these woods a month if need be, until there ain't no hope at all. Meantime, Faren's got no clothes, and we don't have food. You understand, don't you, Terry? We've done all we can today."

Terry had chewed his lower lip raw. He nodded tersely. Arn helped him to his feet. Faren looked on silently, her face blank, in the doldrums herself. With Arn in the lead they made their way slowly down the mountain to Walkout Town. No one had the strength to say a word.

The mists of Walkout Town had cleared beneath a blazing sun. They stopped at a spring and drank, and lay down. Terry closed his eyes for a minute. Then he got up. He looked spectral, as if his heart were missing. He began to call Josie, his voice echoing.

"Terry, that ain't no use. She's dead. I saw her die. I don't think she suffered none, if that's any—"

Terry stopped calling and stared at Arn, tears running down his cheeks as he tried to get his breath.

That's when they heard the baby cry.

"Good Lord," Faren said. "Where's that coming from?"

Terry took off, running across the rosy green littered with croquet wickets, stumbling over one he didn't see, falling; he got up and started to run again, going toward the hut in which Josie had lived.

The baby continued to cry.

Arn said reluctantly, watching Terry, "Reckon we got to find that baby, and put it out of its misery."

"For God's sake, Arn!"

"Faren, it has to be some Walkout's kid. Odds are it's a freak. Do you want it to—"

Terry, on the green, stopped suddenly, with an incoherent cry.

"Arn, look!" Faren said.

They saw a robed figure emerging slowly from one of the huts. The Walkout had the baby in one arm.

Faren, limping from a stone bruise, Arn's jacket flapping around her hips, led him at a jog toward Terry, who was staring at the Walkout. They couldn't make out his face, although he seemed to be looking at them, waiting. He acted as if he didn't know what to do with the baby.

Terry said incredulously, "I think that's—"

The Walkout sat down heavily, nearly collapsing, but didn't drop the baby. Faren gasped and ran. She reached the robed figure and took the baby from him. He lifted his hand and pushed the cowl back from his face and lay back. His other hand was out of sight, perhaps useless. His eyes were glazed from nightlong pain. But he had a smile for his son when Terry kneeled beside him.

"You made it," Whit said gratefully. "Thought I was—the only one."

There was blood on the robe, on Whit's right hand.

"What happened to you, Colonel?" Arn asked him.

"Oh—" Whit searched for an explanation. "Shot, I guess." He touched his left shoulder. "Here."

Terry said, his voice cracking, "Who shot you?"

"Long story," Whit said. "Don't know if—you'll believe it."

"I'll believe anything now," Arn muttered.

Whit looked at Faren, who was examining the baby in the soggy blanket. "Is she okay?"

"Just wet and hungry," Faren assured him. "And isn't she a little beauty?"

"My sister," Whit said, smiling, awed and proud.

Terry straightened and glanced at the baby, then looked in disbelief at his father.

"What's that, another long story?"

"Yeah," Whit said, closing his eyes, breathing deeply but without discomfort.

Arn said, "Colonel, can you make it? We got a ways to go yet."

"I'll be all right. Slept a couple of hours in the hut. Faren, there's a dry blanket in the perambulator, and a baby bottle. But the milk's not good."

"I'll find something around this place for her tummy; juice, maybe canned milk." She crooned to the redly squawling infant. "Yessss I will! Don't you worry about a thing, cutie."

Terry said stonily, "What are we going to do with a baby?"

Whit gave a slight shake of the head; he didn't know. Faren, holding the infant against her breast, shot him a look and then turned to her husband. Arn's jaw sagged a little when he comprehended the gleam in her eye.

"Don't you say a blessed *word*, Arn," Faren told him. "She's perfect. She's beautiful. And she needs us."

"I can't think of two people I'd rather have looking after her, Arn."

"Has she got a name?" Arn said, still in shock.

"Laurette," Whit told him.

Arn tried to think of something else to say. He settled for, "That's some pair of lungs."

They all listened to the baby crying, as if the sounds she made had a certain sanctity.

"And we need her, don't we, Arn?" Faren said.

Arn looked at her steadily for a long time, and stopped squirming.

"Yeah," he said. "Maybe we do."

"Well," Faren said, "I'll just get her out of this wet dress, and then we'd better be on our way."

Terry turned and walked away from them. Whit, grimacing, sat up.

"Where're you going, son?"

"Not going anywhere. I'm staying here."

"Why?"

"Because—" he stopped several feet away, hands clenched, but wouldn't face them. "I have to—wait for Josie, that's all."

"Kid," Arn said, "there ain't nothing left of Josie, take my word for it."

"No!" He was close to breaking then. He sniffed several times and got his voice under control. He looked at them with eyes flushed by fever, by his passion to be understood. "If dad got out, then Josie could've too." He cut Arn off before he could speak. "And maybe you don't know *what* you saw in the chateau! I don't think she's dead, that's all, I just d-don't believe it! And—and *look* at this place, it's deserted, there's nobody who can take care of her when she—"

"Terry," Whit said firmly, "we've all had a rough time, and you're just making things worse."

"Your daddy needs lookin' after by a doctor, and the baby—"

"I don't care! Go on! I'm staying. You can't *make* me go."

Faren gazed thoughtfully at him, then looked at Arn. She whispered something Terry couldn't hear. Then she went into the hut behind them and after a while the baby stopped crying. Arn apparently decided to ignore Terry. He kneeled beside Whit.

"Why don't I have a look at that shoulder? Maybe

there's somethin' I can do that'll make it easier on you."

"Thanks, Arn." Whit paid no further attention to his son either.

So they were going to treat him like a kid. Hurt and indignant, frightened and dismayed, Terry walked across the broad croquet lawn, stooping to pick up a mallet. Fortifying himself, if only symbolically. The sun was full in his face but he shivered. He knew he was sick; nevertheless he wasn't going with them now no matter what. Josie was coming back. He would wait for her.

Bocephus barked gruffly and Terry turned to see that Arn had come halfway across the mossy lawn toward him.

"Okay," Arn said. "We're goin' now. We talked it over, and you can stay, if that's what you want. I'll leave Bo here for company. Be back this time tomorrow. Maybe by then you'll be satisfied."

"Okay," Terry said, surprised.

"One more thing. Don't go in the woods, or I'll never find you."

Arn rejoined Whit and Faren, who had washed and put on a Walkout's robe. She carried the swaddled, sleeping baby. Bocephus sat down beside Terry, who put a hand on his collar. His father turned with a wave of his good hand. Arn had made a sling for him, but he was obviously still in pain. His movements were slow and his head was down; Terry felt a pang of regret not to be with him. He watched until they were shadows amid deeper shadows, until no trace of them remained. Terry began to cry and momentarily hated himself for it; but to cry felt good, and it let out much of the hurting. Calmed, he could think more clearly.

He was hungry, and Bo had to be hungry too. In one

of the huts he found jerked venison for the hound to chew on. The meat was unappetizing to Terry, but a larder of fruit and nuts he discovered filled his belly. There was more cool water to drink.

He was too tired to move around much, and he had no curiosity about how the other Walkouts had lived. They had been freaks, but Josie was his love. He avoided her hut and stayed outdoors, resting with his back against a tree while Bocephus dozed on his side, drawing flies. Much of the time Terry looked at the pale sky, expectantly, willing Josie to appear in an elegant spread of wings, more beautiful than any ship under sail. Squirrels played in the branches above his head. He saw an eagle. So much to remember, all of the sweet moments concentrated into one image, her green eyes on him, watching, somewhere. The lengthening day brought clouds, thunder, rain. He crept then into Josie's hut, stared at the empty saddle-bed, lay down on the bearskin she had provided, his head aching and burning. Bocephus occupied the doorway.

A wind that shook the hut awakened him, in darkness. The saddle-bed swayed and creaked. He sat up dizzily, half-blinded by a flash of lightning. Bocephus was yowling, far from the hut.

Someone was there.

With a hand on the saddle-bed, his heart trying to squeeze into his throat, Terry pulled himself up.

"Josie?"

The fever had broken, he was wet all over. Lightning again. He saw the glare of a curved handax, the tall goatman standing in the doorway, his narrow head thrust forward, cornucopiae of horns waxen in the shrinking light. Terry had dreamed, but of nothing like this.

"Taharqa!"

The goatman turned and left the hut, although his
after-image remained fixed for a few moments on Terry's retinas. Terry scrambled after him, into another
blast of lightning, and earth-shaking thunder.

"Have you seen her? Do you know where she is?"

The Ethiopian turned and looked at him, the goat's
face oddly jeering in the brilliant silver light. How,
Terry wondered, had he escaped the chateau? Or had he
gone there at all?

"Take me to Josie!" Terry pleaded.

The goatman slowly raised his ax; Terry's blood chilled.
But it was not a threatening gesture; he moved the ax
slowly in the air, beckoning.

"Do you want me to follow you?"

Bocephus came up behind Terry, thrusting his nose
into the hollow of a knee; Terry jumped. When he
looked again for Taharqa he saw the goatman moving
uphill through evergreens restless as the sea, horned
head gleaming beneath a polished pewter sky. Terry ran
to keep up, but was unable to match the black man's
barefoot stride. He didn't think about where he was
going, or even if it was sensible to follow (*Don't go in
the woods,* Arn had told him). But was it accidental that
Taharqa had found him in Josie's hut, and wanted him
to follow? Maybe she had fallen from the sky, maybe
she was dying—no, it couldn't be. If Taharqa could get
to her, he would have brought her to Walkout Town.

She was all right, then. She had come through alive.

Anticipation sharpened Terry's reflexes, he felt strong
and happy. And when he fell too far behind, lost track of
Taharqa, the goatman always paused until Terry had
him in sight again.

Wind, lightning, thunder, but no rain. He was thoroughly lost, but it didn't matter. He was going to Josie. This was her home, the wild wood.

At first he didn't recognize the place to which he had been led. The wind was milder at the crest of this treeless hill, stars were visible behind thinning dark cloud.

"Where are we?" he said, going down on one knee to catch his breath. Bocephus flopped down beside him. But the goatman stood tall against the sky, handax sheathed, his own chest barely moving as he breathed.

Taharqa pointed to something Terry couldn't see, a short distance away in the darkness.

"Is it Josie?" He lunged eagerly to his feet and jogged, hurting from a stitch in the side, in the direction Taharqa had indicated.

Then he came to a panicky stop at the lip of the quarry. Stared into its depths, at the square of pool some sixty feet below. Looked up at the silent Ethiopian.

"No! God! No!"

Taharqa slowly lowered his hand, turned his back on him.

Terry slumped down at the edge of the pool. He had seen Faren leap from almost the exact spot where he was sitting. He had been about to follow her, but Josie had pulled him back.

Terry lifted his head and cried, *"Is that where she is?"*

The goatman had vanished.

Terry shuddered. He sat for a long time with his head on his knees, hurting so bad he didn't want to move. The wind had died. Faraway lightning flickered soundlessly beneath the clouds around Tormentil Mountain. Was the chateau still there, and would it be there forever?

He could find out.

This time she wasn't hovering in the air, ready to seize him.

She was on the other side, or just below the surface of the eerie pool, waiting for him.

If he had the courage to go to her.

Josie.

He was ready now. On his hands and knees he leaned forward, looking down, fascinated, remembering how it had appeared to him, that swarming, dreadful green pool . . .

You don't have the protection, Josie had warned him.

Yes I do! I have *you*, Josie.

Ready, he thought. His throat closed. He couldn't breathe. He leaned out a little farther, over the brink.

The green pool wasn't there.

In its place was the universe. He saw it whole, in stunning clarity. Not the blackness of space, the chaos of creation, but the blue of beatitude, the peace of eternity.

He knew then why Josie had summoned him, he knew where she was now. She had wanted him to know, and not grieve. She was not lost, nor in torment. She lived in beauty, quick as light. So did all the others, he was sure, those unfortunate souls who had populated the Well of Sorrow. Something stirred in the night beside him. He withdrew from the edge of the quarry. His cheek was brushed, devotedly. It was a fleeting touch that would never be repeated: maybe it was only a memory. His eye was drawn to a particular star in a field of stars. He didn't know what was different about it, but his heart felt good; and so he watched till morning.

JOHN FARRIS

NIGHTFALL

Suddenly Angel moved. Three weeks of catatonic trance ended. His eyes focussed, his hands reached out and he killed.

Escaping from the institution, Angel went looking for his wife. As he went, he killed – sometimes for a reason, sometimes just because he felt like killing.

Down in Mississippi Anita waited. She had protection – very professional Mob protection. She also had former flyer Clay Tomlin about the place. He'd come home to rest up and fish and think about a future and a career that had just fallen apart.

All of them, about to face the dark avenging Angel of Death . . .

'One of the giants of contemporary psychological horror'
Peter Straub

POST A LITTLE HAPPINESS

Post·A·Book

A Royal Mail service in association with the Book Marketing Council & The Booksellers Association.

Post-A-Book is a Post Office trademark

JOHN FARRIS

SON OF THE ENDLESS NIGHT

When he killed her – he used a tyre lever – he left very few bones unbroken in her body and her head. Afterwards he claimed he was possessed.

The authorities were unimpressed.

But later, in the cell, the priest watched as the entity took control once more. Watched as his head swelled and blackened, the charred skin splitting as white flesh and soft flexing bone burst through, as obscenity and hot bile spurted from the lipless contorted mouth.

Then the priest knew the name of the Enemy he faced, and shuddered.

'John Farris has a genius for creating compelling suspense'

Peter Benchley

NEW ENGLISH LIBRARY

HORROR AND SUPERNATURAL FROM
HODDER AND STOUGHTON PAPERBACKS

JOHN FARRIS

☐	05900 6	Minotaur	£2.95
☐	41729 8	Nightfall	£2.95
☐	40575 3	Son of the Endless Night	£3.50

JAMES HERBERT

☐	38999 5	Moon	£2.95
☐	40937 6	The Magic Cottage	£2.95
☐	42668 8	Sepulchre	£3.50

STEPHEN KING

☐	41143 5	It	£4.50
☐	39249 X	The Bachman Books	£4.95
☐	05769 0	Pet Sematary	£3.50

All these books are available at your local bookshop or newsagent, or can be ordered direct from the publisher. Just tick the titles you want and fill in the form below.

Prices and availability subject to change without notice.

Hodder & Stoughton Paperbacks, P.O. Box 11, Falmouth, Cornwall.

Please send cheque or postal order, and allow the following for postage and packing:

U.K. – 55p for one book, plus 22p for the second book, and 14p for each additional book ordered up to a £1.75 maximum.

B.F.P.O. and EIRE – 55p for the first book, plus 22p for the second book, and 14p per copy for the next 7 books, 8p per book thereafter.

OTHER OVERSEAS CUSTOMERS – £1.00 for the first book, plus 25p per copy for each additional book.

NAME...

ADDRESS ....

....